RUMORS

Catherine Mann

Delacorte
Press

Published by
Delacorte Press
The Bantam Doubleday Dell Publishing Group, Inc.
666 Fifth Avenue
New York, New York 10103

Library of Congress Cataloging in Publication Data
Mann, Catherine.
    Rumors / Catherine Mann.
      p.   cm.
    ISBN 0-440-50037-0
    I. Title.
  PS3563.A5353R8   1988
  813'.54—dc19   88-4566
                                                           CIP

Manufactured in the United States of America

December 1988

10 9 8 7 6 5 4 3 2 1

BG

This is for
Janie and Al Micallef
and their great big Texas hearts.

Prologue

■ From *The Hollywood Daily,* June 5, 1938:

CAPPY DESMOND DIES AT SEA
"Hollywood Daily" Founder
Succumbs to Heart Attack

Charles "Cappy" Wentworth Desmond, patriarch of *The Hollywood Daily,* died of an apparent heart attack aboard his yacht, the *Regina Renata,* early Sunday morning. He was 57 years old.

The *Daily*'s owner collapsed suddenly at approximately 2:10 A.M. in the ballroom area of the 120-foot luxury vessel, during one of his celebrated weekend cruises for show business notables.

According to Mr. Desmond's sole heir, daughter Renata, 18, her father's heart attack came without warning. "He was his usual vigorous and robust self all day and evening," noted Miss Desmond, who was aboard the yacht. "Father was laughing and joking with his guests only the moment before this tragedy occurred."

Mr. Desmond was stricken as the yacht cruised off the coast of Baja California. Attempts to revive him on board were to no avail. He was pronounced dead at 4:15 A.M. in Rosarita Beach, Mexico.

Guests aboard the *Regina Renata* at the time of Mr. Desmond's collapse included director Peter Hopkins, actress Alisa Hudson, costume designer Jeffrey King, *Daily* gossip columnist Letty Molloy, choreographer Beanie Parker, singer Flora Roberts, columnist Sammy Rollins and *Daily* reporter Harvey Stinson.

Born in Manchester, England, where his family owned a large woolen mill, Mr. Desmond emigrated to the United States shortly before World War I, settling in Los Angeles. He began speculating in real estate and by the early 1920s owned major parcels of coastal land extending from Monterey to San Diego. In 1929, recognizing the need for a show business industry newspaper, he founded the *Daily* and guided its growth in the face of later competition as the preeminent voice of the Hollywood community.

Mr. Desmond, a lifelong bachelor, adopted his daughter, Renata, in 1920. Miss Desmond, who was graduated from L'École Sumaar in Switzerland and later attended the University of Paris, will assume her father's position as publisher of the *Daily* and president of Desmond Land Corporation, Inc.

"My father has been grooming me to one day walk in his footsteps. I am only sorry that my time has come so soon," Miss Desmond stated. "Father was a brilliant man and it is so tragic that he was taken in his prime, at the height of his career."

As word of Mr. Desmond's death spread, messages of condolence and sympathy began arriving by the hundreds at the *Daily*'s offices from prominent citizens of the entertainment industry and other well-known personages around the world.

Miss Desmond requests that, in lieu of flowers, donations be sent to the Cappy Desmond Scholarship Fund, Box 23, Hollywood, Cal.

Funeral services will be private.

·I
The Assignment

1

1985

■ Kate Brannigan found the row marked 3 D-E-F and allowed herself a silent Hallelujah. All three seats were empty. She'd be flying to the West Coast in semiprivacy. At least she had that to be thankful for.

She shoved her carry-on bag up into the overhead compartment, slammed it shut, flopped down onto the window seat, and willed her body to go limp.

Rest—Kate was in desperate need of it. But now, as usual, she found it impossible to relax. Her spine felt like a tightly coiled spring. It had been that way for weeks.

Kate was hoping the trip to Los Angeles would make a difference. She needed a change of pace. She needed a great deal more than that, really. But just getting away from Washington, D.C., would be a start. And seeing Sara was bound to boost her spirits.

Sara! A half smile crossed Kate's lips as she fastened her seat belt, thinking about her dear friend Sara—with her sprightly, self-deprecating sense of humor and her seemingly endless supply of compassion. She'd been Kate's savior during so many emotional storms over the years. Always there to listen and advise, despite her own hectic life.

The wife of a top-notch film producer, Sara was also the mother of twins. And she had her own star in the Hollywood galaxy. She'd recently been named chief of television production for Culver Studios. Kate sometimes wondered where in the world little Sara found the energy to do it all.

She closed her eyes now and pictured the Silversteins. Short, perky Sara, her husband Mark, and their teenage twins, Jackie and Jennifer. Family—that's what they were to Kate. Or the closest thing she had to it.

Family. She turned the word over in her mind as the flight attendant demonstrated the use of the oxygen mask.

Painful memories still brought tears to her eyes. Visions of her parents. Remembrances of her mother planting bulbs in her prized tulip garden. Taking a spin around the block on her bicycle. Her father sitting in his favorite after-dinner chair, correcting English lit. papers. Both parents smiling proudly as Kate received her diploma that sunny June afternoon on the grounds of Vassar.

And then her father's sudden, unexpected death. Her mother's final days in the dark, musty bedroom at home in Rochester. And Kate, at twenty-four, feeling so helpless, so alone. The two people she cared most about gone within two years of each other.

As the huge jetliner lumbered slowly to the runway, Kate struggled to blot the unsettling scenes from her memory and concentrated once again on her California visit. R and R, that's what it would be. And some pretty upscale R and R at that.

Staying in the Silversteins' pink guest room was always a luxurious treat. The raw silk Austrian draperies, an airy shade of powder-puff pink. The cushy down comforter on the spacious queen-sized bed. The cozy sitting area with two comfy overstuffed calico chairs and the pink and white striped chaise longue. There Kate and Sara would talk for hours, as they always did after a few months of separation.

Six months this time. Kate hadn't seen Sara since last March when all four Silversteins had visited D.C. during the twins' spring break from junior high.

Kate wondered now about Mark. He'd seemed his own cheerful, dynamic self as she'd toured the Smithsonian with them on that drizzly Saturday afternoon. But Sara had taken Kate aside and instructed her not to mention "the business." So Kate had been careful to avoid the subject of Hollywood and films—particularly Mark's recent film, *Expectations*—the one he'd gone way over budget on. The movie had taken a nosedive at the box office. And some critics predicted that Mark's career was headed in the same direction.

Sara had said very little about *Expectations.* But recently she'd mentioned another movie Mark was involved in. And Kate was looking forward to hearing more about it. *Who knows,* she thought, brightening. *Maybe he'll be in the midst of shooting and I'll finally be able to visit the set.*

Mark had been promising Kate she could watch him make movies for the longest time. But somehow it had never worked out. Secretly she thought he was just too insecure to let her hang around and ask questions, though she'd never admit that to Sara.

The only thing Kate wasn't looking forward to at Sara and Mark's was the black-tie dinner party scheduled for Sunday night. That particular evening Kate knew the Silversteins' sprawling Bel Air mansion would be teeming with narcissistic Hollywood braggarts. Puffed-up producers, writers, and network executives. The kinds of characters that never appealed to Kate, particularly not now when she was feeling so unsure of herself.

She would attend the party, of course. In fact she had packed her favorite crepe de chine dress just for the occasion. "A perfectly ultra-chic affair, my dee-ah," Sara had joked over the phone. "Can you believe—Taylor has agreed to wear a tux?"

Taylor Evans, Sara's younger brother, was the reason for the Sunday night soiree. Basically it would be a publicity party, launching the TV series in which Taylor would soon debut as the star. Kate still couldn't understand that.

Taylor Evans—an actor? Well, he was certainly handsome enough. Tall and sturdily built with rough-hewn Tom Selleck good looks and a healthy crop of wheat-gold hair. But in personality, Taylor seemed the antithesis of an actor. He was by no means an extrovert. Mild-mannered, almost shy—that's how Kate would describe him. And he was so immersed in all that higher-self Far Eastern philosophy.

Kate remembered how, back in the late seventies, Taylor had taken off for India and stayed a couple of years, studying with several high priests—searching for the meaning of life. And, until just recently, he'd presided over a rustic retreat in Santa Barbara called Westwinds. An emotional healing ground for high-stress victims was what Sara called it.

Kate wasn't clear on exactly what Taylor's disciples learned at Westwinds. But she had once met a female correspondent for *Time* magazine who'd spent two weeks there and couldn't say enough about the mystical powers of Taylor Evans. She'd even referred to him as her "psychic mentor."

So the fact that Taylor, the highly evolved guru, would do an about-face and start acting for a living seemed a bit odd to Kate. But then, she thought as the silver 747 queued up into take-off position, what is Hollywood but a backdrop for the odd and the ridiculous? She'd ruled out living there long ago. At least that's what she told herself.

After the School of Journalism at Columbia, Kate Brannigan had had her heart set on becoming a respected print reporter. She'd worked hard toward that goal, turning out free-lance pieces for a number of major magazines. Some might say she'd already succeeded. But not Kate.

The way she saw it, she'd stopped smack in the middle of her ascent to fame. Clipped her own wings, maybe. She hadn't done a lot of thinking about it then. She'd merely followed her instincts and run from the hurt. From New York. From Cary Eckhardt. For the first time in her life Kate's work had come second to healing her own heart.

But it hadn't worked. Because here she was again—running. Hoping to heal. And wondering why, no matter what she did, her personal life always wound up a total shambles.

As the sleek wide-bodied jet finally lifted off the runway, Kate's blue-violet eyes grew moist and she pressed her flushed cheek up against the cool glass of the window.

God, just take me away from all of this, she thought. *Help me find my way to some kind of life that works.*

Would distancing herself from D.C. be the answer? Was it possible that all the tension and inner turmoil she'd been carrying around with her for weeks would dissolve in sunny California? Simply evaporate like the morning dew?

No. In her heart Kate knew feelings like this didn't just disappear with a quick change of scenery. People spent years in analysis trying to cope with problems half as serious. Kate had never gone to a psychoanalyst. But she could certainly recognize an emotional crisis without anyone telling her what it was.

Kate Brannigan was thirty-five. Over the past decade she'd lived like a modern-day nomad, in four different cities. From her home-

town of Rochester to Hollywood. Then back east to New York and
on to Washington, D.C.

Her life thus far seemed as rootless—as soulless—as a congested
freeway, with Kate forever battling to beat the traffic. Pursuing her
career at reckless high speed, without regard for her personal safety
or peace of mind. Now she'd somehow missed the correct turnoff
and wound up in the middle of nowhere.

Kate was lost. Twice she'd fallen in love. She'd suffered a massive
broken heart once. And never had she felt more confused and deserted than right now.

Her biological clock was ticking away like a time bomb. She had
maternal instincts but no man to share them with. And no prospects
at the moment.

Being in California would help, she hoped. She wasn't sure how
much. But she knew she had to take back control of her life.
Restructure it somehow. Find a new direction. Stop dwelling on the
past.

Her mind, though, kept reaching back—almost two years—to
Cary and New York. Kate could still remember with devastating
clarity that bitter cold night when he had left.

It was two weeks before Christmas. Cary had just returned from a
working trip. And after his perfunctory kiss Kate had asked him
about spending Christmas with their friends, the Jamesons, in Glen
Cove, Long Island, as they had the year before. It was then he had
told her he was leaving. Merry Christmas and good-bye. Just like
that.

He'd announced his intentions matter-of-factly, looking directly
into her eyes. "Kate, you know I've been spending a great deal of
time in San Francisco researching the new book. Well, I've met
someone . . ." His face was expressionless. He didn't even have the
decency to apologize for the abruptness, the awful timing. It was
over, that's all. Two years of her life. Gone now. Ended. Cary was
moving on. She didn't even get a vote.

She'd refused to notice the inevitable clues. Cary's long trips to
the West Coast. Their infrequent lovemaking. His sudden lack of
interest in her work. Kate had been oblivious of it all. She had to be
told.

He'd packed and left the same night. Moving like an automaton on remote control, she'd thought. So detached. So unemotional. How could he do this without considering her feelings? How could he just walk out? Surely he'd come to his senses. Return and beg her forgiveness.

But a month later, Cary married the twenty-three-year-old, gorgeous, athletic, charming Pamela Reines. Heiress apparent to the Reines' Jewelry fortune. Once Kate accepted the fact that Cary wasn't coming back, she felt absolutely purposeless. Work became an effort. For the first time she began missing her magazine-assignment deadlines. Finally she stopped accepting new work for a while and tried refocusing her life.

It was a horrendously difficult task. She felt betrayed and used up, unable to go on. And yet she knew she would. She'd learned too much from Cary Eckhardt to let a personal crisis infringe on her career. Even if the crisis was over him.

Kate asked herself the same question over and over again during those first few weeks without him. What would she be doing if she hadn't met Cary? She honestly didn't know. Cary had influenced her career direction to such a degree that she felt like an extension of him. It was as if he had given her a part of his own mind. And that he couldn't take back. He'd left her, yes. But he'd taught her a lot as well.

First impression. The night they met. Elaine's, on an unseasonably warm summer evening. That face. Famous, yet so familiar— she'd already seen him on every major national news and interview show. She was taken with Cary Eckhardt immediately. Not with the man but with his aura of celebrity. His book, *A Political Travesty,* had been a mega-bestseller for weeks. And of course she knew the story of this fiery but brilliant journalist. How he'd been hired by the President of the United States as a speechwriter. How he'd won President Laurence Bennett's total confidence and had been promoted to special White House media adviser. And how, through his very own White House keyhole, Cary Eckhardt had first spied the now-famous scandal. How he initially tried to ignore it, failed, sought to stop it, failed, and quit his post. How he had succeeded in exposing the rottenness at the core of the administration he had ably served and defended.

Not since the *Post*'s Woodward and Bernstein blew the lid off

Watergate had the country been so jarred by a political scandal. As Eckhardt reported it, the U.S. Secretary of Energy had been on the take, accepting millions of dollars from a group of oil-rich sheikhs. In exchange he'd silently squashed the fledgling synthetic fuel industry in the United States. And the entire insidious scheme had originated in the Oval Office.

Cary Eckhardt's scathing exposé broke in *The Washington Post* in August. By year's end the Secretary of Energy had resigned, and the President faced the prospect of impeachment. And Cary Eckhardt had a half-million-dollar advance to write what became *A Political Travesty,* a detailed account of his White House investigation.

Mark Silverstein had been among those vying to option Cary's bestseller for a movie, and he was trying to woo the author over dinner at Elaine's when Kate Brannigan suddenly appeared at their table. She'd been having a drink with a friend nearby. Saying hello to Sara's husband was uppermost in her mind, of course, but she'd recognized Cary Eckhardt, too. She found herself brimming with curiosity as he stood up and extended his hand.

Later she'd learned Cary was equally curious about her. He'd had his eye on her since she walked into the restaurant half an hour earlier. He'd noticed her striking red hair. And he liked the way she was dressed, in a purposely rumpled turquoise shirtwaist, tight enough to show the outline of her shapely thighs. But what really piqued his curiosity was the way she carried herself. A little proudly, maybe arrogantly. She wasn't a beauty—not in the New York glamorous way. Yet he saw something temptingly arousing in her. A smoldering sexuality, he surmised.

And she was the only reason he'd allowed this Silverstein hotshot from California to keep him at Elaine's so long. It was nearly eleven o'clock when Kate finally walked over to their table. She could tell immediately that Cary was impressed. First he insisted she sit down. Then he urged her to order a drink. No? Well, coffee at least. She accepted.

Within the first five minutes she learned he was newly divorced, and by the time they all decided to leave he'd offered to share a cab with her to the West Side.

Kate demurred. His celebrity aside, she wasn't particularly attracted to Cary Eckhardt at first. He had a long, pensive face with deep, dark eyes and a brooding mouth. He couldn't have been much taller than she was. He was undeniably bright, very fast on the uptake. But he seemed a bit puffed up. The media high had gone to Eckhardt's head, Kate decided. Besides, he was probably too old for her. Forty-four, she'd read. No, thanks.

He called, though. She knew Mark would probably give him her number if he asked. So she wasn't all that surprised when Cary invited her to lunch. And she went. If nothing else, she figured, she could pick his brain. Maybe even come up with some new editorial contacts.

Kate was frustrated with the direction of her own career at the time. She'd been writing free-lance magazine pieces in New York for more than a year. She loved the city but had begun to fear she would never get what she wanted here. The winner's circle. That's what she hungered for. Trading quips with Jimmy Breslin and Pete Hamill. Hanging out with Tom Wolfe, Jim Wolcott, and Marie Brenner. The Manhattan superstars of the printed word. The keenly in-the-know, stimulating dozen or so who could mold public opinion in the city . . . and the country, for that matter. Journalists with true insight. The ones who observed the passing scene, analyzed it, and reported it—immortalized it—in their own unique and authentic voices. Kate wanted entrée to their world. She wanted to hear what they said. And bring similar discernment and imagination to her own magazine pieces.

That, she knew, was the real reason she'd agreed to meet Cary Eckhardt at Maxwell's Plum. She was after his mind and his crowd, the people he could introduce her to. He was probably after her body. She wasn't about to give it to him, not unless and until she wanted his. But if he wasn't overly obnoxious, perhaps they'd see each other again. And maybe Cary Eckhardt could provide what she wanted most.

Kate got what she was after. And so did Cary. But it wasn't the calculated trade-off they'd each intended to make that rainy afternoon. To their surprise, they liked each other. They discovered similar drives, attitudes, and tastes. Despite Cary's hectic travel schedule to promote the book, they managed to spend a good deal of time together that first month. Lunches, dinners, movies, the theater, parties. And to Kate's amazement, he didn't come on strong. It puzzled her at first. Only later, after they'd decided to live together, did he explain.

"You were too good to be true," he announced one night after they'd made love for hours. "I didn't want to risk bad sex and ruin a good relationship."

"Bad sex?" Kate protested, poking him lightly in the ribs. "What did I look like, the ice queen?"

"Baby," he assured her, brushing his lips over the splash of freckles on her upturned nose, "you looked like the goddess Athena come to take me to Libido Never-Never Land. I just couldn't believe one woman could be so gorgeous, bright, and a good lay to boot. There had to be a snag somewhere."

She tickled him behind the ear. "There wasn't?"

"Haven't discovered one yet," he teased, running a finger playfully up her thigh. Kate nuzzled her face into his chest and they began making love again.

Cary had needed an anchor. He was growing weary of one-night stands and fleeting affairs. Deep down, it was a solid relationship that he wanted. And Kate was his solution. By the time she moved into his spacious twelfth-floor apartment on West End Avenue, he was totally infatuated.

A year later, when the idealization period had passed, Cary was faced with the real Kate. The workaholic who habitually wrote late into the night, often passing on lovemaking to meet a deadline.

"My God, I've created a monster," he would tease, finding her hunched over her typewriter at two A.M. And in a way he had. For Cary had opened the doors for Kate, introducing her not only to his stellar media friends but also to the most important editors and publishers in town. He had paved the way. It was up to her to prove herself, of course. She knew that, couldn't forget that, not for an instant. Work would be her salvation.

Kate Brannigan wasn't writing for *Self* or *US* magazine any longer. Now her byline appeared in the handful of prestigious publications that mattered: *The New Yorker, Vanity Fair, Esquire, New York, Rolling Stone, The New York Times.* Her forte was the political profile. Cary had seen to that. Helping her to formulate questions. Working with her to refine, shape, and hone each piece. Even Cary was a bit amazed. She caught on quickly.

By their second year together, Kate had become so consumed with work that she didn't notice when Cary began to wander. She still loved him very much and was totally satisfied with their relationship. It was warm, comfortable, accepting. She had no complaints and assumed if Cary did, he would air them. But that was not the case.

He was working on a new book, which meant a great deal of travel. But Kate was understanding. And soon she came to enjoy being alone. During the week she needed the time to write, and it was easier not having to apologize to Cary when she disappeared into her office. Besides, on weekends they made up for lost time. Or so she had thought. Until that cold night in December.

Sara, as usual, had come to her rescue that Christmas. Insisting that Kate spend the holidays with her, Mark, and the twins in Aspen. And it had helped. Dear Sara. They'd been fast friends since freshman year at Vassar. And in all the intervening years they'd never let each other down. When Sara got pregnant during senior year, it was Kate who soothed her, reminded her she had a choice, helped her compose the letter to her parents, and stood there proudly as maid of honor when she married Mark.

These days it seemed that Sara was doing more than her share of the hand-holding, Kate thought now, gazing out over the Potomac. *Here it is, more than a year since Cary left and Sara's playing emotional paramedic again.*

This time because of Seth. Seth. She could see him now. Wrapping his arms around her. Holding her tight. Secure. Safe. Loved. And *trapped,* Kate reminded herself so emphatically that she almost spoke the words aloud.

You can't go back to him, an inner voice insisted. *No matter how much you want him and how much he loves you. It's totally unrealistic. Face it. You met him on the rebound. And he's far too young. Ten years, Brannigan! You'll overpower him. He'll hate you for it. It will never, never work. Why can't you accept that?*

Kate knew the answer even though she'd denied it for weeks. The truth was, without Seth she felt lost. Empty. And, okay, insecure. He had added such joy to her life, releasing a kind of adrenaline in her that she'd had no idea existed.

Seth Arnold had unlocked so many secret compartments in

Kate's heart and mind that it was almost as though she'd discovered a new person within herself. Even at this point, Kate was still convinced that before she'd met Seth she'd never really experienced the feelings which accompany contentment. And she knew she'd never been so happy as when they were together.

But then—she'd ruined it. Walked away and left him. Couldn't help it. Couldn't help herself.

And now, as she settled in for the long flight to Los Angeles, Kate wondered what *would* help. What did an unmarried woman, bordering on middle age, do when she hit yet another dead end? How many times could you fall in love, or think you were in love, and then have it all blow up in your face?

Sara would have some insight, she knew. And she was grateful for that. Her effervescent college chum had an uncanny way of making even the bleakest times seem just a little brighter. And with that comforting thought, Kate Brannigan rubbed her weary eyes, yawned, and fell mercifully asleep.

2

■ "Kate Brannigan . . ."

The pudgy man with the tinted monocle repeated the name, rolling it over his tongue as though savoring the silken seductiveness of a marvelously fresh Colchester oyster. Then he took a slow sip of his vodka gimlet, lifting his eyes over the rim of the glass to continue the concentrated stare he had fixed on the tall redhead before him.

She wasn't a beautiful woman. Not in the traditional sense of the lovely creatures who often pounced on him at chic gatherings like this. But then, he was certain she wasn't an actress. Too straightforward and totally unaffected, without a trace of narcissism. Not a model either. She didn't have the bones or the body. She was too well rounded, appealingly so, but she'd photograph heavy.

The face was also far from perfect. Forehead a bit too high. Cheeks a little chubby. The eyes, however, were absolutely stunning. They were blue, deep blue mixed with violet. Widely set and strikingly intelligent. Definitely her best asset. But, he had to admit, the hair was rather magnificent too. A wondrous shade, the color of ripe persimmons, freshly cut in the sunshine. Soft, hastily combed curls spilling down to caress the shoulders of her royal-blue crepe de chine dress. The longer he looked at her, the more eager he became to know who she was.

"Kate Brannigan," he repeated once again, wondering where he'd heard her name before. Normally he wouldn't be quite so curious. In his position he met so many people he forgot more names than he could remember. But there was something about this woman. She had a certain quality. A wholesomeness which he found quite refreshing. And though he couldn't put his finger on it, a definite allure.

Kate shifted on her feet and fidgeted with her chunky silver necklace, realized what she was doing, and stopped abruptly. She was beginning to feel distinctly uncomfortable. Still a bit groggy from jet lag, and certain she wasn't looking her best, she was now being stared up and down by the odd duck with the monocle.

Of the three dozen or so Hollywood insiders clustered in the oh-so-perfect living room of Sara Evans Silverstein's Bel Air mansion, Kate had selected this man, Jerry Lindner, as the least likely to prattle on about his latest three-picture deal or the most recent executive axings at the major studios. He looked a bit eccentric, perhaps. But she knew Lindner by reputation; he was a serious journalist. West Coast bureau chief for *World* magazine, the most popular weekly news publication in the country.

Now she was beginning to question her choice. Since she'd introduced herself, Lindner had repeated her name twice and was examining her face as though it held a clue to some hidden treasure.

"Ahhhhh-hah!" Lindner almost bellowed now, his face lighting up like the Rockefeller Center Christmas tree. "I've seen your by-line. Good work too. *New York? Rolling Stone? Vanity Fair?*"

"All of the above. I free-lanced out of New York. Years ago," said Kate, flattered.

"And didn't you work out here at one time, for *The Hollywood Daily?*"

"Briefly," Kate murmured evasively, feeling her freckled cheeks beginning to flush and knowing that within moments her naturally rosy skin would resemble a stop light. "Many, *many* years ago. More recently I've been living in the Washington, D.C., area. Politics." Before he could continue interrogating her, she added, "I thought *World* already did a profile on Taylor Evans. So what brings you here?"

Lindner let the hint of a smile cross his lips and nodded in the direction of an imposing, elegantly—if unfashionably attired—sixty-ish woman at the center of a clutch of people across the room.

"Her," he announced.

Kate's head turned in the direction he was indicating and a look of surprise registered on her face.

"Renata Desmond," Kate mumbled, astounded.

"Yes," Lindner was saying. "The magazine is doing a—"

Kate didn't hear the rest of his explanation. She directed her eyes back to Jerry Lindner. But it was Renata Desmond she continued to see. Standing there in the vintage dress of brilliant scarlet with the huge shoulder pads and the sweetheart neckline. Looking as smug and stylish as she had—let's see, how long had it been? Seven—no, eight years ago.

At the far end of the room, near a gigantic Hockney painting splashed in pastels, Taylor Evans was pinioned by the piercing gaze of the regal figure in scarlet.

"Tell me, Taylor," Renata Desmond commanded. "Exactly what is your TV series all about?"

Inwardly, Taylor Evans was squirming.

He was beginning to have doubts, serious doubts about the wisdom of agreeing to do this TV stuff at all. Had he made a big mistake? So far, the acting itself was challenging, even satisfying. But this unrelenting publicity garbage which accompanied it—an absolute bore.

Taylor's amber eyes returned the stare, defiantly. He wasn't really interested in talking to this demanding female who looked like she'd stepped out of a 1940s time capsule. She was arrogant and coolly direct. Her manner suggested she was accustomed to having her questions answered, her orders carried out. Taylor was tempted to comment on her abrasiveness. But that would be honest. Honesty wasn't the medium of exchange at a party like this. The image, the facade, was what counted. With conscious effort, Taylor forced himself to relax, willing himself into a state of quiet calm, keeping his studied smile intact.

She went on. "The *Daily*'s readers—"

Ah yes, the trade paper heiress. So this was the fabled Queen of Hollywood, the dragon lady who ran *The Hollywood Daily* with an iron fist encased in a velvet glove. No wonder her vibes were so powerful; they radiated from her like stray megawatts. Even the deep, throaty voice had a hypnotic pull.

As she continued to speak, he caught a certain sexual surge as well. Hell, this is crazy, he told himself. He'd heard she preferred women. Even if she was bi, she wouldn't come on to him—not here, not now. Would she? This was his sister's home. They'd just met. So why did she keep staring like that? Taylor was beginning to suspect that here in Hollywood people like Renata Desmond made the rules.

He would stick exactly with the script. This party was all about publicity. His publicity. And sister Sara would be very disappointed if he blew his chances for a piece in the *Daily*.

"Thanks for asking, Renata. The series is called *Ki & Company*. the *Ki* is from the word *aikido*, which, as you may know, is the most stylized of the martial arts. A totally nonviolent form of self-defense."

"Fascinating," she said.

He plunged ahead. "And this character I play, Justin Kane, he's a private investigator. Sort of a Robin Hood who champions the underdog. No weapons, though. Just *aikido*. And he chose the name Ki & Company because *ki* is the universal energy flow of which everything, including man himself, is composed. It's all a matter of tapping into it, using our *ki*, converting spiritual power into physical force." He stopped to wait for a sign that she understood. "Follow me?"

"Certainly," she lied.

"Of course, Justin Kane always triumphs," he added, flashing perfect white teeth beneath a carefully trimmed wheat-gold mustache.

"Of course," she repeated.

Outside, two red-jacketed parking attendants snapped to attention in the circular driveway to the sprawling white stone mansion. A British racing green Jaguar was pulling up to a quick stop. The license plates were Texan. And so was the driver, who stepped lightly from the car, took the small white ticket from the valet, and unfolded to his full six-foot, three-inch height. Taking the arm of his passenger, a lanky platinum blonde in a long white dress, he strode briskly toward the large double oak doors. Leaving the parking boys to wonder if he were a director, producer, or chief of a major studio. He was none of these, but could have been all three.

R. B. McDevitt exuded confidence and money. And well he should. He was, after all, the owner of one of the ten largest bank holding companies in the nation. Listed by *Fortune* as among the twenty-five wealthiest Americans, R.B. mined his millions from a dozen or more sources, from oil to pharmaceuticals. Then there were those few ventures in which he measured his reward in both fun and profit. In that category, his first love was raising magnificent Egyptian Arabians on his vast ranch in the Texas hill country.

After his horses came Hollywood. R.B. had begun dabbling in the movie business because he loved the glamour factor the town offered. His ambitions, however, went far beyond the few films he had produced to date.

That was one of the reasons why he'd cut short an African safari just to be here at this intimate dinner party. Without question, this was an "A"-list affair, a much-prized invitation on what's called "the Bel Air circuit"—the homes of the studio bosses, major stars and producers, the most sought-after directors, the handful of others who comprise Hollywood royalty. This in itself wasn't why R.B. had flown halfway across the globe to eat dinner. He was here mainly because this evening was in honor of his good friend, Taylor Evans.

But there was another, equally important reason as well. For months now, R. B. McDevitt had had his eye on Selwyn Studios. If there was valuable intelligence to be learned to aid him in launching a takeover, he knew he'd nose it out here.

"R.B., it's been too long!"

Sara Evans Silverstein stood in the open doorway, and as the tall Texan with the curly, light brown hair stepped inside he encircled her with his warmest bear hug. "I'm so thrilled you could make it," Sara enthused after R.B. introduced his date. "The guest of honor is right over there." She gestured toward the far end of the living room, where Renata still held Taylor captive.

R.B. and the platinum blonde began circulating, working their way through the crowd, renewing acquaintanceships and making new ones.

From her vantage point in the marble-floored foyer, Sara watched the two of them for a moment, then shifted her glance over to her handsome brother. *Good, he seems to be holding his own nicely with Renata Desmond. I still hardly believe he gave in and agreed to do the series,* she thought.

Taylor had never acted before in his life. But when the pilot script for *Ki & Company* crossed her desk, Sara had known at once he should do the role. Taylor Evans *was* Justin Kane. From the commitment to Far Eastern philosophy to proficiency in aikido, the character and her brother were one and the same. It took her six

months, but somehow she finally talked him into an audition. It
went splendidly. And like many before him, he caught a touch of the
show business bug. He left behind his well-ordered, peaceful, icono-
clastic life in Santa Barbara and came to chaotic, crazed Hollywood
to take his shot.

He'd be a star. She knew it. And it didn't hurt that Sara Evans
Silverstein was the president of TV production for Culver Studios,
which was producing the series. Hers was the perfect position from
which to guide her brother's newfound career. To give him and his
show the special treatment crucial to the survival of a budding new
series. Odds against new programming making it were ten to one.
Good publicity was among the imperatives. And Sara knew how to
get it.

This private little confabulation of the town's top image makers
could do wonders for Taylor's future. If all went well, this single
party would do more for the series and its star than a million-dollar
advertising campaign. The potential influence on Taylor's career of
the gossipers and preeners in Sara's living room was worth at least
twice that. Arrayed here on her costly Chinese rugs, sipping champagne from her Baccarat stemmed crystal were the people who
could overnight make Taylor Evans's name as recognizable as Don
Johnson's or Robert Redford's. The owners, editors, and columnists
of several of the most influential publications in the country. *People,
TV Guide, World.* The Hollywood trade papers—*Variety, The Hollywood Reporter, The Hollywood Daily.* The national newspaper syndi-
cates.

Television, of course, was also represented. *Entertainment Tonight, PM Magazine, 20/20.* Sara was delighted to see that even
Margo Green had shown up. Her weekly celebrity profile show was
always in the Top Ten in the Nielsen ratings. In a matter of months,
Taylor would be perfect for her.

Peppered among the journalistic entourage Sara had gathered
were two Oscar-winning producers, the president of the network
that was airing *Ki & Company* as well as a smattering of highly
respected directors, authors, and screenwriters.

Sara was on a first-name basis with all her distinguished guests.
She had personally telephoned each one. That's the way it was done.
A casual invitation to an entertaining evening in Bel Air. A chance

to trade shoptalk with the best of the breed. To make new contacts. Renew old ones.

It was business, Hollywood-style. Work camouflaged as play. The soft sell. There were no press kits. No speeches. No direct references to Taylor's show when Sara introduced him to her friends. But they all knew why they'd been invited. Why she had gone to the trouble of bringing together this stimulating and powerful mix of personalities. Why the exquisite dinner, from the velvety purée of asparagus soup to the buttery, tender *gigot d'agneau rôti* to the lovely mousse of chestnut cream in chocolate cups. Why the lingering afterglow of hundred-year-old cognac and coffee. They all knew Sara wanted something in return. And she was certain not one of them would let her down.

Gliding toward the kitchen, Sara paused momentarily at the large chinoiserie mirror next to the curving staircase to check her appearance. She did not like what she saw. She never did. The strapless green-sequined Oscar de la Renta evening gown was stunning. Her sandy-blond blunt cut looked *très chic,* she knew. And the emerald earrings Mark had given her for their last anniversary were perfect.

It was the rest of the package Sara couldn't abide. Herself! Her body. She'd always been considered petite. But with the recent acquisition of fifteen pounds, Sara now called herself a "puffy petite." Then there was her face, her nose in particular. Despite two rhinoplasties ("Second one was only the tip," she'd insist defensively), the copious nose still looked out of place on her elongated face. A chin trim hadn't worked the miracle Sara had hoped for, either. ("Look at this thing," she half joked to Kate after the surgery. "You could still hook a wet towel on it and mop up the floor.")

Her friends were used to Sara's self-deprecating sense of humor. It had been, she'd once confessed to Kate, the only thing that got her through grade school, where everyone thought for sure she was Taylor's adopted sister. "How could such an Adonis be related to this *mieskeit?*"

"This *what?*" Kate had asked.

"*Mieskeit . . . mieskeit.* You know, an ugly. A bow-wow. A woof-woof." Sara shrugged. "Taylor got all of Mom's *goyisheh* white-bread looks. I inherited Aunt Hester's weird bone structure and Daddy's skin. Problem is, it just doesn't hang right."

Marrying Mark Silverstein had helped Sara's self-confidence. Not that she'd been unpopular at Vassar. She had, in fact, been class president two years running and a hot ticket in school theatrical productions. True, their vows were exchanged when Sara was three months pregnant. ("So, it was a shotgun wedding! Who cares? I sure enjoyed the bang," she admitted to an astonished Aunt Hester after the ceremony.) But becoming Mrs. Mark Silverstein had made a big difference in Sara. Kate noticed right away.

"Of course he's good for me," Sara agreed with her. "He's Jewish, so I'm finally legit. Evans? What kind of a name is that? Know what it was before?" Kate didn't. "Yavanowitz. Yavanowitz, for God's sake. How the hell Daddy got *Evans* out of that, I'll never know. Did it years ago, for 'business purposes,' he claims. But I think he's always been sorry. And now he's overjoyed 'cause there's going to be a yarmulke under his little girl's roof. Wait till I become a genuine Jewish mother!"

Though she would never admit it, even to Kate, Sara knew that meeting Mark at that Princeton dance during her junior year was the best thing that had ever happened to her. She adored him. Yet she'd never been able to convince herself he really loved her. And recently he'd become so distant. Of course, things hadn't exactly been going his way, careerwise and . . .

Oh, there he was! Mark with . . . was that Clarence Bradford of the International News Syndicate? *God, yes, it is!* she reassured herself without turning around to stare. She could see the two men reflected in the mirror. Talking animatedly. Accepting a caviar hors d'oeuvre from one of the circulating waiters. *Go for it, honey . . .* She said an anxious prayer that Mark would hint that several studios were bidding on *Possessions,* his newest script. It wasn't true, of course. But if it ran in Clarence Bradford's syndicated Hollywood column, it would be accepted as truth. And Mark would get another shot at the brass ring. *Poor sweetheart, he's been so blue lately.*

"Sara, I've got to talk to you."

She turned to find Kate Brannigan guiding her swiftly down the hallway toward the powder room.

"Why didn't you tell me Renata Desmond would be here?" Kate implored as she locked the door behind them.

"Omigod!" Sara clasped her hand to her cerise-lipsticked mouth.

"Kate, sweetie. I'm *so* sorry. I just—it just didn't occur to me. I mean, it's been so long since you were—" Sara paused, catching herself before the offending word slipped out.

"Fired? Not long enough," Kate said firmly, turning to the mirror and fluffing out the soft red curls with her fingertips. "I don't know, Sara. Just seeing her rankles me."

"Sweetie, what could I do? By the time you decided to fly out all the acceptances were in. And I had to invite Renata. *The Hollywood Daily* is the most important trade publication in the business, you know that. She's an unadulterated bitch. But she's got clout, Kate, tremendous power. I'd sure hate to have her as an enemy. Jeezus, I even hired her snooty girlfriend to cater tonight."

"Quintana Jaye? The British jabbertalkie?" Kate said, with a wry smile as she spun around to face her apologetic blond friend.

Sara burst into laughter. "One and the same, my dear. Lord, I'd all but forgotten that nickname we had for her. She does run off at the mouth, doesn't she? You should try working with her. It's like having a conversation with a magpie!" She laughed again, joined now by Kate.

"I'm so glad you're here," Sara said, basking in the warmth of their frivolity and hugging her best friend. "And we've got so much to talk about. I just . . . oh, I forgot to show you—" Sara closed her deep-set hazel eyes and waited. "See?"

"See what?" Kate asked, wondering what she was missing.

"The liner. I had it done. Permanent. Great, huh?"

"Terrific," agreed Kate, who could hardly tell the difference and wondered why in the world her friend had bothered.

"Decided to do it a couple of weeks ago," said Sara, turning to the mirror to examine her eyes. "A tattoo artist in the Palisades. Five hundred bucks. But, imagine! I never have to apply eyeliner again."

"You save some time putting on makeup," Kate commented, trying to sound enthusiastic.

"Yeah, got it down to three hours now. Not counting twenty minutes for the adhesive tape," Sara joked, leading Kate from the powder room. "Now come along, Ms. Brannigan. You just forget all about Dragon Lady Desmond out there. We're in for an eight-course feed, courtesy of Quintana's ridiculously pricey Par Excellence. That is, if Quintana hasn't forgotten all about us with her constant chatter! Let's go see what the old broad's got cooking."

It never failed. Sara had magical powers to calm whatever storms threatened Kate, and once again she found herself feeling a deep gratitude for her friend's gift. "Sara," Kate said now as they walked together toward the kitchen, "I've been meaning to ask you. Brandy St. John. Is she going to be here?"

Sara shook her head. "Not tonight, sugar. I know you two are pals. But if that gorgeous Swedish creature were here she just might steal brother Taylor's thunder. The spotlight is his tonight. I don't want anybody upstaging him."

"How's her series going?" Kate persisted. What a transformation the trembling, undernourished girl she had met in the ladies' room of that dumpy Greenwich Village restaurant had gone through. Brandy had been a top photographic model for the past several years. And now she was about to debut as an actress.

"Show's great. Brandy's a natural in the role—and she's working her barely-there derriere off. Everyone on the production side is happy so far. The network loves the pilot. It's a definite go for later this month."

"Terrific. I can hardly wait to see her," Kate said, following Sara through the kitchen doors.

"We'll do lunch, the three of us. Does she know you're in town?"

"No. I didn't alert anyone."

"So much the better. Shall we surprise her, then?"

"Yes! That'd be great!"

"By the way, lady," Sara whispered to Kate as they approached Quintana Jaye, an auburn-haired, Rubensesque figure hovering over freshly baked popovers. "I have a surprise for you, too. Pay specific attention to the gentleman on your left at dinner. He has a date, but it's nothing serious. Our tastes differ, I know, but try to like him. Believe me, he's very special."

No doubt about it, he was good-looking. But Sara had been wrong, Kate decided, as soon as she'd had five words with R. B. McDevitt.

That Texas twang. Right out of central casting. And his taste in women? How could Sara even imagine me being attracted to a man who dates pneumatic bubbleheads like this platinum number? Kate sipped the Laurent Perrier in silence and attempted to ignore R.B., which turned out to be impossible.

He had shifted in his seat, ignoring the blonde, to face Kate. She could feel his curious glance sweep over her upper torso as he said, "So you're the brilliant reporter Sara keeps telling me about?"

Reckon I am, pardner, Kate was tempted to quip. But she simply said, "Yes," without looking directly at him.

"Well," R.B. continued through his most engaging grin, "Your pal Sara sure got one thing wrong."

"And what's that?" Kate asked coolly.

"She told me you were very attractive. Should have said ravishing. And Irish too, I'll bet?"

Lord, I think I'll throw up, Kate thought. "How'd you guess?" she asked a bit sarcastically.

R.B. reached for his champagne glass and held it up to hers for a toast. "To L.A. and beautiful ladies," he enthused as the glasses clinked. "How long you here for?"

"I'm not sure." Kate placed her glass on the table and studied it, turning the stem around and around in her hand.

Come on, Brannigan, lighten up, she scolded herself. *It's only a dinner party. And he's not that bad.*

But just then R.B. reached across the table to skewer a pat of butter with his fork. He jabbed the entire square on a hard roll and took a huge bite.

Yes he is! Kate turned to the producer on her right, hoping to engage him in conversation.

R.B., however, was persistent. "So tell me, Kate," he said after inhaling the roll, "how long have you been writing?"

"Since journalism school."

"Columbia, right?"

"You guessed?" she asked, mildly surprised.

"No, ma'am." He shook his head. "Did my homework. Bad habit of mine."

One of hundreds, no doubt. "So what else did you find out?"

"Not enough to satisfy my curiosity." He grinned. "That's why I'm asking the questions."

Kate busied herself with the endive salad in front of her.

R.B. finished his in less than forty-five seconds.

"So where is it you do your writing these days, Kate?"

"Wherever I land."

"Vagabond, huh?" he chuckled. "Gal after my own heart. Listen," he went on as she nibbled the salad, "a pal of mine runs the L.A. bureau of *Forbes* out here. And he was just telling me there's a staff position about to open up. Maybe it's something you should consider."

Kate turned to look at R.B. in utter amazement. Was he serious? Why in the world would she want to take a drone staff position with *Forbes*? And where did he gather the audacity to even suggest it?

"Well, that's very nice of you, R.B.," she said without enthusiasm. "But I'm really not interested in anything permanent right now."

"That bad, huh?" His tone was sympathetic.

"I beg your pardon?" Kate's cheeks were beginning to flush.

R.B. leaned in closer. "Listen, Kate, I don't mean to get personal or anything . . ."

"You already have," she murmured so softly he didn't hear.

"But it seems to me that right now you're sort of, well, ah—mad at the world."

"At myself," Kate blurted, immediately regretting it.

"Even worse," he replied in a low voice. "Now look, here's my advice . . ."

Advice! Kate couldn't believe her ears. Where did this egotistical character get off? Who did he think he was anyway? Ten minutes into a conversation and he was giving her advice.

"I hope you don't mind, but Sara told me you're a little disenchanted with D.C. and . . ."

Oh, Lord, what else did she tell him?

"And I can't say I blame you, 'cause the way I figure it all politicians are, well, let's just say they're less than gentlemen. But, Kate, point is, you're probably at some sort of crossroads right now, juggling your career and all. So, in my opinion, the best thing you can do is to stay here in L.A. as long as you can stand it. Have lunch. Swim. Do you play tennis . . . golf?"

"No."

"Okay, so go to the beach. Zone out under the sun. Let your brain fry. Treat this town like the Silly Putty Land we both know it is.

Then, when you feel like it, you take a drive up north to Santa Barbara and have a talk with brother Taylor."

Kate just stared at R.B., dumbfounded. She didn't know whether to laugh or confront him. Her Irish temper was pushed to the boiling point. And it was all she could do to control her tongue. After a few seconds she managed to sputter, "But I thought Taylor had relocated to Los Angeles for the series."

R.B. shook his head vigorously, then said in a conspiratorial whisper, "Temporary move. Between you and me, Kate, the acting won't last. Taylor Evans was born to do what he does at that retreat. Put people's psyches back in working condition. Make them find the good that's inside and go with it. And, pardon me for saying so, but I think you could do with a little of Taylor's therapy. He still owns Westwinds, you know. He's there every Sunday to meet the newcomers. And anytime you want to go, I'd be happy to oblige."

"Thanks," Kate said, her jaw set in stone. She was stunned at R.B.'s rudeness and growing angrier with each moment. She knew her face must be fire-engine red by now. And she had to caution herself to cool down.

At the same time, Kate was aware of another feeling welling up inside her. One she'd never have imagined possible. Kate was flattered. What woman wouldn't be? During the last several seconds she'd finally figured out whom she was sitting here listening to. She knew she'd recognized the name from somewhere when Sara first mentioned R.B. But now the man was clearly coming into focus. He might be longwinded and obnoxious and a chauvinistic jerk. But he was R. B. McDevitt. *The* R. B. McDevitt—worth millions. Kate had read about him in several business publications over the years and remembered being impressed.

R.B. was apparently one of those rare geniuses who had perfected the technique of the corporate takeover to a high art form. He owned dozens of companies all over the world. Sports, too. Didn't he own a baseball team? Or was it football? Anyway, he lived on a palatial estate, or ranch, she supposed, somewhere in the heart of Texas. And now here he was, this keenly intelligent, highly aggressive millionaire, paying more than a little attention to her.

Well, what's so bad about that? Kate asked herself, raising the flute to her lips once again. She took a long, cool sip and smiled almost contentedly. All of a sudden she decided to start enjoying herself. And the slight dizziness from the champagne didn't hurt. In fact, it felt pretty damn good.

As liveried waiters began to clear away half-empty bowls of soup, a series of conversations started to swirl like mini-whirlwinds across and down the dinner table. When the main course was served, the conversations grew in their intensity and power, and the dining room filled with fabulous tales, famous names, and hilarious word-play, along with the savory scent of roast lamb, garlic, and herbs.

Those seated at the elongated glass-and-chrome table began letting down their guards, luxuriating in the sunny glow of the full bodied Zinfandel, which followed the champagne. Everything in the room—the setting itself; the drink; the fine china and gold flatware and exotic floral centerpiece; the aromatic, exquisitely presented meal—it was all combining to produce that liberating, soaring, positively inebriating sensation found only at the very best and most successful social gatherings.

They felt privileged to be able to share in this delicate moment, yet at the same time they felt *entitled;* it was their due, their reward, as paragons of their chosen professions. They were the American Dream come true. They had made it; they stood now at the summit. And it was only right that they pause to bask in the rarefied atmosphere, to feel that pleasant lightheadedness together, to survey with one another their exalted status and the glorious view. They were drunk with themselves.

"Hey, R.B.!" came the taunting voice of an esteemed editor from the opposite end of the table. "How about those Longhorns? Coming on pretty strong this season. Took the Bears last Sunday. Any regrets now about selling out to Renata?"

"Regrets? You jokin'?" R.B. countered, leaning forward on his elbows. "Why, Sunday was some kinda freak accident, like one a' your mudslides that eat whole houses out here. Only time that team's gonna win again is on turkey-trot day. All they know is foul. Can't run. Can't throw. Can't tackle. I could hardly get 'em headed toward the right goal post."

A rally of amused titters followed. Then all eyes focused on Renata Desmond. Her perfectly painted scarlet lips drew back in a slow, self-righteous smile. "Odd that a cowboy like Mr. McDevitt doesn't know anything about breeding and training," she said icily. "It's taken me three years to turn that bunch of ill-mannered shitkickers into a cohesive team. But I've done it. And this season you're going to see a Longhorns team worthy of the name—for once. All they needed was a good coach, some talent . . . and patience. A word apparently not in Mr. McDevitt's vocabulary."

Spoons clinked. Forks were put to rest. Waiters silently daubed chestnut cream onto fragile glass dessert plates. But no one spoke. Not a word for at least ten seconds.

"Tell ya what, Renata, honey," R.B. replied at last. "Ten thousand says your weak-kneed Longhorns don't win more than four games this season."

Excited eyes shifted back to Renata, who refused to look at her challenger. "Twenty thousand."

"Done."

When normal chatter had resumed, R.B. grumbled under his breath, "Cockleburred bitch."

Kate turned to her overbearing dinner partner and smiled. "My sentiments exactly," she softly agreed.

Directly across the table *World* magazine's Jerry Lindner noted the surreptitious comment and smiled knowingly.

3

■ Kate was running late when she arrived at Kathy Gallagher's restaurant in West Hollywood. She approached the maître d' near the bar, hoping she looked composed.

She followed the man toward a far corner, wending her way through the mélange of business suits and tennis warm-ups, oversize jackets and baggy pants, off-shoulder dresses and designer jumpsuits. California apparel usually amused her. Here you found such an odd mix of attire almost any time of day or year. But this afternoon Kate was hardly conscious of the colorful, eclectically arrayed crowd as she approached Jerry Lindner's table. She was too curious about why he'd invited her to lunch.

"I'll get right to the point," he said crisply after they'd ordered drinks. "I'm interested in you."

Kate inadvertently raised her eyebrows.

"Professionally."

She held back a chuckle of relief, then replied, "How's that?"

Lindner was observing Kate closely through his monocled right eye. "Renata Desmond," he said.

"You've got to be joking."

"Not at all. Our annual Woman of the Year cover comes up in November. Don't ask me how, but the vote swung Renata's way. My boss back in New York wants a big Hollywood takeout. About how she runs the oldest trade paper in town, and all that crap. A three- or four-pager, at least, on the queen and her hallowed Hollywood empire."

Lindner reached for a cigarette and lit it with a flourish. Then his eye moved back up to Kate's face, as he tried reading something from her expression. He was disappointed.

"That's all well and good, but how do I fit in?" she inquired calmly.

Lindner busied himself for several moments straightening a wrinkle in the tablecloth. He seemed to be deliberately attempting to build the suspense.

"The story's yours, if you like," he said finally. "I'm off to Europe for some much deserved R and R at the end of the week. Planned it ages ago, before this Desmond piece came up. That's the way they operate in the New York office. Do this yesterday, know what I mean? But I struck a deal with Russ Stevens, that's my boss. I'm allowed to hire someone to do the piece." He paused to stare directly into her eyes. She found the effect unnerving. "Interested?"

"Why me?" Kate asked, purposely not answering the question. "Why not someone on your staff?"

"Because they're all playing catch-up on fifteen different assignments." He scrutinized her face once more. "And because you have a working knowledge of the *Daily* already. You might be able to tap your old contacts there."

A wry smile worked its way across Kate's full pink lips. "Maybe," she said offhandedly.

"Look, I had the feeling you might be interested in some freelance work, that's all," Lindner said pointedly. "This pays pretty well. Three thousand, plus expenses. I know the task isn't what you're used to, journalistically speaking. But it'll be a change from politics. And it might be a kick. I shouldn't think you'd find it very difficult. Hell, most of the work can be done by phone."

She was still being cautious, revealing very little. "What's the tone of the piece?" she asked.

"Depends on what we come up with. But let's face it—we're not in the running for a Pulitzer here. I mean, I know there must be more than a few skeletons in the Desmond boudoir. But getting anything on her that'll stick would be analogous to bringing down a Mafia Don. She's a powerful lady. Finding somebody willing to rat on Renata won't be easy. However, don't let that impede your attempts to do so."

Kate smiled. "Sounds like you're not exactly a fan."

Lindner stalled, sipping his drink. "Let's put it this way, Kate. The entire idea bores the hell out of me. Unfortunately, though, Stevens is absolutely fascinated with Renata and her empire. He sees it as real Hollywood dynasty material, you know? So probably no matter how you write it, he'll turn it into a golly-gee testimonial. Puff stuff. To tell you the truth, I'm glad I'm leaving the country."

So am I, thought Kate. *So am I.* This was exactly what she needed. Something to keep her in Hollywood for several weeks. A reason to pick up the phone. Make a few new contacts. Sniff around for more work.

And the subject? It was absolutely tantalizing. There would be no puff piece, not if Kate could help it. She was certain that with a little luck and a lot of effort she could uncover some unscrupulous details about Renata Desmond that would sizzle the New York editor's eyeballs. The very thought was enough to make Kate's pulse race a bit faster. She suspected that was exactly why Lindner wanted her.

"So, what's the verdict? I gotta get back and read travel brochures," he joked.

"Yes," said Kate determinedly. "Yes, I am definitely interested, Jerry. I'm glad you thought of me."

"Great," he said with obvious enthusiasm. "It's not as if you just fell off the turnip truck, Kate. To tell the truth, Stevens wasn't nuts about me farming this out. But when I mentioned your name, he bit right away. Had I not succeeded, it might have been bye-bye Lisbon and Florence." He raised his glass. "So here's to the bitch of Hollywood. May her glorious empire crumble before our very eyes."

Kate chuckled as their glasses clinked.

"Now," Jerry went on, withdrawing a slim notebook from the inside pocket of his snug tan jacket. "I do have a few items for you to follow up on. Let's start with the personal stuff. Quintana Jaye. We're not after *Enquirer*-like bedroom habits. But the piece can certainly allude to a long-time live-in relationship here.

"As we both know," he continued, "Quintana's been camping out at Renata's Trousdale estate for more than ten years. What we don't know is how much of Quintana's catering service Renata owns. Obviously, Renata got her started. I mean, Quintana was a cackle-brained typist on the *Daily* when they met. A year later her company was whipping up soufflés for all the 'A' soirees in town. Not to mention the way she has the studios covered, catering most of the big premieres and parties. Renata has pulled strings for her British darling, no doubt about that. Wouldn't it be nice to find out just how much her take is?"

Kate smiled but said nothing. She was enjoying this immensely.

"As for the *Daily* itself, Renata's owned it outright ever since her daddy died. You remember: Charles Wentworth Desmond. 'Cappy,' they called him . . . nickname from his buddies at the old Babylon Yacht Club. No kidding, that was the name of it. Flamboyant old bastard, too. Used to throw these famously licentious bashes aboard his yacht. The *Regina Renata*. Is that too much? True, I swear. Can you imagine growing up surrounded by the old man's kind of life-style? Anyway, old Cappy kicked off in the late thirties, I think. Aboard his boat, fittingly enough. Heart attack. Better check the obits. Renata wasn't even twenty yet. But she took command of the *Daily* and everything else, I gather, almost immediately."

"How much do we want on her childhood?" Kate asked, jotting down some notes.

"Oh, whatever seems debauched and flagrant enough to print," Lindner joked. "No, seriously, I think she went to school in Europe. She'll fill you in on all that during the interview."

"Interview?"

"Yeah. I spoke with her at Sara's party and she's salivating already. The woman must eat her own clippings for breakfast. Can't get enough publicity. So she's yours whenever you like, Kate. I told her someone from *World* would be in touch. Here's her publicist's card. Call whenever you're ready for a nauseating afternoon."

"Will do," said Kate, already visualizing the moment. She could hardly wait.

"Then there's the Fort Worth Longhorns. Renata's football team. Bought it three years ago from R. B. McDevitt. The Texan you sat next to at the party. Seems Renata's always had a thing about foot-ball. More likely it's her ultimate ego trip—you know, competing in a man's world, in the super-macho arena of professional football. Word is, she seldom attends an out-of-town game. You might ask her about that."

"What about real estate?" Kate asked, remembering articles she'd read about Renata's land company.

"Right," Jerry said, flipping a page of his notebook. "All that's a little sketchy. Cappy came from England. Heir to a woolen-mill fortune. Parlayed it into real estate and made a bundle. By the twen-ties he owned miles of California coastal land. The twenty-nine crash didn't make a dent in his net worth. When he started the *Daily,* he was already a millionaire a couple of times over. But we don't know exactly how much of the land Renata sold off. All of its holdings are privately held, under the Desmond Land Corporation, Inc. Try to nail down a ballpark figure on the combined worth, okay?"

Kate nodded. "Anything else?"

"Ah, yes. The *pièce de résistance.*" Lindner sat back in his seat and fixed her with a dramatic expression. "This is the only thing we've got going that might provide some sort of edge."

Kate leaned forward attentively.

"Renata's building a monument to herself," he said.

"She's what?"

"Building a monument. Buying immortality, Hollywood-style," he teased.

"Jerry, what are you talking about?"

"*The Hollywood Daily* Center for Education and the Arts." He waited for her reaction. He wasn't disappointed.

"The *what?*" Kate exploded.

"Too much, huh?" he said, laughing. "It's Renata's newest project. And she's buying up the southwest corner of Hollywood and Vine to put it on."

"But what exactly is it?" Kate asked, fascinated.

"A zillion-dollar facility for teaching, filmmaking, special effects, directing, acting. Anything to do with movies. There'll be a film library. A Hollywood museum. And a number of theaters for screenings and legit plays. The largest of which will bear her name. The Renata Desmond Pavilion. Nice ring, huh?"

"You mean like the Dorothy Chandler Pavilion downtown at the Music Center?" Kate asked, astonished. "Where the Academy Awards are always held?"

"Right you are. And our modest little Renata has her heart set on switching the Awards venue to her pavilion in the near future."

"How near?" she asked.

"Oh, five years, maximum, I'd say. The question is—"

"Where is she getting all the bucks? Right?"

"Right, exactly. This venture will cost a mint. And as far as I know, Renata has no investors. But she's already started buying up the land. Surreptitiously, of course. There's nothing on the street about any of this yet, Kate. So when you go snooping around, be careful."

"No question," Kate agreed, scanning the hurried notes she'd jotted down. "Does that do it?"

"Just about," he said. "Except for one more formality. Uhhh, Kate . . ."

She looked up from her notes to see that his face had grown serious all of a sudden. "What?"

"Uh, this might seem to come from left field. But is there anything I should know about your experience at the *Daily*? Anything that might turn around and, uh, well, bite me in the ass. I mean, I know you were there for a short time and that you left under—"

"Duress?" she cut him off, but smiled good-naturedly. "I was fired, Jerry. Plain and simple. But without good cause. You can ask Joe Birnbaum. He's still managing editor there. That was centuries ago, though. And I certainly have nothing to be ashamed of."

Lindner chuckled. "It's okay," he assured her. "Just something I had to ask—to cover myself. I knew you'd been canned. But being fired in this town has nothing to do with your talents or productivity. We all know that. And I already spoke with Birnbaum. Gives you a clean slate, plus. The guy thinks you're terrific. Why don't you call him? Have lunch. He could be helpful."

"I'll do that. Anything else?"

"For now, no. I'm off to Portugal on Friday. But there's no reason you shouldn't start in on this right away. Come on over to the office tomorrow morning. I'll set you up with a desk and phone. When I'm gone, you'll be able to use mine."

As they walked out of the restaurant together, Jerry raised his voice to combat the heavy traffic noise on Third Street. "I think you'll have some fun with this, Kate."

"I'm sure I will," she replied, handing her ticket to the parking attendant.

Minutes later, as Kate turned the Peugeot onto Sunset Boulevard, she caught a glimpse of herself in the vanity mirror and realized something with a start. She was smiling. Smiling. And happy. Kate felt sensational. She hadn't thought about Seth once in the last two hours. But it was more than that. She had just been handed the ultimate challenge.

An exposé on Renata Desmond. Kate knew firsthand how ruthless the woman could be. Now it was just a matter of finding several people who were willing to talk about Renata's unsavory tactics. It would take some digging. But Kate had the time. And she would be well paid.

"Hallelujah!" she whooped with a burst of enthusiasm as she pulled away from a stop sign. What could be better than being paid for an assignment that offered such a wellspring of vindication? Kate was ecstatic at the thought of interviewing Renata face to face.

And as she headed toward Culver Studios to meet Sara, a hot, heady surge of joyous anticipation bubbled up inside her. She felt like a racehorse at the gate. Eager and anxious.

For years stories had been circulating around Hollywood about the implacable Renata Desmond. There were dozens of accounts as to how, like a steamroller in fast forward, she had simply obliterated the careers of those who got in her way. Rumors, some people called those accounts. But Kate knew differently. And she was willing to interview anyone who could help her prove that. It would be an arduous task, but well worth it. Kate was determined to put the rumors about Renata Desmond to rest. The facts about the woman, she knew, would make much better reading.

4

■ Renata sat at her antique vanity table smoothing cold cream on her face. It was a late-afternoon ritual she always enjoyed, removing, then reapplying her makeup. A rejuvenating process that left her feeling totally invigorated and ready for the evening's activity.

As she reached for a tissue, she heard familiar footsteps approaching. Then the unmistakable rustle of taffeta and petticoats, as Quintana swooshed into the spacious bedroom suite.

"Da-da!" the *zaftig* caterer announced, raising her arms in triumph. "You like?"

Renata glanced at the floor-length magenta gown out of the corner of her eye. "Hmm. A bit Scarlett O'Hara-ish for my taste. What's the occasion?"

"Celebration!" enthused Quintana, spinning ungracefully around in the cumbersome dress. "This little number is my present to me . . . my reward for hard labor. Darling," she continued excitedly, flouncing on the four-poster bed, "I've just learned that our Par Excellence has grossed almost double last year's quarterly earnings. Isn't that utterly jolly?"

"Quin, that's wonderful," Renata replied, with an uncharacteristic show of enthusiasm. Then she frowned into the mirror, meticulously brushing her eyebrows.

"Ah, redoing thyself for a 'do,' I see," Quintana observed, walking over to the small liquor cabinet near the window. "I was hoping we could at least sneak a cocktail together." She poured Stolichnaya into a glass tumbler.

"Quin, it's only four-thirty in the afternoon," Renata objected. "Besides, I have an appointment with Templeton Haight in less than an hour. And after that, a dreadfully dull dinner at the Thorntons'. Select charities meeting."

"So why not beg off? Plead a migraine or something."

"Please," Renata said sternly, "you know I never allow myself to—"

"Shirk responsibility," Quintana said, finishing the sentence she'd heard so many times over the years.

"That's right."

"By the way," Quintana announced, sitting back down on the bed, "your little bet with R. B. McDevitt has spread around town like a forest fire. I overheard a conversation today at Hillcrest and—"

"Overheard? Honestly, Quin, the way you must strain to overhear things I'm surprised you don't lose your balance and fall off your chair. How is it you always seem to pick up on what people halfway across the room are saying?"

"Oh, my! Are we in a touchy mood today!" Quintana joked from the bed. "Are we still smarting from the confrontation with that big bad Texas bull?"

"Nothing of the sort," Renata said smugly. "McDevitt is a total horse's ass. Just jealous he was stupid enough to sell me the team. I handled him!"

"And with great style, my dear." Quintana raised her glass in approval. "Even I was impressed. So you're confident the Longhorns will start paying off this year?"

"They damn well better," Renata replied icily.

Quintana tapped her short fingernails on the tumbler for a moment, watching Renata's face in the mirror. "I've another tidbit to share, darling. Are you aware of who'll be writing your cover story for *World*?" she asked with a playful smirk.

"No," Renata said, carefully stroking mascara onto her lashes. "But I suppose you overheard that too."

"As a matter of fact, I did." Quintana stood up abruptly. "But I don't want to bore you with secondhand information so . . ." She headed for the door.

"Wait a minute," Renata commanded without turning to face her. "Who?"

"Who? Hmm, let me think," Quintana teased. "Name escapes me. But it's someone who's only just arrived in town. Redhead. Female. I'm told she was at that party for Taylor Evans the other night—"

"Don't play coy with me, Quin," Renata snapped, slamming the mascara wand down on the table. "Are you telling me that Kate Brannigan—that no-talent reporter—"

"Ah, yes, Ms. Brannigan. How could I have forgotten?" Quintana cooed. "Finally got up the courage to slink back to La-La Land. Can't imagine how she landed an assignment after your little black-ball operation."

"Quintana!" Renata protested, hiking her throaty voice up an octave. "That's enough."

"Sorry, darling." She stepped back over to the liquor cabinet. "But I do love gossip, you know. Nothing like being able to keep tabs on the players. And who's plugged into whom, if you get my drift. Which leads me to the obvious." She paused, adding a splash of vodka to her glass. "Mr. Taylor Evans. I assume you've managed to finagle an evening with him?"

Renata stroked dark contour powder under her cheekbones, determinedly silent.

"So . . . when's the big night, lovey?" Quintana persisted. "When's the hunk expected for dinner?"

"Next Wednesday," Renata answered finally. "Alone."

"Naturally. What's on the menu? Something aphrodisiacal? Oysters? Rhinoceros horn?"

"Perhaps."

"You'll be disappointed, you know. He's absolutely zero in the sack. At least that's the word around. Lives like a monk, I've heard. Runs some kind of center for the emotionally disturbed up north. And I think that—"

"Darling, I don't particularly care what you happen to think on this matter," Renata replied coolly as she got up. "And Taylor's center is not a hiding place for crazies," she continued, opening the door to her massive walk-in closet. "It is a rather charming hotel in Santa Barbara, where he holds seminars for those who want to get in touch with their inner selves. At his tender age, you see, he has become a sort of spiritual healer. A high priest for yuppies, you might say."

"Is that so?" Quintana responded, unamused. "Then why's he gone Hollywood all of a sudden?"

"A change of pace, I suppose," Renata replied, browsing through the vast array of evening attire before her. "Everyone likes to shift gears from time to time, you know." She paused dramatically, examining a red linen Chanel suit. "Even me."

Quintana knew she should be used to Renata's dalliances by now, but she couldn't help feeling insecure. She'd never understood her lover's need for an occasional male partner. And she never failed to feel threatened by it. "Which explains why you must dabble in the land of male genitalia, I suppose," she rejoined with increasing annoyance.

Renata turned to glare at her for a moment. "Why don't you take your insolent, filthy tongue and stick it in a Cuisinart, Quintana?" How she resented the woman's relentlessness at moments like this. Push, push, push. Needle, needle. Until she struck a nerve.

"Very amusing," Quintana rejoined, walking toward the doorway. "But may I remind you, darling, that you are a full-fledged senior citizen." She stopped to face Renata, an expression of mock-pity on her face. "And still philandering, just like your dear old dad."

"Vicious bitch!" Renata hissed, slipping out of her black silk dressing gown as Quintana left the room. She stepped in front of the floor-length mirror and held up a navy-blue evening suit. Like all of Renata's garments, it was cut in the style of the 1940s. Her favorite decade.

It was during the forties that Renata had come into her own as a businesswoman. Assuming control over her father's companies after his death. And she never felt so efficient, so alive, so powerful as when breezing about town in her stylish suits with their nipped waists, broad shoulders, and flared skirts. The square-toed shoes with ribbon bows. The short, white gloves for daytime. Elbowlength, with long, cap-sleeved gowns for night. The small, veiled hats for afternoons. Larger, plumed versions for evening.

Setting the suit aside, Renata surveyed the upper shelves. Her eyes came to rest on a delicate ostrich-feathered hat, similar to the one Myrna Loy had modeled for *Vogue* in 1942. The hat, like all of Renata's vintage clothing, was in perfect condition. She removed it from its plastic box with utmost care.

Renata had never considered changing her style. Her long, angular body was perfectly suited to the forties' look. Over the years, it had become *her* look, her signature. An essential part of her inimitable presence.

The look also bestowed upon her a certain youthfulness. It was as though Renata Desmond, the beautiful, tall—five feet, eight inches —young woman with the glowing, milk-white skin and the flashing emerald eyes had not really changed since her twenties. Dressing now as she had then helped make her well-preserved face and body appear years younger than her six and a half decades.

Renata slipped into a sheer red silk blouse, the broad-shouldered navy suit, and square-toed navy pumps. Then she resumed her position at the vanity table and quickly swept up her hair Dorothy Lamour-style. She crowned it with the ostrich feather hat.

But as she surveyed the ensemble in the floor-length mirror before leaving, there was a telltale furrow on her brow. Renata was still thinking about Quintana's caustic exit line. *Still philandering, just like your dear old dad.*

Damn, she thought, as she picked up red gloves and a beaded antique bag. *How dare she compare me to that alcoholic old pervert?*

Fifteen minutes later Renata sat impatiently across from Templeton Haight in his high-rise Westwood office. As always, her posture was pencil-straight, her body motionless except for the turning of the ring.

As she listened to the balding man behind the cluttered glass-topped desk, her fingers were busy. Around and around she twisted the large diamond ring on her right hand. Around and around. With ever-increasing fury.

The ring was heavy, masculine. A five-carat diamond set in a thick gold band. It was the kind of ring a man of wealth and power would wear, as indeed "Cappy" Desmond had done during the final decade of his life. The ring was the single personal possession of her father's that Renata had kept.

During the entire time Templeton Haight had been talking, Renata continued twisting the ring with such force and intensity that she now felt the skin break. Then a sticky wetness in the separation between her fingers. Blood perhaps? She didn't bother to check. Instead, placing her elbows on either side of the winged armchair, she cut off the vice-president of Desmond Land Corporation in mid-sentence.

"What do you mean we're not as solvent as we thought? Are

you telling me that you botched the sale of the Pebble Beach estate?"
Renata was incredulous. Templeton Haight was indisputably the
most competent financial manager on the West Coast. That's why
she had employed him for more than twenty years. He couldn't be
letting her down now. Or could he?

"Templeton?" she demanded.

"Botched is a very strong word, Renata," he replied, shifting uncomfortably in his cushioned leather chair. He was a short man with
a diminutive round face and a huge belly that made his limbs seem
stubby in comparison. He had what Renata referred to as an amusing body. "A dead ringer for Humpty-Dumpty," she'd once chuckled with Quintana.

She was not laughing now. And Templeton Haight was doing
everything he could to avoid her penetrating glare. His eyes played
nervously across his desktop, to the compact Mickey Mouse televi-
sion/radio near the telephone. Its screen filled Mickey's protruding
tummy; two tiny speakers were ensconced in his commodious ears;
and the station selector was displayed on the irrepressibly happy
rodent's smile.

Oh, how Templeton loved gadgets! And oh, how he'd been able to
accumulate so many over the past two decades! His home in Beverly
Hills was littered with gadgets. Extremely expensive one-of-a-kind
items. Talking picture frames that lectured on the significance of the
Renoir and Van Gogh hanging in the living room. In the kitchen, an
elongated cylindrical machine with an ultrasonic eye whose sole
function was to seed watermelons.

At his beachfront getaway in Malibu there were cushy chaise
longues that not only provided body massages but folded themselves
up neatly for storage at the touch of a button.

He had enough paraphernalia to start his own oddball museum,
his friends often chided. Templeton ignored their sarcasm. To him,
each carefully selected object was like an individual badge of honor.
Proof that Templeton Haight, the bus driver's son from Portland,
had made it. And then some.

Which was why he squirmed now in the face of Renata's pointed
question. Never before this afternoon had Templeton felt himself in
such jeopardy. During that one millisecond the thought flashed
through his mind. *Bankruptcy.* It was possible.

He shuddered. Templeton sat on the board of more than a half-dozen major conglomerates across the country. He was a sought-after speaker on the college lecture circuit as well. And had picked up a number of honorary doctorates during his travels. Now, all of that could be reduced to sheer mockery. He could see the headline in *World* magazine already. "Haight Resigns in Total Disgrace—Loses All!"

"Templeton," Renata repeated petulantly, "do you hear me?"

"Yes, yes, of course," he answered with a feigned assurance. It was one of the reasons Templeton had lasted so long under Renata. He seldom, if ever, lost control. Inner turmoil was never externalized. He had two bleeding ulcers to show for it, but he always maintained the correct stoniness of George Washington on Mount Rushmore.

"And yes," he went on, "I'm afraid we have lost this sale. But we still have a number of options," he lied.

"Options? Options at this late date?" she scoffed. "Templeton we have just lost thirty million dollars—cash. Escrow was supposed to close in a week, and all of a sudden they're not buying? How, may I ask, do you propose we get around that?" She spoke slowly and deliberately, the words trailing out in a prolonged hiss. "Or have you finally hit upon the gadget that turns you into a magician?"

"Not yet," he replied with a pinched smile. "I thought perhaps another buyer. I have a number of—"

"Too damn late!" she interjected. "You know we need the thirty million by early November to get the rest of the property for my Hollywood Center. And you also damn well know that every minute we drag our feet on that deal, the more impossible it becomes to keep our plan under wraps. Must I remind you that we are fighting the calendar? If word leaks that we're doing the buying, the price will shoot up as if gold were discovered at Hollywood and Vine!"

She lowered her voice to a conspiratorial whisper. "Templeton," she said, holding his eyes with a hypnotic stare, "we need the money in less than three weeks, or the Center will not materialize. That . . . cannot . . . happen."

Templeton nodded slowly.

Two years earlier Renata had ordered him to buy up the entire block on the southwest corner of Hollywood and Vine. He'd set about the task efficiently and surreptitiously, using the names of straw corporations. Five parcels of land in all. Four purchased. One to go. But it was the biggest and most critical.

And then that damned screw-up with the Swiss millionaire he'd sold the Pebble Beach estate to. Check that. Almost sold. Hell, how was he to know Lasseur would back out at the last minute, claiming some trumped-up currency transfer problem?

The real problem, however, was that Renata was running out of money. He had to find a way to raise the cash to finance the final parcel of land; otherwise she could be out her Hollywood Center. Worse than that, it was conceivable, even likely, that the Desmond Land Company might be forced into bankruptcy.

Over the past two years Templeton had done Renata's bidding and sold off most of the corporation's larger holdings in order to finance the land for the Center. And often he'd sold at below-market value, for the quick cash. When even this did not produce enough capital, he'd robbed Peter to pay Paul. The entire company was leveraged to the hilt. Once the land was theirs, they'd have no trouble finding a bank to underwrite construction, and all would be well; but until then, they teetered dangerously at the brink.

So far Renata knew nothing of this.

Templeton thought back to the night they'd planned their strategy. How he wished he could have that night back now.

It had begun over a cozy, confidential chat in Renata's dining room. Quail for two at the magnificent mahogany table. He still remembered the tremendous glow of self-confidence he'd felt when she'd confided her dream to him and entrusted it to his care.

"We're going to pull this off together, Templeton," she'd assured him over cognac and coffee. "And it will change your life, I promise you. *The Hollywood Daily* Center for Education and the Arts. It will immortalize us and bring Hollywood back to the luster and glamour of the forties. We'll be heroes, you realize that, don't you? We'll each get a star on the Walk of Fame."

Now Templeton saw only that he would have to work some wizardry to save their collective asses.

"A second mortgage on your home," he ventured, as if thinking aloud. "No, out of the question. We'd get ten million, tops. Not nearly enough . . ."

Renata was watching him closely, suspicious of where he was trying to lead her.

"But perhaps if you corraled a few investors for the Center . . . then you could—"

"Also out of the question. We've been over this too many times already. You know this is to be my Center. Mine. And you know very well that the egomaniacs in this community who might invest in it would insist on grabbing a share of the glory, too. No. Definitely, no."

"All right then," Templeton said calmly, placing his clammy hands carefully on the desk. "Consider instead going public with the *Daily*. I know we've discussed this before as well, and you've always refused. But we desperately need the cash, Renata, and doing so could bring in a great deal very quickly."

He stopped. Renata was already shaking her head vigorously back and forth.

"I am not about to risk losing control of the *Daily*, Templeton, not now, not ever. If you think I would even consider going public, you are clearly having a wet dream with your eyes wide open."

Templeton brightened, laughing softly—a gesture of approval and understanding. He'd known she would refuse both suggestions. He'd merely been paving the way for the one idea he figured she might accept, if he timed it properly. It seemed that time had come.

"Well then, Renata," he suggested, in a hopeless tone, trying to sound as though their options were exhausted. "You have one other choice."

She regarded him skeptically, saying nothing.

"You should seriously consider selling the team."

He waited the full three seconds it took her to respond. Listening to his heart thump hard against his chest. And then he had the answer he'd hoped he wouldn't hear.

"Sell the Longhorns? Over your expired carcass, Templeton," she announced, rising up from her chair. "Now may I suggest that you do some more thinking about this"—she stood over him, playing up the drama of the moment—"because, my dear Mr. Vice-President, if I lose the Center, you're going to lose a lot more than your job. I'll see to that."

Templeton Haight did not doubt her for a moment.

5

■ Sara Evans Silverstein's impeccably manicured hands grabbed at the side of the cold marble sink in an attempt to steady herself. The wave of nausea had overwhelmed her. She'd rushed here, to her executive powder room, barely able to walk. And now she couldn't stop shaking.

Warily, Sara looked up into the black onyx-bordered mirror and examined her face. It was pale and drawn. The force of tears had sent ripples of mascara trickling down her cheeks. Telltale lines of red were etched in her deep-set hazel eyes. She thought she looked old. Maybe ten years older since this morning, when she'd arrived at Culver Studios brimming with her usual energy and enthusiasm.

And why? What had happened in that brief amount of time? And had it really happened? Sara asked herself now, the queasiness still rippling through her stomach. Yes. Yes. It had. A truckload of *tsuris,* that's what had happened. And she'd been totally off guard when it did.

She was so happy when Mark phoned to ask her to meet him for lunch. Her hectic schedule didn't allow them much time together during the week. He was making an effort to see her. She was glad. And also surprised he'd chosen the studio commissary.

Mark hadn't set foot on the lot in more than six months. Ever since *Expectations* had gone eleven million over budget and died a terrible death at the box office. Suddenly, Mark Silverstein, the Hollywood *Wunderkind,* the thirty-six-year-old writer-director whose second film had garnered a best-screenplay Oscar nomination, was out in the cold. Poison. Persona non grata. Not only at Culver Studios but in every production house in town.

Mark had spent the last few months licking his wounds, preparing a new script, and leaning a great deal on his wife. Sara had held up well, balancing her new job as the studio's President of Television

Production with the requisite show-business socializing and her responsibilites at home with Mark and their twin girls. She'd done it all with the aplomb of a professional juggler. Without being asked, she had been cast in the role of superwoman. And she found she loved it, thrived on it.

Then the call from Mark. And the lunch. And the stiff, awkward, horrible conversation.

"So how's it goin'?" he'd asked listlessly when she joined him at the small square table in the corner.

"It's going." She shrugged, sipping her iced tea, afraid to seem enthusiastic. Too much jubilation about her work might backfire, considering his current state of affairs. *Downplay it, kiddo,* Sara told herself.

"So, like what?" he asked, impatiently tapping the tabletop with his short, square fingers. "Good things or bad?"

"Well, good," she began, keeping her excitement in check. "The first *Vs. the Odds* hour is finally completed. You know, the Brandy St. John series about the woman attorney. I'm screening it this afternoon. Kate's coming. Like to join us?"

"Ah, no. I think I—I mean, I have an appointment with Hubbard this afternoon. He's got a group of investors from Arizona. They might be interested in *Possessions.*"

"Honey, that's terrific!" Sara enthused too loudly. "Why didn't you tell me earlier?"

"Just came up." Mark looked unusually depressed this afternoon, as if he were in pain. "And well—I, Sara, there's something we need to talk about. It's that I, ahh . . ." Silence for a few seconds.

"Yes, what is it, Daddycakes?" she whispered, hoping he'd loosen up a bit at the mention of her pet name for him. But to Sara's dismay, he didn't smile, not even a little. Mark hadn't been himself in months, so she wasn't unduly alarmed. *Maybe it's just being here on the lot,* she thought. *He's still insecure. Nervous about running into the wrong people.*

That, it turned out, wasn't the problem at all. When he finally said the words Sara was stunned at first, unable to accept what she had heard.

"You expect me to believe this? It's a joke, right? Like the time you came hobbling back to the house in Aspen and told me you'd broken your leg?" She tried to laugh. But what came out was a weak little guttural sputter.

Mark said nothing. Her questioning eyes searched his strong, tanned face. The face she'd caressed and kissed for so many years. It was set in a stony expression, immobile and so very cold. She knew then. It was no joke. Sara felt as if she had been hit by a piledriver.

He wanted out. Their thirteen-year marriage. Over. He'd decided. And he couldn't manage to say much more. No, it wasn't another woman. No, Sara hadn't done anything wrong. She had, in fact, been wonderfully supportive. But he just couldn't stay there anymore. In their Bel Air home.

"Why not? It's a big place. Twelve bedrooms. You can take your pick," she countered, still striving for lightness. But inside she was falling apart.

"I'm going a little nuts, I guess," he said. "I need, well, as tritely California as it sounds, I need some space. Time to work things out by myself."

"But, Mark," she implored, finally serious, "you never said anything before. And we haven't had a chance to discuss it. Couldn't you have waited until tonight? Can't we, please, talk later on when—"

"*When? When* is the question, Sara," he said, raising his voice for the first time. "When are you ever home? Eleven o'clock? Midnight? Finally back from meetings and cocktail parties and screenings and dinners? There's no time at home, Sara. You hardly have five minutes to kiss Jennifer and Jackie good night."

After that Sara couldn't say much more, and certainly nothing that would dissuade him. He said he'd already packed his bags and moved in with a friend. Sara didn't inquire as to who the friend was. She just hoped it wasn't a woman. Yet by the time Mark gave her a quick little hug good-bye and rushed off without a backward glance, she still hadn't thoroughly comprehended the reality of her altered life. Her mind had heard and understood the fact that he was leaving her. Her heart hadn't. It was too clean and quick. Too surgical. Marriages didn't just end over lunch. It couldn't be happening.

Once the nausea struck, Sara realized that it truly was. This was no Hollywood fabrication, not a movie of the week, not business as usual. This was real, and so was the pain, the hurt, the humiliation.

She sensed it would get worse before it got better, that she was only beginning to deal with the mental anguish that would follow. Her man. Her lover. Her best friend. The father of her two beautiful daughters. Mark was gone. Even at his weakest, he had still been her anchor, the only one she'd ever clung to. She wasn't sure she could go on without him.

"Is it show time yet?"

It was Kate's voice. *My God, she's here. Oh, yes, the screening.* "Uh, in a minute. Have a seat."

"Sorry if I startled you," said a somewhat puzzled Kate when her friend finally emerged from the bathroom. "Your secretary let me in. Guess I have an honest face. Hey, what's with the dark glasses? Sara, are you going Hollywood on me at this late date?"

"Hardly." Sara emitted a strident little laugh as she sat down at her desk and reached for the telephone. She'd promised herself she would not reveal a thing to Kate, not here. She didn't trust herself. Tonight, safely at home, she could unload all of it on her best friend. Then she could afford to crumble again.

"Laurie? Check with Projection Room One will you? See if everyone's set for *Vs. the Odds.*"

"Sara," Kate said, getting up off the striped raw-silk couch and walking over to the desk. "Sara, are you all right?"

"Of course. Fine. Want to use the *power* room before we leave?" she asked, lamely using a favorite pun of theirs. "How was lunch with Lindner? What was it all about, anyway? He's got the hots for you, right?" The words tumbled out in a rush.

"Sara, can the kibitzing, will you?" Kate said emphatically, leaning over and planting her hands firmly on Sara's sleek teakwood desk. "There *is* something wrong, isn't there . . . isn't there?"

Sara said nothing but instead reached up and slid the dark glasses down the bridge of her nose briefly, then pushed them back in place again.

"Good heavens, Sara! What is it?"

Sara looked up ruefully at her dear friend. "Not a pretty sight, as you can see. *Mieskeit* in mourning." A single teardrop made its way down her cheek.

"You've got to tell me." Kate had both hands on her shoulders now. "What in the world happened?"

Taking a deep breath, Sara slumped back in her chair. "It's Mark
. . . he's leaving me." She choked it out. And she began crying
again, harder this time. No use in holding back now. She told Kate
about the fateful lunch.

Men—they're such total jerks, Kate was thinking as Sara sobbed
through the painful story. *How can they so easily mess up a perfectly
well-directed life?*

"The only good thing," Sara whimpered, wiping her eyes and
examining the tissue, "is that I now have permanent eyeliner. Can
you imagine the mess? If only husbands were so permanent." She
blew her nose noisily.

Kate sat down on the desk and handed Sara another tissue. "Listen, hon. This isn't your fault. None of it."

"Yes it is. It's *all* my fault. Look at me, Kate. I mean really look
at me."

"I know what you look like. You look terrific when you're feeling
good. You're very stylish and always beautifully groomed and—"

"Groomed! A stupid poodle can be beautifully groomed. What
about attractive? What about pretty? I'm not that. I never will be
that. And I'm fat. Fat, Kate. I've gained fifteen pounds. More than
fifteen probably. When I couldn't fight my way into my jeans any
more, I stopped weighing myself. All those cockamamy parties and
dinners. I look tired and worn out. See these bags under my eyes?
It's like somebody dumped a couple pounds of ground coffee in
there. I'm a wreck."

"Sara, will you quit berating yourself?"

"No! I won't. Don't you see? That's why Mark is leaving me. I
don't do it for him anymore. He's found another woman."

"He told you that?" Kate asked, holding her breath.

"He didn't have to tell me. I know. It's instinct. Someone younger
and prettier." She made a crazy-lady face. "He wouldn't have to go
far."

Kate had heard enough. "Now you stop that, Sara. Stop that right
now. And listen to me. He loves you. He didn't deny that, did he? Of
course he didn't. He loves you and he still wants you—"

"He doesn't want me!" Sara protested. "Kate, we haven't made
love in weeks. And who can blame him? Look at this body. Who
wants to hump the Pillsbury Doughgirl?"

"Dammit, Sara, it isn't the end, you hear me? He'll be back. Mark's too smart to walk out on an intelligent, dynamic, loving lady like you. He's just down on himself right now. The man has lost his way. He feels like a failure. And his male ego just can't take the dependent role he's fallen into with you."

"But he's not dependent on me, he's—"

"Sara, you know he is. At least he has been since *Expectations.* Just like he was when you first married. You think he wasn't intimidated by your family? How many fathers give their daughters multi-million-dollar mansions in Bel Air for a wedding present? Mark had a hard time living up to your life-style, Sara. You know he did. We've discussed it so often. Then, finally, he made it on his own. He was in charge. He was getting the glory. It was even okay when you went back to work producing that TV series. But when you got this hot new job, and then Mark hit the skids, and you had to take care of him again . . . and let's face it, you know your folks were ready to pay the bills too, if need be—"

"But they didn't have to," Sara said weakly.

"No. But they could have. And Mark couldn't. Oh Sara, it's such a lousy cliché, and it's not your fault. You can't help it that your father owns half the Silicon Valley. But think of Mark and what it must have done to him all these years. You knew when you married him he'd always be struggling to get out from under the shadow of your family. Where are his folks from anyway? Detroit?"

Sara nodded her head yes. "The suburbs. Livonia."

"Okay. Livonia. His father was a janitor or something, wasn't he?"

"Chief maintenance engineer of a large auto parts company."

"And your father runs his own computer chip company, raking in the millions. Sugar, it's not that Mark doesn't love you. He just feels he can't measure up."

"Yes he can. He has. He's already proven that. Now he wants out. He only married me because he had to . . . and for the money. I've known it for years. I just never admitted it. Why else? You know damn well nobody on campus could believe I'd landed him. He was editor of *The Daily Princetonian,* for God's sake. And damn good-looking—in a runty sort of way." She half smiled now, enjoying the stab at Mark's Achilles' heel—his height.

"That's better. You *should* get angry. Get it out of your system," Kate encouraged. "Go ahead, call him names. Come on—do it!"

"Okay. He's a jerk."

"A rat," Kate urged.

"A bastard . . . and a schmuck," Sara fumed.

"A *pisher* and . . ."

"No, no." Sara waved a hand. "Not a *pisher,* honey. That's somebody young. Mark's a *putz.* He's a real *putz.* And a shithead. And an asshole. And a no-good son of a bitch. And I hate him. I really hate him!" Tears gushed out now in a waterfall.

"Good. You go ahead and hate him. Hate him as much as you want to. Think about all the lousy things he's ever done. All the times you wanted to strangle him," said Kate reassuringly. "Just remember it isn't your fault. And he'll be back—that is, if you still want him."

"I just can't believe it's happening." Sara smiled sardonically through her tears. "If somebody pitched this script at me, I'd throw it right in the toilet. What the hell am I supposed to do now?"

"Nothing. Just carry on as usual, and don't go bonkers. Give him time to think things through and see he's made a mistake."

Sara scrunched up her face and reached for her compact. She looked sad and tired. "You're staying aren't you, Kate? For a few weeks anyway?" she asked, daubing a light cream makeup base under her eyes.

"Of course I'm staying. What do you take me for—a deserter?" Despite herself, she felt a twinge of pleasure—and a little guilty for that—at being able to rescue Sara for once. It's about time, she thought, that she had a chance to return the favor. "In fact," she continued on breezily, "you might have a long-term boarder in the pink guest room. I've landed a job."

"What?" They were walking swiftly toward the projection room now. Sara stopped short just outside the door. "That's fantastic, Kate. How did . . . wait a minute, Lindner—right?"

"Indeed," Kate said, a note of triumph in her voice. "I'll tell you all about it later, but it's a cover story for *World* . . . a piece on Renata Desmond."

"You . . . writing about Renata?" Sara sounded almost like herself again. "How deliciously ironic!"

"A challenging and intrinsically rewarding undertaking, I'd say." Kate winked as they entered the projection room.

She followed Sara to the deep-set leather seats next to the volume controls reserved for the chief of TV production and her guest.

Her emotions firmly in check once more, Sara chatted briefly with the series' producers. Kate sank into the lush seat and closed her eyes for a moment, luxuriating in the seductiveness of Hollywood, its private screening rooms, the sense of belonging to the most glamorous club in the world. And she let her thoughts wander back to the last time she'd taken a job in this town.

How excited she'd been that afternoon! She could still remember what she was wearing. A white pleated skirt with a kelly-green blazer and a striped polyester blouse, which Sara had assured her looked just like silk. Her hair was short then. Tight curls cropped close to her head. She must have looked pathetically young and naive.

But Joe Birnbaum, managing editor of *The Hollywood Daily,* had taken her seriously. He'd read all her clips and liked them. It was her second interview with him. And how lucky for her that Birney, as everyone called him, was best friends with her favorite journalism professor at Columbia.

"Well, kid, ya got the job. Can't turn down the old prof's star student, can I?" Birney had announced, peering up from under his visor. He had a standard uniform for work. The green visor. A light blue oxford-cloth shirt with rolled-up sleeves. When it was chilly, a vest. And there was always a pencil tucked up over his ear. When they'd first met, Kate had thought how much Birney looked like one of the harried newspaper editors in the classic play *The Front Page.*

"The prof says ya got a pretty good track record with that paper back in New York. Rochester, wasn't it? How many years there?"

"Three."

" 'S a long time to stick with a hometown daily," he said offhandedly.

"My mother was very ill and alone," Kate explained. "I really couldn't leave. She died earlier this year. Cancer."

She didn't tell him about her father's unexpected death only months after she'd graduated from journalism school. He'd suffered a fatal stroke. "Cerebral vascular accident," the doctor had announced. An accident that had shaken Kate's world to the core. At the time she wasn't sure she'd ever recover from his death. She was certain her mother never had.

"Sorry," Birney said, a bit embarrassed, then went on quickly. "Here you'll find it a bit different from your ordinary newspaper city room. Even though you'll still be on the business beat like before, the 'business' here has a lot more glitz and glam than what you're used to. Some pretty sharp but sleazy characters out there with roving eyes and limousines. What we print here can make or break projects worth millions. You just keep your eye on the straight and narrow. Understand?"

Kate nodded. If she didn't quite, she would very soon.

"Now," Birney continued, "first point of business is getting your contacts in order. Harvey Stinson, he'll be your boss. Been covering the beat since the forties. Been askin' for an assistant for almost that long too. Harv'll be helpful. Introduce ya around. Get ya started." He paused somewhat dramatically, Kate thought, and his face took on a look of gravity. "But remember one thing. If you ever think you're in trouble on a story . . . or anything . . . you come directly to me, hear?"

As it happened, Kate took Birney up on his offer. Harvey Stinson did not prove to be helpful. And he certainly didn't go out of his way to introduce her around. During her first weeks at the *Daily,* she felt like a neglected puppy dog at his feet.

Harvey was a tall, lean, angular man. His skin was dry and coarse, and his polyester jackets were flecked with tiny white specks of dandruff. He had an abrasiveness about him that put Kate off.

But she did her best to overlook his bad manners and learn as much as possible. Although Harvey made no comment on her first few pieces—they concerned executive shufflings at the major film studios—Kate knew Birney was pleased. And that was enough for her. By her third week she realized the truth. She had really been hired to pick up Harvey Stinson's slack. Already she was producing more than he, while Harvey did not vary in his established routine of arriving late and lunching until well past three in the afternoon.

Kate didn't mind the workload. More stories meant more exposure, more opportunity to know and become known. Harvey could be out to lunch permanently, as far as she was concerned. But it wasn't Harvey Stinson's work habits that caused Kate to walk into Birney's office on a buoyant spring afternoon just before Easter. It was something else. Something she felt Birney ought to know.

At first the managing editor clearly didn't believe her. "Kate, do you realize how serious a charge that is? Have they been passin' the Wheaties at the parties you've been attending? I thought you were a straight arrow."

"Birney, I do know, and I am serious," she said, ignoring his ridiculous cocaine accusation. "I have it on very good authority. Max Steiner, Goodwin's chief of production—okay? He's mad as hell and might even go to the SEC. He swears that Harvey knew about Newsome Food's intentions to take over the studio . . . a week ago. I mean, Steiner didn't say so, but he probably leaked it to him himself, thinking that if Harvey broke the story in the *Daily* . . . well, obviously Steiner was hoping the leak would wreck Newsome's bid and protect his own job."

She reached into her large leather handbag. "But Harvey sat on it. And now two of his best buddies . . . here, I have their names and the dates of the stock transactions. They each bought five thousand shares of Goodwin Studios stock on Thursday, at thirteen per share. Today, after Newsome announced its acquisition, it went up to twenty-five."

Although Kate didn't know it, there'd been other complaints in recent months about Harvey Stinson. Screwups on names, dates, sometimes box office grosses. But never anything major, never anything like this.

As Kate saw it, Birney had no choice. If the Securities and Exchange Commission got wind that a *Daily* reporter had traded on inside information, there'd be hell to pay. And what if this wasn't the first time? He had to tell his boss, Renata Desmond. She'd probably fire Stinson. And that was too bad, because the old guy—he was sixty-four—had put in an entire career at the *Daily*. And Kate hated to see a loyal trooper booted out in disgrace.

She slept fitfully that night, wrestling with guilt over having nailed Stinson. Would word leak back to him? Would he provoke an ugly confrontation with her? Would the other *Daily* staffers see her as an opportunist, scheming to get Stinson axed in order to claim his job as her own?

The next morning, hurrying through the arched doorway of the old Spanish-style building on Hollywood Boulevard, which had housed the *Daily* since its inception in 1929, Kate fought against the impulse to go directly to Birney's office. Summoning every ounce of self-control, she decided to wait. Wait until he contacted her. His call came shortly after lunch and she quickly made her way to his office, trying not to appear anxious.

"Ahhh, Kate . . . I have somethin' that's not so easy to explain to you," he began sheepishly.

"Yes?" More than anything else, his strange demeanor aroused her curiosity. Kate had never seen Birney like this. So subdued, so— tame. Whatever Renata had decided about Stinson must be weighing heavily on poor Birney's soul, she figured. His night was probably spent struggling with demons of his own.

"Well, it's that—y'know how much I like your work, Kate. You're a very able reporter. Better than that. You're good, damn good." He hesitated. "But y'see, I got budget problems. All of a sudden. Nothin' I suspected when I hired you. And, well, I know this is short notice, Kate, and it's all our—my fault. Should have paid more attention to the payroll overload before you came aboard. I had just hired a coupla more stringers, y'see. Toronto . . . Nashville. And I, uh, well, I really can't afford havin' two business reporters on staff just now. So—"

"You mean I'm fired?" Kate heard herself blurt out.

Birney winced. "Let's say, *let go.* More like being laid off. We'll pay you through the end of the week, of course. But I won't expect you to finish up your assignments. You're free to go . . . whenever. And, Kate, I just want you to know this is no reflection on you . . . and that, well . . . I'm just damn sorry it had to—"

Kate didn't listen to the rest. She was concentrating on swallowing hard to clear away the dull, aching lump in her throat. And trying not to cry. Call it whatever you wanted, it amounted to the same thing: She had been fired. And it wasn't possible. Nobody in her family had ever been fired. It was beyond imagining. It was . . . it was a disgrace.

Kate's eyes met Birney's. And she knew he could see the stinging wetness threatening to come tumbling down her freckled cheeks. But she couldn't just get up and walk away. Not yet. Harvey Stinson! With the shocking news of her own fate, she'd shoved him to the back of her mind. More than ever now, she had a right. And she had to know.

"So Stinson stays?" she asked.

"Yep," Birney mumbled. "Looks that way."

"Did you tell Renata? What did she say? Surely she can't—"

"Kate, listen kiddo," Birney cut her off. "The Stinson matter is out of your hands now. Y'did the right thing tellin' me. And I'm handlin' it. That's all I can say. 'Cept I don't want you gettin' any crazy idea that you bein' let go has anything to do with Harv . . . okay?"

Kate nodded, but she knew it wasn't okay. She was positive Birney was covering up for somebody. And her every instinct told her that the *somebody* was Renata Desmond.

Harvey's excuse about the budget was a bunch of hogwash. Kate's firing was just too coincidental, and she was certain he would never have done it on his own.

Only the week before she'd heard from Professor Kagan, her old journalism teacher, that Birney was amazed with her "splendid progress" and delighted with her reportorial skills. No. It had to be Renata. Some sort of collusion existed between her and Stinson. Harvey was being protected. And Kate was being canned.

It just isn't fair . . . it just isn't fair. The words kept echoing inside her head as she left Birney's office. *There must be a way to uncover what's really going on. And I'm going to find it.*

I'll go to the authorities, she decided, sweeping the contents of her two desk drawers into a small cardboard box. *The police. No . . . the district attorney's office. Maybe the SEC.*

But she knew she had to speak first with Max Steiner over at Goodwin Studios. She needed him to back her up. Without Steiner to corroborate the story, nobody would believe her.

I'll call him. No, I'll go over to the studio and see him in person. After all, didn't he say, Stop by anytime? If he isn't there, I'll just wait.

By three that afternoon Kate was speeding over Laurel Canyon in her second-hand Volkswagen and rehearsing what she would say to Steiner. She wasn't sure he'd be willing to go along with her. In fact, she thought he probably wouldn't. But she was determined to convince him.

By three-twenty she was standing, nearly paralyzed in astonishment, in front of the graying receptionist at Goodwin Studios.

"I'm sorry, Miss Brannigan," the dour, middle-aged woman was repeating. "As I said, Mr. Steiner is not here. He handed in his resignation this morning."

"But he . . . I wanted to . . ."

"Perhaps you'd like to speak with his secretary. I can—"

"No. No. That isn't necessary. Ah . . . thank you," Kate said, turning numbly away.

It was at that moment she realized the tremendous force of Renata Desmond's stranglehold on the Hollywood community.

Still stunned, walking aimlessly through the executive parking lot past the gleaming Jaguars, Porsches, Rolls-Royces and Mercedeses, Kate noticed a man in paint-spattered coveralls. He was crouched in a vacant spot, hurriedly brushing over a nameplate, covering up the bold white letters with sweeping strokes of black paint. EINER, was all Kate could make out of the banished name. My God, she thought —it's as if the man himself has disappeared.

But as a trained reporter, Kate was certain she could track Max Steiner down. And she spent the next week trying to do so. The papers, including the *Daily,* reported that Steiner had departed Goodwin Studios in order to set up his own production company. But nobody could tell her where it was headquartered. And the handful of executives she knew had Steiner's home phone number were unwilling to divulge it to her.

Finally she asked Sara's husband, Mark, to intercede. Several days later he came up with Steiner's unlisted phone number. But each time Kate dialed it, she got an answering machine. She left at least two dozen messages. Steiner never once returned her calls.

In despair, Kate gave up. By then she wasn't even so sure Steiner had told her the truth. Maybe he'd deliberately lied. Set her up. Maybe he'd had some grudge against Stinson and used her to try to get Harvey fired. If that had been Steiner's plan, the whole thing had backfired on him.

And on Kate. But she hadn't yet experienced the full impact of the explosion.

Once she got her self-esteem back up to a healthy level and went job-hunting, she found that all doors were mysteriously, unalterably closed. No one wanted to hire the woman who'd been canned after just four months on *The Hollywood Daily*. Her credentials, the recommendations on her résumé—they made no difference. For Kate Brannigan, Hollywood was padlocked. Period.

Renata Desmond had seen to that.

Suddenly the lights dimmed in the screening room, and Kate roused herself back to the present.

"Terrific opening," she whispered to Sara as gigantic colored letters flashed onto the screen, spelling out *Vs. the Odds*. Then a series of quick cuts. Brandy St. John, looking incredibly gorgeous and intelligent, in a courtroom, in an office, walking up the steps of city hall.

Smiling affably, Kate settled back to enjoy her good friend's TV performance. And she made a silent promise to herself. This time in Hollywood she would stay. She would stay for as long as she liked. She would fit in here. She would be a success. Despite Renata Desmond. Or perhaps because of her.

6

■ Kate plopped her tan leather briefcase down heavily on Jerry Lindner's desk, with a disgruntled sigh. There were no messages. She'd been gone most of the afternoon, and not one of the two dozen people she'd tried to reach earlier that morning had returned her call.

Lindner had been away in Europe for more than a week now. And still Kate hadn't unearthed anything startling, or revealing, or even halfway interesting about Renata Desmond.

She'd interviewed more than a dozen people already. Most of the studio chiefs, television and record company executives she'd contacted were willing to give her a half hour. After all, a possible mention in *World* was worth that. But they'd all proved disappointing. Heaping nothing but praise on Renata. Handing Kate the same pat quotes she could have lifted from the thick press packet *The Hollywood Daily*'s public relations firm had messengered over.

Not that Hollywood suffered from a scarcity of leads about Renata Desmond's ruthlessness. Kate remembered hearing, for instance, about Chet Werner, the advertising executive. Werner was Vice-President of Marketing at Ingram Studios for five years—until he was abruptly fired. Apparently Werner had altered the studio's trade ad budget, shifting more ads over to *Variety* and fewer to the *Daily*. Renata promptly used her leverage—ordering an unflattering portrait of the studio's recent marketing strategies and making it clear privately to studio executives that more of the same could be expected if Werner remained at his post. Good-bye, Chet Werner.

One of *World*'s reporters had told Kate about Tracey Lawson, the soap-opera actress. Tracey claimed that Renata had ruined her chances for a starring role in a big-budget movie. Because Tracey had rejected Renata's advances.

Tales of the woman's vindictiveness pervaded clandestine conversations everywhere. One of the most frequently repeated concerned Jean deMornay, the celebrated chef at Le Bijou in West Hollywood. At the urging of the stars and studio brass who loved his cooking, deMornay started a catering business in the fifties.

And he did extremely well until Quintana Jaye launched Par Excellence. Within a year she'd stolen almost all of deMornay's accounts. The "A" parties and significant premieres. The private luncheons, bar mitzvahs, and weddings. Eventually deMornay filed for bankruptcy and retreated back to Le Bijou's kitchen. Everyone knew who was really responsible: Renata Desmond.

But deMornay was now a permanent resident of Forest Lawn. Tracey Lawson wasn't interested in risking Renata's fury again by talking to Kate, and neither was Chet Werner. Stories like theirs about Renata were always carefully put "off the record." None of them could be documented. In short, they were worthless.

Today Kate had spent the afternoon at the Academy of Motion Picture Arts and Sciences research library sifting through piles of newspaper and magazine clippings. Looking for a lead. Some hint. Any reference to a person she'd not yet thought to call. Surely there must be *someone* in Hollywood willing to expose a chink in Renata Desmond's steel-plated armor. But after four hours she had nothing except bleary eyes—and the nagging fear that she wasn't doing enough. The same relentless sensation she always had when tackling a challenging project.

Kate slumped back in Lindner's swivel chair and stared at the long list of names on the legal pad in front of her. Forty-five . . . fifty? She'd called them all, more than once. She'd even cornered some of them briefly at screenings or press parties. "Certainly." "Call me tomorrow, darling." "Be happy to talk to you." That's what they always said. Anything to get away, to avoid her call the next day.

Maybe Renata had gotten to all of them first. Obviously the more nosing around Kate did, the more steps Renata would take to protect herself. And in the case of Templeton Haight at the Desmond Land Corporation—well, there was simply no question that Renata had scared him off.

Haight had made the mistake of picking up the phone the first time Kate had called. Delighted with her luck, she'd tried every-

thing she could think of to convince him to submit to an interview.
And he'd been most cordial, all but promising his cooperation.
When she called again, Haight's secretary had informed Kate that
the answer was a flat no. The same answer she'd gotten from every
staffer on the *Daily* except Birney—and even he had given her nothing really substantial.

Kate glared at the phone, thinking about her upcoming meeting
with Renata. It was scheduled for Friday morning at the Desmond
estate in Trousdale. Now she was considering putting it off.

How could she confront Renata unarmed, without the necessary
ammunition? She wasn't ready! She needed something more. Something to show Renata that all her efforts to thwart Kate's investigation had been in vain—that not *everyone* in this town was scared to
death of her! Right now Kate's only secret weapon was her knowledge of the *Hollywood Daily* Center that Lindner had mentioned.
That might knock Renata off-balance a little. But it wasn't nearly
enough.

Kate refused to give up. She was certain that if she kept looking,
she would find what she needed. Solid evidence of Renata Desmond's malevolence, her underhanded tactics, her bullying stranglehold on the entertainment business. Sooner or later she'd uncover
the damaging information to wound the queen. Without it, Renata
would control the interview. She would walk all over Kate.

Besides, the longer Kate put off the interview, the longer Renata
would have to stew—wondering what Kate was coming up with,
whom she'd talked to, how much she really knew.

Yes, Kate decided. It was clear now. Postpone the interview. She
flipped through Lindner's Rolodex. It wasn't yet six o'clock. She
could still reach Renata's press agent at Laurence & Ferber.

A piercing buzz startled Kate. The intercom line. Quickly, she
reached for the phone.

"A Mr. Arnold here to see you."

"What?" Kate said, astonished.

Kelly, the receptionist, lowered her voice to a muffled whisper.
"Says he knows you, that you're friends."

"I do—I mean, we are. I, ahh . . . of course, send him in." She
stood up, briskly smoothing out her wrinkled gabardine pants,

readjusting the light blue silk blouse. She hadn't looked in a mirror since lunch—no time now.

Within seconds he was standing in the doorway. Seth Arnold.

Kate caught her breath. For just an instant the memories came flooding back—the long, peaceful walks along the Potomac, the quiet late-night dinners, the silly disagreements. The touch of his skin as they made love. The Georgetown apartment they'd shared—so still and empty once he'd left.

But she had been the one to ask him to leave. The one who'd broken it off and said, "No, I can't live with you anymore. Not now, not ever. Please go away. Please make it easier—on us both."

She'd fled to California, hoping that would make a difference. And she thought it had. The past two weeks she had successfully distracted herself, thought less about Seth. She'd convinced herself she'd forget. In time.

But looking at him now, Kate knew she was a long way from forgetting about Seth Arnold. She was still terribly attracted to him. His robust, well-toned body and dark good looks. His features—more rugged than handsome. The strong, angular jaw and aquiline nose. And those sensitive, warm brown eyes. There was a maleness about Seth that Kate found absolutely magnetic.

But it was more than that. There was a bond between them. She couldn't explain it. She only knew her feelings for Seth ran much deeper than she'd ever expected.

"It's good to see you, Kate."

The sound of his husky voice sent an uncontrollable thrill through her. She tried to say something in reply, but the words wouldn't come out.

"Lady executive I see," he went on, teasing her now, sensing her uneasiness. "Nice office. Impressive."

"Not really mine." She laughed nervously. "This is merely a facade. I'm back to the reporting trenches."

"I know. Did some checking."

"Oh."

He turned to close the door. And then he walked over to her, taking those long graceful strides she knew so well. Basketball strides. Varsity forward, University of Pennsylvania. "Jewish jock," she could remember him joking once. "Not many around. Better hang on to me."

"So what brings you to L.A.?" Kate asked uncomfortably, backing away from him a step. She sat down on the desk.

"Business," he said, standing close to her. "Land down in Newport Beach Dad wants me to check out. But the real reason is you. I need to talk to you, Kate. Can we go somewhere? Take a drive?"

"Seth, haven't we been through this already? What else is there to say?"

"A great deal. And I can't believe you don't think so too. Kate, I've missed you. It's been more than three months, and I've thought it all through." His hands were on her shoulders now, his eyes searching for some sign that she hadn't been able to forget him, either. That she still cared as much as he did.

She knew it would be easy to give him what he wanted. Part of her ached to reach out and cling to him, to wrap her arms around his tall, hard body and not let go. He was, she knew, the only man who'd ever loved her. Really loved her. Unconditionally. And deeply.

But, my God, he was so young. When she was fifty he'd be forty. Kate couldn't imagine how they could bridge a vast chasm like that. And there were other problems—ambition, for one. Seth would never understand her driving, ambitious spirit, her tremendous need to accomplish and succeed. To make something of her life. And she would never understand his lack of it.

You know this can't work, she cautioned herself all over again. *Cut it off now. Tell him you have an appointment. Tell him there's someone else. But tell him something. Fast. Before the old wounds are reopened, and the pain begins anew.*

Seth's lips swept down on hers then, touching briefly. And she felt molten inside. Her resolve was melting like ice under the white heat of a California sun. But somehow, quickly, she broke away and pushed herself up off the desk.

"Seth, I just wasn't ready for this . . ." She escaped to the far side of the office, near a floor-to-ceiling window, and stared out at the towering superstructures that comprised Century City. But she saw nothing. Her mind was thousands of miles away—in Georgetown, where she'd shared her life with Seth Arnold for eleven wonderful, carefree months.

No. She couldn't dwell on that, couldn't permit herself to remember those happy times now. He was here. And what was she going to do about that? Push him out of the office and slam the door? "All right," she sighed, turning to face him. "We'll go somewhere. To talk. Ahh . . . the beach would be nice now. Not too crowded."

"I'm ready," he said, quickly joining her at the window and taking her arm.

She smiled up at him, then shook herself free and stepped over to the desk. "I just have to make a couple of calls first."

Brandy St. John hung up the phone, obviously disappointed. "That was Kate. She can't make it tonight."

"Oh, too bad," said the attractive, fiftyish woman sitting on the cantaloupe-colored couch. "Can you do it another time?"

"I sure hope so," Brandy said, with a heavy sigh. "My schedule is just so impossible. But I really want to see her before the tour."

"Well, I'm sorry, dear. I know you were looking forward to it."

"Yes," Brandy said, sitting down on the couch. She'd been looking forward to the coffee date for more than one reason. Not only was she anxious to spend some time with Kate, Brandy was very eager to slip away from this wearisome practice session with her agent, Monica Chase.

The six-thirty appointment at the Old World would have been the perfect out. *If only Kate hadn't called,* Brandy caught herself thinking as she arranged her skirt over her knees. Being stood up would have been better than sitting here—going through this silly charade one more time.

"All right, dear. Let's try it again, shall we?" Monica coaxed, rising from the couch to turn on the videocamera. Then she sat down again and gave Brandy a reassuring pat on the hand.

Brandy shifted uncomfortably and recrossed her long tanned legs. She was trying to relax, but it was difficult. Three hours they'd been at it already—running through the same questions over and over again. The ones she'd have to face in a scant few weeks when the network shipped her off on tour to promote her new series. Five cities—all major television markets—were listed on the itinerary, and she would be bombarded by print, television, and radio interviews in each. She wasn't looking forward to any of it. In fact, she was terrified.

As a photographic model, Brandy had never had to do interviews. But now, as an actress, the game was altogether different. The network wanted her out there beating her own drum—and she wasn't sure she could do it. Delivering well-rehearsed lines in a scene was one thing, but being grilled by a total stranger in some unfamiliar studio was quite another. Even sitting here and going through the motions with her dear friend and agent Monica Chase was unnerving. Brandy was trying hard, but she felt she wasn't being nearly animated or convincing enough. They'd boo her right off the air.

"Ladies and gentlemen," Monica began, playing talk-show host, "I know you'll recognize today's guest immediately. Her face has been on dozens of magazine covers all over the world. She's done many, many television commercials—you'll remember her pumping iron in those Streamline Shape-up ads and as the gorgeous femme fatale in those delicious spots for Reminiscence Perfume. Brandy St. John is here to tell us about her new television series set for this fall. Let's give her a big welcome."

"Thank you," Brandy said, striving to seem relaxed. "It's so nice to be in Boston."

"We're delighted to have you here. But tell us, Brandy, how is it you made the transition from modeling to acting so quickly?"

Monica had warned her about this one. What some interviewers might try to do is intimidate her—make her out to be another blond bubblehead gone show biz, another flash in the pan bound for failure as an actress.

The thing to do, she remembered, was emphasize that she'd studied with Stella Adler, one of the more highly respected acting coaches in New York, and to stress the special significance of *Vs. the Odds.* Much like *Cagney and Lacey,* it was a breakthrough show. Her character was presented as a believable career woman, a lawyer who'd dedicated herself to helping other women whose causes she believed in.

"Well . . ." Brandy began, immediately aware that she'd already made a mistake. "Never begin an answer with *well,"* Monica had urged earlier. "Merely a waste of air time."

"I really enjoyed modeling," Brandy forged ahead. "But there was an opportunity to do a small role in a television series two years ago, and I liked the work. So I decided to study acting. And Stella Adler helped me to . . ."

Monica followed up with a number of questions about Brandy's early acting experiences. The off-Broadway play she'd costarred in. The guest shots on *Love Boat* and *Hotel.*

Answering the questions, Brandy looked directly into Monica's eyes, just as the agent had instructed her to. And as the interview progressed, she began to notice Monica's expression beginning to change, ever so slightly. At first Brandy thought she was just imagining it. But, no, now she could see it plainly. There was—yes—there was a definite flicker of approval in her agent's calculating gaze.

". . . and the network is positive that *Vs. the Odds* is just what viewers are looking for—a series with substance." Brandy finished her answer with an easy smile, but her mind was racing forward, hoping this would be it. A good take, at last. The one Monica could turn over to the network's publicity chief. The woman had insisted on seeing a tape of one of these practice Q & A sessions before the tour began.

Brandy knew the pressure was on Monica to produce a good take, one that showed she could handle herself on the media tour. And she very much appreciated her agent's concern. But this was the second long afternoon they'd spent together, going over and over the same endless list of questions. And each time it became more difficult for Brandy to make the answers seem fresh.

At the moment, however, she was beginning to feel a bit more confident. And it had everything to do with the way Monica had just winked her approval.

"Brandy St. John!" the agent continued. "Such an unusual name. Is it your real name, Brandy?" Her tone exuded cattiness.

Brandy smiled with amusement, just as Monica had suggested.

"No, I can't say it is," she confessed playfully. "My real name is Brenda Vreesen. My manager and I changed it some time ago. She thought I needed a bit more glamour."

"But why Brandy St. John?" Monica prodded.

"Well—" Brandy began, then quickly stopped herself, "Brandy is

my manager's favorite drink. And she thought for a last name that
. . . it's a little embarrassing, but she thought I had a rather an-
gelic-looking face—" Monica nodded encouragingly. "And we considered Angel or Angelique for a last name, but they just sounded
too silly." She laughed. "So finally we hit on St. John."

Monica was beaming by now. "And what about Brenda Vreesen's
family? Didn't I read somewhere that you were born in Sweden?"

"Yes." Brandy nodded, considering her words. If handled correctly, Monica had said, this answer could evoke great sympathy
from viewers. But she had to be careful not to milk it too much. And
to segue quickly back to the series—which was what the network
wanted. The more often she mentioned *Vs. the Odds,* the better.

"I lived in Stockholm for only three years, though," she continued. "You see, my father, who was an importer, died. And my
mother brought me here to the States to live. In Denver. She passed
away when I was seventeen. I live in New York City now—and in
California while I'm doing the series. We're shooting *Vs. the Odds* in
and around Los Angeles and . . ."

Brandy had been over this answer so many times that by now
she'd convinced herself it was true. And she wondered, as she stared
into her agent's wide-set eyes, does Monica buy it? Isn't she the least
bit dubious about my past?

If so, Monica hadn't let on. And for that Brandy was grateful. But
at the same time it made her feel guilty. Monica had always been
straightforward with her—even from the first day they'd met. It
wasn't fair to repay her this way—keeping her in the dark. But what
else can I do, Brandy asked herself as she continued answering the
question. I certainly can't tell her the truth.

The savvy agent, however, was well aware of the prevarication in
what she was hearing. She'd known for some time that there must be
another version of Brandy St. John's past. The young woman was,
quite simply, an enigma.

There was no explaining her appearance in New York at such an
early age. Here was this Swedish vision fending for herself since high
school? Completely on her own, no one looking out for her? It was
just too incredible.

No doubt about it, there was definitely something mysterious
about the girl. Monica would never forget the first time she spotted

her. It was a muggy July in New York. And when she entered the dry cleaner's on East Sixty-fifth Street, Monica was daydreaming about her lovely "country chalet" set high in the Hollywood Hills. With its massive French windows, glorious view, Spanish-tiled Jacuzzi, and inviting heart-shaped pool.

It was one hundred five degrees that afternoon in Manhattan—even hotter inside the dry cleaner's. And there were three other people in line ahead of her. Monica was having trouble breathing, and she could feel the perspiration streaming down her back. For two skirts and a jacket, it wasn't worth waiting. She was about to leave when she caught sight of the statuesque blonde behind the counter. In an instant Monica forgot completely about the heat.

Those bones. Look at those exquisite bones. In all her years running the Chase Agency, Monica had seen bones like these only twice. Veruschka had them. And, to a lesser degree, so did Twiggy.

But this girl was simply astonishing. She had high, refined, angular cheekbones. A sleek snip of a nose—an aristocratic nose, Monica called it. Brilliant azure eyes and a gloriously well-defined chin. All framed in a halo of thick, natural blond hair.

The girl's face was powerful. And sensitive. It had depth. And deception. She could be sixteen or twenty-six, Monica thought. A naive waif or a seductive temptress.

Monica stood riveted in that inferno reeking of dry-cleaning fluid, her adrenaline surging. Think of the possibilities! She hadn't seen a face with such promise in years. In her rapture she decided the girl was Christie Brinkley, Daryl Hannah, Lauren Hutton, and Cheryl Tiegs all wrapped into one.

And she was tall. Five ten, plus. Maybe six feet. Even now, with a minimum of makeup and after hours in this steambath, she had an allure about her. An aloof sensuality. A quality Monica was most anxious to tap—please, God, let it transfer onto film!

She'd have Nita arrange for test shots immediately. As early as tomorrow perhaps. Monica knew there was a reason her psychic had advised her to spend July in New York. This had to be it. Within months, this wondrous child-woman could be the talk of the modeling world.

But to Monica's astonishment the child-woman wasn't interested. Politely, she took Monica's card and slipped it into her pocket, but she didn't call. Monica returned to the cleaners twice more to urge her to stop by the agency. To no avail. It was soon apparent the girl wanted no part of the modeling business.

Monica was dumbfounded. Each year thousands of young women from all over the world made the pilgrimage to New York in hopes of catching the eye of Monica Chase. Hers was the best agency in the business. Acceptance as a Chase model usually guaranteed a lucrative modeling career. Yet here was this stunning, enigmatic walking work of art. With unbelievable potential. Working in a dry cleaner's, for heaven's sake. Refusing even to test.

Monica knew she couldn't force the girl to accept fame and fortune—and, not unimportantly to Monica's calculating mind, bring to her agency an additional measure of both—so she stopped pursuing her. But she never forgot her. So it was with tremendous pleasure seven months later that she welcomed into her office a shy and obviously nervous Brenda Vreesen.

The girl sat primly on a slender, white-lacquered art-deco chair facing Monica's desk and explained her change of heart matter-of-factly. She had thought it over. And now she was eager to try.

Not until much later did Monica learn why Brenda—by then, Brandy—had changed her mind. Her friend Kate Brannigan, the popular journalist, had talked her into it.

Once Monica began acting as Brandy's personal manager as well as her modeling agent—a more comprehensive role she played for a handful of her top girls—she made it a point to meet Kate. By inviting her to lunch she hoped to gain additional insight into Brandy, particularly the girl's mystifying background.

Kate, however, seemed to know very little—either that or she was very good at playing dumb. Interesting that Kate would say she'd met Brandy through a mutual friend, though. Brandy had already told Monica that she'd met Kate by chance at a bookstore.

Somebody was varnishing the truth, and Monica feared it might be Brandy. She had little time to play Agatha Christie, however. Too much needed to be planned in Brandy's future to waste energy dwelling on her past. Brandy would open up when she was ready and Monica didn't want to risk losing her to another agency by prying into her background.

Besides, Brandy was a joy to work with. Always prompt and

energetic, never a complaint despite grueling fourteen-hour days on the set. While the series was in production, she was a house guest at Monica's Hollywood Hills aerie—and a welcome one. Monica found it such a pleasure having her around.

When she was around. In recent weeks Brandy had been working doubly hard. To increase her exposure, the network had arranged for her to guest on two episodes of the new series *Ki & Company;* that meant many extra hours beyond the filming of her own show. Monica knew she was under tremendous pressure. The additional burden of preparing for the promotional tour wasn't helping, that was for sure.

But Brandy was holding up very well. And as Monica turned to the camera to conclude their mock-interview, she knew the network would be pleased with this latest take.

With genuine enthusiasm Monica got up and turned off the camera. "Well, that was quite wonderful, my dear. I think you deserve a nice glass of chilled chardonnay. Then we'll play it back and have a look-see."

Brandy watched Monica reach for two stemmed glasses from the wooden runners over her bar.

"Don't worry," the good-natured agent said, noticing her protégée's troubled expression. "Perrier for me. I'm not about to blow five months of AA in one afternoon."

"That's not what I was—"

"Oh, of course it is, Brandy. I know you're concerned. And I appreciate it very much. But I can manage. In fact I'm doing quite well."

"Yes, remarkably, I'd say," Brandy offered, accepting the cold glass of wine.

"So, enough about Monica the lush," she said with a wry smile as she sat down. "Let's take a look at the tape."

"You're sure I was okay?" Brandy asked tentatively, as Monica rewound the cassette.

"Yes, I am sure. Very sure. You were one hundred percent better this time, as you will see in just a few seconds."

"I don't think I want to see it."

Monica shot Brandy a look of surprise. "But you must. How else will you learn?"

"Couldn't you just watch and tell me about it?" the girl asked sheepishly.

"I could. But I won't. Because I know what's best for you." Monica flicked the VCR to "play."

Brandy watched the interview in silence, frowning at herself on the screen. "Lord. That was pitiful, Monica," she said when it was over. "I'm just terrible. How can they expect me to tour? I look like a klutz. I just can't do it."

"Yes, you can. And you will," Monica said gently. "And they'll love you. Now why don't you have a nice splash in the pool and then we'll have a leisurely dinner."

She watched Brandy pad toward the guest bedroom to change. She was confident the girl's anxiety would pass. Monica was used to these occasional outbursts of insecurity. In fact, almost all her girls displayed the same lack of self-confidence on occasion.

It was bewildering, yet it seemed the most magnificent-looking women were often the very ones who thought least of themselves. It didn't matter how frequently you told them they were fabulous. Or how many times they saw their own sensational images in magazine ads or TV commercials. They knew those images were manufactured by the finest makeup artists, hair stylists, fashion designers, and photographers money could buy. *They* didn't buy it. Inside, they were still fat, unattractive wallflowers. Or unpopular, rangy child-monsters. Unwanted and unloved.

With Brandy the problem was more pronounced than usual—because her work was all she had. Aside from Kate Brannigan, Monica knew of no close friends. And she was almost positive Brandy never dated. Or, if she did, she never talked about it.

Brandy was twenty-four years old now. And Monica would bet money that she'd never had a lover.

That's one lonely young lady . . . The thought troubled Monica. Yet there was little she could do, she told herself, running a hand through her silver-streaked hair. Certainly she wasn't the one to set an example in the relationship department. Two divorces. A series of ill-fated affairs.

Ah, life's a bitch . . . and then you die, she mused, getting up. She followed the mouth-watering aroma of chicken in mustard sauce to the kitchen.

Well, Monica, life certainly holds a major challenge for you in the coming weeks—getting Brandy St. John through this damned tour successfully.

She wasn't at all sure it was possible.

7

■ "Sara, my God!" Taylor said in disbelief at the sight of her.

She said nothing until she'd hoisted herself up the three steep steps to her brother's sparsely furnished dressing-room trailer. "So?" she waited for his reaction.

Taylor kept staring at her.

"You know," she said nonchalantly, glancing around the modest trailer, "you could do better than this. Star of your own series, and everything. You ought to talk to the big cheese."

"I think I'm looking at her—but I don't recognize her."

"Okay . . . okay," Sara said, plopping down on a cushioned wicker chair. "So you're not crazy about the new hairdo. Don't tell your sister, it'll hurt her feelings." She smiled up at him impishly.

"It's just that it's well—so . . ."

"Gorgeous, right?" she interjected before he could say anything negative. "Well, Kate likes it anyway."

"She does?" Taylor asked, amazed.

"Yes. She says it's . . . ummm, trendy,"

"And what else does she say?" Taylor coaxed, with a little laugh.

Sara smirked. "That it looks like I stuck my finger in an electric socket while standing in a puddle."

It did. Sara's sandy-blond blunt cut had been hacked away (probably by some ultra-chic stylist who kept a machete on hand, Taylor thought). It was all choppy now, with a smattering of singular spikes, riveted as if they'd been frozen in midair. And the color was all wrong for her. A bright silvery platinum shade, except for one muted green streak on the right side.

"Why did you . . ."

"Because I needed a change. A drastic change. So I went to a new hairdresser—and *voilà!*" She raised both arms and gave Taylor a big Gloria Vanderbilt grin. Secretly, Sara wasn't sure she liked her new look either—not as much as she had sitting in Pelo Nafti's chair. But he'd come highly recommended as an image changer. And Sara was convinced she needed a total revamping.

"Well, it'll take some getting used to," Taylor said now, sitting down crosslegged on the carpeted floor across from her. "Actually it does make you look a little younger," he offered, wondering if she'd believe him.

She didn't. But she loved him for saying so.

"Planning any more, ahh, renovations?" he asked hesitantly.

"The works. Starting at the top and moving down. Next I'm having my mind vacuumed—so I can forget about Mark."

"Heard from him?

"No," Sara said, quickly closing the subject. She wanted to talk about Mark, but not yet. Well, maybe she didn't want to at all. But she did. She knew she did. That's why she was here.

Sara hated feeling desperate like this, hated having to lean on her younger brother. When they were both growing up, it had been different. In those days Taylor was the emotional one—forever locking horns with Dad, erupting into tantrums, then spilling all his troubles to big Sis while she made with the patient "there, there" 's.

Taylor had rebelled against practically everything and everyone in his youth. Parents. Choate. Stanford. They'd all been relieved when he made it through UC–Santa Barbara. But even then the rebel in him had not died. After graduation he'd turned his father down flat, rejecting the offer to become Vice-President of Evans Products, the family business.

Offended to the core, Martin Evans had almost disowned his only son. Yet it had become clear, even to his disappointed parents, that Taylor had no appetite for the entrepreneurial *Star Wars* of the Silicon Valley. Computers, software, microchips—to him these were words from an impenetrable foreign language. His chief interests at the time were women . . . and the martial arts. He'd been a devoted student of karate and aikido since childhood.

A few months after college Taylor took off for the Far East, winding up in India. He stayed two years, studying Eastern philosophy and religion at an ashram near New Delhi under the tutelage of some high priest or guru, whose name Sara still couldn't pronounce.

The Taylor who returned to the Evans's sprawling Palo Alto estate had developed a distinctively new persona. He had achieved manhood at last, but the change was more fundamental than that. In place of the rash, hot-headed youth, there was a calm, reflective human being radiating inner tranquillity. Now he was patient and clear-thinking, at peace with himself—and determined to pass along the principles of spiritual renewal that he himself had benefited from and absorbed.

Within half a year—and with the blessing, astonishingly, of his parents—Taylor opened Westwinds, the Institute for Emotional Rejuvenation, in Santa Barbara.

Almost overnight it became a haven for fatigued and disillusioned competitors on life's fast track. The workaholic baby boomers, the burn-out cases that show business and other stress-ridden industries produce en masse. Now they turned to Taylor, who taught them how to meditate and how to look into themselves. How to examine their lifetime goals and short-term motivations. Most importantly, he gave them in abundance what they hungered for beyond all else— positive reinforcement, caring, love. Brother Taylor, the rebellious brat, had become a self-styled guru.

And here was Sara. Always the stable one, the "good little girl," Daddy's favorite and Mommy's joy. Strong, capable Sara. The high-powered studio executive. *Barely hanging on.*

Thank God her brother was always there for her. Not that she called on him often. In fact she'd never visited Taylor on the back lot before. She didn't like barging in on him when he was working. But it was almost seven-thirty, already dark outside. She knew that *Ki & Company* had wrapped for the day—and for her the past several days had been impossible. She just couldn't go home to Jackie and Jennifer, not yet. She had to talk it out.

"What's wrong, Sara?" Taylor asked gently, sensing her need to confide. "Company war games? Or personal?"

"A little of both, I guess. Really want to hear this?" she asked, knowing he would. "I won't even go into what happened earlier in the week, but first thing this morning I get the word there's a problem with *Vs. the Odds.* Technical stuff. Bad sound in several scenes of Show Two. We have to reshoot." She sighed wearily and swung her legs up over the side of her chair. "Total *mishegoss.* Means a week at least. Screws up the entire schedule. And will probably put us over budget."

"That is a bummer," Taylor sympathized, waiting. He knew there would be more. It took a great deal for Sara to approach him with her problems. Only once since he'd moved down to L.A. had she poured out her heart to him. And that was when she was reeling from the impact of Mark's sudden departure. If she'd gone out of her way to come to his trailer, she had to be hurting. Badly.

"And," Sara went on, shaking her head in disgust, "some total schmuck at the network has decided to play hide and go seek with the show. They're airing the two-hour pilot on Tuesday night. But the series—are you ready? They've slated it for the dead zone. Sunday night. Seven o'clock!"

"Up against *60 Minutes*?" Taylor asked, astonished. That was instant death for a new series; even he knew that much.

Sara nodded, laughing grimly. It was so dumb. So absolutely ridiculous. All the hype. All the build-up. The three-hundred-thousand-dollar advertising campaign. The tour. The extensive publicity on Brandy. Reshooting. Reworking. Reshuffling. Overspending. And for what? To bury the show before it even had a chance to breathe.

"That's insanity," Taylor said. "They have to be nuts."

"Oh, they are. All network executives are certifiably *meshuggener*. It's a prerequisite before they get a title—the crazier they are, the higher they land." They both laughed. At last she was beginning to unwind. The day had drained her energy, but now it felt good just to sit here with Taylor. Even though it would change nothing but her mood, and that only temporarily.

"Well, is this written in stone?" Taylor asked now, getting up to fetch them each a bottle of mineral water. "I mean, the season's hardly begun. Aren't these schedules subject to change?"

"Sure. Things could change. In TV the only certainty *is* change," she said, accepting the bottle and placing it against her cheek, momentarily enjoying the dewy coldness. "But my guess is, it won't. I predict that *Vs. the Odds* really is going up against the odds—Mike Wallace and Andy Rooney. Can't explain why. Just intuition."

Taylor resumed his semilotus position and regarded her warmly.

"Mine tells me there's more on your mind than work. What is it, Sara?"

"Nothing . . . nothing more. I was just too churned up to go home, and—"

"And I don't believe you for a minute."

"Well, you should," she said defensively. "Your psychic batteries are on overcharge, that's all. I'm fine."

Taylor said nothing but just continued to look at her inquiringly with his lambent amber eyes.

Sara squirmed uncomfortably. She set the bottle on a plastic side table. "Okay. But you'll think I'm the one who's *meshuggeneh.* Fair warning?" He nodded and she sighed heavily. "Taylor, I think Mark is doing coke. A lot of it."

He frowned, considering her words. "You think? What kind of evidence?"

"He withdrew twenty thousand dollars from our joint account last week. And another ten thousand yesterday."

"And that means he's using the money to—?"

"It only means something because of who I've discovered he's been spending a great deal of time with. Maybe living with . . ." Sara stopped herself before the anger within her swirled up and took over the way it had earlier that afternoon. She had wanted to scream then. And to strangle Mark and that low-rent singer he was sleazing around with. Two Grammys. Big deal. The slut was a notorious druggie—everybody knew that.

"Who?" Taylor asked skeptically.

"Niki Erickson!"

"You're not serious?"

"This afternoon over lunch," Sara continued, "I had the good fortune to learn that Mark was with her in Malibu last weekend. A real blow-out. Erickson was freebased out of her mind, as usual. So was he."

"What makes you think they're living together?"

"Mark told me he's staying with a friend near the beach in Venice. Erickson rents a house on Brooks Court, just steps from the water. I checked." She stood up quickly and began pacing the short distance of the trailer. "It's just too much, Taylor. And I've had enough *tsuris* for a lifetime already. I know what you advised: 'Be patient.

Let him get whatever it is out of his system.' But this—this is unbelievable!" She was shouting now. "He's probably already wiped out his own bank accounts. And if he's going to continue—"

"Wait a minute, Sara." Taylor did not yell, but his words pierced her mounting hysteria. "Now stop it. And sit down." She did. "Take a moment. Just breathe deeply. Don't say anything," he commanded.

Why was it so difficult for him, seeing her this way? If he appeared to be maintaining control, that was not how he really felt. He'd helped so many people through personal crises before. Seen them at their worst. His good friend R. B. McDevitt had nearly turned himself inside out when he got divorced. Ranting, raving, cursing himself—cursing his wife, Lalli. But Taylor had guided him through. Slowly winning R.B. over, using the principles of meditation and self-acceptance.

With Sara it was different. How could he sit here and watch his only sister throw herself into such a frenzy? The separation was eating her up inside. And it made him feel sick, knowing what she was going through.

His first impulse was to nail Mark against a wall. Find out if Sara's suspicions were justified. And if they were, to force Mark into setting things straight and stop treating his sister so cruelly. But that was all out of the question. Mark had his own crises, his own set of problems to deal with.

Taylor could do nothing more right now than try to make things a little easier for Sara. He wished to hell she'd taken up meditation. He'd suggested it often enough, but she'd always put him off, saying it wasn't her style. Sara could be stubborn. And strong—most of the time.

"All right," he said softly. "Feel better?"

She shrugged. "With a new life, I might."

"You'll get through this, Sara," he said, reaching over to touch her hand. "But you've got to stay in control. Now tell me, what do you propose to do about all of this?"

"Divorce him. I've already spoken with Arthur Crowley."

"Sara, my God! Why don't you just call the L.A. *Times*? You know as soon as Crowley files, your personal life will be public property. The story will show up in every gossip column across the country. Besides, you're not even sure that Mark—"

"As sure as I can be without a deposition, Taylor. What do you want me to do, drive out to Venice and yank the broad out of his arms?"

"Not necessarily. But I could."

"No way," she said flatly. "I don't want you checking up on my husband. He knows where to get hold of me. Pretty soon he'll have to anyway," she added with a sardonic smile. "He'll run out of money."

"Promise me one thing, then, all right? Promise me you'll wait at least through the weekend before you do anything about filing."

Sara thought for a moment. He was right. And she'd known he would say exactly that. Probably that's why she'd come. To be reprimanded. And restrained. "All right," she agreed, getting up. "Got yourself a deal, doc. How much for this session?"

"Gratis, dollface," he said, standing up to hug her. "Just a little love—and respect. Meaning, keep your promise. And no impulsive moves, okay?"

Sara nodded. "But . . . there is one condition," she added, with mock-seriousness.

"And what's that?" he asked, smiling.

"Brunch with me and the twins on Sunday. I promised I'd take them to the Egg and the Eye for omelets—and they'd love to see their handsome uncle."

"Fine, but make it early, can we? I have a date at noon."

"Oh?" she asked, sounding pleased. "Anyone I know?" As a rule Taylor was quite secretive about his personal life, and Sara was always eager for details.

"You might," he said teasingly, anticipating her reaction. "She's an actress. Tall . . . blond . . . blue eyes. Name's Brandy. Brandy St. John."

It was clear and balmy in Santa Monica, the kind of early evening that made Kate want to reach out and hug the air because it smelled so clean and felt so refreshing. The sun was just minutes away from setting. And from their vantage point as they strolled high up on the Pacific Palisades, Kate and Seth could see a smattering of diehard sun worshippers still stretched out on towels on the rippling white sand below. Beyond loomed the outline of the colorful Santa Monica Pier, where Kate had taken Sara's twins, Jennifer and Jackie, for a carousel ride the previous Sunday.

Despite the occasion, Kate felt at peace. It was so comfortable here, walking with Seth and watching the tide slip in. Saying nothing, just being near him. It felt right somehow. It always had. But it was a fantasy, she knew. A future linked to Seth was out of the question. Ultimately she'd be frustated and unhappy, and so would he.

"Kate," Seth began finally, catching her hand in his, "listen to me now. I don't have a big speech prepared. What I want to say is very simple and straightforward. I've spent a great deal of time alone— just thinking about us. The separation probably did us both some good, but I love you too much to lose you. I'm more sure than ever we can work things out."

"How?" she asked, concentrating on the whitecaps of the incoming tide below. "We've discussed this, Seth. So many times. The obstacles are still there. Age. Me. I don't know my own mind right now, or what I want to do. I feel like I'm in some kind of limbo. I don't even have a job."

"You're working now. Maybe that'll turn into something. And who the hell cares if you don't have a permanent job? So what? You're a respected journalist. A bona fide success. You could even go back to politics if—"

"No way! Never again!" she interjected, resolute.

"Kate, please. That was only one experience. One congressman in the entirety of Washington. You can't let Ed Mitchell color your attitude about politicians forever. You were damn good as his administrative aide. I'm only saying that you could work for another congressman—or even in the White House—if you put your mind to it."

"But I don't want to," she said firmly.

"All right. But whether or not you're working isn't the issue. Listen, I don't care if you never work again. You know I can support you. The family company is solid. We're constructing two new shopping centers, one of them near Bethesda. Dad is piling more and more responsibility on me. Wants me to take over in a few years when he retires. I'm finally settling down, Kate, and I've been working very hard. That stuff doesn't matter, though. What matters is us. Two people who love and trust each other."

She stopped to look directly into his eyes, fighting back the fierce desire to wrap her arms around him and just be loved. How easy it would be to press her lips against his, bury her face in his broad chest, and melt into that wonderful fantasy world she'd allowed herself to create back in Georgetown.

Back then Kate had deluded herself, believing she could have it all. Seth. Two children. A spacious home somewhere in the country, with her own separate office. A nanny to care for the kids while Seth was off working. She could, Kate had convinced herself, have marriage and work. A balanced life. Total bliss—at last.

Now she saw the dream for what it really was. A grand delusion. During those deliriously carefree months in Georgetown, Seth had become her anchor—a grounding force. But somehow everything had gone haywire and she didn't know what she felt for him anymore. Except that she was still attracted to him, more than she wanted to be at this moment.

"Can't you see?" Kate said finally, almost pleading. "I don't *know* what I want right now. Can't you understand that?"

"No." He placed a finger over her lips. "All I can see is the most beautiful, kind, intelligent woman in the world. And I don't care how old she is. I don't care if she's sixty-five. I want her . . . for my wife."

Kate's heart skipped a beat. She'd thought about it plenty, being Mrs. Seth Arnold. But he'd never said that before. In fact, no one ever had; it was her first proposal. A man had actually said he wanted her for a lifetime. And as he stood there smiling down at her in that sincere, adoring way of his, the brilliant sunset over his left shoulder, she wanted him so too.

The fiery-red orange globe was disappearing into the vast azure Pacific when he bent down to kiss her. His strong thighs pressed tightly against her, his arms encircled her shoulders. And for a brief moment nothing mattered except their entwining, caressing strength. When his lips touched hers she was beyond control, beyond thought. She kissed him back, again and again, lost in the warm glow of caring and tenderness where she felt safe, comforted, and so very much in love.

"I'm serious, Kate," he said softly now, touching her cheek with his fingertips. "Since we broke off, I've examined this relationship inside and out. And I know that when we were together, we had something very few people are ever lucky enough to find. Tell me— tell me when you've been happier or more energized. More yourself. Tell me you didn't mean it when you said you loved me more than any other man in your life." Gazing at her with an intensity that sent a thrilling shiver down her spine, he said, "Kate, I love you. I know there's nothing better out there. And there's nobody else I want. I just want you. Will you marry me, love?"

Yes. No. Maybe. I don't know. Oh, please don't make me decide . . . She wanted him, yes. So much. For the good times they always had together and his incessant optimism. For his strong, hard body next to hers at night. For the life they could share together. For the children they might . . . But still she knew it was wrong.

The red flags were waving everywhere, warning her: *He's so young —careerwise and in every other way. You need someone older, more sophisticated. If you marry Seth you'll be bored within a year. Trapped. Suffocated. And by the time your first child is in kindergarten, you'll look like a grandmother. If you aren't certain, don't risk it, Brannigan. Don't take that step.*

She felt terribly torn and confused—and yet a year ago Kate might well have said yes immediately. Because a year ago everything had been different, everything had been sailing along on course. And Kate was feeling wonderful about her life.

It had been a totally new life for her. Relocating from New York to Washington, D.C., was Kate's desperate attempt at reinventing herself. After Cary had left, she'd needed a change—and Congressman Edward Mitchell of Manhattan had provided the means.

Mitchell was a young, aggressive first-term Democrat. She had been assigned to do a profile of him for *New York* magazine shortly after Christmas, and although she'd pulled no punches in the piece, he'd nonetheless been impressed with her savvy. A month later he'd phoned on the long shot that she'd accept a position on his staff.

By March Kate was living in Washington and working for Mitchell. She admired the young congressman and his politics, and she knew she could be an asset to him. But she didn't fool herself about her motives—they were more personal than career-minded. Kate needed a new perspective. She hoped Washington would provide that.

For the most part it did. She adapted to Mitchell's organization almost effortlessly. She wrote his speeches, supervised several on his staff, and saw to it that her boss was armed with every bit of research available on the crucial issues and legislation before Congress. Often she worked late into the evening with Mitchell, briefing him on materials she'd read and digested and helping him to decide which way to lean on pending legislation. She loved the responsibility and tackled her duties with inexhaustible energy.

At that point dating didn't seem very important. She was extremely busy and often attended social functions on Mitchell's behalf. Weekend nights Kate was happy to stay in and catch up on some reading or rent a movie to watch on her VCR.

There were few men she was attracted to anyway—and they were usually married or so consumed with their own careers that relationships came a distant second. Occasionally the lack of companionship did trouble her, but not often. She had adjusted to the life of the Washington workaholic remarkably well.

Seth Arnold changed all that. They met at the athletic track near her apartment where she ran three miles every morning, her way of charging up for the day.

She'd seen Seth on the track a number of times but hadn't paid much attention to him beyond noticing that he ran very fast and kept passing her. So she was surprised when he greeted her casually one morning as she was stretching out. They didn't talk long. But for the next few weeks they spoke almost daily, and Kate began looking forward to seeing him.

She was surprised to learn Seth's age, for he looked at least five years older and had a self-assurance and savoir faire that belied his years. He'd traveled extensively, spoke fluent French, seemed well read and insatiably curious.

Kate told him about her job. He was a real estate investor for his family's Georgetown firm.

Finally, he asked her out. They went to see a Jack Nicholson movie, and at the Chinese restaurant afterward, Kate's fortune-cookie prediction read: "Today begins a lasting relationship." They laughed it off and chattered on. But as their friendship progressed, Kate became increasingly aware of something special about Seth. She wasn't quite sure why, but she felt calmed by his presence.

When she spoke with him, she always came away with the impression that he cared very much about what she was saying. With other men she had dated in D.C. that was seldom the case. Usually they were so wrapped up their own problems and work that Kate found herself doing all the listening.

With Seth it was different. Each time they went out, she returned to her apartment feeling better about herself. A bit more free, a bit less burdened by the pressures she shouldered. Being with Seth gave her a renewed sense of herself, a wholeness. She liked the feeling.

The gap between their ages didn't bother her at first. Few people would have guessed they were separated by an entire decade. And they were, after all, only friends and not lovers. Not yet anyway. She knew that time was coming, though. Call it chemistry or the attraction of opposites or whatever, Kate had never before been so drawn to a man in such a purely physical way. *Primitive instincts,* she warned herself. *Control yourself, old lady—don't go robbing the cradle so fast.*

But Seth was so diligent in his pursuit, so attentive. Barely a day passed without some thoughtful gesture, some little thing to make her pause a moment and smile. To realize how nice it was to have someone care for her. Perhaps a single rose in a bud vase at her doorstep. A funny note or card that arrived with the rest of the mail on her desk. A slim volume of Elizabeth Barrett Browning's poems.

When they made love for the first time, it was the most tender yet uninhibited experience. Kate felt utterly fulfilled. And adored. And voraciously sexy. In the weeks to come it seemed her entire life changed. Even the most routine chore, the most ordinary moment, became more meaningful and enjoyable.

Her love affair with Seth gave Kate a wellspring of energy. She worked even harder, but she had fun, too—wine, pizza, and a blazing fire on a wintry Washington night, horseback riding on crisp, fall weekend afternoons in nearby Maryland. Rock concerts at Wolf Trap. And hours and hours to tell Seth about her hopes, hurts, ambitions, and dreams.

He was the antithesis of Cary. Her time with Seth did not encompass those exhilarating debates about politics or writing. They would never share that particular intellectual chemistry. But what they did share she now felt she couldn't do without: a growing mutual trust which inevitably bonded their love.

Yes. She loved Seth very much. Probably more than she'd ever loved Cary. She'd depended on Cary, learned from him, made love with him. But she'd never felt cherished by him. Or needed by him. Seth—handsome, inquisitive, energetic young Seth—absolutely adored her. His love was unconditional. It didn't derive its energizing force from her status in Washington, who her friends were, where she'd gone to school. He cared only for her. He wanted her near because her very presence made him feel good.

And she felt better living with him than she had alone. Their first few months together were incredibly fulfilling for Kate. She was more exuberant and enthusiastic than she could ever remember. Even occasional sixteen-hour days at Mitchell's office failed to slow her down. Now she had someone to balance her life, someone she'd needed for a long time.

She couldn't remember now exactly when their relationship started to change. But she knew it was around the same time her tenure in Congressman Mitchell's office ended. That had been a horrendous experience in itself and left Kate despondent for weeks.

It had begun innocently enough. A few minutes before midnight one Friday Kate had returned to the Longworth Office Building to retrieve paperwork she wanted to take home for the weekend. She was sure it was on Ed Mitchell's desk. When she opened the door to his office, she quite naturally assumed she would find no one there.

Kate would never forget the embarrassment and the outrage and the disgust that overwhelmed her in that split second. She stood frozen in the doorway. There in the dimly lighted office was her boss, the man she respected so much and had devoted almost two years to—Edward Mitchell, Democratic Congressman from Manhattan—sprawled facedown on his leather couch, moaning his pleasure in short, enthusiastic little gasps.

And the short puff of pulchritude undulating beneath him had her navy-blue dress hiked up to her armpits. Kate could see instantly that it was not Joanna, Mitchell's lovely wife. It was, Kate soon realized, that large-breasted, loud-mouthed lobbyist who worked for the garment manufacturers. Lana something. She'd been around for weeks trying to swing Mitchell's vote on a pending bill.

As an influential member of the subcommittee with jurisdiction over this particular piece of proposed legislation, Mitchell held a great deal of power. In a close vote he was virtually in a position to kill it or let it live on to be recommended to the full House membership.

Lana the lobbyist, wailing noisily as the vigorous young congressman pumped harder and harder, was after a "yea" vote. And that's no doubt what she would get, Kate thought, closing the door silently and backing away in shock.

She caught her breath for a moment, trying to quiet her rage and then quickly left the building. Early on Monday morning she confronted Mitchell.

"What about the garment industry foreign-labor bill, Ed?" she asked pointedly. "When we spoke a few weeks ago, you said you didn't think you'd support it. Any change?"

"Matter of fact," he said, calmly looking up at her from a stack of paperwork, "I've given it some more thought, Kate, and considering all the input from the subcommittee staff, I've decided to go with the manufacturers on this one. It just seems more economically feasible. According to these reports . . ."

Kate listened patiently as Mitchell ran through the charts and figures. She'd already reviewed them. And it was clear to her that, based on that information, Mitchell would be much better off not supporting the bill. If he did, and the bill were to be signed into law, the garment industry would be able to farm out millions more in work to cheap foreign laborers in the Orient and South America. And the garment workers in Mitchell's own Manhattan district would be the biggest losers. Hundreds of them could lose their jobs —and certainly wouldn't vote for Edward Mitchell come next election.

He couldn't be serious, she thought, fearing she already knew the awful truth. This was much more important than a quick lay. There were so few reasons to support this bill. And so many reasons not to.

"Ed, listen," she began when he'd finished, "this could be a very damaging move for you. Think of the garment workers. If this bill passes, they'll blame you. You really shouldn't—"

"Kate," he said, shaking his head as if lecturing to a wayward child, "you're overreacting. What we're talking about here is dollars and sense—s-e-n-s-e. And, given the big picture, it makes much more sense, economically, to give the manufacturers their head on this one. Okay? Now I know you mean well, but—hey, we have far more important things to discuss this morning."

She walked over to the door and slammed it shut, then turned to him. "No, we haven't, Ed!" she said, her eyes burning. "We have nothing more important to discuss. I want you to know something. I saw what went on—on that couch Friday night, with that slutty lobbyist."

"Kate . . . that—" he started to respond.

"And I want you to know something else. If you vote for that bill, I walk. You know very well you were opposed to it from the beginning. And now all of a sudden you change your mind. Well, we both know why, don't we? This isn't a question of getting your rocks off, Ed. It's a question of integrity. And I can't continue working for someone who doesn't have it." She stood there in front of him defiantly, arms crossed.

Mitchell rose slowly from his chair and glared at her. "Is that so, Ms. Self-righteous? Now you listen to me. Nobody makes the rules in my camp but Ed Mitchell, get it? And I'll support any damned bill I see fit to. I'll even go you one further, Kate. You don't have to quit. You're fired."

Within the hour Kate was standing on Pennsylvania Avenue, without a job. She was still stunned. Had she been too hasty? Had she made a mistake? No. Her gut instinct told her she was right. Still, she couldn't bring herself to believe that a smart guy like Mitchell would jeopardize his career over something so insignificant as a roll on the couch with an ambitious lobbyist. There had to be more to it than that.

Several weeks later Kate got her answer. As she sipped her morning coffee, there it was staring back at her in *The Washington Post.* Congressman Edward Mitchell was under investigation, said the Justice Department, for allegedly accepting kickbacks. Among the several groups accused of paying Mitchell under the table for favors was the Manhattan Garment Manufacturers Association.

So she'd been right—there had been more in it for good ol' Ed. Kate felt vindicated, in a way. Yet she also felt used and disgusted with politics and politicians. Even the ones you thought you knew well, the ones you trusted and worked your butt off for, could reward your loyalty by turning out to be nothing but double-dealing thieves.

As much as anything, the whole rotten affair had been a blow to her ego. Here she was, the streetwise journalist being duped by a two-bit congressman. She should have smelled the corruption in Ed Mitchell from the very beginning. Oh, well, maybe it was a lesson. Kate resolved never to get involved in politics again.

So there she was, thirty-five and once more in search of a new direction. Frustrated and depressed since her firing, she'd been moping around for more than a month, still at loose ends about what to do with her life. And what to do about Seth.

It wasn't until Kate stopped working that she'd had the chance to take a really good look at who Seth was. Now it finally struck her how young he was and how little ambition he had for himself. He often seemed like a child to her, a little boy in search of instant gratification. His greatest pleasure seemed to be spending time with her. He was forever looking for a new diversion, something "fun" for them to do together. He said it was to take her mind off her problems and brighten her mood, but she secretly suspected he just liked to play.

He seldom went to his office. And that bothered Kate, especially now that she was at home so much. With Seth underfoot all the time, she felt smothered. And guilty as well, because he was so good to her.

Dear, sweet, loving Seth. It wasn't his fault, but he couldn't give her what she wanted and needed most now—activity, challenge, the stimulation that those exhausting days in Ed Mitchell's office had provided. Without them Kate felt empty and more than a bit lost.

She was addicted to work. As surely as an alcoholic needed a stiff morning drink, Kate needed a job or a project to charge her up. To make her feel significant and needed, and to revive her failing self-confidence.

She tried often to make Seth understand, but how could he? His perspective was entirely different. His cure for the doldrums wasn't meaningful work, it was a *vacation*. He whisked Kate off to Bermuda. It didn't cure anything, but by the time they returned to Georgetown, she had come to one important decision. She just couldn't go on this way.

She couldn't live with Seth any longer. He was leaning on her. And in her unrelenting state of depression, she was only pulling him down.

He didn't want to leave. He tried for days to change her mind, but she would have none of it. When he'd exhausted his arguments, he glumly packed up his belongings and left. Once he was gone, she'd felt tremendous relief, then overwhelming loneliness—and, finally, a terrible, gnawing loss.

She cried for days, until she could tolerate her own lethargy no longer. Forcing herself to make decisions, Kate gave up her apartment, stored her furniture, and gratefully accepted Sara's invitation to the West Coast.

Seth had left a number of messages, but Kate hadn't called back. She missed him. And she loved him. But he wasn't the answer, she knew that. For both their sakes, she had to stay away from him. She had to be strong.

And yet here she was with Seth again. Three thousand miles from Georgetown. She was still trying to be strong, trying not to show how vulnerable she really was.

"I love you too, Seth," she murmured, looking up at him with eyes blurred by tears. "I always will. But don't you see? It's never going to work. I can't marry you. Please, please, try to understand."

He couldn't; she knew that. But he didn't demand further explanation. They said little on the drive back to Century City.

After he had guided the car to a stop in front of the sleek tower on the Avenue of the Stars, Seth said, "Just think it over, Kate. You know where to reach me." He brushed his lips lightly against her cheek. She climbed slowly from the car. And then he was gone. She watched the rented black Mustang disappear into the steady stream of rush hour, feeling utterly abandoned.

The *World* office was empty when she returned to collect her briefcase, and Kate was glad. She didn't want to talk to anyone. She didn't think she could. Her mind was still elsewhere—with Seth.

She moved like a sleepwalker, packing assorted lists and notes into her briefcase, locking the huge glass double door behind her, taking the elevator down to the cavernous underground parking lot. Aware of nothing but a nagging sense of loss. She'd probably just made the biggest mistake of her life. What in the world was wrong with her?

It wasn't until she was inside the Peugeot that Kate noticed the two pink message slips in her hand. The ones she'd hastily scooped up off the desk. Now she scanned them. The first was from R. B. McDevitt. He'd left two phone numbers, one with a Texas area code.

The other message was far more intriguing. "Letty Molloy," it read. "Call at home as soon as possible. Urgent!" And then the number. *Urgent? Who in the world is Letty Molloy? And what does she want with me,* Kate wondered, backing out of the parking space.

Then her pulse quickened as she remembered. She had seen the name Letty Molloy several times earlier that day, when poring over yellowed newspaper clippings at the Academy Library. Letty, Kate knew, must be at least eighty years old by now. In her heyday, though, she'd gone neck and neck with Hedda Hopper and Louella Parsons. Letty Molloy was the town's dowager gossip, retired for the past several years, but she had kept the citizenry of show business informed since the early thirties. For nearly half a century Letty Molloy's celebrated column had appeared in *The Hollywood Daily.*

8

■ Kate had to laugh at herself. In the last half hour she'd changed clothes a dozen times, discarding outfits faster than a nervous teenager before a first date. Skirts, blouses, pants, and a number of jackets were strewn over the bed where she had tossed them while trying to figure out exactly what to wear.

Now, dressed in a pair of tan gabardine slacks and a beige cotton knit sweater, she worked quickly, placing the clothes neatly back in the closet. When she'd finished she checked her makeup and hair once more in the mirror. Then she sat down on the chaise lounge, picked up a copy of *Vogue* and shook her head, wondering why she'd ever agreed to this ridiculous outing in the first place.

Too late now, an inner voice reminded her. She glanced at the clock radio. It *was* too late, figuratively and literally. Almost noon. R. B. McDevitt was supposed to have picked her up at eleven-thirty, sharp.

Kate flipped through the magazine distractedly, not really seeing the luxurious ads for designer furs and fragrances. She was thinking about what a mistake she had made. Here she was submitting herself to a two-hour drive with R. B. McDevitt. Cooped up in a car with a man she hardly knew, all the way to Santa Barbara. Whatever would they talk about? The idea seemed less and less appealing.

It was Sara who had urged her to return R.B.'s phone call. And by now Kate had managed to convince herself that the only reason she'd accepted his invitation was to appease her matchmaker friend. And to finally see Brandy, who would be at Westwinds with Taylor. That, in itself, seemed reason enough to make the trip.

But there was another reason Kate had agreed to accompany R.B. One she found so unsettling she could barely admit it to herself. She was mildly intrigued with the loud Texan. Yet she wasn't quite sure why.

The man could be totally obnoxious. And officious. And there was something about him that made her distinctly uncomfortable. But he did exude a certain kind of maleness that she found rather appealing. Not like Seth. That was different. With R.B. there was a sense of controlling strength that appealed to Kate. He was just so darn sure of himself. She admired that in a man, even though, as in this case, she did not admire the man.

His green Jaguar roared into the circular driveway promptly at one.

"Sure am sorry about being late," he apologized as soon as she was in the car. "Problem with one of my planes."

"How many do you have?" Kate asked, fastening her seat belt.

"Le'see . . ." He pulled at his chin with his free hand. The other one was maneuvering the Jag around several hairpin turns toward Sunset Boulevard. "About twenty-five now, I guess. Rent them out. Mostly to private companies for charters, junkets. My new one, though, a Falcon 50—a real little beauty—has a fuselage problem. Had to leave her in Texas for some surgery. But"—he turned to flash a wide grin at Kate—"that's all taken care of and now we're on our way to Westwinds."

"Let me get this straight. You flew all the way to Los Angeles this morning just to get in your car and drive all the way to Santa Barbara? Isn't there an airport that's closer?"

"That's not the point," R.B. replied, adjusting his sunglasses. "It's a gorgeous drive. I love being behind the wheel. It's like therapy, you know? Besides, if I'd flown there directly I sure wouldn't be sitting here next to you."

He'd caught Kate off guard. She folded her arms, trying to think of an appropriate comment.

"Does that make you nervous?" he teased.

"What?" she asked, too quickly.

"That I like spending time with you. For a moment there you seemed a little fidgety."

Kate assumed her best fake smile. "Not at all. I was just sort of . . . ahh, settling in."

"Shouldn't be too long a drive." He flicked on the Fuzz Buster and floored the accelerator. "We'll be there in about an hour."

"An hour? I thought it took two!"

"Not with me driving. You see, Westwinds is really this side of Santa Barbara. In Montecito. But I do like to move along at a pretty good clip."

"I see you do." The speedometer registered eighty-five miles per hour.

"So tell me, Kate, how's it going for you here on the West Coast? Slain any dragons yet?"

"Not exactly," she laughed, loosening up a bit. "But I might have one on the hook." She told him about the Renata Desmond piece for *World.*

R.B. was enthusiastic. "Gotta say I envy you there. What I wouldn't give to be able to drag that nasty viper through a little of her own dirt. You've got yourself a plum assignment, Kate."

"I think so." She was gazing out the window at the picturesque Pacific coastline, glad they were taking Highway 101 instead of the freeway.

"Won't be easy, though," R.B. went on. "Renata's one slippery character. Don't try tangling with her girlfriend, either. Real bull dyke if I ever saw one."

"Thanks for the tip."

"And, Kate, it goes without saying . . . if you need any help, I'd be happy to—"

"Oblige, right?"

"S'right." He chuckled.

"Tell me about Westwinds," she said, purposely changing the subject.

"Well, jeez, I can hardly do it justice by describing it. But the setting is phenomenal. Lots of trees and gardens. Very relaxing. The whole place is perched up on a hill. The main auditorium is a replica of a Buddhist temple Taylor visited in Mount Koya, Japan. Carved out of cedar. There are a number of other buildings scattered around the grounds. And the bungalows, of course."

"People live right there?"

"Yeah. Nothing like the Beverly Hills Hotel bungalows. In fact the life-style at Westwinds is pretty rustic. But you adjust fairly quickly. What happens is, people usually sign up for a week or two. Each day is broken into various workshops and group sessions.

From five to, say, twenty people in a group, depending on what you're doing. Meditation. Encounter. Role-playing—"

"Role-playing?" Kate interrupted. "Sounds like acting."

R.B. shook his head. "Not even close. It's well—you'll just have to experience it for yourself."

In my next life, maybe. "So, is that how you first met Taylor—at Westwinds?"

"Sure is. Heard about the place from a buddy of mine. A banker out of Fort Worth. I flew over and met Taylor the next day."

"You did? That soon?"

R.B. nodded. "Stayed a week the first time. Came back a bit later and checked in for a month."

"A whole month?" she asked, amazed. "Why? I mean was your life . . . were you upset . . . stressed out—"

"A little of both, I guess," he said stiffly. And she noticed his jaw tighten ever so slightly.

Kate thought for a moment, wondering whether her initial snap judgment of R.B. had been unfair. Maybe there was an ounce or two of sensitivity lurking behind his tough-guy image.

"Business or personal problems?" she prodded.

"A little of both there too." He was staring straight ahead. The lines of his face were etched in a somber expression.

"I'll, uhh, understand if you'd rather not talk about it."

"D'rather not," he said tersely.

They drove in silence for a few minutes. R.B. flipped on a George Winston tape, which seemed in keeping with his sudden contemplative mood. But it wasn't long before he was talking again, asking Kate all sorts of questions.

She answered each one, without elaborating. She told him about Vassar. Meeting Sara. What a rebel Taylor had been as a teenager.

She didn't say much about her parents, just that they were no longer living. Neither were his, he said. And went on to describe how close he'd been to his father, who'd passed away only recently.

After that they were both quiet for a time. Later she asked him about his work, told him she'd read articles on McDevitt International, and let him brag about all his publicity for a while. When he inquired about Washington, D.C., and her decision to move away from politics, she gave him only a sketchy outline. She said nothing of the men in her life.

Just as they were approaching Westwinds, stopped at a red light, R.B. turned to her—a thoughtful expression on his face. "You know," he said, looking deep into her blue-violet eyes, "I've got a feeling you've been through a lot more than you're willing to admit. My instinct says you're a survivor, Kate—just like me."

"Well, thank you . . . I guess," she replied, averting her eyes.

"Believe me," he insisted as the Jaguar swung up the steep, eucalyptus-lined drive to the retreat, "it's a compliment."

Kate mulled that over for a while. And then she decided what it was she really disliked about R. B. McDevitt. The man had a most distinct and annoying idiosyncrasy. Every time he opened his mouth, he seemed to be patting himself on the back.

They arrived at Westwinds just as Taylor was finishing up a lecture inside the awe-inspiring auditorium. And not long after that, Kate and Brandy managed to slip away together for a stroll around the bucolic estate.

"Just let me look at you," Kate said, giving the exquisite blonde a once-over. "Ah, you're gorgeous, as usual."

Brandy was draped in a light blue gauze dress that was belted at the hips, emphasizing her long, slender body. She wore silver drop-earrings and a matching bracelet. But little makeup.

"And you look wonderful," Brandy enthused, eyeing Kate's tailored gabardine slacks. "Lost some weight, haven't you?"

"Couple of pounds. Never enough," she said, remembering how she'd struggled through a few more stretch exercises than usual that morning. "Thigh flab—if I could only wish it away."

"Still jogging?" Brandy asked, leading Kate in the direction of a lush Oriental garden.

"When the mood strikes me—which isn't very often these days."

They stopped to admire a cluster of bonsai trees.

"Lovely here, isn't it?" Brandy observed. "And so peaceful."

"Uh-hmm . . . although, I must admit, I'm not into all that higher-self mumbo-jumbo."

"Me neither," Brandy confessed, relieved. "Don't take this

wrong, but that's part of the reason I'm so delighted you're here. I didn't know how to squirm out of that group meditation session."

"I sure did!" Kate laughed. "Besides, R.B. and Taylor probably want some time together. So it works out perfectly."

"What's the story with Seth?" Brandy wanted to know as they continued walking.

"It isn't."

"Lost cause?"

"No question," Kate said firmly. She went on to tell Brandy about Seth's recent visit and her decision not to marry him. "But that's history," she concluded, with forced enthusiasm. "I want to know all about you. Acting. Being a star!"

"Star?" Brandy gasped. "Not so fast. Let me get the series off the ground first. Do you know how many of them fail, Kate? Like about ninety-five percent a season."

"Not yours, kiddo. You're special. You'll see."

"I hope you're right. Actually doing the series—the acting—is well, quite enjoyable. Hard work but fun, you know? It's the publicity I can't abide."

"Like the upcoming tour?"

"Sara told you? It's less than ten days before it starts. I'm scared to death!"

"Well, don't be," Kate said authoritatively. "Just remember what a knockout you are. That'll stun them for starters. Then dazzle them with your brainpower. They'll all be astonished to find out you're brilliant as well."

"I hope so," Brandy mumbled, unconvinced.

"Well, Taylor certainly caught on right away. I've never known him to be seen with a woman whose IQ was under two hundred," Kate joked.

"He's nice," Brandy said softly.

"First date, isn't it?"

She nodded. "We met when I did his show. And I didn't really like him at all. But . . . well, he went out of his way to be nice to me."

"I'm sure," Kate teased.

"No, I mean he did something that . . . I just don't think most men would do. It was . . . oh, never mind."

"What do you mean, 'never mind'? Now that you've piqued my curiosity, I'm just supposed to dismiss it? Come on, you have to tell me."

Brandy stopped walking and looked directly at Kate. "Okay. But this is really embarrassing. Promise you won't repeat it?"

Kate studied the odd mix of mischief and apprehension on Brandy's face. "Of course. And you know I keep my promises."

"Yes. I know that." Brandy said poignantly. "All right. It happened my first day on the *Ki & Company* set. I was playing this young woman whose husband has been murdered. And the scene that morning was a simple one. All I had to do was walk into Justin Kane's office, sit down, and deliver a couple of lines. I knew them backward and forward."

Brandy shook her head, as if she were reliving the distressing moment. "We'd rehearsed the scene perfectly. But when the camera started rolling and the director called for action, I stepped through the doorway and immediately tripped over a cable. You should have seen me, Kate. I went flying. Crashed into a heavy brass floor lamp and smashed the bulb to bits. Bruised the heck out of my leg."

"Poor baby," Kate offered, stifling the urge to laugh out loud. "And Taylor helped you up?"

"He did more than that. He saved me from going to pieces. It wasn't that anyone actually laughed. But there were all these muffled snickers. References to 'dumb bimbo'—things like that. And I was absolutely mortified. I guess Taylor sensed I was ready to fall apart."

"So what did he do?" Kate urged.

"Nothing!" Brandy said proudly. "He just went on like nothing had happened. And everybody else followed suit. After that, he went out of his way to make me feel at home—hey, quit laughing."

"I can't help it," Kate said, as they made their way over a wooden footbridge. "I mean it must have been awful at the moment, but think of the mileage you'll get out of that story at cocktail parties—or even interviews, when you're famous."

"There you go again."

"Sorry, pal," Kate said, draping her arm over Brandy's shoulder. "As far as I'm concerned, your star-studded future is locked in."

"I'm glad one of us is so positive."

"Now, tell me about Taylor. How do you like him—I mean other than as a friend?"

"Hmmm. He's, well, he's more than I expected. At first glance he looked like a carbon copy of all the male models I've worked with. You, know, great bodies, huge egos, vacuous brains. But he's not like that at all, as I'm sure you're aware. And I . . . ahh, I like him—"

"How much?" Kate probed.

"I don't know. I mean—"

"I mean, are you attracted to him?" Kate interjected playfully. "Is he a turn-on?"

"We haven't gotten that far," Brandy said crisply.

"I know, but—"

"Kate! I'd just rather not discuss it, if you don't mind."

"Sure, that's fine," Kate said, backing off. "Just my old reporter's instinct rearing its ugly head. Sorry."

"It's all right," Brandy said coolly.

Kate didn't know how to proceed after that. So she rambled on about Taylor a little longer. Telling Brandy how his parents had virtually disowned him at one point, then turned around and financed Westwinds a couple of years later.

"There's something very special about him," Brandy said evasively as they stopped at a fishpond full of prized koi.

"Seeing anyone else?" Kate asked casually. "Any old beaux from New York—or new ones out here?"

"I've hardly had time," Brandy explained, bending down to get a closer look at the exotic fish. But Kate knew she was purposely avoiding the issue of men. Just as she always did.

It seemed odd to Kate that Brandy never opened up about her personal life. The two had been friends for almost five years. And during that time Kate had poured her heart out to Brandy on more than one occasion. Sputtering expletives about some hack editor or an impossible assignment. Blubbering through her tears over Cary and, more recently, Seth. But Brandy never seemed to *need* to talk about her life the way Kate did.

There was, in fact, very little Kate knew about Brandy's social life —or her family, for that matter. Just that she'd left home when her mother died, trading Denver for New York.

Strange, what good friends we are, Kate mused to herself, *when we have so little in common.*

"Tell me more about R.B." Brandy urged as they headed back toward the auditorium.

Kate shrugged good-naturedly. "What's to tell? He's rich. He's arrogant. He thinks the world of Taylor. And he's definitely a male chauvinist pig."

"You're kidding! I didn't get that impression at all."

"You had a two-minute conversation with him, Brandy. Try an hour or so in close quarters, like his car. Do you know the man actually refers to his airplane as a *her*?"

Brandy giggled. "Well that's not so unusual, is it? He seems nice, Kate, not to mention good-looking. And Taylor says for all R.B.'s money he's really very down-to-earth."

"That's because Taylor probably has just as much money," Kate chuckled. "No, hon, I'd say R. B. McDevitt is definitely not a contender for my heart."

"That's too bad," Brandy said wistfully. "I was hoping he'd take your mind off Seth."

"No contest."

"Oh, I wouldn't be too sure, Kate," Brandy teased as they ascended the steps to the auditorium. "I'd say R.B. is definitely interested in you. And from what Taylor tells me, he's the kind of man who gets what he goes after."

Taylor insisted on giving Kate a grand tour of the facilities at Westwinds, as she knew he would. R.B. and Brandy trailed a few paces behind, swapping Hollywood and Texas stories, as Taylor deluged Kate with an endless monologue about the hundreds of "friends" he and his counselors had been able to help at this hilltop retreat. She listened politely.

But when he drew her aside in his office and suggested that she, too, might benefit from a couple of weeks of "emotional restoration," Kate lost her patience.

"Listen, Taylor," she said sternly. "I'm fine. I know R.B. thinks differently, but—"

"Actually, Kate, it was Sara who mentioned that you—"

"Maybe so," Kate interrupted hotly. "She may have told you I've been a little depressed, but this pep talk was R.B.'s idea and you know it. For some reason, he has me pegged as a wounded bird."

"Kate, that's not true," Taylor insisted with a smile. "He thinks you're very strong—"

"Well, I am, dammit!" she retorted, angry with herself for being on the defensive. "And I don't need you and R. B. McDevitt to start orchestrating my life. I've gotten along on my own for a long time, and I'll continue to do so."

"Hey, I didn't mean to upset you," Taylor apologized, getting up from his desk.

"I know," she replied with a weak smile. "I guess I'm just a little sensitive about—"

"Forget it," he said, leading her toward the door. "Only a suggestion. Everybody's different, Kate. What worked for R.B. here at Westwinds wouldn't necessarily work for you, anyway."

You've got that right, Kate thought as they strolled outside to the parking lot, where R.B. and Brandy were waiting.

The four of them drove into Santa Barbara, where they walked along the ocean for a while, then over to a bustling pier lined with restaurants and shops. It was a typical cloudless California afternoon. "One you'd give your heart and soul for," R.B. enthused, raising his arms to the sky.

They drifted along, munching on giant-sized waffle ice cream cones, poking around gift shops, and finally stopped at the end of the pier to watch some city kids try their luck fishing.

Any other time Kate might have enjoyed herself in this carefree setting, ambling along on a double date. But at the moment she was only pretending to have a good time. Laughing on cue. Offering witty comments. Even smiling at R.B. once in a while.

No one noticed the furtive way she kept checking her watch. And late in the afternoon, when Taylor suggested they all drive over to the popular Presidio Cafe for any early dinner, she played her disappointment to the hilt. Explaining that she had a previous engagement back in L.A. An interview of sorts with Letty Molloy. Had any of them heard of her? No? Well, she was an elderly woman and Kate just couldn't beg off at this late date. Otherwise she'd love to stay for dinner.

Kate did this with such sincerity that even Brandy seemed to buy it. As did R.B. "Little lady's got to work," he said in a patronizing tone that infuriated Kate. "Besides I have to fly back to the ranch."

When Kate and R.B. finally pulled away from Westwinds in the Jaguar, a surge of relief swept over her. She didn't even mind the ride back, during which R.B. did most of the talking. Whatever the man had to say at this point, it didn't matter to Kate. She had already tuned him out and written him off.

Pompous jerk—trying to redirect her life. Giving Taylor the impression she was a basket case. What complete audacity. Any redeeming qualities Kate might have stumbled across in R. B. McDevitt's flawed character had suddenly vanished. The man was impossible. A complete egomaniac.

As he walked her to the door back in Bel Air, R.B. suggested dinner the next week. Kate said she'd have to check her calendar. She knew he wanted an invitation to come inside the house, but she didn't offer one.

"You'll have to excuse me, but I just have time to change and get across town to Letty Molloy's."

"Do it!" he said, then kissed her quickly on the forehead. "See you soon."

"Not if I can help it," Kate muttered to herself as she walked inside and firmly closed the door.

9

■ "Over here, my dear. Nothing to be afraid of. I've been waiting for you."

The voice was deeply guttural and authoritative. Almost masculine. It came from the imposing figure seated on the overstuffed, slipcovered chair in the darkened corner.

Kate moved with some hesitancy. The last rays of daylight streaked through the high stained-glass window, cutting a single illuminated path across the antiquated parlor. She squinted into the darkness but still couldn't see clearly.

"Come, come, sit down across from me," commanded the voice impatiently. "I'm quite harmless, really. Whatever you've heard has been greatly exaggerated. Except the titillating tales of my romantic escapades. Those are true, every last one."

Kate eased onto the paisley-print settee, waiting for her eyes to adjust. Finally she focused on the mysterious figure in front of her. Letty Molloy was draped in a faded dress of lavender lace, which was far too large and so threadbare that Kate surmised it had been purchased decades earlier.

How pitiful, Kate thought, without altering her cheerful expression.

A slender woman, with a bony, wide frame, Letty had been called stately, even regal, in her day. But now she had the look of someone who had lost too much weight too fast. She wasn't hunched over or arthritic, as Sara had led Kate to believe, yet there was a sickly pallor about Letty Molloy. Her skin had a yellowish cast, wrinkling up into thousands of tiny, sallow crevices. Her cheekbones were high but her jowls hung limply, giving her the appearance of someone permanently despondent. She wasn't at all what Kate had expected.

"Miss Molloy, I'm so—"

"Surprised, right?" exclaimed Letty, emitting a deep, guttural guffaw. "Oh, it's all right, my dear. Truth is, most people figure I'm kicking up daisies by now. And the rest of them wouldn't believe I'd wind up looking like this . . . like the remains of Big Bird after a crash diet. Ha, ha, ha."

Kate smiled politely. "I was surprised to hear from you."

"Yes! Bet you were! Glad you dropped by, too. Not often I entertain these days. Oh, that reminds me—you'll take tea of course. Raymond. Raaaymond. Attaboy, just wheel those little goodies right over here. Needn't stay. Miss Brannigan will do the honors, I'm sure."

As Letty's dull-eyed servant retreated to the kitchen, Kate picked up the chipped ceramic teapot from the wooden cart and began to pour. "You indicated over the phone that you might have some information about Renata Desmond," she said, hoping she sounded matter-of-fact.

"Honey, I've got information that's gonna knock your socks off and rocket them clear to Timbuktu," said the older woman, reaching for a sticky, cream-filled napoleon and taking a substantial bite. "Love these little devils, don't you? Have one. You see, dearie, I know more about Renata Desmond than the rest of this town would like to forget," Letty continued between chews. "By the way, bet you're not having much luck snooping around, are you?"

"Not exactly," Kate admitted, adding more cream to Raymond's intoxicatingly strong tea.

"Well, Kate—may I call you Kate? Good. I've got an earful for you. And you needn't even take notes. Never mind why. Just trust me. That's key here, dearie. You've got to trust Letty. I know that's not the rule in this town. Trust is something that went out with the first television screen. But to me it's key. Always has been. And I trust you, Kate."

"But you don't even know me."

"No," Letty agreed, scooping up a tiny cream puff and popping it into her wide mouth. "But I know a great deal about you. I know you're trying to get the goods on Renata for *World* magazine. And I know why it's so important to you. I might look like a feeble old bird, honey, but there's nothing flappin' in the breeze upstairs. The old noodle is still operative."

Kate wasn't so sure. She'd heard rumors that Letty was either

senile, or suffering from Alzheimer's disease. At any rate the octoge-
narian gossip had been cloistered away in this musty, run-down
house off Hollywood Boulevard for years. Chatting only occasionally with loyal cronies like Mary Martin and Bette Davis.

"Now, I'm certain you're skeptical. And well you should be,"
Letty announced, placing her cup and saucer on the cart with an air
of finality. "Skepticism is the mark of a good reporter, my dear.
Never assume! Assumptions are the termites of relationships. Like
that? Can't remember who said it. Oh, yes. It was that fellow who
played the greaser on television, in that show *Happy Times,* or was it
Days? Yes, that's it. *Happy Days.* What the heck's his name? Henry
something. Wendler? Willner—?"

"Winkler."

"Right you are. Henry Winkler. 'Assumptions are the termites of
relationships.' Bright boy. Wonder if he's still in the business. Let's
see now, what were we talking about?"

"Skepticism."

"Very important. Glad you reminded me. I know you're skeptical,
Kate. Probably you think I don't have a working brain cell left.
Well, I can assure you, the doctor says my gray matter is intact. It's
the body that's going. ALS. You've heard of it? Didn't think so. Lou
Gehrig's disease. That's what most people call it. And let me tell
you, it's no picnic. Degeneration of the nerves, which control the
muscles, as you know. Pretty soon, they tell me, I won't even be able
to walk. Or eat. Or talk, I suppose—"

Letty trailed off and stopped talking, staring dreamily at the cut-
glass chandelier overhead. Caught up in her own private, morbid
reverie.

This is it, thought Kate. *Your chance to take off. Exit. Vacate. Slip
by old Raymond the butler and never return. Just get out of here fast,
before you waste any more time. Sara was right. The woman has lost
it. She's bonkers.*

"That's it, dear, do come a little closer," Letty said, startling
Kate, who was about to push herself up off the settee. "I want you to
get a good look at my dress. Real lace. Faded now, of course. That's
because it's so old. This is one of my favorite frocks from the thirties.
And what I want to tell you is . . . how I got this bloodstain on the
sleeve."

As Kate's eyes focused on the purplish spot just above Letty's elbow, the old gossip continued to talk. She talked nonstop for more than twenty minutes. And not once did she lose her train of thought. It seemed as though she didn't even pause to take a breath. Her story about the bloodstain on her sleeve was so dramatic and intense and thorough and emotional that it unfolded effortlessly, like the very best performance of a Shakespeare tragedy.

And, though reluctant at first, Kate was held captive. As she listened to the sordid details of Letty's story, her doubts about the woman's mental agility began to melt away. And by the time Letty stopped talking, Kate's jaw had dropped noticeably.

"Better clap your trap, dearie. Raymond isn't too swift with a fly swatter," Letty chortled, folding her long, yellowed fingers in her lap. "Well, what do you think of my little report? Quite a revelation, isn't it?"

"More like a time bomb," Kate said, still shaken by Letty's graphically repugnant descriptions. This information, this completely reprehensible, abject tale not only shed shocking new light on Renata Desmond, but in print it could also ruin her. Sandblast her ivory image. Disgrace her. Bring her down. Letty's story was far more than Kate had hoped for. It provided the edge she needed for her place in *World*. And it could trigger the end of Renata's stranglehold on the Hollywood community.

But—skepticism again. Could Kate believe it? More important, could she prove it?

Almost as if reading Kate's mind, Letty interrupted. "There is, of course, one area that will be troubling, my dear. And that is evidence. At this late date we have, sad to say, only three eyewitnesses left. Aside from me, that is. Alisa Hudson, the actress. She was there. So was Sammy Rollins, that bumbling columnist who still works for Renata. You know him? Treacherous little man, such a weasel. And the third party . . . someone you're not too fond of, I'm afraid. Stinson. Harvey Stinson. Your superior during your brief tenure at the *Daily*, wasn't he? A real bastard, that one. But he could be convinced to tell the truth. They all could be. That, my dear Kate, is your mission. Get them all to swear to it. Corroborate my facts."

"I'll try, Miss Molloy—"

"Letty, for heaven's sake. Call me Letty. We're old friends by now. And you'd better try, my dear Kate. You'd better break your cute little whatsits trying. You know why? Because you now have the hottest piece of information any reporter in this town has ever latched on to. Damn all the fuss they make about that skulduggery that goes on at the studios. Happens all the time. This is different. This is unique. This is Hollywood at its most debauched, with Renata Desmond center stage. And you, Kate Brannigan, are the first reporter to learn the truth. Now take the truth, Kate, and run with it!"

·II
The Investigation

10
Beverly Hills, California
1920

■ The arrival of Renata Nadia Desmond at Shangri-la, the fifteen-acre, hilltop estate of Charles Wentworth Desmond, sent ripples of shock and astonishment radiating throughout the Hollywood community. In the 1920s single parenting was hardly in vogue. And even if it were, Cappy Desmond was a most unlikely candidate to seek out the role of fatherhood. Cappy was a notorious womanizer. A confirmed bachelor. Why in the world would he adopt a baby girl?

"Unbelievable!" "Absolutely ludicrous!" "Cappy playing daddy? Hey, who's been passing the joy powder?" The exclamations of skepticism fueled cocktail-party gossip for weeks. Finally, the tale turned full circle: A consensus formed to the effect that Cappy Desmond must have started the incredible rumor himself.

"That Cappy, what a card!"

After all, hadn't he previously orchestrated some of the town's most fabled and wicked pranks? Once, hosting three dozen of his celebrated neighbors for a weekend at Shangri-la, feeding them sumptuously in the forty-foot oak-paneled dining room, followed by billiards in the basement and dancing in the grand ballroom . . . graciously, he bid them all good night, only to tiptoe upstairs to a hidden gallery above the guest bedrooms. Concealed eyeholes offered a glorious overview of the beds. Douglas Fairbanks and Mary Pickford had not been amused when, on the patio over coffee the following morning, Cappy casually alluded to their sexual calisthenics of the night before.

Another time, the predawn fire drill aboard his yacht . . . Cappy had invited his usual complement of a dozen or so for a frolicsome cruise, and they'd docked in Avalon on Catalina Island, partied for hours, and retired very late.

Around five in the morning, in total darkness, Cappy began clanging the ship's big brass bell and hysterically screaming, "Fire! Fire!"

Once the dazed but terrified group was herded ashore, Cappy and his yacht swiftly vanished into the watery blackness, leaving his guests marooned in various states of dishabille for a full hour. Charlie Chaplin threatened to sue over that one.

He never did, of course. For despite Cappy's boisterous, often crude sense of humor, despite his outrageous antics and flagrant flaunting of his newly acquired millions, the man had undeniable charm. Hollywood, in its way, loved him all the more for it.

And he was English—in an age when all things English were automatically considered superior. The English theater was then thought to be the highest possible expression of dramatic art, and English actors were coveted for screen roles. An English accent— "Shakespeare's tongue"—was like money in the bank, especially as the talkies revolutionized the motion picture industry in the late twenties. American actors practiced emulating the clipped tones of aristocratic British speech: It didn't matter so much what was said; what counted was *how* it was said.

Cappy Desmond sounded just right, even when he was being vulgar and short-tempered. He had flair. He fit right in. He had the money. A debonair elegance when he strode into a formal dinner party with a ravishingly lovely starlet on his arm. A dignified British aggressiveness as he proceeded to acquire vast holdings in Beverly Hills and Bel Air.

He was accepted by the Golden People. That small group of Hollywood élitists who had decided to make the twenties roar. Studio executives, producers, writers. And stars like Rudolph Valentino, Barbara La Marr, Theda Bara, and Harold Lloyd. They lived like kings and queens—after all, the public expected it. And, like royalty, they conformed to no codes of conduct other than those of their own devising. They reveled like pagans—some, like satanic demons— whooping it up for days on end with unbridled abandon.

Had he not been a real estate tycoon, Cappy Desmond might well have become an actor himself. A self-proclaimed "ham," he was at his best center stage. And he was handsome—a slender six footer with merrily mischievous brown eyes. He bore a slight resemblance to his good pal, the famed actor John Gilbert. When the two went on the town together, Cappy liked to boast that he was Gilbert's older brother. No one challenged the assertion, even after Cappy added what was to become his personal trademark. His mustache. A long, meticulously groomed line that perked up into curlicues at the ends, giving his visage a look of permanent optimism.

The proud, often overbearing Englishman was, no doubt about it, one of Hollywood's most eligible bachelors. And one of the most sexually voracious. An unending parade of glamorous actresses paid nocturnal visits to the dashing millionaire's extravagantly decorated, fifty-room Spanish mansion. Its exterior was painted a blushing pink, and small wonder. The servants gossiped that their master sometimes entertained as many as three ladies at once in his bedroom suite decorated in black marble and black leather.

Certainly this pasha's pleasure palace was no place to raise a child, came the raised whispers in Cappy's select circle of friends. Surely this adoption business was a bunch of nonsense. Surely.

But then there arrived the elegantly engraved invitations to Renata Nadia Desmond's "coming out" party. "In celebration of my daughter's first year on earth . . ." Cappy Desmond, it became clear, was quite serious about being a daddy.

"About time I became a father, don't you think?" he bellowed above the calliope that warm Sunday afternoon. His eyes shone as he surveyed the gaiety of the carnival party that swirled around him on three acres of manicured lawn adjacent to Shangri-la's formal gardens.

More than five hundred of his affluent friends and acquaintances had motored eagerly past the gatehouse on Angelo Drive. Downshifting their Stutzes and Appersons into second as they ascended the steep, palm tree–lined private road to the cobblestoned forecourt.

Heads turned as Cappy's more famous guests made their entrances. Buster Keaton and Will Rogers pulled up within seconds of each other. Gloria Swanson stepped gracefully from a Rolls-Royce Silver Ghost, dressed in ecru lace. Rudolph Valentino emerged from his custom-built Voisin tourer. A gaggle of children gathered round to examine the car's coiled-cobra radiator cap.

Behind the sprawling mansion, dozens of bright-eyed preschoolers, dripping ice cream, queued up for pony-and Ferris-wheel rides. Their impeccably attired parents waved and resumed their adult conversations while savoring huge wisps of pink cotton candy washed down with sips of chilled champagne cocktails.

"A bit ostentatious for an infant's debut, don't you think?" sniggered a slickly groomed actor dressed in summer whites. "Ostentatious as hell, darling," agreed his ingenue companion. "But that's Cappy's style. The showier the better . . . and then some."

"He says he adopted the kid because he doesn't have an heir," Jake Selwyn, a fiftyish studio chief, was explaining to his wife as their merry-go-round steeds pumped rhythmically up and down. "Every man of means needs someone to leave his legacy to."

"That's a bunch of malarkey and you know it, Jake," Martha Selwyn replied, shifting her ample behind uncomfortably in the wooden saddle. "I say the whole thing smacks of no good. If the man wants a child, why in heaven's name doesn't he get married?"

"Simple," said Jake, turning slightly to steal a furtive glance at the half-bared legs of the shapely young brunette on the pony just behind. "He probably doesn't want a wife. Who can blame him?"

Martha grunted. "More likely," she countered, seeing her husband's preoccupation with the brunette, "he's impotent!"

"Martha, mind your tongue!"

"Jake, mind your eyeballs!"

"Spanish, don't you think?"

The slender woman's dangling earrings tinkled ever so slightly in the soft breeze as she whispered the words to her escort. They were hovering over baby Renata, a tiny vision in white lace nestled comfortably in her handcrafted white lattice crib.

"No . . . no. Not at all." The man yawned, accepting another stemmed crystal glass of bubbly from a clown-costumed waiter. "Skin's too light." He bent down low to take a good look at the child. She stared back fearlessly with big green eyes flecked with gold. The man made a cooing sound and stroked her surprisingly long hair, which was perfectly straight and jet black. "Portuguese perhaps. Or Italian. Maybe a cross."

"Or maybe a cross between Cappy and a hot-blooded Italian *si-*

gnorina," giggled the woman as they strolled together now toward the calliope.

"A possibility, my dear. A distinct possibility."

Nothing Cappy could say would quell the conjecture. Wherever he'd gone, for months, he'd caught snatches of these whispered and urgent conversations, even among his boating buddies at the Babylon Yacht Club. It didn't surprise him. He rather relished the endless theories and opinions about the truth behind his fatherhood.

But eventually, as he'd predicted, the talk died down. The astute and affluent moved on to newer, hotter topics. And Miss Renata Desmond was accepted into the fold.

It was quite obvious to all that she hadn't altered her father's lifestyle. Her presence at Shangri-la, in fact, assured Cappy's friends of even more of the elaborate parties and outings he delighted in overseeing.

Everyone within a five-hundred-mile radius of Beverly Hills knew that June fourth was Renata's birthday. For each year Cappy staged a spectacular celebration. A wondrous, imaginative event that was awaited with mounting anticipation by the most overpampered and hard-to-please sybarites in southern California. By mid-May they were sifting anxiously through the morning mail in search of the coveted gold-embossed envelope. Everyone invited attended. Renata's birthday party was a Hollywood must.

One year it was a magnificent masquerade ball. An affair that kept every available costume designer and expert seamstress working round the clock for weeks. No ordinary costume would do, and it became something of a competition around town to see who could outdo all the rest in extravagance and creativity.

Hollywood should have heeded one of the oldest show business truisms: The kid always steals the scene.

An hour after the party began, the guest of honor made her grand entrance. Little Renata stepped lightly from a magnificent miniature silver carriage pulled by eight matching, plumed, ivory-white ponies. She was dressed in a floor-length white organza ball gown trimmed in blue satin ribbons. A diminutive Cinderella. With her handsome Daddy playing the Prince . . .

The next year, Cappy had a huge stage constructed at Shangri-la for his darling girl's big day. The highlight of that party was a specially commissioned musical extravaganza, a madcap romp titled *My Little Renata,* and featuring the Ziegfeld Girls.

But it was the summer of 1926 that Cappy thoroughly overwhelmed the town. In celebration of Renata's sixth birthday, he took over a mile-long strip of Hollywood Boulevard and staged an afternoon of "adventuresome family sports." Cappy was dressed as the mighty Grecian god, Zeus. Renata as a darling little Aphrodite. Together they commanded their own Mount Olympus atop a set of bleachers, surveying their excited domain of mere mortals below.

The tension mounted. Then the shrill bleat of a bugle. The crowd hurried to find seats, and there soon came the rumble of heavy horse-drawn chariots. It was a day at the races! Including a neck-and-neck contest between two ostriches ridden by dwarfs. And the grand finale . . . an ever-so-close race between an elephant and a camel.

"Well, what did you think, angelface? Not bad for a spur-of-the-moment shindig, huh?" Cappy roared at his own joke as he wheeled their fire-engine red Pierce-Arrow back toward Beverly Hills.

"I loved it, Daddy," the worn-out little girl managed weakly.

He gave her a look that seemed to Renata to say that he wanted more from her—which made her little heart sink even lower. More than anything, she hated disappointing her father.

"Daddy, that man you were talking to—was he right? Did they really used to have chariot races at the Tournament of Roses parade?"

It was all she could think of to say, but the question appeared to please him. "Oh, yes, sweetheart. Why, back before you were even born, in '06 . . ."

But by then Renata wasn't listening anymore. Her father's words were lost in her troubled thoughts. The same troubled thoughts that always welled up inside her during these huge gatherings. In truth, she hated these spectacles her father found so amusing. All those people. Pointing at her. Staring. Other children her own age reaching out to touch her . . . as if she weren't even real.

When she was little more than a toddler, it had been far easier. Then she could nestle safely into her father's lap and lose herself against his large, comfortable frame. Then it didn't bother her so much when some strange adult, usually stinking of alcohol, insisted on kissing her or stroking her or patting her on the head.

But now Daddy said she was becoming a "little lady." He expected her to make friends with everybody—to laugh and talk and carry on the way he did. But she just couldn't. Every time she tried, she failed miserably. Her mouth opened but words wouldn't come out. Her knees felt wobbly and funny, as if she were going to fall. And sometimes her right eyelid acted strange, sort of jumping up and down like it was never going to stop.

Renata prayed no one would notice her odd behavior. Especially not her father. Often she'd overhear him making the excuse to his friends that she was "just shy, you know—going through a stage." But she knew it was more than that, more than shyness or a feeling that would go away in a little while. And she longed to tell him how she really felt. But she was afraid. Afraid that if she revealed the awful truth—about how thoroughly she disliked the birthday parties, how they made her all hot and cold and sick inside, about how she really didn't like playing with the other children, didn't want to go to that school on Wilshire Boulevard anymore, even if it was only half days . . .

If she told her father all of this, Renata was desperately afraid he would be so disappointed in her, so *angry,* that he would send her away. And for good, back to the orphanage he said she came from. Even though she couldn't remember what it was like there, it must have been terrible. And lonely. There she would have no one. Not even Consuela, her nanny. No one to love her, not even a little bit. That would be horrible. She couldn't bear it. She needed her father's love—she'd never been more sure of that.

For despite the gala birthday parties and the beautiful clothes and the other things he showered upon her, the little girl already harbored grave doubts about her father's devotion. She'd had them for some time. She wondered why she saw him so infrequently. Were other daddies always so busy? The only meal they shared was breakfast, and Cappy's evenings were routinely consumed with business or social plans. A quick good-night kiss was the most she could expect during the week, and on weekends there were always other grown-ups around. Dozens of them, dropping by for brunch in tennis whites or decked out in formals and tuxedos for elaborate evening parties. On these occasions, when Cappy insisted on introducing her to everyone, showing her off like a rare and delicate jewel, Renata still couldn't believe he really truly loved her.

Even at her young age she was constantly monitoring his actions, on the alert for the smallest signs of his affection. She did this imperceptibly, hardly aware herself that she was habitually keeping score —counting every one of the smiles and kind words her father allotted to her. And continually feeling cheated, deprived. By the time she was five years old, Renata was convinced that Cappy would really have preferred a boy. Maybe it was the way his face flushed an excited red and his laughter rang loudly across the vast lawns of their home when she watched him roughhousing or playing catch with his friends' sons. Or the way he seldom looked at her as she sat beside him at football games. She could tell he was dissatisfied with her. Why did she have to be a girl?

True, those Saturday afternoons at California Field were some of her happiest. Because then it was just the two of them. Rooting for the University of California Golden Bears while munching on popcorn and hot pretzels and sipping hot chocolate. Daddy nearly always explained the plays to her, though keeping his eyes fixed rigidly on the scurrying players in their leather helmets and soiled jerseys. Despite his coaching, however, she never really understood the game. Not like a boy would. And she sensed her father knew that— and resented her for it. Did he wish he could do something about it? Would he like to send her away and adopt a boy instead?

She got up the courage to ask him about it once when they were having breakfast on the patio. "Daddy," she began as he skimmed the front page of the *Los Angeles Times,* "would you ever . . . I mean . . . did you ever want me, ummm . . . not to be a girl?"

Cappy lowered the newspaper with a startled expression. "What, honey? Whatever do you mean?"

Renata's lower lip trembled slightly as she met her father's puzzled gaze. Now she'd done it. She'd started to ask and she had to finish it. But she was suddenly terrified. "Well . . . I just thought maybe sometimes you'd"—minuscule drops of water formed at the corners of her large green eyes— "that you'd rather have a . . . a son."

In one swift motion Cappy reached down and scooped up his bewildered daughter to cradle her in his arms.

"Sweetheart. You know how I adore my little angelface. I could have adopted a hundred little boys—but I picked you instead. You know why?"

She shook her head. A small smile poked through.

"Because of sugar and spice and everything nice—that's what little girls are made of. And my baby girl is the nicest little girl anywhere on this planet. Now eat your pancakes." And then he placed her again on her chair and went back to his paper.

Still, she was not completely reassured. The pangs of apprehension continued to stab at her. Would he always love her like this? Would she trip up somewhere, displease him? Like today at the party—did he notice that she really wasn't having a very good time, that it had been such a struggle for her? She couldn't say anything, could she? No. No, that would be too much of a risk.

"But you know what I said to the man—about your outfit?" Cappy was asking her as he maneuvered the Pierce-Arrow up his private road to the forecourt. "Renata? Are you listening, honey? You know what I told the *Herald* reporter about what you should wear?"

"No . . . no, Daddy. What?" she asked, not at all sure of what he was talking about.

"Well," Cappy went on, now guiding his daughter up the Spanish tile steps, "I told him that my little lady would decide herself what she wanted to wear in the pictures."

"Pictures?"

"Yes, precious. Like I said in the car." He stooped down to Renata's eye level. "The paper wants to do a four-page layout— that's lots of pictures. All of them of you, here at Shangri-la. Pictures of you riding around the gardens in your train, some shots in your little thatched cottage, and maybe Consuela could help you make some cookies. You could bake them in that pint-sized oven I had sent over from France. And Jojo—you'll want to pose riding him around his ring. Now maybe you'd like to get a brand-new outfit for . . ."

Renata said nothing. She just looked at her father, dazed. She couldn't. Couldn't possibly do that. Pose for all those pictures? For strangers who were coming to gawk at her? She felt a sense of panic, an urge to flee and hide. If she refused, Daddy would know her secret—he'd know she was only pretending, that she didn't really like all the things he wanted her to. That she didn't want to be around the other people. That she just wanted to be like other little girls, just wanted to be with her daddy or with Consuela. Or be left all by herself, alone.

"They want to call the article, 'The Luckiest Little Girl in the World.' Isn't that something?" Her father's words echoed in her ears. His face was so close now. His nose was almost touching hers, and she could see his gold-capped tooth at the back of his mouth as he smiled. "Just think, angel. You're the luckiest six-year-old on the face of the earth."

And then she couldn't help it. The tears started flowing down her high, beautifully chiseled cheekbones. Her frail little body began to shake. She could taste the saltiness as she gasped for breath. When she tried to speak, no words came out at first. Only the heartbreaking sobs she'd been holding inside for such a long time.

Finally she managed to say, "I—I know, Daddy. I k-know."

Her father swept her into his arms and hugged her close to him. "There, there, sweetheart," he soothed her. "Too much excitement for my little girl for one day. Consuela will give you a nice hot bath and tuck you in. We'll talk more about the pictures tomorrow."

In the morning Renata was feeling no better. She stayed in bed until well past eight o'clock, purposely missing her ritual breakfast with her father. Once she heard the Pierce-Arrow roar down the driveway, she tossed off the sheets and soft lamb's-wool blanket and got up. Reluctantly she allowed Consuela to dress her for school.

All day she weighed and balanced her alternatives. Daddy had been so nice last night when she cried. He didn't get mad. And he didn't say anything else about the dumb picture-taking. Maybe if he knew how much she didn't want to do it, he wouldn't make her. And if he didn't, then maybe she could risk telling him about all the rest.

If she could only do that—just tell him. Then maybe he wouldn't make her go to another party ever again. He was such a good Daddy. And she loved him so. If he would just forget about all those other people, all those friends of his that she couldn't stand being

with. Then it would be wonderful. Then it would be just the two of
them. Together. Always.

Later that evening he asked, "Well, did my best girl do some
thinking today?" Renata was in her pajamas, perched on Cappy's
bed, watching as he adjusted his bow tie in the mirror.

"Oh, yes, Daddy. I did. I thought about lots of things," she said
brightly, sliding back and forth on the sleek black satin bedspread.

"I mean about the pictures. What have you decided to wear? Or
should we go shopping?"

She stared hard at the floor. "Daddy, I . . . um," she stumbled,
then blurted out abruptly, "I don't think I really want to do the
pictures. Could you just tell the man from the paper—"

"Sweetheart! What do you mean, you don't want to pose for the
pictures?" Cappy chuckled as if his daughter were making a joke.
He was inserting gold monogrammed cuff links into the French cuffs
of his tuxedo shirt. "Of course my baby wants to be featured in the
Herald. It's the chance of a lifetime—or at least of a childhood." He
turned to look at her. "Do you know how many little girls would
give their eye teeth to be asked? And the paper picked *you*. Little
Renata Desmond. Aren't you pleased?"

She was concentrating now on the bunny faces on the toes of her
slippers. "Oh, yes, of course I'm pleased, Daddy. But—but I just
don't want to do it. Please. Please don't make me."

"But why not?" he demanded, slipping into his striped dinner
jacket.

"Because . . ." Her voice weakened, almost to a whisper. "Because I just don't like to do things like that, that's why. And I don't
feel—"

"Renata," he said firmly, moving to the bedside, "I can't believe
my ears. You've never acted like this before. Now let's just stop this
silly talk and—"

"It's not silly, Daddy, it's not!" she protested. "It's how I feel."
The force of her own voice scared her, and immediately her eyelid
began fluttering uncontrollably. "I don't want to. And I won't. And
that's that." She looked up at him, struggling to control the convul-
sive eyelid and so afraid of his reaction that the rest of her body
began trembling as well.

Cappy's face reddened and he glared at her in silence. She'd never seen him like this. Mad. Her Daddy was really mad and it was all her fault. She cowered before him. Was he going to hit her?

"You listen to me, you little prima donna," he said, grabbing her by the shoulders. "I don't know what's gotten into you, but you will not talk to your father that way, understand? And if I say you're going to be in the damn *Herald,* then you are, by God—you're going to be in it. So just get that straight."

He was shaking her now, his fingers digging into tender flesh above her narrow shoulder blades. Spikes of red-hot pain shot through her small neck, and she felt as if she were going to choke. "You're acting like a stupid spoiled brat," he said, finally releasing her. "And an ungrateful one at that."

Grabbing suede driving gloves from the bureau, he stalked out and slammed shut the bedroom door. Renata collapsed back on the black satin, sobbing. He hated her now, she knew it. She'd been bad. So very bad. How long would it be, she wondered, before he sent her away?

Cappy never mentioned their confrontation again. And three days later Renata posed prettily for the pictures. Dressed in a frilly pink pinafore her father had selected and looking "just like a little princess," as the photographer cooed. Inside, though, she was churning, on the verge of tears with every forced smile. She said little but got through it. Cappy loved the layout.

Loved it just as he did taking her shopping. Showing her off in elegant restaurants. Parading her to his friends' palatial estates on golden Sunday afternoons.

After their confrontation over the newspaper photos, Renata never again let on that she was an unwilling participant in her father's unceasing efforts to show her off to the world and his social circle. But neither could she force herself to be outgoing and effervescent—though it was plain that's what her father wanted.

Sometimes he urged her, "Be a little nicer to the other children, dear. They'll think you don't like them." She would smile back at him and pretend to try, but the truth was she *didn't* like the other children, or their parents. They were intruders. Unimportant and silly.

Renata's reticence did not go unnoticed. The gatherings she and

Cappy attended were peppered with clandestine conversations critical of her behavior.

"A bit shy, isn't she?"

"Shy? Aloof is more like it. Acts like a damn little dowager."

"Well, the kid's spoiled rotten. And it's no wonder. Look at how her father flaunts her about. Terribly stuck-up. I'd say he's in for a hell of a time as she grows up."

The prediction proved accurate. Cappy *was* in for a "hell" of a time. But it had nothing to do with Renata's truculence—and it happened long before she grew up.

It was shortly after Renata's ninth birthday that Consuela sheepishly approached Cappy. She asked to talk to him in private. He was about to step out to meet friends for dinner at the popular Café Montmartre but saw the woman was clearly distraught. Her usual cheerful demeanor had been replaced by a furrowed brow.

Curious, Cappy led her to the library. His daughter's nanny seldom made demands on his time. Perhaps she wanted a raise. New furniture for her room. A vacation to visit her family in Guadalajara. Whatever the woman wanted, she was entitled. The child loved her dearly. And Cappy knew Consuela was worth twice the thirty-five dollars a week he paid her.

But once the troubled nanny began to explain the reason for her concern, Cappy realized there would be no simple solution. He was faced with a problem money alone would not solve. He listened with mounting unease as Consuela searched for the right words in halting, broken English.

"So, sir, I, eh, don' know what to do. I see the *pelo*—it's there, you know? Ah . . . between . . . between the *piernas*—eh, legs." Ashamed, she averted her eyes. "And the child's *pecha.* She have the, ah . . . *tetas pequeñas* there. Like should not be. Not yet."

"Consuela," he interrupted impatiently, "I don't understand. Are you telling me that my daughter is"—the words stuck in his throat—"is developing breas—signs of womanhood?"

The abashed woman nodded gravely. Afraid to meet his gaze, she sat perfectly still on a leather wing chair, her hands clasped together tightly, the short, chubby fingers white. Her face burned with embarrassment.

It took Cappy several moments to accept what Consuela had told him—and then he was filled with revulsion. Never in his life had he heard of anything so appalling. Pubic hair at the age of nine? And breasts? Consuela had said Renata's chest had already enlarged a full inch since her birthday. What would be next? Menstruation?

He couldn't conceive of it. The woman must be hallucinating.

Cappy stood up abruptly, tugging on his finely tailored red vest. "Thank you, Consuela," he said stiffly. "I'll see that the matter is attended to. That will be all for this evening."

The nanny hoisted her heavy body up off the chair with a silent sigh. "Oh, one more thing," he added as she shuffled toward the large redwood doors. "Not a word of this to the other servants—or anyone. Understand?" She nodded solemnly.

The next week was like a nightmare for Cappy. Three different doctors who examined Renata confirmed Consuela's report. The girl was maturing far ahead of her years.

"Your daughter has a very rare condition," Dr. Burgess, chief gynecologist at St. Augustine's Hospital, explained to Cappy in private. "For lack of a better name we call it 'precocious puberty.' It's related to an overabundance of the female hormone progesterone. I've read of a number of documented cases, some of them treated with testosterone injections to balance the system out. But results vary, Mr. Desmond. Hormonal therapy could have damaging effects on the child now—and later in life."

"Well, then, what else can you try?" Cappy demanded.

Dr. Burgess rested his chin on his clasped hands. "Usually," he said evenly, "we recommend no treatment at all. You see—"

"No treatment?" Cappy gasped. "But what should I . . . Renata, what will happen to her? How much more obvious will this become? Will she have to start wearing a bra? Will she have her periods? The girl's only nine years old, Dr. Burgess. There must be something you can do now!"

The doctor shook his head sympathetically. "Believe me, Mr. Desmond, it's best not to. In time the condition will most likely correct itself. As the child grows, you see, her body will catch up to her hormone level. She may menstruate earlier than most, but over the years things should pretty much level off. And by the time she's in her teens, she'll be no different from other girls her age. The one thing in—"

"But I don't care about five years from now," Cappy almost shouted. "I care about *now*. And next month. I can't believe you're sitting here telling me there is nothing—"

"Mr. Desmond, please. I can only recommend what I believe to be safe. And in this case, it is nothing. Fortunately your daughter is quite tall for her age. So the physical incongruities will not be quite so obvious as they would be if she were smaller. I suggest that you do sit down and explain this to her. Or, if you like, I will do so myself. Your concern now should be not with reversing the condition but with helping Renata to cope with it."

Cappy marched from the hospital seething with rage. The next week he took Renata to New York for more doctor appointments, more examinations, more humiliation. The child was growing increasingly withdrawn. She didn't complain and she didn't cry. But even Cappy realized that his confusion and frustration over her physical abnormalities—not to mention the endless procession of doctors peering and poking at her body—were only adding to Renata's distress.

Yet he couldn't bring himself to explain fully the condition to her. "Growing up a little soon," was all he managed to say when she asked what was wrong. "Don't worry. You'll be fine."

By the time they returned to Shangri-la, however, Cappy had lost hope. Hormonal therapy or any other treatment was out of the question, he'd been told over and over. Finally he had to face the facts. His little princess! His sweet beautiful daughter was turning into a prepubescent hairy beast. With tits, yet. Good Lord. It was disgusting.

And it didn't matter how tall she was. He noticed now. Others would notice too. There would be talk. Nasty cracks behind his back: *Freak!* They'd call Renata a freak. And they'd laugh at "the luckiest little girl in the world" and all her fancy parties and expensive shows. They'd laugh at her—and at him.

He couldn't bear it. The decision to send Renata away was so effortless and automatic that Cappy might as well have been negotiating a real estate transaction—that's how quickly he made up his mind. It was obvious to him that she could not remain at Shangri-la, where she would be a constant embarrassment, a walking reminder of his overwhelming sense of guilt. No, she could not stay—and Renata would just have to accept that fact.

The only question was where to send her. The farther away, the better, Cappy determined. And within two weeks Renata was enrolled in an exclusive Swiss boarding school in Lausanne.

That September, he hired a multilingual governess to escort his daughter abroad. It was with a tremendous surge of relief that Cappy resumed his peripatetic social life—as if nothing had happened.

No one in his circle was surprised that the gregarious, good-looking bachelor had finally tired of his parental responsibilities. And few inquired further once he announced the girl was away at school. It was as if Renata Desmond had dropped into a monstrous crater and had disappeared.

11

■ "Kate! Kate, wake up. Wake up right now. Look at this!" Sara was leaning over the bed, thrusting the morning *Los Angeles Times* at her sleepy friend.

"Wha . . . wha time is it?" mumbled Kate. Her tongue felt fuzzy. She propped herself up on her elbow and blinked at Sara, a vision in a rumpled cotton nightgown, her spiky new hairdo askew. "My God, you look like a porcupine in heat. What is this, a fire drill?"

"No, it's more important than a fire drill. More important than a fire. It's a macabre little development I knew you'd want to know about, even though it's only six-thirty. Look at this headline. I was right. Letty Molloy is *meshuggeneh* . . . check that, *was.*"

Kate yanked the paper from Sara and stared at the boldfaced headline: VETERAN COLUMNIST LETTY MOLLOY POISONS SELF.

"Good God, I don't believe it! I was with her less than twelve hours ago and she seemed . . ."

"You said yourself she seemed a little skittish. 'Not exactly all there at times,' if I may quote you."

"True," Kate agreed, skimming the obituary quickly. "But I also said I thought what she told me might be worth following up on."

"Now you know you were wrong, I guess," Sara sighed, sitting down on the bed. "Anybody who swallows a bottle of laudanum for a bedtime snack has got to be nutso."

"Wait a sec, did you see this—on page three?" Kate asked, excitedly.

"Page three? Sweetie, TV execs aren't in the habit of reading beyond the first three lines of a story," Sara joked, looking over Kate's shoulder at the letter which the *Times* had reprinted.

My Dear Renata,

I want to take this opportunity to thank you for all my years on *The Hollywood Daily* staff. And to tell you how very sorry I am that your kingdom must crumble. You see, my dear, there are no real fairy tales in Tinsel Town. Only sagas of greed and mere mortals who mistakenly think they can control the lives of others forever.

Letty

"What the hell does that mean?" asked Sara, totally confused.

"I'm not sure. The paper dismisses it as the mere ravings of a doddering old woman. Renata is quoted as saying she's totally mystified by the letter. For me, it might be all the more reason to believe Letty Molloy was telling the truth. But I just don't know . . ."

"Okay Sherlock," Sara teased, crossing her arms authoritatively. "If you'll share the *juice,* Watson here will give you a readout."

"Oh, no you don't," Kate said, padding to the bathroom on bare feet. "Never betray an informant's confidence."

"But your informant is dead!"

"My story isn't, though," Kate sputtered through a mouthful of toothpaste. "Make you a deal. If it doesn't check out, I'll do a treatment for you. The stuff I got from Letty Molloy would make great television!"

Two hours later at *World* headquarters, Kate was still debating whether or not Letty's sordid tale had, indeed, come straight from Fantasyland.

By early afternoon she'd almost convinced herself that the whole thing was too far-fetched. The old gossip had been suffering from a debilitating disease and wanted to cause a stir on the way out. Well, Kate wasn't going to put her reputation on the line, snooping around for a scandal that didn't exist. No. She wouldn't follow up. It was a waste of time.

Then the mail came. And among the items addressed to Kate was a thick beige envelope containing a six-page letter written in a spidery, longhand scrawl.

Kate checked the bottom of the last page, and caught her breath. It was signed "Letty Molloy."

"My God," Kate murmured, sitting down. There was something

chilling about receiving a letter from a dead person. At first she was so appalled she didn't want to read it. Once she did, she wished she hadn't.

"My Dear Kate," it began. "Remember our conversation on Sunday when I told you not to take notes? That was because I'd already written this for your reference. Just in case you thought I'd made the whole thing up, I've documented every last detail here again for you."

Kate skipped through the six pages briefly and found that, indeed, Letty had done just that.

"Now you go to it, dear," the old woman had concluded. "With this, you will be able to unmask Renata Desmond for the loathsome hypocrite she is. And with your expert urging I'm certain Alisa, Sammy, and Harvey will all corroborate my facts. You just show them this and tell them Letty says it's time to give Renata some of her own medicine. I'm quite confident that you'll see to it, dear— and now, thank the good Lord, I can at last rest in peace. Letty."

Kate read the letter twice, pacing around the spacious office. Then she picked up the phone and dialed Celebrity Service.

"Hello, this is Kate Brannigan over at *World*. Do you have a contact number for Alisa Hudson?"

"My God!" Renata exclaimed. She'd spun around just in time to see the rotund figure in corduroy overalls and a red plaid shirt zooming toward her like a rocket.

"Move! Move!" Templeton yelled, waving his stubby arms up and down hysterically. "Can't stop," he said, sailing by Renata as she backed into the bookcase. He barely missed her.

Templeton was zipping along like lightning. Much faster than he'd expected. The hidden track he'd just had installed throughout his Beverly Hills mansion was butter-smooth. According to the manual, he could be doing up to thirty miles an hour. Right now it felt like sixty. Something had gone awry.

The remote control in his hand. It was supposed to move the rudders on the bottoms of his high-topped boots. It was supposed to make him stop on command. It wasn't working.

An expression of naked panic stretched across Templeton's face. Frantically he clicked the button again and again. He was headed toward the north wall—going straight for the prized suit of armor he'd paid three hundred thousand pounds for. The only suit of armor in the world that walked and talked, it could recite the history of the United Kingdom in thirty minutes flat. His inventor friend, Lord Brimley, had spent four years working on it. And now, oh no . . .

There was a terrible crash as Templeton rammed head-on into the life-sized metal suit, and both he and armor clattered clumsily to the hardwood floor.

"Oww . . . uhhh . . ." he moaned from beneath the rubble.

"Will you tell me the meaning of this?" Renata demanded, tapping her square-toed, black patent-leather shoe.

Stunned, Templeton glanced around at the now incapacitated suit of armor. There were limbs everywhere. A gauntlet had flown clear across the room. The visor had tumbled over to the spot where Renata continued tapping her foot. Still dazed, he rubbed his head and examined the gash on his right wrist.

"I'm sorry, Renata. Honestly, I am. I didn't know you were down here. My houseboy didn't announce you. Or maybe I missed it on the intercom. See, I was testing my new track and I—"

"I don't care what you were doing. I don't care if you turn this place into a roller rink. I don't care if you fly around here like Peter Pan. But I will remind you that we have business to conduct. It is seven o'clock, Templeton. The appointed hour."

"I know. I guess I just got a little carried away and—"

"Shut up, Templeton. Quit whining. You look like a superannuated six-year-old in that stupid railroad getup. Do you know that? What is it that possesses you to act like a raving maniac?"

"Just happy, I guess. We have cause to celebrate, Renata." With some difficulty, Templeton managed to push himself up off the floor. "I have wonderful news to share," he said, struggling now out of the offensive ruddered boots.

"It had better be wonderful. It had better be stupendous, considering what you've already put me through, you idiot," Renata said huffily, as she sat down on a Wainscot chair.

"Yes. Yes. I'm sure you'll agree that it is stupendous and all those other superlatives we know and love so well," said Templeton, sitting down beside her and activating a floor button with his silk stockinged foot.

"Visual aids?" she asked sarcastically, as a large movie screen descended from the ceiling.

"But of course, Madam President," Templeton replied. "I want you to savor all the details of the most ingenious financial scheme in the history of the Desmond Land Corporation.

"Templeton, if you are wasting my time, I'll . . ."

"Please, Renata," he cautioned, activating the videotape. "This is important. I have found a way to breathe life into your *Hollywood Daily* Center for Entertainment and the Arts. If you find this plan to your liking—and I'm certain you will—by 1991 you can rest assured that the celebrated Academy Awards ceremony will most definitely be held at The Renata Desmond Pavilion."

"What's going on, cutie pies?" asked Kate. She put her heavy briefcase down on the gleaming glass-topped bar. Sara's twins, Jennifer and Jackie, were sprawled out in front of the television, watching music videos.

"Not much doing, Aunt Kate," said Jackie, looking up briefly.

"How's tricks with you? Still playing supersleuth?" asked Jennifer, as Kate poured herself a diet soda.

"Sure am," said Kate, collapsing on a gray sectional couch beside them. *Though not very well,* she thought. Kate hadn't gotten through to Sammy Rollins or Harvey Stinson. And Alisa Hudson's manager wasn't returning her calls.

"Any luck?"

"Not exactly. Where's your mom?"

"Out!" replied Jennifer crisply.

"Yeah. She had a fight with Dad," added Jackie.

"Another phone fight," said Jennifer " 'Cause Dad keeps dipping into the almighty bank account. And he wants to see us. But she won't let him. She's just jealous because he doesn't want to see her."

"Don't be dumb, beanbrain," said Jackie. "She's punishing him. Haven't you ever read a psychology book?"

"Girls," Kate interrupted, "I think you're being too hard on your mother. She's going through an awful lot right now and—"

"She's been going through it for weeks now, Aunt Kate," complained Jennifer. "When's it going to stop? When is she going to quit running around like a hyperactive chicken?"

"You shut up," said Jackie, swatting her sister on the behind. "Mom's upset. Can't you understand that? Don't you know that's why she's acting a little strange?"

"A little strange? More like completely wacko," Jennifer corrected her sister. "You saw her this morning. In that hiked-up leather skirt and that dumb vest over that flashy T-shirt. She actually went to work that way. Can you imagine what they're saying around the studio?"

They were saying plenty. And not only at the studio. Just that afternoon Kate had bristled when she overheard a conversation in the elevator at *World* headquarters.

"Seen Sara Silverstein lately?" an editor had asked a reporter. "What a disaster. Looks like she just inherited a flea market."

"Yeah, from Pelo Nafti," the reporter chuckled. "Talk about a Svengali. I wouldn't let that guy loose on my mother-in-law. He's the worst."

Kate knew they were right and she was anxious to speak with Sara. But not in front of the twins.

"So where'd your mom go?" she asked, hoping to change the direction of the conversation.

"Vroooooom . . . Vroooooom." Jennifer reached out, holding imaginary handlebars. "Romeo of the leather world, who else?"

"She means Jimmy," Jackie sighed.

"Not just Jimmy," Jennifer insisted. "Jimmy Z!"

"I know who you're referring to," Kate said. "I met him last night."

"What does she see in him, anyway?" Jackie asked. "He looks wasted."

"You know what she sees in him, all right," snapped Jennifer. "You saw it as well as I did. How could you miss it with those tight black leather pants he pours himself into? What a pack that guy's got. He might as well advertise. Probably does."

"That's enough, Jenny," Kate said. "I'm sure your mother has her reasons. She probably just wanted to get out of the house."

"Yeah, and into Jimmy Z's pants!" snapped Jennifer, getting up abruptly. "I'm going to bed."

"Me too," said Jackie, trailing behind.

Poor kids, Kate thought, watching them traipse upstairs. On the surface they seemed to have everything. Money. Private school. All the right friends. And they were cute, if not actually pretty.

The twins looked exactly alike. Sara's imposing nose. Mark's sparkling blue eyes. Short, straight sandy hair. They dressed alike too. Oddly enough, they seemed to enjoy that. Probably just because they liked fooling people, Kate reasoned. It certainly wasn't because of similar personalities. The two girls were always at odds. And since Mark's unexpected departure, the lines had been clearly drawn.

Jennifer was Daddy's girl. And Jackie, Mother's darling. Who knew why, or how, kids chose up sides? Maybe the parents were to blame. Kate just wished that during this trying family crisis the twins could find comfort in each other. It was clear they weren't getting much from Sara.

"Anybody up? Kate!"

"Sara, I didn't hear you come in," Kate said, startled.

"How could you hear anything with that blasting?" her friend shouted.

Kate reached for the remote control and turned down the volume.

"Since when are you watching MTV?" Sara asked, heading for the bar.

Was she walking funny, or was that just Kate's imagination?

"Since your two teenagers got me addicted," she chuckled, watching Sara pull the ring off the top of a can. "Beer? You never drink beer."

"I do now," Sara said flatly, plopping down beside her friend on the couch. She looked bedraggled. The tight jeans and tank top were not becoming. The circles under her eyes were darker than usual. And her lipstick had all been eaten off—or something, Kate thought. She'd never seen Sara looking so disheveled or tired or depressed.

"Wanna talk?" Kate asked.

"Okay. Shiksas first." Sara smirked.

"Not much to report. Very little progress on the Renata front, aside from the fact that Madam Desmond does pocket half the take from Quintana's catering business. Real shocker, huh? On the personal front, I miss Seth but I know I can't call him. Because I'll just hurt him again. End of story. You've heard it all before."

"Yes. But I like repetition. It's soothing," Sara said, half closing her eyes.

"Want to sleep?"

"Can't."

"Tonight I'll bet you could."

"No way! Mark called again. I'm bound to lie awake replaying the whole conversation over and over."

"What did he say?"

"What the hell does he always say? He needs time. Just be patient. He can't explain the missing money. He'll replace it. Can he see the girls? Never mentions me and how I feel."

"He knows," Kate said reassuringly.

"But doesn't care." Sara took a swig of beer.

"Yes, he does, but—"

"Oh, forget it, Kate. Just can it, all right?" Sara practically yelled, getting up for another beer. "I've had enough of trying to believe what you say about Mark. I've waited. Almost a whole month I've waited. And the schmuck is still carrying on, saying the same lousy things. It's useless. You want to know how useless? I filed today." She leaned over the bar, waiting for Kate's reaction.

"Oh Sara, I'm so sorry," she said.

"Well, I'm not. He's a stupid jerk-off and he doesn't deserve me," said Sara, walking around the room. "I'm pretty hot stuff, you know? I've changed, Kate. And everyone notices. You can't believe the way people are looking at me, like I'm different. Like I'm a new person now."

"And why do you think that is?" Kate asked hesitantly.

Sara sat down and leaned over toward her friend. "I think it's because I've finally found myself. Finally I have an image. Pelo has helped me discover—no, what does he say?—*release* the real me. I've broken the chains of mediocrity. It's style, honey. Style. For the first time in my life I've got it. I'm dressing with vision, Kate. Because I'm a futurist. A trend-setter. Someone other women want to emulate."

Kate couldn't hold back. She had to say something. She consid-

ered her timing: Sara so tired and drunk and all. But if not now—
when? Sara was deluding herself. Someone had to stop her. Fast.

"I wouldn't be so sure about that," Kate began.

"About what?"

"Your new look. Other people liking it. Women wanting to emulate you."

"Why not?"

"I've heard different."

"What do you mean, *different*?" Sara asked, shocked.

"Sara, I'm not telling you this to be cruel. I'm telling you because
I care for you and I don't want to see you get hurt anymore. The
word around is that you're acting like a looney tune, Sara. At first,
with the punk hairdo, you just seemed a little eccentric. But now,
you've done such an about-face from your conservative days that
everyone's trying to figure out why you're backpedaling. Honey, it's
as if you swallowed a pill to become an instant teenager—and barely
missed. I—"

"Is that all?" Sara said icily, standing up.

There was total silence as the two women locked eyes. And for a
brief moment it seemed as though they'd never shared anything,
never really been friends.

"There's more," Kate said, leaning back exhausted. "But I don't
want to tell you right now."

"Don't. Do me a huge favor and don't ever mention it again.
Because I don't want to hear your theories about how I look or what
I'm trying to do, understand? I don't need some Mickey Mouse
reporter who doesn't know a Don Zaro from a Claude Montana
sitting in my house telling me how to dress. You wouldn't recognize
an original if the designer himself helped you squeeze your chubby
hips into it."

"Sara, I've only repeated what I heard other people say. It's fine
to make changes. But don't you realize what Pelo Nafti is doing to
you? His tastes are far too extreme. You can't—"

"I can do anything I damn well please, Kate. And for your information, I've never felt so young in my life, thanks to Pelo. He's
taken years off me. And if you want my opinion, you could use a
little work yourself. After a couple of sessions with Pelo, you just
might look less dumpy."

"Oh, wonderful," Kate retorted, getting up on her feet. "So then maybe I could start dating one of the Hell's Angels too, right? We could go out drinking and riding together. You, me, Jimmy Z, and his friend, Johnny Stud! Can't wait."

"Jimmy is *not* a member of the Hell's Angels, dammit," Sara shouted. "He is an actor and a damned good one."

"I'll bet he is but not in front of a camera," said Kate, her Irish temper rising. "Just what you need while your family is falling apart —a twenty-two-year-old actor without a last name."

"Jimmy's age is insignificant and so is his profession," Sara said with amazing calm as she walked toward the staircase. "I just know he's warm and male. Right now, that's what I need. And you know what?" she said, pausing to turn around. "I think that's what you need too."

Quintana Jaye bustled into Renata's private study without knocking. She was carrying an armful of pastry boxes that threatened to stain her peach-colored dress.

"I bear dessert for tonight's seduction feast," she announced a bit belligerently. "Mouth-watering chestnut roulage and dreamy chocolate truffles. Enough to tempt even a stoical mustachioed guru."

"You needn't have bothered." said Renata, setting aside the ledger she'd been studying. "He's canceled."

"Again?"

"Again."

"That makes three times," Quintana remarked, a definite note of optimism in her voice.

"Don't be so smug. I'm determined."

"And so, it appears, is our Mr. Evans, though not to have you, I'm afraid," Quintana shot back cattily.

"What *are* you talking about?" Renata demanded, taking off her reading glasses. "Quit teasing."

"But I'm not teasing, dear one," Quintana said, sashaying over opposite her lover, and hiking her cumbersome girth up onto the desk.

"Careful where you sit," warned Renata, pulling a handful of documents out from under the crush of Quintana's backside.

"Oh, what's this? Private papers? Trying to hide things from your significant other? You know secrecy is a nasty habit, lovey. We always share everything, remember? Except men, of course. Despicable creatures, all of them. Come, let's have a look," she said playfully, reaching out.

"Mind your own business, Quin." Renata yanked the documents away and inserted them into the ledger. "Now what's this drivel about Taylor Evans?"

"No drivel, darling. Not a speck of it. I have news. Real gossip-like news. Best kind, don't you think? Oh, but you look so tense, pussycat. Let me help!" Quintana stood up and began rubbing Renata's temples.

"Mmmmm, feels wonderful," she sighed. "All right, enough of your little games, Quintana. What about Taylor?"

"About Taylor? Oh, nothing, really. He's so unimportant in the scheme of things, you know, love. We're so much better off forgetting about him, aren't we?" Dexterously, Quintana's long, smooth fingers traced a path down Renata's neck and began to slowly massage her shoulders.

"Oh, darling girl. How deliciously inviting you are," she whispered, close to Renata's ear. "Can't we just be together and you stop all this nonsense about the ever-so-mystical man of the moment you've fixated on? He's merely a flicker in the frying pan, lovey. A lump in the pudding. Just like all the rest."

"Nevertheless," said Renata, her body moving to the rhythm of Quintana's affectionate, silken touch. "I want to know what you know."

"Oh, all right. If you must," Quintana relented. "What I heard is that Mr. Taylor Evans and Ms. Brandy St. John are swiftly becoming an item."

"Who says?"

"Pleasure-dove, it's the buzz in the finest circles around town. You know I cater to those circles. Those circles feast on my *quenelles ambassade* and my *côte de veau en papillote* most every night. And those circles are so very garrulous when they've indulged in a drop of wine as well. So—"

"So he's sleeping with her?" Renata asked, not bothering to hide her irritation. Automatically she began twisting the heavy five-carat ring on her right hand—round and round again.

"That, my sweet, has not been clearly defined as yet. But you can safely assume he would like to. And let's face it, bow lips, most men do get what they want."

"So do I," exclaimed Renata, unabashed.

"Yes, I know, lovey. And sometimes I do too," said Quintana longingly, as she surveyed the statuesque beauty she'd fallen so hopelessly in love with. "Do you know how desperately I want you?" she whispered into Renata's ear.

"Please, Quintana, I'm hardly in the mood," Renata objected with a wave of her hand. She stood up abruptly, snatched the ledger up off her desk and walked briskly from the room.

"It's no use, you know," Quintana called after her. "You'll never have him."

"Oh, yes, I will," Renata shouted as she ascended the marble staircase to her bedroom. "Never say never to me."

12

■ "How you doin', superstar?" R. B. McDevitt shouted into his cellular car phone, without waiting for an answer. "Just got back from Hong Kong. Heading up to San Francisco in an hour or so. Got to see a man about some stock. You free for dinner?"

"Yes, but I'm wiped out. How about a rain check?" Taylor had been up since four that morning and the last thing he wanted was a five-course Italian dinner at the Villa Taverna, no matter how comfortable R.B.'s private jet might be.

But later that evening there he was, strapping himself into the soft glove-leather seat next to R.B. and sipping Calistoga water from Waterford crystal.

"What do you think of this little baby? Three engines. Full bathroom, too!"

R.B.'s newly purchased Falcon 50 climbed swiftly up through sun-streaked smog and leveled off at thirty-seven thousand feet. And, for a few moments, both men were silent, gazing out at feather-light clouds. Like huge dollops of whipped cream, they hung suspended against the clear cerulean background. A captivating ethereal mix of blue and white.

It was a rare moment of tranquillity. Each man preoccupied with his own private world. Silent, yet connected by their friendship.

Tired as he was, Taylor was glad to be in R.B.'s company. Their time together was always rewarding. A bond existed between them. One that cut through the facade of macho-male talk, allowing a free exchange of ideas. They had similarly affluent backgrounds and a deep mutual respect.

The two had taken to each other instantly five years earlier when they'd met at Westwinds. R.B. was going through a painful divorce. His world was crumbling. At thirty-nine he felt fifty. And for the very first time he had stopped running his companies in order to concentrate on his personal life.

It was something the wealthy Texan could never have imagined doing, trying to "find himself." That was for teenagers, not grown men. But four years into a bad marriage with Lalli McBain and he'd known he had to make some changes, starting from the inside.

He didn't have much of a choice. Lalli had left him. He knew in his heart he'd driven her away. And he felt absolutely lost without her. R. B. McDevitt had never experienced such pain.

He'd virtually fallen apart during the first few weeks at Westwinds. Then, piece by piece, Taylor had helped him reconstruct. The result was a much stronger individual. A man who had begun to trust in himself and rely on his instincts with a certainty he'd never had before.

"No matter what I accomplished," R.B. had confessed to Taylor, "the banks I established all over Texas; the petrochemical companies, the deals in the Orient and Europe; the newspapers, Lord, I've got 'em in five major cities. But it didn't matter. I never felt like *I* did it. There was this little voice always reminding me that I'd fooled them again and maybe I wouldn't get away with it next time. I guess that transferred to Lalli. I was always on the go, chasing down a new deal, trying to prove myself. There was little time for her. No time for us."

Self-confidence was what R.B. had now. The key ingredient that had been lacking in his marriage. It was a gift that had always eluded him. Money had come easily. Power too. But now R.B. had a new perspective. Now he believed in himself. Sometimes, Taylor thought, a little too much.

"So what stock are you chasing down?" Taylor asked, spearing a succulent shrimp from the Lucite tray between them.

"Movie stock, brother. Gonna pull a little raid on Selwyn Studios."

"Selwyn? I thought that was a family-owned operation."

R.B. shook his head. "Nope. Lotta people assume that because old man Selwyn launched the company more than sixty years ago. His grandson, Teddy, runs it now. Majority stockholder. But Selwyn Studios is as public as they come. New York Exchange. Fair game!"

"And this is a particularly good season?" Taylor inquired, fascinated with R.B.'s business acumen.

"You betcha. Teddy's managed to consistently lose money since he stepped in as Chairman of the Board five years ago."

"But I thought Selwyn was the most successful studio in town."

"Used to be. Take a look at their annual report and you know different," R.B. said, handing Taylor a slick black and gold catalogue with the Selwyn Tiger on the cover.

Taylor scanned a page listing quarterly losses. "Not too impressive."

"Except to me. Teddy Selwyn is a master of mismanagement. His speciality is diversification. Since he took over, he's purchased a publishing company, a record company, a toy manufacturing firm, and most recently, a fast-food chain—Gobbles. Sells turkey balls on a skewer, or something."

"Turkey burgers, I think," Taylor laughed.

"Same difference. Throw-up food. The chain is going belly-up, just like all of Teddy's acquisitions. Look at those figures. Selwyn Studios' stock dropped twenty-two points in six months. It's down to eight now. Scoop-up time."

"And just how much are you going to scoop?"

"Much as I can. Get myself some allies who own large blocks. And together we'll press Teddy to the wall."

"Force him out?"

"Damn right. Any stockholder who looks at Teddy's track record has got to vote against him in a proxy fight."

"You think it will come to that?"

"Probably. And by the end of the year, I ought to be sitting pretty in the boardroom with my own group of good ol' boys as directors."

"But you don't know anything about running a studio, R.B."

"Doesn't matter. It's like any other corporation. Divest yourself of all the leeches, sell everything that's terminally ill, and start doing what you should be doing. In this case, making big box-office pictures. Course I'll have to nab some heavy hitters from the other major studios. Make sure I've got some talented men behind me."

"And women?" Taylor chided.

"Sure." R.B. grinned roguishly. "We'll have some secretaries, receptionists." He laughed. "Seriously, Taylor, I've been thinking about Sara. Maybe she'd be interested down the line?"

Taylor sighed. "I'm not sure you'd be interested in her. Remember how you felt when Lalli left?" R.B. nodded. "That's where Sara is."

"That bad?"

"Maybe worse. She's got this image problem. Shows up at her studio looking like a punk rocker who deserted the band."

"No kidding? Sounds like she needs a vacation."

"She's on one. A one-way trip to never-never land. I'm surprised she still has her job."

"She'll snap out of it. Your sister's got the inner strength of a crusty ol' mule."

"I used to think so too."

"Now, here's an idea. How about if I invite Sara and the twins down to the ranch for my sale over the weekend? Real big doings this year. Got more than a hundred Egyptian Arabians on the block. Black-tie dinner Saturday night. The works. You ought to come too."

"Thanks, I'd like to, R.B. But my weekends are spoken for."

"Brandy, huh? How's that going?"

Taylor sighed. "Okay, not great."

"What's the problem, boy?"

"Well, for one thing, she's shy . . . I mean withdrawn . . . or something. I really don't know."

"Worst kind, the aloof ones, aren't they?" R.B. commiserated.

"Yeah," Taylor agreed with a bittersweet smile. He was thinking about the party he was going to attend with Brandy later that week. He felt addicted to her. It was as though she'd cast a spell over him.

The bright lights of San Francisco were in sight now. And the sleek steel-gray jet began its descent.

"Say, brother, speaking of ice maidens—in this case a real cold fish—" R.B. said, fastening his seat belt, "I hear you actually had the stomach to step out with the goddess of greed herself the other night."

"Renata Desmond?"

"Now, how the hell do you explain that?" R.B. inquired, incredulous.

"You should ask Sara." Taylor shot R.B. a knowing look. "She encouraged it. Your basic publicity ploy. But as it turns out, Renata wanted a lot more than I was willing to offer."

"And did she get it?" R.B. emitted a full-bellied laugh.

"Not a smidgen. We went to a boring roast for Bob Hope, at the Century Plaza, after which I took her home. She insisted on touring me through most of the forty-two rooms. I declined an after-dinner drink. She put the move on me in the library. I vanished into the night. End of story."

"Hah! Not for that viper. You'll hear from her again. Damned female is totally unscrupulous. She'd do anything to get what she wants. And apparently she wants you."

"Not anymore, I'm sure."

"Don't be. By the way, old buddy, any idea how long Kate Brannigan will be staying with Sara?"

Taylor looked surprised. "No more than you do. Aren't you two dating?"

"Well, yeah, sort of." R.B. cleared his throat and thought for a second. "But she's, ahh . . . pretty vague about her plans. When I called and suggested lunch this week, she took a rain check. Got the feeling she meant sometime in the spring of 1999. Not real encouraging."

"R.B.!" Taylor admonished. "Since when do you need encouragement?"

When Kate got back from her date, around midnight, Sara was still up.

"How'd it go, Cinderella? Was he everything you hoped for?" Sara called from the top of the stairs.

"Hardly," Kate said, referring to the record producer Sara had fixed her up with. "Not exactly my type." Kate had always disliked blind dates and after tonight's experience she'd decided *never again.*

"So?" Sara inquired, watching her weary friend trudge up the steps. "What'd you do?"

"Ehh," Kate groaned, taking a right into Sara's bedroom and collapsing facedown on the bed. "You don't want to know. I met him at a recording studio where he was ostensibly winding up a session. That was eight-thirty. I swear he forgot I was there entirely until about ten, when I finally tried to beg off. But he insisted on dinner."

"Where?" Sara sat down next to her.

"Nucleus Nuance."

"Very nice," Sara approved. "Shows he has some taste."

"Taste? Taste?" Kate repeated, with a stricken expression. "Sara, I'm sorry to sound so ungrateful, but your pal Jay has all the taste of a cave dweller, with a matching vocabulary. He is terminally confined to one-syllable conversations, mainly about rock stars. I couldn't wait to get home."

"Okay," Sara agreed, mildly miffed—but determined not to show it. "So he wasn't perfect. There are plenty of others who—"

"Hang on!" Kate interrupted, rolling over on her side to look at Sara. "I just don't think I want to go out at all for a while. It isn't fair, really." She shook her head despondently. "I just can't seem to stop thinking about Seth."

"You mean tonight—?"

Kate nodded. "As soon as I met this guy, Jay, *zap!* The Seth memories started their parade—in full technicolor. And being with someone else, even for a quick dinner, makes me feel—well—just rotten," Kate confessed, burying her head in the pillow.

"Sweetie, listen," Sara urged, touching Kate's shoulder gently. "The only way you're going to be able to let go is to see other men. I know I'm not exactly an expert on this—with Mark and all. But, honey . . . Kate, look at me. I just hate seeing you so blue. And I think maybe you could use a little professional help. Laura Bernstein in Beverly Hills is an excellent psychologist. I've heard she's—"

"Sara!" Kate objected.

"Now just hear me out. What's so bad about talking to an expert? Someone who specializes in—"

"No. I'm not at that point. Anyway I haven't the time."

"If you have the time to make yourself sick over Seth, you have the time for Dr. Bernstein."

"I am not making myself sick!" Kate said, getting up. "I'm just a little tired, that's all. You know I appreciate your concern. But I don't need to see a shrink, Sara. I can take care of myself just fine."

* * *

The following day Renata removed her red hat and gloves as she sat down behind the Chippendale desk in her office. She adored luncheons like the one she'd just attended. This time, the Women in Show Business had honored her with their annual Hollywood Woman of the Year Award.

It had been a festive affair in the enormous Grand Ballroom of the Beverly Wilshire Hotel, with stars like Linda Evans, Michelle Lee, and even Angela Lansbury on hand to sing Renata's praises and congratulate her. More than one hundred fifty women had shown up for the gala event to sip cocktails, munch on fruit salads, and do their usual double takes as Renata took her place at the dais.

She'd gone out of her way to startle them today. A bright royal-blue bolero suit, its high-waisted skirt accentuating her firm breasts. The glittering silver braid outlining her sleek curves and the red suede wide-brimmed gaucho hat with two pom-poms topping the ensemble off with utter perfection. She had wowed them. Surefire photographs for the "Click" page of the *Herald Examiner.* Perhaps she'd even make the "View" section of the *Los Angeles Times.*

Renata leaned back thoughtfully and made a steeple with her fingers. Things were certainly coming together. In an hour she'd meet with Templeton to finalize their new fund-raising plan. It was risky, but Renata thrived on risks. This one would pay off, and how.

The Hollywood Daily Center for Education and the Arts, featuring the Renata Desmond Pavilion. The mere thought made her tingle with anticipation. Soon the Center would be a reality, and Renata Desmond would begin receiving the kind of national recognition she so justly deserved.

She felt high. She felt delirious with pride and power. She got up and paced around her antiques-filled office. It was large. Sparsely but elegantly furnished. And dominated by an Andy Warhol portrait of Renata herself.

She never tired of the portrait. Warhol had captured a certain omnipotence in her smile and a vague necromantic quality in her deep emerald eyes. It was the quintessential piece to set visitors off balance. Renata enjoyed doing that.

She'd gone out of her way to redecorate the office after her father's death, refusing to set foot on the highly glossed hardwood floors until all of Charles Wentworth Desmond's belongings had been removed. Aside from a yellowed photograph of him aboard the *Regina Renata,* not a trace of *The Hollywood Daily*'s founder remained.

Renata never so much as glanced at the photograph. In fact, she assiduously avoided looking in its direction. She'd only left it there for appearances. Why give anyone reason to talk about her lack of respect for dear old Cappy?

"Here we are, Miss Desmond, all of this week's trades," announced Renata's aging, blue-haired secretary, placing a pile of trade papers on the desk.

With a regal nod, Renata silently dismissed the woman and sat down. She flipped through the back issues of the *Daily*'s rival publications, *The Hollywood Reporter* and *Variety*. Her eyes traveled quickly, scanning headlines and columns, on the alert for stories her own paper might have missed.

The *Daily*'s managing editor, Joe Birnbaum, was usually quite thorough in these matters. But once in a while he buried a front-page story inside the paper or, worse yet, missed it entirely.

Nothing gave Renata more pleasure, on these occasions, than walking imperiously into Joe's office and dressing him down. It was an intoxicating experience, an incomparably delicious high, of which she never tired. Unfortunately, this afternoon Renata found no reason to confront Joe.

But something irksome caught her eye. In Army Archerd's column. "On hand at the Academy screening of *Windfall,* television newcomers Taylor Evans and Brandy St. John."

Renata threw the paper down on the desk. It was the third time she'd read a reference to Taylor and Brandy that week. So Quintana had been right. So what? Perhaps they were merely seeing each other for the sake of publicity.

It happened all the time. An actor and an actress "dating" just for the media. Together they had a far better chance of turning up on *Entertainment Tonight* or in *People.* Often these celebrity couples didn't even like each other. Perhaps that was the case with Brandy and Taylor.

But even if it wasn't. Even if Taylor were smitten with that dumb-looking blond Swede, the affair wouldn't last long. Renata would see to that. And for his own good. After all, she knew she could be far more valuable to Taylor Evans than that second-rate actress. Renata could help build his career. Renata could make sure he got the kind of attention he needed.

She leaned forward, placed her elbows on the desk and folded her hands. Her emerald eyes focused hard on the offending line in Archerd's column as she concentrated. Then, almost instantaneously, her frown disappeared and her bow-shaped lips stretched out in a smug smile.

Renata reached for the last button on her sleek pearl-gray telephone. Within seconds the blue-haired secretary appeared, notebook in hand.

"Martha, see that Mr. Rollins reports to me at once."

As Martha closed the door behind her, she could hear Renata Desmond's deep, throaty laugh.

Kate couldn't believe her luck. She'd been trying to get in touch with Joe Birnbaum for days. Now, here he was, hunched over a plate of eggs and chicken livers at the counter of Musso & Frank's Grill.

"Ahh . . . sorry I didn't get back to ya', Kate. Matter of fact, I was going to call this afternoon. Place has been like a zoo, ya' know? Vacations. Illnesses. Temperature goes down to sixty-five here and— *boom!*—three cases of pneumonia," he explained, with an edgy little laugh.

"Do you have a few minutes?" Kate inquired, a bit hesitantly.

"Sure. Sure. Siddown. Havacupa coffee," he invited, motioning to the counterman.

Kate slid into the wooden swivel chair and considered what she was about to say.

"So! Ya' look great, kiddo," Birney chattered on. "Big time stuff, huh? *New York* magazine. *Vanity Fair.* Real success story."

"If you say so," she smiled. "And now I'm working on the Renata Desmond piece. Life does have its little ironies."

"Couldn't live without 'em, kid," said Birney.

Enough small talk, Brannigan. Get to the point. "Uhh . . . Birney, I've run into a dead end on some factual stuff. About Harvey Stinson and Sammy Rollins, specifically. Do you have any idea how long they've been working on the *Daily?*"

"Years, ya' mean? Not really. S'gotta be forever, though. I think they helped stucco the walls."

"I don't mean to put you on the spot, but . . . is there some reason Renata keeps them on? I mean, they're both well into their retirement years. And you know as well as I do that the town is filled with writers who are much more competent."

"Loyalty, kid," Birney said offhandedly, biting into a piece of sourdough bread. "Renata's funny like that. Look at me. Been there almost twenty years."

"But you're talented, Birney. And it's no secret that Sammy Rollins is a, well, a joke in this town. I remember when Natalie Wood died."

"Don't remind me," Birney interrupted. "Listen, Kate, it was my mistake. Shoulda caught it."

"But you didn't. And people are still laughing. Sammy's opening paragraph about Natalie's travel plans—the same day her obit was all over the front page. It was a glaring, embarrassing error, Birney. I'm surprised Renata kept Sammy on. It just—"

"Kate, I don't have any answers for ya'. Like I said—loyalty."

"Maybe it's more than that, Birney," she urged. "Maybe something happened between Sammy and Renata a long time ago. Maybe they have a little deal."

"Like what kind of a deal? What the hell are you fishin' around for, Kate?" he asked, raising his voice.

"I just thought, uhh . . . I thought maybe there might be a better explanation for Sammy and Harvey's presence," Kate said evenly.

"Nothin' I know of."

"Okay, then," she countered, "let's talk about why I was fired. You know it had nothing to do with the budget. It had to do with Renata protecting Harvey Stinson. She even managed to have that studio executive axed. Max Steiner. I searched for him for weeks. Why, Birney? Why? What's Harvey Stinson got on Renata Desmond?"

"I don't know what you're talkin' about, Kate," he insisted through clenched teeth.

"I think you do. You're a smart man, Birney and—"

"If I were smart I wouldn't be sittin' here with you at all, pal.

Case you didn't know, Renata's put out the old *silenzio* order. Nobody talks to *World* except her. Looks suspicious, me sittin' here with you, Kate. Quite frankly, if someone spotted us, I could be canned."

"You know that wouldn't happen."

Birney shook his head, perplexed. "You're a good reporter, Kate. The best. Knew it when you were working for me. But you've gotta do yourself a favor on this one, kiddo. Stick with the facts from the publicist. Don't go nosin' around for anything else."

"Birney, I—"

"No, Kate," he warned. "You're totally off base. And that line of questioning better stop here, understand? You go meddling in Renata Desmond's private affairs, and you're going to get hurt. I wouldn't want to see that happen."

"Brandy St. John?" Sammy Rollins exclaimed, astonished. "That's like trying to pin a rap on Pam Dawber or Mary Tyler Moore. You're talking America's newest sweetheart here."

"I'm talking journalism, Sammy," Renata corrected, enunciating each syllable carefully. "Jour-nal-ism. It's a word you have yet to fully comprehend. But I'm convinced you are the man for this job."

"I'm a columnist, Renata," Sammy protested, leaning forward in the Chippendale wing chair. "Not a mudslinger."

"Actually you're neither. But since you are in my employ, you will carry out this little task, Sammy, posthaste," she demanded.

"But I don't know the first thing about how to do this, Renata. You need a professional to—"

"Oh, but I thought you were one." She smirked.

"You know what I mean. You need a private investigator."

"Or an investigative reporter, which I'll grant you, you are not. But you do have contacts, Sammy. Use them."

"My contacts wouldn't stoop so low as to—"

"Yes they would. Your contacts would push a peanut down Hollywood Boulevard with their collective noses if you threatened to stop mentioning them in your silly column. So use a little leverage, Sammy. And use it fast."

Sammy squirmed uncomfortably in the chair, crossed his legs and smoothed his comb-over. He was a small man, but his belly hung out over his Gucci belt, belying too many good meals in too many fine restaurants.

"Nobody knows anything about Brandy St. John," he whined, "She hasn't been in town long enough."

"Nonsense. She's a public figure."

Begrudgingly, Sammy reached for the manila folder on Renata's desk and glanced through a smattering of recent newspaper and magazine clippings.

"She's from Denver, for crissake. A nice girl from Colorado."

"So? Take a trip! You like expense accounts, Sammy. If need be, hire someone to help you. But use cash."

"All right. I'll do it, on one condition—that my byline does not run with whatever I find."

"I'll make that decision when you deliver, Sammy," Renata retorted with finality. "Good day!"

Back in his own office, Sammy paced back and forth, fuming.

Then he picked up the phone.

"This is Sammy Rollins," he said, when the receptionist answered. "I'm returning Kate Brannigan's call."

13
Lausanne, Switzerland 1929

■ At first glance, L'École Sumaar gave the impression of being something out of a fairy tale. The boarding school was set high on a mountain, overlooking the enchanting town of Lausanne, Switzerland and the shimmering ice-blue waters of Lake Geneva.

The grounds sprawled out over several acres. And the structure itself bore a striking resemblance to the romantic castles little girls spend their idle hours reading and dreaming about. A castle with peaked turrets and small arched windows, all enclosed by a high, thick wall of rough-hewn stone. There was even a moat. It was the kind of castle from which that ravishing fairy-tale heroine Rapunzel had thrown down her long mane of golden hair so that her prince could latch on to it and climb up.

But this castle, nine-year-old Renata Desmond was soon to find out, was not one in which childlike fantasies came true. The student body at L'École Sumaar was a clique-ish sort. Most of the girls had been enrolled there since their sixth birthday. And it was always difficult for a new girl, an outsider, to break in. For Renata Desmond it was more than difficult.

Sitting across from the severe-looking headmistress, Madame Rouard, that first morning, Renata felt as though she'd been sentenced to prison.

She shifted on the straight-backed chair uncomfortably as the headmistress busied herself with a checklist. A fat woman who smelled of bleach bustled into the office and deposited two regulation navy-blue jumpers and crisp white blouses on the large wooden desk. "Size eight," she announced, then left.

Renata felt like crying, but she knew better. She sensed that the headmistress would not be sympathetic. And she was right.

Madame Rouard was tall and skinny and quite homely. She reminded the timid girl of a mean-looking chicken hawk she'd once seen in a puppet show. Madame had a sharp-beaked nose, round wire-rimmed glasses, which kept slipping downward, and a shrill, abrasive voice.

"We hope you will be happy here, Renata," the headmistress announced while removing her glasses. She bent the frames in slightly, then firmly planted them back on top of her beak. "You will be rooming with Hannah Krug, the daughter of a respected pharmaceutical manufacturer in Germany. Hannah's roommate went home recently. A, ahh . . . touch of the flu. Hannah is a bit older than you are, Renata, but I'm certain you'll get along very well indeed. Now, let's get you settled."

Renata trudged along behind Madame Rouard, up two flights of steep stone steps to a cramped corner room with a window seat, two small desks, and bunk beds.

"You unpack now, my dear. Lunch is at noon precisely. You'll meet Hannah and the other girls then. Lights are out at nine-thirty every night. And we're up at seven sharp each morning. On weekends you may take the bus into town, but never alone. Our girls always travel in groups of four, with a teacher-escort. We have one hundred and thirty-eight girls here. From the finest families all over the world. And they all speak English, so you should feel right at home. I know you will find L'École Sumaar a very fulfilling experience, Renata—if you abide by the rules. And I'm certain that you will."

Renata wasn't certain of anything, except that she wanted to go home. She was tired and shaken from traveling all the way to Switzerland and heartsick over the way her father had abruptly dismissed her.

"But of course you must go to boarding school, Renata," he'd commanded when she'd objected. "I can't imagine you not wanting to take advantage of this opportunity. Any other little girl would jump at the chance to live abroad. You are becoming far too spoiled, you know. This will do you good."

As soon as Madame Rouard left the room, Renata flung herself down on the bottom bunk and began sobbing uncontrollably. She was so tired. And so confused. Terrible things were happening to her body. Her nipples were enlarged and tender. She actually had breasts now. They were growing bigger every day. And that awful curly hair—down there. She kept shaving it off, but it continued to grow back, even thicker.

The night before Renata left Shangri-la, Consuela had sat on her bed and explained about bleeding and what to do in case it happened. The frightened little girl had listened attentively and finally collapsed into her nanny's soft, comfortable lap and cried herself to sleep.

Renata had cried all the way to Europe. On the ship she'd gotten seasick, which made her even more miserable. Now she had to dry her tears and try to look happy so that no one at L'École Sumaar would suspect there was anything wrong with her.

Lunch was taken in the cavernous dining hall, filled with sturdy, long wooden tables. Convivial chatter and girlish giggles swirled around the room as steaming platters and dishes were passed. Renata kept her eyes on her plate and said little, praying she wouldn't draw attention to herself. But soon Madame Rouard was clanging a huge bell, silencing the room, and introducing her.

Oh, no! Renata's stomach did a flip-flop. She had to stand up. Madame expected it. She tried to smile but couldn't. She burned with embarrassment. What if the girls noticed something funny about her. What if they noticed her breasts?

Introductions over, she sank into her chair, visibly shaken. She was seated next to her roommate, Hannah Krug, a hefty girl with chubby cheeks, a lumberjack appetite, and a barrage of questions.

"Who's your father? What does he do? Why are you here?"

"To go to school," Renata said, watching Hannah reach past two girls for a bowl of boiled potatoes.

"No, I mean what did you do? Didn't you get in trouble? Pull off some outrageous umm . . . *der Streich* . . . I mean, prank?"

Renata looked at the German girl blankly.

Wouldn't you know I'd get stuck with a dummy, thought Hannah, shoveling potatoes and bread into her mouth simultaneously. "Come on," she chided, "you must have done something. My best trick at home was setting fire to the maid's ahh, *die Schürze* . . . oh, you know—apron."

Another of Hannah's "tricks," Renata learned later, was pushing her former roommate, Tatiana, out on the ledge in a snowstorm and leaving her there for hours. Tatiana's "flu," to which Madame

Rouard had referred, was really pneumonia, compliments of Hannah.

"We're better off without her," Renata overheard Hannah saying about the ailing and banished Tatiana. "She talked too much."

That criticism could certainly not be applied to Renata. She barely said a word and kept to herself as much as she could. Classes were easy. And she quickly came to understand that L'École Sumaar was more an institution of orderliness and restraint than it was an establishment of enlightenment.

The school had been founded in the late nineteenth century by René Sumaar, an internationally known bon vivant of the French aristocracy, who'd had the great misfortune of marrying four times. The divorces had sliced unkindly into his inheritance. And the marriages had left him saddled with twelve very rich, very spoiled daughters.

Disgusted with an ever-changing stream of nannies, governesses, and the high tariff that accompanied both, Sumaar decided to open his own boarding school. If he could interest other wealthy parents in stabling their own little terrors there as well, the school might prove a stroke of financial genius. And it did. Within a year of its grand opening, Sumaar's boarding school was filled to capacity. Over the next twenty years it tripled in size.

Although castle-like in appearance, L'École Sumaar was actually more like a citadel designed specifically to keep its inhabitants in captivity. There was good reason for the moat. It served as the ultimate discouragement, should some young lady consider a clandestine escape.

In the school's thirty-five-year history, not one runaway had been documented. And that statistic was L'École Sumaar's single, most popular selling point. The school had a reputation for taming some of the wildest young women. The products of aristocratic, materialistic parents who had long since given up on the fine science of child psychology.

"Blasted little hellions," Madame Rouard was fond of saying, behind closed doors. Often she said much worse. She was curious about the new girl, though. Such a retiring, obedient child. Perhaps rooming her with Hannah the Barbarian hadn't been wise. Oh well, at least she'd get broken in quickly.

I wonder though, thought the headmistress as she sipped ginger tea by the fire in her small but immaculate quarters, *whether the poor child will survive.*

Renata was wondering the same thing. Life at L'École Sumaar was bearable, at best. She was almost always alone. She didn't make friends because she rarely spoke to anyone. During the daily afternoon activity hour she chose to stroll about the vast acreage by herself. Every evening after dinner she sat down at her desk and wrote a letter to her father, begging to be allowed to come home. And every morning she ripped it up.

Hannah, oddly enough, completely avoided her. For that, at least, Renata was grateful. And she was beginning to think that somehow she could endure L'École Sumaar until the Christmas break. So far no one had noticed her condition.

She was careful never to disrobe around Hannah. And each morning, in the privacy of a toilet cubicle, Renata would take a long strip of white muslin and wrap it tightly around her breasts. Once she slipped on her blouse, she looked as flat-chested as the other girls her age.

The worst time was showering. There was no way to avoid taking off her clothes in front of the other girls then. The shower room was huge. But it did have separate stalls. About twenty of them. So it wasn't too hard to hide, especially if the room wasn't crowded.

Renata carefully chose the least popular time of day to shower, just before dinner or bedtime. Usually she selected the last stall in the row and kept her towel and clothing close by. One night around nine o'clock, quite certain she was alone, she dried off hastily, then walked across the room to examine her body in the full-length mirror.

"Mein Gott . . . die Brüste!" The whispered gasp came from nowhere, shattering the silence.

Startled, Renata clutched at her towel and froze, statue-still. Then slowly she turned around. But saw no one. And heard nothing, except her own short breaths.

"Aw, come on, busty. Let's have another peak. Show us what we're supposed to look like when we're all grown up." The accent was British this time.

Then, all of a sudden, there were more voices. Chanting, "Yeah.

Take it off. Take it off." And whistling. And now she saw them, clapping and stepping out of the shower stalls. There must have been fifteen girls, all laughing and pointing and forming a circle around her.

"Big Tits Desmond, that's what they call her back home."

"Sent her here so she could hide. But there's no way you can keep a secret like that from us, honey."

Hannah stepped to the center of the circle and reached for Renata's towel.

"No. Don't. Don't do that. Leave me alone," pleaded the frightened girl, turning away.

But her strong German roommate spun her around and yanked hard, gashing Renata's flesh with a long fingernail as she tore off the towel.

"Think you're so smart," Hannah jeered. "I knew it all the time. Knew you were a freak."

Renata cowered against the tile wall, hunching forward in an attempt to cover herself. "Please," she sobbed. "Please don't."

Smiling superciliously, Hannah moved in closer, like a huge tiger stalking a helpless bird. She raised both hands and placed them on Renata's breasts.

"Just a little feel, love. Ohhhh, you're so sexy," Hannah taunted as the other girls stood there snickering.

"What's this?" came a shrill, commanding voice from the doorway. "What is going on here?"

Hannah backed off. Everyone scurried for the toilets. Before Madame Rouard could figure out what was happening, the shower room was empty. Except for Renata. She stood there, grasping the towel and shaking.

"It is exactly nine twenty-seven, miss," said the headmistress, staring down at her. "You have only three minutes before lights out. And that goes for the rest of you little busybodies as well," she shouted, with a sweep of her arm toward the closed toilet cubicles.

Renata was terrified of returning to her room. Afraid of what Hannah would do to her. The German girl was at least a foot taller and much stronger than she was. Renata's heart pounded fiercely as she opened the door.

Hannah was already lying on the top bunk. "Weirdo. Freak. Monstrosity. Just my luck to be bunking with a circus act," she complained loudly. Then she rolled over and was silent.

Renata lay awake all night, waiting. Knowing she'd have to defend herself against Hannah. Not knowing how she would do it.

But Hannah didn't bother her that night. And she never once touched Renata again. She was too busy making sure everyone else in the school knew her roommate was "a deformed queer."

Renata Desmond's premature puberty became the talk of L'École Sumaar. And the timid girl was a perfect target for ridicule. After a couple of days she resigned herself to the stares and the whispers and the muffled giggles.

At first she told herself she deserved it. She'd always known something awful would happen to her, even when she was living at Shangri-la with her father. And she must have displeased him. He'd sent her away. Her unhappiness was meant to be.

If she could just get through the next two months, she told herself, and go home for Christmas, maybe everything would be okay. Maybe Daddy would take her back. And then one day she would grow up to be normal, as Consuela said.

But as the days passed and the jeers and jokes about her continued, Renata's attitude began to change. The misery and self-loathing she'd been accepting as her just due started to dissolve. She got angry. She burned with resentment every time one of her classmates turned around to stare. She bristled with rage when she overheard a group of girls gossiping about her on the bus into town.

And she made a decision. She would fight back. She even had a plan.

In the library late one afternoon Renata summoned up every ounce of her courage and approached the most popular girl in school. Francine Devereaux was eleven years old and the sole heir to the Devereaux wine fortune. The word was that Francine was worth millions.

Her parents had been killed five years earlier in an avalanche, while skiing in the French Alps. And Francine had been much on her own since then, aside from the loose supervision of her aging Aunt Clarissa, who resided in Paris.

All the girls looked up to Francine. She was a born leader. Even Madame Rouard said so. President of her class, lead soprano in the all-school chorus, features editor of the student newspaper, and chairman of any number of committees. There was no doubt about it. Francine led the pack. Even the older girls deferred to her wisdom and power.

"Yes?" Francine asked, when Renata tapped her on the shoulder. She'd been reading a history book at a deserted table.

"I wonder if we could talk," Renata began, trailing off but trying not to lose her courage. This was her only chance. With Francine's help she might be able to turn the tide.

"Talk? About what?" the sophisticated French girl inquired. Renata noticed her bright red fingernails. Francine had thick, curly chestnut hair, brilliant black eyes, and a magnificent smile. But she wasn't smiling now.

"It's personal," Renata answered, with a weakened voice. "I need your advice."

"But of course," agreed Francine sympathetically. "Let's go to my room."

The two girls talked for several hours. And several days later Renata Desmond had what she wanted. A new identity. A new persona. She even looked different. She was walking with her head held high now, shoulders pulled back and eyes directed haughtily forward. She seemed proud of her body.

The talk about her suddenly changed. Now there was a look of awe in the eyes of the girls who whispered as Renata strolled through the hallways. Some of them waved and said hello. A couple of them sidled up next to her and walked along. Gone were the condescending comments, the snickers, and the jokes. Now every girl in the school wanted to make friends with Renata Desmond. Because of what they'd heard about her.

They'd heard that Renata's early puberty, the fact that she already had breasts and pubic hair, was no freakish thing, no accident of nature. It was something she had planned.

Back in California she had a friend whose father was a gynecologist. Together, the two girls had pilfered a bottle of experimental hormone pills from his office. And they'd taken some, hoping to speed up the development of their bodies.

The pills had worked very fast. And Renata was pleased with the results. So she kept taking them. She knew the more grown-up she looked, the more boys would be attracted to her. And Renata had all sorts of boyfriends where she lived in Beverly Hills. Older boys. Some of them in their teens.

The girls knew that this was true, because one of them had heard it from Francine Devereaux. Rumor had it that Renata could even get pregnant—if she wanted to.

Overnight, Renata the rejected misfit had been transformed into a charmed princess in the eyes of her fellow students. Now they wanted to emulate her. They sought her out. Some of them took her aside and asked how they too could procure hormone pills.

And now Renata had a best friend—Francine Devereaux. The two were inseparable. They spent many hours talking about boys and Renata's erotic escapades with the opposite sex in California. Francine saw to it that her friend was appointed to a number of committees and invited to all of the secret parties that took place after lights out.

Within the next several months Renata's popularity soared. When her periods started she made the most of it by explaining to Francine, in graphic detail, exactly what womanhood was like. She knew the rest of the school would hear the story the next day, in an exaggerated version.

She started wearing a bra. She stopped shaving. And she began to carve out an image for herself as an exciting, experienced daredevil.

It was Renata who would slip into the dark kitchen late at night to steal a dozen sweet rolls. It was she who sketched a hideous caricature of Madame Rouard on one of the bathroom walls. Once she'd even had the courage to sneak into the quarters of the stern English literature teacher, Mademoiselle Pruitt, and short-sheet her bed.

With each prank, Renata knew, she commanded more respect from the other girls. What she was learning during those early months at L'École Sumaar was that she possessed a talent in the art of manipulation. And she soon began to use it to make her peers look bad. Especially the ones who had caused her such embarrassment and pain.

For Mary Frances Claire, who had been the first to snub Renata in the dining hall, some powdered laxative. Secretly, Renata slipped the fine white particles into the girl's milk. Poor Mary Frances couldn't attend classes for days.

Another time Renata took great pleasure in strangling Oscar, Madame Rouard's pet poodle. Now that she was a leader, she commanded the attention of her timid classmates and made them watch as she carefully used a sharp knife to cut off a patch of the dead dog's white corkscrew curls.

Later that afternoon, she hid the knife and the piece of bloodied dog fur in the pocket of her roommate's heavy winter coat. The next day Hannah Krug was expelled.

There was not one peep in Hannah's defense from the other girls. They wouldn't dare cross Renata. They were too afraid. Renata Desmond had assumed a controlling position at L'École Sumaar. And she was playing it to the hilt.

But all of Renata's newfound self-confidence dissolved within a few hours after her arrival home for Christmas vacation. Consuela took one look at the young girl's overripe body and burst into tears. Cappy Desmond kissed his daughter perfunctorily on the cheek and then sat down to a silent dinner with her. Before she woke up the next morning, he was off to northern California on a business trip.

Renata saw her father only two more times before she returned to school. Once on Christmas Day for about an hour. Stiffly, he presented her with a new bicycle and a wad of money. "Consuela will take you shopping tomorrow. Get some pretty things," he said, with a tight-lipped smile.

She saw him again at breakfast on New Year's Day. After that he was off to the Rose Bowl game. An event he used to take his little girl to, when he loved her. But no more.

Renata sulked in her room for a while, then decided to roam around the house. She wound up in Cappy's bedroom, where out of curiosity she snooped about, looking in all his closets.

Sitting down on the slippery black satin bedspread, she opened up the drawer of an antique lacquered side table and rummaged through it. First she pulled out a small box full of long, skinny, light yellow balloons. Or were they? She tried to blow one up, but it didn't budge. So she pocketed it for further investigation.

Next she found a slim red volume filled with pictures. Black and white photographs of men and women who were . . . what were they doing? Renata caught her breath. *My goodness,* she thought, *these people don't have on any clothes.*

Hastily at first, she thumbed through the small book. Then she slowed down, reading some of the captions and scrutinizing the limbs and body parts of the couples in the pictures. *This is it,* she thought, closing the book momentarily without losing her place. *These people are "doing it."*

Nervous now, not wanting to be caught, she scanned the room and held her breath, listening carefully. Not a sound. Renata was absolutely alone with her discovery.

She glanced down at the book's red cover. Embossed in gold ink was the title *Erotic Positions.*

She wasn't sure what *erotic* meant so she quickly scurried downstairs to the immense library and looked it up. "Arousing or satisfying sexual desire," she read. *Wow!*

Finding the dirty book was the best part of Christmas. Wouldn't Francine be surprised?

The very first night back at L'École Sumaar, Renata presented the new treasure to her friend. Francine was more than surprised. She was insatiably curious about the photographs, and more than a little turned on.

"Look! Look at this one!" she squealed in delight. "Can you really get pregnant like that? What does it feel like? Doesn't it hurt?"

Renata did her best to fake her way through all the answers.

Finally Francine stopped asking. After they'd gone through the book twice, she put it down and said, "Let's try some."

"Huh?"

"You know," replied the French girl, unbuttoning her navy-blue jumper. "Let's take off our clothes and try it."

"But . . . but we can't. We're both girls," Renata objected, trying to hide the fact that Francine's suggestion was making her uneasy.

"Doesn't matter. You know what Mademoiselle Pruitt says, 'Imagination is the key to rewarding life experiences.' We're about to have one—maybe more," giggled Francine. She stepped out of her panties. *"Vite, vite,* Renata! Hurry up!"

Reluctantly, Renata started taking off her shoes. "Are you sure about this?"

"What are you, *une poule mouillée*—a sissy?"

"No, I just wanted to make sure you were ready for this," Renata replied, trying to sound grown-up. "I mean you've never done anything like this before—have you?"

"No. Have you?"

"Only with boys!" Renata lied.

"Well, I have to get broken in somehow," Francine coaxed as she took Renata's hand and guided her to the bed.

14

■ "I don't believe this driveway," squealed Jennifer excitedly. She stuck her head out the open window of the shiny russet station wagon and looked back over the winding gravel road. "How long is it anyway, driver?"

"He's not a driver, Jennifer," Sara corrected in an irritated voice from the front seat. "His name is Hank and he's R.B.'s foreman and he went out of his way to pick us up at the airport."

"That's okay, ma'am," said the tanned, husky man at the wheel. "Driveway's eight miles long, Jenny. And those are live oaks and post oaks alongside there. Pretty sight, isn't it?"

"Sure is," Jackie answered for her sister. She was gazing out at the glorious blaze of reds and golds. "I didn't know leaves turned colors in Texas."

"Oh, I'll bet there's a lot about Texas you didn't know," teased Hank. "Like where you are right now."

"Oh, yes, I do. We're in south Texas."

"Almost right. What we really call it is the Texas hill country, because of big hills up there, see 'em? If you want to get more specific, we're just north of the Pedernales River and Wolf Creek. Not far from LBJ's ranch. You remember him?"

"Wasn't he Vice-President, or something?" asked Jennifer.

"And President," Kate added, leaning her head back on the soft brown leather seat. It was good to be getting away from Los Angeles, even for two days. Even if it meant having to be civil to R. B. McDevitt. Besides, she'd never been to a horse auction. And the weekend would provide a well-needed diversion for Sara, who had recently, and inexplicably, been dropped by Jimmy Z.

"How many acres are there?" asked Jackie as the station wagon slid throught the arched wrought-iron entrance to the ranch.

"Oh, about seventy-five thousand, give or take a few."

"*Wow!* How'd R.B. get so much land?"

"His family had lots more than that way back when. Four hundred and fifty thousand acres in the late 1800s. See, Grandpa McDevitt came over from Scotland. Didn't have much money, but he started herding up wild cattle he found in the bush country here. Moved the cows up the Chisholm Trail to Abilene, Kansas, where they were shipped to markets in the East. R.B.'s grandpa really helped launch the cattle industry here in the States."

"So is that how R.B. got all his money?" Jennifer inquired with keen interest.

"Well, no, not exactly. What happened was that R.B.'s father, B.J., started digging for oil. And he hit it big. So with that money he started a bank in Breedwell, Texas, and then he began lending money to other men who were drilling for oil. And when R.B.—"

"What's B.J. stand for, anyway?" Jackie interjected.

"Quit butting in, A-hole," complained Jennifer. "Can't you see the man is—"

"Shut up lard-ass," Jackie said, reaching over to shove her sister.

"Girls, watch your language!" insisted Sara, totally exasperated.

"Initials don't mean anything in Texas, girls," Hank continued. "R.B., B.J., H.R.—just like names, but they don't come from them. R.B., now, he was real smart. He established banks all over the state. Did you know he owns one of the ten largest bank holding companies in the country?"

"What's a bank holding company?" asked Jackie.

"Don't they teach you anything at Crossroads?" Sara snapped. Her back ached, and she longed for the end of the interminable driveway.

"The reason you have bank holding companies," Hank went on to explain, "is because in Texas there are no bank branches. So R.B. owns about thirty-five banks, like the B Bank of River Falls and the B Bank of Fort Worth. And he also owns a holding company called Breedwell Bank Shares. And that bank holding company owns the stock of all the other banks."

Jennifer let out a whistle. "Boy, that's a lot of money," she said as Hank pulled the station wagon up in the circular driveway.

"Sure is," said Sara, opening the door. "And the rich banker is available, too," she whispered to Kate. "Some smart journalist ought to snap him up."

"Quit *hocking* me," Kate warned with a disapproving smile and walked on ahead.

"Oy, vey!" Sara groaned, taking a step. Every muscle burned. She made a silent vow never again to exercise and followed Kate into the huge ranch house.

It was an imposing, two-story structure of hand-hewn white Austin stone built in the late nineteenth century. The walls were four feet thick and the ceilings eighteen feet high.

Once inside the vast foyer, the first thing Kate noticed was the glazed red stone floor. The stones were a deep purplish-red. A crimson color. Large and unevenly cut. But there was something earthy and sturdy about them, something almost reassuring about walking on that great expanse of stone floor.

Kate followed it to the main living area, which was dominated by a massive sandstone fireplace. A long plank of unfinished native oak served as a mantelpiece. The furniture was modest. Brown tweedy couches and roomy leather chairs. She counted five huge area rugs. Each one was of good quality, but most were worn and some faded.

The creamy stucco walls were covered with shoulder mounts of white-tailed deer. Trophies taken by R.B.'s grandfather almost a century earlier. And in a far corner Kate saw a handmade oak cabinet, which, Hank pointed out, was R.B.'s prized possession. It contained seventeen unique branding irons. One from each of the ranches his grandfather had purchased so many years ago.

There was a reassuring sense of warmth and comfort and history in this splendid old room. Without even realizing it, Kate felt immediately at home.

"Uhh," Sara groaned, collapsing into a beige leather chair. "Can't move. My new trainer, Kurt the Nazi, has realigned my body. I shall never be the same."

"So?" said Kate, sitting down as the twins followed Hank into the kitchen. "I thought that's what you wanted. A revamp, a total change."

"I do. I do," agreed Sara, bending over to massage her right calf. "But perhaps I've been a little extreme. Maybe I should just have a lipectomy."

"A what?"

"You know, have my fat sucked. It's the latest thing to—"

"You mean a liposuction? Sara, are you crazy? You don't need to do that."

"Yes, I do. Look at these Jell-O–pudding arms. Not to mention my saddlebag thighs. Kate, I have so much cellulite I could franchise it. And sucking is the perfect solution. The surgeon makes these tiny incisions and—*zap!*—vacuums away the fat. Fast. Simple. And painless."

"You don't know what you're talking about, Sara. I've read about that procedure. It's fairly new and it can be painful. And what about the residual effects? Your skin might not shrink back properly. You could be left with unsightly dimpling and—"

"All right, already. I get the point. But I'm willing to take my chances. With a face like mine, who needs a body like this? Anything would be an improvement. I've already made an appointment."

"You'll be sorry."

"Not half as sorry as I'll be if I keep buying larger sizes. My closet looks like Tiny the Elephant's sartorial fantasy."

"Sara, you're impossible," Kate said, chuckling.

"So are you." Sara countered, carefully hoisting herself up off the chair. "If you were the smart cookie I used to know, you'd admit the only reason we're here is because R.B. has fallen madly in love with you. And you'd give him a chance."

"Not interested." Kate got up and locked arms with Sara as they strolled toward the kitchen.

"Listen to me, honey, you could get interested real fast. For starters, consider what the man has accomplished. He's strong, Kate, and smart. You need somebody like that."

"My heart, unfortunately, is otherwise engaged."

Sara shook her head. "Time to reel it in, sweetie. You've been in the dumper too long. Let's talk reality here. R.B. is a catch. You heard what Hank said about—"

"About the legendary McDevitts and their oodles of land and money?" Kate said in an exaggerated tone. "I don't care, Sara. I really don't. The man simply does not appeal to me. Besides, I got a

little turned off by Hank's speech. Sounded a bit canned, don't you
think? I wouldn't be surprised if R.B. put him up to it."

"What the hell do you mean, you're having trouble with Komack?
I thought you said he was our ace in the hole."

R. B. McDevitt was angry, which made him look even more ridiculous. He was sitting smack in the middle of a sprawling green
velvety pasture, astride his favorite Egyptian Arabian stallion,
Prince Razi. Shouting expletives into a cordless telephone. It was
not one of his better moments.

R.B. prided himself on the peacefulness of the Clear Fork. When
there, he was usually able to disconnect from the stress and strain of
business. And he liked nothing better than to rise early, breakfast
with his ranch hands, and spend the rest of the morning exercising
his prize dappled gray stallion.

Time was tight this particular morning because of the elaborate
black-tie dinner and auction later on. But R.B. had managed to steal
away from the hubbub for half an hour, leaving the details of the
forthcoming extravaganza to his capable staff of thirty-five.

He needed the time alone. And mounting the powerful prize-winning stallion always provided an incomparable thrill. Prince Razi
moved with the grace of a ballet dancer and the arrogance of a
pharaoh. Putting the sleek Egyptian Arabian through his paces had
an almost therapeutic effect on R.B. And there was an unspoken
rule at the Clear Fork. When R.B. was exercising Prince Razi, no
interruptions. Except in the case of an emergency.

This was one.

Nothing less could have pried Mrs. Phelps, R.B.'s longtime secretary, up off of her ample bottom and sent her charging out to the
pasture, phone in hand. A long-distance call from Miles Durville
this early on a weekend morning spelled trouble.

Begrudgingly, R.B. held the phone to his ear and listened to his
financial consultant.

Within seconds he learned that the emergency was one Archie
Komack, a wealthy New York restaurateur who owned a large block
of Selwyn Studios stock.

"So what's the problem, Miles?" R.B. ran a hand through his
curly light brown hair. "You think Komack smells a deal?"

"Hard to tell, R.B. Only thing he'll say is that he wants to meet with you."

"Well, dammit, Miles, you know that's impossible. I've got this sale all weekend, and I have to be in London Monday night. I'm sure you can handle this. Try a little incentive bargaining. Send him theater tickets. Or some booze. Yeah, a little Glenlivet. Better yet, some Cristal champagne. Ought to impress the hell out of Komack."

"Already tried, R.B. The Cristal is SOP. Went out last week. No sale."

"For God's sake, man, use your imagination, then. Send his wife a Bloomingdale's gift certificate. Do something."

"Komack's not married."

"His girlfriend, then—"

"The girlfriend's a him."

"What? Well, I'll be a son of a gun! You mean to tell me old Archie is 'light in the loafers'?" R.B. had to chuckle. "You're on your own there, buddy."

"Nice pass, R.B. But we've got a serious foul-up here. In case you've forgotten, Komack owns 1,238,000 shares. That's two percent of Selwyn. Without it, we're not going to get to first base. If you want this studio as badly as I think you do, you'd better be here Monday."

"Gotta think about that, brother. You see what else you can do to swing the pansy our way and report back, hear?" He signaled Mrs. Phelps to retrieve the phone.

Damn. R.B. knew he'd have to postpone the London trip. And that could jeopardize the next purchase of Brompton Pharmaceuticals he'd been working on for more than a year.

But Selwyn stock was more important. Running a Hollywood studio had been R.B.'s lifelong dream. The ultimate power trip, he supposed. Now he was this close. So he'd have to compromise. He'd have to fly to New York and cater to the whim of some swishy limp-wrist who wanted to play games.

Games! That's all it is, anyway, R.B. thought as he wheeled Prince Razi toward the stables. *High-roller games. You choose your goal and you pay the price.*

Sometimes he felt like cashing in. He could do that. R. B. McDevitt could afford to live wherever he pleased. The South Pacific. Scandinavia. Certain parts of the Orient appealed to him. And he'd always wanted to spend a year in Scotland. Trace the family tree. Get back to his roots.

He knew if he took that step, though, he wouldn't want to do it alone. He'd want to share it with someone. A woman. A very special woman.

If only Lalli hadn't—

Lalli is gone. Forget it. Just block it out.

He didn't think about her often. There was little time for nostalgia or melancholy in R. B. McDevitt's life-style. But he couldn't deny the gnawing emptiness. It was like a vacuum, a bottomless pit inside his soul that ached to be filled up.

There had been many women over the past two years. Most of them beautiful. Some fairly bright. But not one with the intelligence or spirit of Lalli McBain. He missed her snappy repartee, her perspicacity, her tenderness. He missed her in his bed.

Four years of marriage. And how he had abused it. Taken her for granted. Traveling for weeks at a time on business. Rarely inviting her along. And the heated arguments about children. All the times he'd refused to see a doctor, insisting it was her fault she couldn't conceive.

Well she'd proved him wrong. Married that college professor and had a son ten months later. Now they were all happy as clams living somewhere in Maine.

"And how are you this morning, sir?" a leathery skinned groom asked, taking the reins as R.B. dismounted Prince Razi.

"Great, Rusty, just great. Couldn't be better!"

"Four twenty-one left to go in the fourth quarter. It's 31–17. And the Longhorns are trailing. No one really expected the Cardinals to be fourteen points up this late in the game. Here comes the play-in from the sideline. The Longhorns are huddled up back at their own thirty. Third down and four. What do you look for here, Woody?"

Quintana Jaye fired a handful of cheese-coated popcorn at the television screen. "We look for the Longhorns to score, you imbecile."

"Hush," ordered Renata, punching up the volume.

"Brocato's been moving real well to his right," came the color coordinator's deep baritone as the camera zoomed in on the red and blue team's number seven. "And I'd look for some play action, with the Longhorn receivers flooding the right zone."

"I'd look for the Longhorns to start playing football," complained Quintana, raising a frothy margarita to her iridescent pink lips.

"Will you please shut up!" hissed Renata, her cold emerald eyes fixed on the screen.

"You know, Woody," play-by-play announcer Brad Hunter was saying, "nobody expected the Longhorns to have this kind of a month. They're three and one and tied top of the division with the Giants. What's made the difference?"

"Well, Brad, Fort Worth has always been tough defensively. But the past three years they haven't been able to put any points on the board. Drafting speedster wide-receiver Dwight Smith gives them a deep threat, though. And the trade in the off-season for veteran quarterback Don Brocato has given them the leadership they were lacking—"

"Speaking of Brocato," Hunter interrupted, "it looks like he's having trouble understanding the signal again. That's happened twice already in critical situations today and—"

"Damn," Renata murmured.

"The thirty-second clock is running down," Woody Campbell said, excitedly. "And it looks like they're going to have to—yes, number seven, Don Brocato is calling time out. He's trotting to the sidelines. He looks angry."

Renata swung her legs down off the four-poster bed and slipped into a pair of white satin mules.

"And while the Longhorns take time out at Busch Stadium in St. Louis, we'll take time out for our stations along the—"

Renata moved quickly to the door.

"Oh, lovey, don't be miffed. It's just a bit of bad luck. They'll win again next week, you'll see," Quintana soothed from the bed, propping herself up on an elbow.

Without responding, the statuesque brunette made a haughty exit, her purple floor-length silk robe rustling in the autumn breeze.

"Lovey, where are you going?"

"To make a phone call."

"Why don't you make it here—" Quintana slipped off the chestnut-colored satin comforter and hustled to the door. "Renata, why are you so upset?" she shouted. "They've won three games already. That's a hell of a lot better than last season. Renata. Renata! Oh, forget it."

Quintana Jaye raised a hot-pink slippered foot and gave the sturdy pine door a swift kick, slamming it shut.

The sun had just begun to set in the Texas hill country. And R. B. McDevitt's festive gathering was already under way. There were more than six hundred people. A sparkling crowd. Hand-beaded designer dresses and sequined shoes. Small plumed hats, some of them veiled. A smattering of furs and enough emeralds, amethysts, and sapphires to keep Tiffany and Cartier in window displays for months.

A long white awning stretched out, welcoming this procession of sartorial splendor. The guests strolled leisurely up the luxurious, thick, royal-blue carpet. Liveried waiters, offering tall flutes of Dom Perignon, stood at attention on either side of the entrance.

R.B. was situated just inside, greeting his guests and accepting a profusion of compliments.

"Absolutely magnificent. I've never seen anything like it," cooed a short woman in magenta lace and diamonds.

"Fascinating! This thing must be twenty feet high," her husband agreed, giving the tent a once-over. "Looks as big as Texas Stadium."

The sprawling white tarpaulin measured seventy-five hundred feet in circumference. At one end stood an enormous proscenium stage and an adjoining runway, both covered in Astroturf.

There were one hundred and ten small round dinner tables. Each one impeccably set with light blue Lenox china. The floor-length tablecloths and napkins were of the finest linen, specially imported from Italy. A stunning arrangement of white narcissus, lavender freesia, star-gazer lilies, and leather fern graced the center of each table.

On each serving plate rested a small package, carefully wrapped in shiny beige paper, and embossed in brown and gold. Gifts for the affluent who had gathered to celebrate their mutual enthusiasm for the Egyptian Arabian breed. And to spend thousands of dollars on the majestic creatures about to parade before them.

Once everyone was seated, a gray-haired man with a yellow rose boutonniere stepped up to the microphone. The fourteen-piece orchestra struck up the theme from *Lawrence of Arabia.* And a regal-looking chestnut-colored stallion proudly took center stage. His head held high. His lustrous coat curried to silken perfection. As if on cue, the stallion cantered slowly down the runway.

"Royal Matala Two, ladies and gentlemen," called the official with the yellow rose. "And isn't he a beauty? A purebred Egyptian Arabian. His sire was Royal Matala One, syndicated for five million dollars. His dam was Royal Laden Princess who foaled Royal Laden, syndicated for three—"

"What is this, an auction or an equestrian beauty contest?" asked Sara, nudging Kate.

They were alone at their table. The twins, worn out from an afternoon of horseback riding, were already in bed. The card next to Sara was marked Harding Johnson. The one next to Kate, R. B. McDevitt. So far she'd managed to avoid him.

My luck runneth out, she thought, frowning at the place card.

"Weird, very weird," Sara mused, watching as yet another horse was introduced. "Down here I guess they treat horses like women, and women like—"

"Careful, here comes Mr. Megabucks," Kate said just in time to turn slightly and flash a counterfeit smile at their dapper host.

"And doesn't he look dreamy? Look at that tux. Must be European," Sara whispered through her teeth.

"How are you gals doing over here? Everything okay?" said R.B., talking too fast for an answer and running his eyes up and down Kate's turquoise beaded dress at the same time.

Her eyes shot darts at him. He didn't notice.

"Want you to meet a buddy of mine from the East Coast." R.B. clapped his arm around a distinguished-looking middle-aged man with salt-and-pepper hair.

Sara's smile broadened.

"Harding Johnson, here, is in the TV business, Sara. Thought you two might have a few things in common. Go ahead, Harding, sit down."

Harding stumbled on the chair leg and lunged forward but quickly grasped the table, steadied himself, and sat down.

"Have a good time now," R.B. said, giving his friend a quick pat on the shoulder. "I'll see you and the gals later."

Gals, thought Kate. *The man lives in the Dark Ages. He probably calls the women everywhere gals. Japan, France, Pago Pago . . .*

She watched him circulate.

So smooth.

And so condescending.

What an obnoxious, pompous ass.

Kate didn't know why she resented R.B. so. After all, he was very gracious. And she could even see how some women might be taken with him. He was tall and quite good-looking. She'd never been partial to curly hair, though. And that gap-toothed smile. If he had so much money why didn't he see an orthodontist? Better still, why didn't he just close his mouth for good?

Out of the corner of her eye, she watched R.B. kiss the hand of a voluptuous woman in a strapless ruby-red dress. Kate wondered if he'd slept with her. Probably he'd slept with half the women there. She wondered what he was like in bed. Probably he was like a jack-hammer. Incredible endurance. Imperceptible emotion.

Not like Seth. Seth was so warm and gentle and loving. So tender when he caressed her. And so free and verbal in their lovemaking. She could almost hear his deep, breathy voice telling her—

"Kate. Kate," Sara insisted, intruding on her private bliss. "Open your gift. Chloë. Don't you love it? The men got Karl Lagerfeld's KL Homme."

"Nice," Kate said, vaguely, observing the perfume bottle in Sara's hand.

I have to call Seth. I just can't stand it any longer.

Yes, you can, she argued with herself. *Seth is a dead-end situation. Forget him. Pull yourself together.*

"Harding was telling me he's with International Cable News, Kate," Sara was saying.

"And doing very well, I hear," Kate said, leaning forward to look directly at Harding. "You've been giving Ted Turner's CNN a run for the money."

"We like to think so." He motioned for the waiter. "Another

Dewar's an' soda, please. The truth is, we're neck and neck with Turner righ' now."

Kate reached for a hard roll, wondering if Harding Johnson had a speech impediment. He seemed to slur his words.

"And just what do you do for the network, Harding?" Sara asked, sticking a fork into the salad of arugula with sautéed foie gras, which had just been placed before her.

"I own it."

Sara disregarded the salad and gave Johnson her full attention. "But I thought ICN was owned by the Dunsworth Corporation."

"I own 'at too," he said, draining a glass of Cabernet Sauvignon.

"Oh. I see." She tried not to sound impressed.

The waiter arrived with the Scotch and soda. Johnson slipped him a dollar and took a big gulp.

Definitely not a speech impediment, thought Kate.

"Tell me, Harding. Do you breed Egyptian Arabians?" Sara wanted to know.

"No. Nothing of th' sort. R.B. jus' thought I might enjoy th' occasion. And . . . I am." His gray eyes were focused on Sara. There was a puzzled expression on his face, which made his eyebrows come together in one straight salt-and-pepper line.

"Is anything wrong?" Sara inquired self-consciously.

"I was jus' won'ering about that ahh—thing in your hair."

"Oh, that," Kate teased. "Actually it's a bird feeder. Sara's partial to parakeets and she thought—"

"Do have some more wine, Kate," Sara urged in a syrupy voice. "It goes to your head so well. Actually, Harding," she explained turning to face him, "this is a designer hair ornament. Fashioned especially for me by Jacquao Quebero. You've heard of him? He does all the stars."

"Hmm," Harding considered, still staring at Sara's head. "It's jus' that you're suchanattractive woman . . ."

Sara's heart raced. *He's good-looking. He owns the Dunsworth Corporation. He's not wearing a ring. So he drinks a little. So what? I've hit the jackpot,* she calculated, breathlessly.

"It jusseems to me that for a woman suchasyou ornamentation isunnecessary," Harding continued.

"Uh-oh," Kate muttered, elbowing Sara, who turned and gave her a questioning look.

"If you'llallow me," Harding was saying, raising a hand to remove the ornament.

"No. Oh, no. Don't, Harding," Sara cautioned, with a stricken expression. "It's a—"

But Harding Johnson could already see what it was.

Suspended from the offending stiffened piece of tulle and lace that he had just removed from Sara Silverstein's head, hung the sleek, blond blunt-cut wig she had been wearing.

Harding's jaw dropped noticeably as his eyes grew wide with amazement. He couldn't stop gawking at Sara, who was now hunched over, trying to hide her own mass of matted, multicolored hair. She looked like a Ukrainian Easter egg.

Kate grabbed the blond wig from Harding and tried to reposition it on her friend's head. But Sara waved her off, then bolted.

"Forgive me, please. I'm sosorry," Harding Johnson implored, stumbling after the mortified Sara, who raced toward the exit as fast as her three-inch heels would carry her.

It was almost one o'clock in the morning and Kate couldn't sleep. Her stomach kept growling. She'd spent most of the evening calming Sara down, reassuring her that hardly anyone had noticed when she'd fled the elaborate dinner party without her wig.

"Oh, right. They thought it was just another bald eagle gliding by," Sara had joked as she got undressed. "I don't know about you, sweetie. But I'm turning in. You go back and watch the pony show."

By the time Kate returned to the enormous tent, the horse auction was well under way. And dinner officially over. She hadn't felt the least bit hungry. But now, lying in bed, she kept envisioning food. A thick chicken sandwich, slathered with mayonnaise. Succulent medium-rare roast beef. A huge baked potato smothered with butter. Hot apple pie with melted cheese. An enormous hot-fudge sundae dripping with whipped cream.

Kate groaned as her stomach growled again. Should she risk going downstairs to the kitchen? The party had broken up a couple of hours earlier and, as far as she could tell, the house was quiet. Surely nobody was around.

Go ahead and get up, she told herself. *The refrigerator's probably jammed with leftovers.*

Moments later, Kate was tiptoeing along the dimly lit hallway. She moved cautiously, stealthily, down the wide, stone steps and through the enormous living area toward her destination. Once inside the kitchen, she ran her hand along the wall, searching for a light switch.

On the descent her palm sideswiped an aluminum bowl, sending it sailing to the tile floor, shattering the silence with a tremendous clatter.

"Damn!" she whispered, finally locating the switch.

The blaze of fluorescent light stunned her for a moment. She stood there, blinking at the array of gleaming copper pots and pans hanging overhead. Then she stooped to retrieve the bowl. And froze in position.

Footsteps. She heard heavy male footsteps, coming from behind.

"Trouble sleeping?" R. B. McDevitt asked, addressing her backside.

Embarrassed, Kate stood up quickly and turned around to face him.

"Oh, hello," she said, yanking on the tie of Jackie's mint-green quilted robe. She'd forgotten to pack her own. This one was far too snug. And too short, stopping just above the knee.

R.B. smiled groggily, amused at the sight of her.

He's enjoying this, the bastard, she thought.

She knew she looked a mess. No makeup. Mascara smudges around her eyes. Hair askew. She managed a fake-smile and attempted to fluff up her matted red curls. Then the robe popped open, and she dropped her arms to give the tie another furious tug.

"Insomnia?" he asked again, still smiling.

"No, ahh, yes—I guess so," she said, flustered. "I was, ahh—just going upstairs." She took a step forward.

"Looks to me like you just got here," he said, slate-blue eyes twinkling mischievously. "Come on, let's raid the refrigerator. I can't sleep either."

"No, really, I was on my way—"

"Back up there to count sheep? Well, stay a few minutes at least. I could use the company."

Probably misses his entourage, she thought, still uncertain of what to do.

He walked over to the refrigerator. After a few moments she joined him.

"What'll you have? Turkey? Cheese? I wonder if there's—yeah, couple of leftover *profiteroles* here in the freezer."

Kate was salivating just looking at the glorious array of food. "Maybe a little turkey," she said, knowing she could easily devour the entire platterful.

"You've got it." He placed several slices of white meat on a small plate and the *profiteroles* on another.

"And perhaps a piece of bread," she added.

"How about two?" he asked, with an infectious grin. "And some mustard?"

"Mayonnaise," she answered.

They sat down at one end of the long plank table.

"Bon appétit," he said as she bit into her sandwich.

Kate chewed nervously and bit her tongue. Damn! If she weren't so hungry she wouldn't be sitting here at all. Well, she'd eat fast. Unfortunately she'd have to talk as well.

She watched R.B. jab his fork into the ice cream and stiffened chocolate sauce. Then asked, "How'd the auction go?"

"Oh, real well. Half a million profit. Can't beat that for a night's work."

"Guess not," she said uneasily. Soon. She would go upstairs soon.

"So what's keeping you awake? Renata Desmond nightmares?"

Kate laughed softly, placing the sandwich on the plate. "Actually I'm making some progress there. One of the *Daily*'s columnists has agreed to talk to me. Sammy Rollins."

"Well, good for you. I hope he gives you something to nail the miserly witch with. When are you seeing him?"

"Monday morning. It's my first breakthrough."

"Tough getting anyone to dump on the old broad, isn't it?"

"Closer to impossible," She noticed his finely tailored tan bathrobe. *Cashmere, no doubt,* she thought. *Nothing but the best for God's gift to women. I wonder who's up there waiting for him in the master bedroom now.*

He finished off the ice cream, pushed the dish away, and frowned.

"Insomnia?" she asked, reaching for the sandwich once again.

"Wish it was only that," he replied, leaning back and stretching his long legs out in front of him. "Just got a phone call. One of my rigs blew over a couple of hours ago. Hurricane in the Gulf of Mexico. A real mess down there. Going to take some time to get it back on line."

"Big losses," she said. "How many barrels a day?"

"About five thousand, I figure. But that's the easy part." he said with a sigh. "Worst is, we lost three men."

Kate stopped eating. "I'm sorry."

"I just wish there was some way to prevent this kind of thing," he said, with a faraway look. "I mean, how the hell do you explain this to their wives and families?"

"I guess there is no way."

"No," he said sadly. "Guess not. Just part of business, like everything else." He got up. "Want some coffee?"

"Coffee, at one-thirty in the morning?"

"It's nine-thirty in London. Might as well start the day," he said, filling the Krups with water. "Say, how's our Sara doing?"

"Sleeping now. Fitfully, I suppose," Kate said. "All my fault."

"Your fault?" He sat back down. "It was my juiced-up pal Harding who pulled that stunt." R.B. started laughing. "He really yanked the wig right off her head?"

Kate nodded and smiled guiltily. "But I'm the one who made Sara wear it. She'd had her hair recolored two days ago. And this time it looked like a psychedelic rainbow. I told her if she didn't wear the wig, I wouldn't come to Texas with her."

"Well, then, I'm glad she brought it along," he said insinuatingly.

Kate nibbled on a piece of turkey and let the comment pass unnoticed.

R.B. shook his head. "I just can't believe a guy like Harding would do that. I mean, he's pretty capable, business-wise. But really shy, you know. Of course, I've never seen him get loaded. Must be the nasty divorce he's going through."

"That'll do it every time," Kate said, surprised at herself for using such a cliché line. Was it because he made her feel edgy?

There was a long, conspicuous moment of silence. After a while he asked, "And what's your schedule like these days? Busy, I guess?"

"Pretty much. I hope to finish the piece for *World* sometime next month." *Oh, no, he's going to ask me out again,* she thought. *What the hell can I say, sitting here in his kitchen?*

"I'll be out of the country for a week or so. Then back West. Why don't we have dinner?"

Their eyes locked.

"Sure. That would be nice," Kate answered, regretting the words as she said them.

She'd get out of it somehow.

15

■ Brandy stepped into the silver silk-satin evening gown and gradually eased it up over her elongated curves.

"Ah, *parfait!*" exclaimed Monica, adjusting the shoulders. "See, I told you the Valentino would work. Morgan Fairchild, eat your heart out. Miss St. John is going to steal the show."

"If I don't pass out first," sighed Brandy, scrutinizing herself in the full-length mirror. The dress was bare-backed, split in a V to the limit. And so tight that it clung to her slender form like Saran Wrap. "I don't know if I'm going to be able to breathe in this, Monica. I already feel like Scarlett O'Hara, after the pancakes."

"Scarlett was the belle of the ball that evening, my dear." Monica slipped a diamond choker, with a magnificent ruby dead center, around Brandy's slender neck and smiled approvingly. "Making a fashion statement is never a picnic. But it is a necessity in this town. And it is high time to start making yours. The paparazzi will be there en masse tonight. A perfect send-off for television's newest star."

"But, Monica, I can hardly move in this thing." Brandy complained, stepping into strappy silver sandals. She took a step and lost her balance. "It's no use," she laughed. "I look like a mermaid with hemorrhoids. I really think I should wear the one-shouldered black velvet that—"

"You will do nothing of the sort," Monica said crisply. "This dress is sublime. You're a standout in it. I spent two hours selecting it. I all but promised Lorenzo you'd show up on the cover of *W* in it. Otherwise he'd never have lent it to me. So wear it you will."

"But it's too tight around the ankles, Monica. I'm immobilized. How am I even going to get into the car?"

"Taylor will help you. I saw a model move like a dream in this dress at the collection show. Take smaller steps. Yes, that's better. Keep your head up, though."

Brandy manufactured a smile and inched slowly back and forth across the room. The dress was stunning but nothing she'd have chosen. And having to toddle around as though her feet were bound together was more than troublesome. It was downright dangerous.

"Very, very good. *Bravissima!*" Monica congratulated, finally. "I know you'll be glad you wore it once you're there. I'm told everyone at Teddy Selwyn's little soirées looks like they've stepped from the pages of *Elle*. And you will hold your own quite nicely."

"I hope so," Brandy said, sweeping her long blond hair up on one side to fasten a silver comb behind her ear. She wasn't excited about the dinner party. But she was nervous. According to Monica, an invitation to Teddy Selwyn's was comparable to being asked to join Prince Charles and Princess Diana at home on New Year's Eve. No one ever refused.

For days Monica had been impressing her with the importance of this party. She'd even managed to procure the guest list and had starred the names of the studio executives, directors, and producers Brandy should make it a point to meet.

"You never know, dear. This singular event could just pave the way to some very exciting developments in your career. There's the doorbell. You look marvelous. Now just relax and have a good time."

Sure!

A half hour later, Taylor wheeled his blue BMW up in front of an immense ivy-covered wall on Palisades Drive. Seven parking valets, wearing bright red jackets, snapped to attention.

"This has got to be something," he said, tossing the keys to a valet.

"What do you mean? The party or the house?" asked Brandy maneuvering herself out of the car cautiously.

"Both." Taylor took her arm and steadied her. "I mean, I've seen estates before. But—just look at this wall. Must go on for a mile and it has to be twenty feet high."

"Guess we're in for a treat." She stumbled on a cobblestone.

"You okay?"

"Depends on what part of me you're addressing. Right now my legs feel as though they've been embalmed in this thing."

"Great dress though," he said, with an admiring glance at her derriere. The V-back was cut so low he could see the top of her baby-skin cheeks. "Uh-oh. Here comes trouble."

Zzzt! . . . *Click!* . . . *Pop!* . . . *Zzzt!* . . . *Click!* . . . *Pop!*

The paparazzi were upon them. At least sixteen still photographers and an assortment of disheveled fans toting scrapbooks formed a circle, trapping Taylor and Brandy inside.

"Oh, God," she said in a weakened voice.

"Easy, sweetheart," he soothed. "Just hang on to my arm. And smile. We're really here for them, anyway."

"Does that mean we can leave after this?" she asked without moving her lips.

"Anything your heart desires, beautiful," he teased.

But within seconds the frenetic photographers swarmed off to sweeter territory. Robert Wagner and Jill St. John were stepping out of a sleek white limousine.

Relieved, Brandy and Taylor moved on to the entrance, where a fierce-looking tiger-head wrought-iron gate swung open automatically. And they strolled inside over a wooden bridge, then down a long eucalyptus-lined walk.

At first glance, Teddy Selwyn's palatial home looked almost bucolic. There were informal gardens and trees everywhere. But as they drew closer, Brandy and Taylor caught sight of the incongruous geometric structure. It was all red oak and tinted glass in the shape of a monstrous geodesic dome.

"Looks like something out of *Close Encounters,*" Taylor commented as they made their way up steep stone steps.

Inside, the walls were all pastels. The paintings all originals. The guests all waiting for their host to make his appearance.

It was understood in favored circles that the heir to Selwyn Studios rarely entertained. And when he did, he was always late to his own parties. Holding a roomful of celebrated personalities captive. Making them wait. It was the highest form of social manipulation. Teddy Selwyn reveled in it.

* * *

"You mean he's always late?" a newcomer inquired of her date.

"By at least an hour, yes. But no one minds. It's a kick just seeing the place. I mean where else could you find a Giacometti, an Oldenburg, and a Lichtenstein all in the same room? Food's always fabulous too," he concluded, popping a slice of caviar-topped kiwi into his mouth.

"Whatever's become of that dreadful little, ahh, what was her name? Missy? Or was it Muffet?" inquired an elegantly groomed woman in red silk.

"Muffet. Why, they're divorced," answered the severe-looking blonde next to her. "It's been a couple of years, at least. Didn't you hear? Teddy had her banished. Part of the settlement. Palm Beach, of all places."

"Gracious. The land of the living dead. Whatever is she doing there?"

"Back to whatever she did before she met Teddy, I suppose. Stripping, waitressing, acting—who knows?" The blonde laughed dryly. "Actually, I hear she got a huge settlement. And a large chunk of Selwyn stock."

"Good grief, what a monstrosity of a house," a science fiction writer told his agent. "Can you imagine living here?"

"Only in one of your scripts, Harry."

"Does he cohabit with someone, I wonder?" Harry asked, accepting a vodka gimlet from a grinning waiter.

"Several someones, I understand."

"Oh." Harry raised an eyebrow. "A nightly dance of nubiles?"

"Yes, but not exactly in the Hugh Hefner sense."

"Teddy's gay?"

"Gay, bi, neuter—all of the above."

"Interesting man."

"He thinks so," said the agent.

"Let's take a look at the famous pool," Taylor suggested, guiding Brandy outside.

"Not so fast," she cautioned, tugging on his arm. "Remember, you're with a fashionable cripple."

* * *

"Remarkable! Now, why didn't I think of that?" a British movie director asked his wife.

"Because you have more taste, Theo," she replied, as they approached the swimming pool. "It's quite pedestrian, really. An appalling eyesore. And totally overexposed. I think it's been photographed by every publication on the planet. Not to mention that dreadful *Lifestyles of the Rich and Famous.* Can you imagine?"

"I don't believe this," laughed Brandy.

Teddy Selwyn's swimming pool was one hundred and fifty feet long, constructed of white marble with gold inlays, and shaped like the Academy Award Oscar. A series of gold-plated tiles formed a halo around Oscar's head. One for each Academy Award a Selwyn Studios production had won. Brandy counted fifty-three.

"Did you see this?" Taylor asked, bending down to examine handprints in the cement nearby. "Dudley Moore. Lionel Richie. John Travolta. Bette Davis, Ann-Margret. Teddy has his own Chinese Theatre here."

"X-rated. Look at this," Brandy laughed. She was standing over the very deep imprint of a full-bosomed female's upper torso.

Taylor scrutinized the signature. " 'Yolanda.' Anybody you know?" he joked.

Brandy shook her head. "Anybody you'd like to meet?"

"No," he said tenderly, drawing her into his arms. "I have what I want right here."

She pressed her cheek against his briefly. And he bent his head down to touch her moist, full lips. But she turned away.

"Not here. I'm sorry, I—"

"Never mind. Let's go inside," he said crisply.

Taylor located a waiter and ordered club soda, purposely ignoring Brandy. He was absolutely wild for her. But she was so infuriatingly cool. Why was he putting himself through this?

She touched his arm and sought his eyes. "Taylor, I—"

He looked at her expectantly. But all of a sudden Brandy stopped talking. Something across the room had caught her attention. And now she stood, transfixed, staring out over Taylor's shoulder.

There was a vague expression on her face, soon replaced by one of unmistakable abhorrence. The color drained from her cheeks, and she began to tremble slightly, eyes still riveted.

"Taylor, take me home, please," she said in a small voice, backing away.

"What? Brandy, what's the matter? What's wrong?" he asked, turning around to see for himself.

It was their host, Teddy Selwyn, easing himself down the last few steps of a white, spiral staircase. Moving with the grace of a small elephant.

Teddy was, in a word, obese. Small-boned but grossly overweight. With thinning strawberry-blond hair. Pasty white skin. And telltale gray circles under his dark ferret eyes. At thirty-four he gave the appearance of a much older man.

Taylor had seen Selwyn before. But never quite like this. The hefty studio chief was draped in a floral print caftan hiding a multitude of flaws. A chunky tiger-head medallion hung from his neck. And a single, long, gold drop earring dangled from his right earlobe.

Approaching the bottom of the stairway, he raised a hand in a gesture of general greeting. And immediately immersed himself in the convivial crowd.

Taylor smiled in disbelief. He guessed now that the stories Sara had told him about Selwyn were all true. *Show business, what a screwed-up industry!* he thought, turning back to Brandy.

But she was no longer there.

Om nahmah shivaya. Om nahmah shivaya. Om nahmah shivaya. Taylor turned the words over in his head, trying to concentrate on his mantra.

Control. He could feel it slipping away. And he had to get it back. Had to stop this frantic behavior. Stop playing these ridiculous emotional games with the twenty-four-year-old teenager sitting beside him in the car.

He had thought she just needed time, understanding. And he'd been more than willing to give her that. But the scenario at Selwyn's party. It was just too much.

Om nahmah shivaya. Om nahma—

What was that noise? The turn signal. The stupid turn signal. He'd driven two miles down Sunset Boulevard and the dumb thing was still blinking and clicking away.

He flicked it off angrily.

She said nothing, just sat there shivering.

He flipped a Beethoven cassette into the tape deck. Anything to diminish the penetrating silence.

They'd been in the car for fifteen minutes and she hadn't opened her mouth. Not even a thank you for rescuing her from that ecstatic pack of photographers.

They'd come running, when she tripped and fell just outside Selwyn's tiger-head gate. Flashbulbs popping rapid-fire, like ammunition from an Uzi. What a sight! Arms and legs sprawling. Dress split in two. Brandy St. John, sophisticated model and rising television star, lying there like an ungainly, comatose Barbie doll. Dazed and defenseless.

The paparazzi had a field day. When he'd helped her up, a few of the unscrupulous had even popped some crotch shots. Those, Taylor knew, would turn up in the least flattering of publications. Catastrophic for her career.

But what did he care?

She was a detached iceberg. Absolutely uncommunicative. Totally uninterested in him.

Om nahmah shivaya. Om nahmah—oh, shit.

"Brandy. For the last time, will you tell me what happened?"

He shoved his foot down heavily on the gas pedal and the BMW lurched forward, up a steep, winding hill. He took a sharp left on Hollyridge Road and a quick right into Monica's narrow driveway.

"Look," he said softly, turning off the engine. "I'm trying to be patient. But you're making it impossible."

Several seconds went by and still she said nothing.

"Brandy!"

He wanted to shake her. He wanted to hold her close. He wanted to slap her. Snap her back into reality. Make her show some sign of emotion. He wanted to kiss her forever.

Taylor Evans studied the enigmatic child-woman sitting beside him for a long moment. She was so fragile and yet so formidable. So naive and yet so stoic. So temptingly lovely and so achingly detached.

He didn't have a choice. He had to let her go.

"Come on, I'll see you to the door."

They walked in silence. She went inside without a backward glance.

16

■ Kate was fuming as she maneuvered the Peugeot out of the parking space. She'd spent the last forty-five minutes pacing back and forth in front of the tennis courts at Rancho Park. Waiting for Sammy Rollins. A call to the *Daily* had set her straight. Not only had Rollins stood her up, he wasn't even in town.

"Away for two weeks," the snippy operator had informed her.

"Weasel!" Kate muttered. She took a sharp right onto Pico Boulevard, barely missing a middle-aged couple in matching warm-up suits.

"Now, where in the world am I going?" She reached into the pocket of her tweed jacket, extracted a torn slip of paper and squinted at the scrawled directions—Hollyridge Road off Beachwood Drive. It would take at least twenty minutes to get there. Maybe by that time she'd be calm enough to face Monica Chase. Kate hoped so. Although right now she felt too frazzled to deal with anybody else's crisis.

Monica the unflappable had telephoned earlier that morning, in near hysterics. Talking so fast that Kate could barely understand her. Something about a party and Taylor. And Brandy locking herself in her room.

"Kate, you must come," the frantic agent had urged in a tremulous voice. "So far I've managed to put the network off, telling them she has a bad cold. But the publicity tour starts tomorrow and you're the only person I know who might be able to talk some sense into her."

Kate was hoping she'd be able to do that, though she couldn't imagine what had happened to Brandy. Probably just a bad case of the jitters, she reasoned. Nothing unusual. But she wanted to help if she could.

By the time Kate reached Wilshire Boulevard, traffic had slowed to a crawl. And as she sat waiting for an interminable red light, her thoughts turned back to the Renata Desmond piece. It was beginning to wear her down.

She'd spoken with dozens of industry heavyweights who knew Renata. Producers, writers, directors, studio executives. But not one of them had given her what she wanted. In Kate's opinion, not one had told the truth. They couldn't afford to. The woman was that powerful.

And Kate was starting to wonder whether she'd made a mistake by accepting the assignment in the first place. At the moment, the entire experience seemed only an exercise in futility.

Failure. The thought terrified her. She wouldn't fail. She couldn't. Not on this one. But her self-confidence as an investigative journalist was beginning to wane. And the last thing Kate Brannigan needed at this point in her career was to start doubting her professional ability.

She had to admit she was at a dead end on the story, though. She had nothing substantial on Renata. Not a speck of information that would illuminate the woman's manipulative, deceitful nature.

And the Letty Molloy letter, the only lead Kate had, was virtually worthless. She'd assumed it would be difficult getting the three witnesses to corroborate Letty's story. She hadn't imagined how difficult. This morning's appointment with Sammy Rollins had filled Kate with optimism. After all, he'd called her. Surely he'd be ready to unload.

What could have happened to him? What did it matter? Kate knew who was pulling the strings.

As much as it frustrated her, she was beginning to think she'd have to turn in a puff piece, after all. Renata Desmond—Hollywood matriarch. Trade paper heroine. The mere thought made Kate cringe.

She still had plenty of time on the story. But coming up with a hook, uncovering something unflattering about Renata, was beginning to look less and less feasible. Nothing less than miraculous, Kate thought as she scowled at the car in front of her.

A half hour later she was standing on Monica's doorstep, smiling pleasantly.

"Kate! Kate, thank God you're here!" Monica exclaimed, greeting her with a peck on the cheek.

"Whatever's wrong?" Kate asked, pretending not to notice the agent's foul breath. Monica seemed perfectly alert, but it was apparent she'd been drinking.

"What's wrong?" the older woman repeated frenetically. "Everything! Kate, I'm absolutely beside myself. Look! Look at this!" she exclaimed, brandishing the "Click" section of the *Herald Examiner.*

Kate sat down on the cantaloupe-colored couch and scrutinized the newsphoto of Brandy. It was a large picture. Five by seven. And most unflattering. There she was on all fours, looking dazed and confused. Apparently trying to push herself up off the ground. One hand clutched at her dress, which had ripped, exposing a portion of her enticing backside.

"Talk About Revealing" read the caption.

"How in the world?" Kate gasped.

"My dear, I have no idea. She won't talk. She won't eat. She's been locked up in her room since yesterday. And we're scheduled on an eight o'clock flight to New York tomorrow morning. Kate, you know I wouldn't have troubled you unless I was truly desperate. I thought since you two seem so—"

"What about Taylor?"

"Him! Nothing. He's become completely uncommunicative. When I telephoned yesterday he was iceberg cold. Claimed he had no idea what came over her at the party. That she'd fled in a panic, tripped, and fallen. I assume they quarreled."

Monica took a breath and considered her words. "Kate, you don't think he made a move—tried anything, do you? Now you may know different, but I swear I believe the girl is quite inexperienced sexually and—"

"Taylor Evans a rapist?" Kate almost laughed. "Monica, you've been watching too many prime-time soaps. Where is she?"

"Upstairs. First door on the right."

Kate started up the beige carpeted steps, a troubled look on her face.

"Good luck," Monica called from the couch encouragingly. "And, Kate . . . thank you."

They were an incongruous pair. The tall, thin woman with the spiky orange hair. And the short, mustachioed man scurrying to keep up with her. The Hollywood version of Mutt and Jeff—in an all-fired hurry. But at bustling Gatwick Airport during the early evening rush, nobody paid much attention.

Niki Erickson and Mark Silverstein had just cleared customs. And they were late.

He glanced nervously at his gold Rolex watch. "You sure we'll be okay?" he asked for the third time since they'd landed.

"Yes, Mark," she replied with sullen self-assurance.

He shrugged, skittering along beside her. "I just don't want to be late, you know? Miss out on being first up. Suppose only a few people show. We could wind up losing big."

Niki shot him a petulant glance. "Mark, please. There'll be more than a hundred people tonight. And we're not going to lose at all. We haven't yet, have we?"

"No," he muttered, dodging oncoming travelers along the crowded corridor.

"So, relax. I told you it's a different scene here in England. They're very civilized players. Like caviar, pâté, and champagne before things get off the ground. Believe me, nobody's going to reach for their wallet before eight o'clock."

Mark checked his watch again. "You sure they know our flight number?"

"Positive. Don't worry. The limo will be here."

It was. A shiny black Daimler, stocked with finger sandwiches, hot coffee, and wine.

The driver had been instructed where to take them. A secluded estate near Oxford. The trip would run less than an hour. With luck they'd make it before the party got under way.

Niki sank into the burgundy leather seat and closed her eyes, a vision of calm in sleek Armani suede. It would be a long night. She needed a catnap.

She wasn't about to get one.

Mark chattered on excitedly, bombarding her with a flurry of questions about the people they were about to meet.

"So, this Viscount Tremley—you know him well?"

Niki answered without opening her eyes. "In passing. I mean, we frequent the same clubs here in London, run with the same crowd."

"High rollers, huh?"

"The highest, pet. They'll hike the ante up a bit here. I told you that. But, believe me, we'll do well. Very well."

"So, how much?" he asked, fingering the thick wad of cash in his pocket.

"Five to start. Maybe more. I'm not sure," she said wearily.

"But that means a big payoff, right?" he asked, full of enthusiasm. "Like around forty grand?"

"You got it, sugar. And that's just one game's take." Niki smiled in the darkness. "Think how much we'll be able to make if we stick around for the week."

"You sure we'll be able to score a few more parties?" he inquired eagerly.

"You better believe it, honey," Niki said as the Daimler raced along the deserted dirt road. She shifted her weight toward the window and nestled into a comfortable position, waiting for sleep. "This gig is going to be better than San Francisco, Acapulco, and Aspen put together," she yawned. "You just wait and see."

Forty-five minutes later Mark and Niki were standing in the richly paneled grand ballroom of Viscount Bryant Tremley's magnificent mansion, sipping chilled Cristal champagne. They'd been among the first to arrive. And as Mark accepted a caviar canapé from a circulating waiter, he noticed that at least thirty more people had shown up.

All of this pleased him very much. Now he was certain it would be a profitable evening.

Things got even better once Mark and Niki had signed up for the night's activities. As they were leaving the registration table, the viscount himself appeared, offering a warm handshake and a friendly smile.

"Just call me Tremmie," he told Mark. "Delighted to have you join us."

He was a distinguished-looking, diminutive man.

Couldn't be more than five four, Mark calculated quickly. He liked Tremmie right away.

The viscount was dressed in a black smoking jacket and a charcoal silk shirt with a bright red ascot at his neck. He was fiftyish, with salt-and-pepper hair, a thinning mustache and a trim physique that belied his years. He seemed sophisticated, without a trace of condescension. And when he suggested a quick mini-tour of the mansion's ground level, Mark and Niki eagerly accepted.

He guided them to the trophy room first, explaining that the mansion had been in the family for hundreds of years. And that he was independently wealthy.

"A dilettante, I'll admit," he chuckled as he stopped in front of a stuffed elephant head mounted on the wall. "I took that one on safari in Africa a few years back. My big-game phase."

As they proceeded to the billiard room, he described an international tournament he'd won in 1975. "Just after a honeymoon in Biarritz, with . . . hmm, Carla? Ah yes," he mused. "Carla . . . my fourth."

"Your fourth? How many have there been?" Niki wanted to know.

"Countless, my dear," Tremmie said with a devilish grin. "No, actually only six. Six very happy women. I made them all rich. But I'll never marry again. Can't afford it." He laughed.

And with that he escorted Niki and Mark back to the grand ballroom, where things were getting under way. There were at least eighty people now. But the crowd had settled into small clusters, and the waiters had disappeared.

"Ah, I'd best leave you here to get on with the main event," Tremmie said.

"Looks like we'll top one hundred tonight," Niki commented, with a sharp look at Mark.

"Yes," Tremmie agreed. "And tomorrow—would you two like to lunch at my club here in town? Stuffy old place, but we might just snare some more players for another party. You are planning on spending the week, aren't you?"

"Okay, okay," Mark whispered to Niki as they made their way toward their group. "You were right. I was wrong. So what else is new?"

"Sara! Sa—ra!" Kate shouted, bounding up the stairs and into her friend's lavishly decorated bedroom.

She always felt like she was visiting royalty in this part of the house. The room was far too large for Kate's taste. Three sitting areas. A magnificent hand-carved walnut bar. A study off to the right. A master bath as big as most living rooms. And a separate alcove for the colossal television screen.

Most of the furniture was in Sara's favorite style, chinoiserie. Just procuring the rare eighteenth-century French antiques had taken years.

"Killed three decorators in the process," Sara liked to joke.

Kate strolled around the room. "Sara?"

The bathroom door was ajar. She tapped on it lightly and caught a glimpse of her friend dressed in a lacy black bra and panties. Sara was busily brushing a dark contouring powder under her cheekbones.

"Oh, stepping out, I see. Who's the victim?" Kate teased. She sauntered over to the bed and sat down. "Okay, so it wasn't funny," she added, flopping over on her stomach. "But if you've got a moment for your best friend—she has a confession to make."

Kate propped herself up on her elbows, waiting for a reaction. "Sara, did you hear me?"

Nothing.

"Where are you—on the moon, or something?" Kate called, rolling off the bed. "Earth to Sara." She marched over to the bathroom, knocked briskly, and pushed the door open.

"Yieek!" Sara shrieked, inadvertently poking herself in the eye with a mascara wand. "Damn!" She reached for the Visine. "You scared me."

"Sorry," Kate apologized. "I just couldn't figure out why you— oh, now I see." She laughed, leaning up against the pink tile wall. "Tell me, Mrs. Silverstein, do you always wear a Walkman in your boudoir?"

"Huh?" Sara removed the earphones.

"What are you doing, learning a fourth language? Russian? Arabic, perhaps?"

"Something much more stimulating. Mood makeup."

"What?"

"Mood makeup," Sara replied in an exaggerated, dramatic voice. "Simply applying cosmetics isn't enough, you know. It should be an emotional experience, *feeling* how one wants to look. And by listening to—"

"I think I smell a Pelo Nafti in the mix," Kate said sarcastically.

"So?" Sara asked, working on her eyelashes again. "The idea is to submerge yourself in the kind of music you want to project."

"Makes perfect sense to me," Kate agreed with a wry smile. "Something wrong with the stereo?"

"Pelo says earphones are much more intimate." She turned around to face Kate. "Tonight I am an ethereal Brahms goddess."

"And who's the lucky god picking up the tab?" Kate joked.

"Harding Johnson."

"What? That *momzer*?"

"Watch your language," Sara warned, laughing. "I knew you'd be shocked."

"He had the nerve to call?"

"Several times before I accepted. That was after the flowers. Didn't you notice them all over the living room? Orchids, gardenias, dahlias. You should see my office. It looks like a hothouse."

Sara walked over to her closet. "He's in town for three days. ICN board meeting."

"So where's dinner?" Kate asked, following her.

"Someplace without a liquor license, I hope." She slipped into a navy-blue Anne Klein linen dress.

"There's always Fatburger. Or Pinks. By the way, R.B. says Harding isn't really an alky. Just a little unnerved about his impending divorce."

"Oh?" Sara said with feigned annoyance. "Well, I can sure count on my good friends to keep me informed."

"I didn't know you were interested."

"I'm not," she replied crisply, adding a string of opera-length pearls.

"And that's why you're decked out like Ms. Ultra-Conservative. Because you're not interested, right?"

"Right." Sara stepped up on a stool and reached for the wig stand on the top shelf.

"Sara, you're not wearing that?" Kate asked, staring at the blond blunt-cut wig. "It's the same one he—wait a minute. Do I read something into this? Are we thinking of perhaps redefining our image for a certain refined, if a bit tipsy, New York millionaire?"

"Kate, will you lay off?" Sara complained, adjusting the wig on her head. "*We* aren't doing anything. I'm just in the mood, okay?"

"Whatever you say," Kate taunted, sitting down on a small white couch. "You're the ethereal goddess."

Sara was anxious to change the subject. "So how did it go with Brandy this morning?"

"How did you know?" Kate inquired, surprised.

"Osmosis! Brandy turns up on all fours in the *Herald.* My brother is walking around like Count Dracula. And Monica Chase sends up a predawn emergency flare. Just call me Clouseau."

Kate chuckled, swung her feet up on the coffee table, and studied the seams of her Sassoon jeans. Soon she was frowning.

"That bad?"

"Pretty sick, Sara. I don't think you—"

"Oh, tell me. I adore being grossed out," she urged, sitting next to Kate.

"You sound like the twins."

"I should only look like them."

"You often do."

"Touché," Sara said, poking Kate in the arm. "Now about Ms. St. John . . ."

Kate thought for a long moment, then said in a serious tone, "This will have to be totally off the record, Sara. I shouldn't even—"

"Since when have I broken a confidence?"

"Never," Kate admitted, with a sigh.

"Kate, it's me, your old college chum. You know whatever you tell me won't go beyond these walls."

Kate got up and paced around. Where should she begin? It was all so convoluted, so unbelievably depraved. That morning when Brandy had first poured out her story, Kate's initial response had been to put it all in print. Write it up for *World* and convince Russ Stevens to run it. Unmask Teddy Selwyn and his sadistic, pernicious games.

But a piece in *World* was out of the question. There was, after all, no proof of Teddy's virulent behavior. Even if the film still existed, trust him to have covered his tracks. A man of Selwyn's stature could not afford to be linked with the kind of debauched butchery Brandy had witnessed.

Kate couldn't imagine enduring a horrifying experience like that. The mere thought of it made her stomach turn. How Brandy had managed to get through all these years without telling anyone was puzzling. The incident had obviously made an indelible mark on her psyche. It had taken her more than an hour to describe that terrifying evening. And by the time she finished she was sobbing uncontrollably.

The rest of the day had been disconcerting for Kate. She couldn't shake the nagging feeling that there was something she could do for Brandy. Some way she could even the score and expose Teddy Selwyn as the ruthless, profligate character he really was.

Although she hadn't considered it before, sharing this dilemma with Sara appealed to her. Perhaps between the two of them they could find a way.

"Sara, this is going to be a little difficult to digest. So just bear with me," Kate said, sitting down again. "You know Brandy left Selwyn's party the other night in a hurry."

"Ran out so fast she fell on her ass, is the way I heard it," Sara piped up, amused.

"Listen, if you're going to—"

"All right, already. You've got the floor."

"Good. The reason she ran was because she'd gotten a glimpse of Teddy."

"Makes sense to me. That guy's got a kisser that would frighten Frankenstein."

Kate shot her a discouraging look and continued. "Brandy had never met Selwyn. Not formally. But she had seen him before, years ago, in New York. And the circumstances were pretty grim. A movie set, of sorts. A snuff film."

Sara's mouth fell open. "Where someone was actually 'snuffed out'—and died?"

Kate nodded.

"Teddy Selwyn's snuff film, Sara. I swear. Maybe he's still producing them."

"And Brandy was in one?" Sara asked, in disbelief.

"Not her. Her roommate. Deede Anderson. They were living in the Village, waitressing. Brandy was only eighteen, new to New York. And Deede, an aspiring actress, had signed up for an improvisational workshop she'd heard about, where the performances were actually filmed. She was pretty shy, afraid to go alone, and invited

Brandy along. So off they went to some loft on Eighth Street, where, sure enough, there was a camera crew. And about a dozen other people."

"Including Teddy." Sara interjected.

"Not yet. First Deede disappeared. Ostensibly to rehearse, and—"

"Rehearse an improvisation?"

"What did Brandy know from scenes or improvs? She sat around waiting. And pretty soon this big guy with pockmarked skin comes over and offers her some pills, Quaaludes."

"She took them?"

Kate shook her head. "Pretended to. Anyway, about half an hour goes by, then Deede and a couple of men appear on the set. A living room, of sorts. Camera isn't rolling yet. But they're going through the improv. Arguing. A love triangle, I guess. But Brandy notices that Deede is acting real strange. Mellowed out and uninhibited. Walking funny, like she's dizzy."

"Or drugged?" Sara added anxiously.

"Right. She must have been. Brandy's sitting near the door and after a few minutes it opens. In walks this huge guy, real blubbery, with reddish-blond hair. And by the way everybody starts fawning over him, it's obvious he's in charge. The cameraman cuts the action. And this fat guy, Selwyn, scans the room—"

"Wait a minute," Sara interrupted, leaning forward. "Why Selwyn?" "He's the only strawberry-blond fatso in New York?"

"Sara, he was wearing that ostentatious tiger-head medallion. And Brandy's almost certain she remembers him being called Teddy."

Sara shrugged as Kate continued.

"So now Teddy takes over and starts directing. The camera rolls. And things start getting messy. Both of the guys go for Deede at once. Her blouse comes off. Then her skirt. And eventually everything else. She's—"

"What the hell is Brandy doing?" Sara demanded impatiently.

"Trying to figure out how to get away. She's terrified by now. Convinced Deede has been heavily drugged. I mean, here's this relatively prim University of Wisconsin graduate, engaged to the dentist boyfriend back in Madison, being beaten and raped in front of an audience."

"My God, I don't think I want to hear any more," Sara groaned.

"It gets worse. Only Brandy didn't stick around for the finale. She spotted the bathroom, slipped inside when no one was looking, climbed out the window and down the fire escape."

"Handy," Sara commented, unconvinced.

"It was," Kate's voice cracked as she talked. "If Brandy hadn't managed to get out of there, it might have been her body that was found the next morning in Central Park, hanging from an oak tree."

A look of revulsion swept over Sara's face. "That's what happened to Deede?"

Kate nodded, her face solemn. "It was all over the papers and TV news, of course. I still can't figure out why Brandy didn't call the cops that night. Too scared, I guess. She sure looked awful when I found her in the ladies' room of that restaurant—"

"Hold it," Sara interrupted. "Instant replay, please. You mean you met Brandy for the first time right after all this happened?"

"I guess I did. But I wasn't aware of it. I was having dinner at this Mexican place in the Village. And when I walked into the ladies' room I saw her sitting on the floor. Her hair was a mess. Her face chalk-white," Kate said, thinking back to that evening so long ago. She could see everything just as it had happened. Even the denim skirt and jacket Brandy had been wearing.

"So you two struck up a conversation and became fast friends, right?" Sara asked facetiously.

"Hardly. She looked so pitiful, as if she'd just thrown up. I asked if she needed help, if I could do anything. She said no. But for some reason I just felt bad leaving her there alone. So I gave her my card. And the next day she called."

"But said nothing about the dead Deede? Doesn't make sense."

"Yes, it does, Sara. She was terrified, afraid Selwyn would track her down."

"Maybe," Sara said, mulling it over. "So she called, and then you two became fast friends."

"Sort of. We met for coffee and she said she was tired of waitressing. Wanted to find a new job and a new apartment. She moved in with me for a short time and—"

"Somehow I never saw you as the waif-of-the-week type, Kate. Must have been your latent maternal instinct," Sara said lightly.

Kate smiled. "You know, I'm still not sure what it was. Just something about her that seemed so fragile and so, well, needy at the time, I guess. She did find a job, at a dry cleaners. And rented a small apartment on the West Side, not far from mine. And then, you're right, we did become fast friends. I often wonder if I'm the only friend she has."

"Are you sure she's telling the truth?" Sara wondered.

A look of total surprise suffused Kate's face. "Why on earth would she make up something like this?"

"I don't know. Attention, maybe. She is an actress. And you said yourself she's a little strange."

"I said mysterious—not demented," Kate replied defensively. "Of course she's telling the truth, Sara. I have no doubt about that. And I think you'll agree that I have a pretty good bullshit detector."

"Best I know of," Sara said almost apologetically. "So, she's okay now? I mean for the tour and everything?"

"I think so. But Monica knows nothing about this, Sara. I told her Brandy was just suffering from a severe case of frazzled nerves."

"You know who would kill—pardon the pun—for this information, Kate?" Sara said with a conspiratorial edge to her voice.

"Who?"

"R.B. He's trying to take over Selwyn Studios, you know. And anything a little shady about Teddy—"

"Would be more Selwyn shareholders in R.B.'s camp, right?" Kate smiled. "Not a bad idea. I'll think about it."

"Just don't think too long." Sara got up to check her appearance in the mirror. "When R.B. moves, he moves like lightning."

"So I've noticed." Kate stood up and stretched. "What time is your date?"

"Soon. What are you up to tonight?"

"Not much. But I do have something to tell you."

"You haven't told me enough already?" Sara asked, extracting a lipstick from her evening bag.

"I mean about me. The reason I came looking for you in the first place," Kate said, watching Sara's reflection in the mirror. "I called him."

"R.B.? Why didn't you tell me? That's great. Maybe we—"

"No. Not R.B. Seth. We're getting back together. He's flying out here."

Sara's face went slack. She held the lipstick in midair. "Oh, no!"

"Your optimism overwhelms me," Kate said derisively.

"Why?" Sara asked, turning to look at her. "You know it won't work. You've told me that yourself a dozen times."

"I have also told you how much I miss him and how lost I feel without him."

"But he's so young. And irresponsible. Not husband material. Those are your exact words. Besides, he bores you. That's what you told me. You want to be dozing off at dinner every night? Don't do this, Kate. You're only going to open the wound and hurt yourself again."

Sara took a breath, surprised by her own vehemence. But she couldn't help it. She knew instinctively that Seth Arnold was absolutely wrong for Kate. And she didn't want to see her make a mistake.

"Sara, you don't understand—"

"Yes I do. I understand perfectly. You're panicking, that's what. You're closing in on middle age, wishing you had a family. And you think Seth Arnold is your last chance."

Kate could feel the color rising to her cheeks. "He is not my last chance," she insisted.

"I know that. But you don't. Kate, you haven't even looked around. You won't let me fix you up."

"Once was enough."

"So Jay Friedman wasn't your type. There are plenty of other fish in the sea," Sara said firmly.

"Not in my hemisphere. Look, Sara, it's easy for you to criticize. You already have kids and—"

"And no husband," Sara reminded her.

"The point is, you've done it. You've had your inning. I haven't even gotten up to bat," Kate said, measuring her words. She knew Sara was just watching out for her. But at the same time, she had a right to love whomever she pleased.

"Look, honey," Sara said, exasperated. "May I be blunt?"

"Aren't you always?"

"You and Seth broke up, how long ago now, four months?"

"Around that, yes," Kate agreed, crossing her arms.

"That is a long time to be without a man. And in my opinion what you're missing isn't Seth Arnold at all. If you loved him so much you wouldn't have left him in the first place. It isn't Seth, Kate. It's sex. That's all. You need to get laid."

"Sara, please!" Kate objected, furious.

"Sweetie pie, forget your straitlaced upbringing and face the facts. You want a man."

"Sara," Kate began, trying to control her rage. "You have it all wrong. I love Seth. And I am going to marry him."

Quintana stood in the middle of the vast lobby, phone in hand. She listened to the ring, impatiently flicking piecrust from her fingernails. And a proud smile played around her mouth giving her a smug appearance.

Wouldn't Renata be surprised?

Earlier in the week a self-indulgent trip to Rancho La Costa had seemed out of the question. As much as she wanted to join Renata she could not afford to do so. Her calendar was bulging with parties to cater.

A bris, two bar mitzvahs, five luncheons, eight dinner parties. And truffles. All those damned truffles.

She'd spent days preparing them, all the while envisioning a huge vat of melted chocolate with Cassandra Goldstein dead center, going down for the count.

It was Cassandra's Beverly Hills soiree she'd made the truffles for. But specifically for the guest of honor, Michael Caine, who Cassandra had insisted "adores the little devils. Really, Quin, we must have hundreds."

The party had gone smoothly enough. A buffet for sixty. But Quintana had watched Caine all evening and he hadn't so much as nibbled on one of the bite-sized morsels she'd knocked herself out preparing.

If Cassandra Goldstein had noticed, she hadn't let on. Late in the evening, however, she'd sought Quintana out. "Far too many truffles, my dear," she'd scolded in the most condescending of tones. "Next time, please don't be so insistent."

Quintana had controlled her temper and carried on in her own

efficient manner. She was used to dealing with the whims of her
egocentric, often maniacal, clientele. But the entire week had been
most trying. And this unexpected escape to the lavish Carlsbad,
California, resort had come as a well-deserved bonus.

Thank God for Janet. If it hadn't been for her capable assistant,
Quintana wouldn't be here at all. Early that morning, the young
woman had returned to work, completely recovered from a bout
with bronchitis. And after one look at her boss, had shooed the
frazzled caterer out the door.

It had taken Quintana all of forty minutes to make her decision,
change into a kelly green warm-up suit, pack her bag, and head
south in her gold Mercedes.

Rancho La Costa was Quintana's favorite getaway. Just ninety
miles south of Los Angeles, it was nestled in a lush natural valley,
surrounded by stately mountains. For those who preferred the exhilaration of physical activity, there was tennis, golf, an Olympic-sized
swimming pool, and a number of diet and fitness plans to choose
from.

Despite her excess poundage, Quintana chose none of these. Her
idea of perfect bliss was a day at the spa. There she would indulge
herself in a stimulating loofa massage, a luxurious ion bath, a colla-
gen facial, an herbal wrap and finally a sunbrella treatment.

She adored offering up her ample body to the deft hands of the
spa's expert attendants. Allowing them to knead and plump and
stroke her weary flesh until she drifted into a state of dreamy somno-
lence.

And she'd never felt more in need of the spa's healing, rejuvenating powers than at this very moment.

"Sorry, ma'am, no answer in 331," the operator informed her.

"Oh? Thank you," she said, disappointed.

Quintana ambled over to the spa and was amazed to find that
Renata had not registered. During the ten years the two women had
been vacationing at La Costa their regimen had never changed. In
the morning they pampered themselves, indulging in a myriad of
soothing beauty treatments. Afternoons they were together in their
suite. And in the evenings they shared a romantic candlelight dinner
of fettuccine Alfredo or chicken Marsala in the Seville Room.

That her lover had varied this well-established pattern more than upset Quintana. It threw her into a momentary state of panic. If Renata wasn't in her room or at the spa, then where was she? Perhaps she wasn't there at all. Perhaps she'd checked out and—but that was absurd.

Quintana marched over to a house phone and rang the room once more. Still no answer.

Very odd indeed, she thought, walking briskly toward the tennis courts. Renata rarely played. But maybe—Quintana scrutinized the faces around the snack bar. No. She took a quick tour of the courts. Not there, either.

Growing more frustrated with each moment, she considered the remaining possibilities. The pool was out. Renata never exposed her body to the sun. But there was the main dining room.

Within minutes she was there, checking with the captain. No, he had not seen Miss Desmond. Just to be sure, Quintana circled the sprawling dining room twice. Weaving around tables and dodging busboys, like a hungry lioness stalking her prey.

A frenzied, desperate look had crept over her face.

She placed another call. Let it ring six times. Then slammed down the phone, like an angry child.

That was just how she felt, angry, anxious, and alone. Quintana had no idea what to do next. But food would certainly help.

She found a table, ordered a cobb salad, and sat there sulking. The euphoria of the morning had long since dissipated. She was annoyed with Renata for vanishing. And feeling quite lost without her.

Quintana was not in the habit of spending time alone. She thrived on the company of others. She needed a lot of people around in order to feel successful. She needed one special person in her life in order to feel alive. For the last two decades that person had been Renata Desmond.

Theirs was an effortless, comfortable pairing. Far more fulfilling and secure than the heterosexual relationships of Quintana's youth.

She had lived with a man once. Carmelo Fiori. An Italian textiles merchant. She'd met him at the London shipping company where she worked. And they'd set up housekeeping in a small flat near Trafalgar Square.

She was very young at the time, in her early twenties. Head over heels in love. And extremely naive. She wanted to marry him. He kept making excuses. She had two abortions, at his insistence.

"As soon as I'm rich enough to marry you and move us to a big house in the country," Carmelo would promise.

He hadn't bothered to tell her about his wife and three children back in Milan.

When she found out, Quintana slipped into a severe depression. Threatened to kill him if he came near her. And seriously considered suicide. She'd lived with Carmelo for eight years. He had been her whole life. Without him she didn't know who she was. Her future seemed nonexistent.

She never got over it. But she did start charting her own course. Quintana set aside her girlish fantasy of marital bliss. Quit her secretarial job. And fled to California. She stayed with a girlfriend, a British actress who had just been cast in a movie. And within a short time she landed a job in the typing pool at *The Hollywood Daily.*

At the staff Christmas party, she met Renata Desmond and took a liking to her. She admired Renata's strength, her striking intelligence, her imperious demeanor.

The next week Renata's secretary was fired. Quintana got the job. Not long after that she moved into Renata's Trousdale mansion. And the two had been together ever since.

The single life had never appealed to Quintana. She rarely even sat down to a solitary meal. Doing so now was enough to put her on edge.

From her table near the immense floor-to-ceiling windows she could see a thick fog rolling in over the golf course. The sun had dipped behind the clouds. And the sudden darkness bathed the dining room in an eerie murkiness, which made Quintana feel all the more alone.

Without finishing her salad, she paid the check and hustled down the stairs. Pausing briefly in the powder room, she ran a brush through her cinnamon-colored hair, refreshed her makeup and rummaged through her bag for the hotel map she'd found in the lobby.

Then she set out for Room 331.

In the back of her mind Quintana knew what was happening to her. But with each hasty step she shoved the feeling farther away. She would not allow it. She would not concede to this overpowering sense of hysteria. There was no reason for alarm. Renata was most likely in her room by now. And all would be well.

When she located 331, Quintana knocked, then playfully stepped aside, hiding.

As soon as the door opened, she yelped, "Surprise!" Then caught her breath. *Oh, my God, wrong room.*

The young woman in the short terry cloth wrapper was tall, slender, and quite beautiful. She had long tousled chestnut hair and stunning black eyes, which now focused on Quintana.

"I'm so sorry," the flustered caterer began, "I seem to have—"

"Michelle? Michelle, darling, is that room service?"

The voice from inside the room was deep, throaty, and female.

Quintana Jaye recognized it instantly.

17
Paris, France
1932

■ Paris, France, was the closest thing to paradise that twelve-year-old Renata Desmond had ever envisioned. From her very first step inside the spectacular rococo residence of Francine Devereaux on the fashionable Rue de Seine, the impressionable schoolgirl was dazzled.

As Francine went upstairs in search of her Aunt Clarissa, Renata stood in the center of the immense reception room, mouth agape.

Everything was trimmed in gold. The ornate mirrors. The marble-topped tables. The chairs, settees, and couches. Even the ceilings, which were high and arched and festooned with an intricate gold filigree.

But Renata was most captivated by the paintings. Or murals, she supposed they would be called. For these joyous bursts of sensual frivolity had not been framed in the traditional manner. The artist had created a series of romantic garden scenes, separated only by an occasional wall panel.

Everywhere Renata looked there were chubby, pink-cheeked cherubs strewn with garlands of flowers. Half-naked women reclining in the shade of a chestnut tree, their ivory-white skin draped in thin, transparent chiffon. Nude men stretched out on the verdant lawn, observing the voluptuous female forms longingly.

She'd never seen anything quite like it.

"Magnificent, is it not, *ma chère?*"

Startled, Renata turned toward the strident, demanding voice coming from the doorway.

Clarissa Devereaux, a petite, birdlike woman, stood there with Francine.

"Auntie, allow me to introduce you to my friend Reny—"

"Yes, yes, of course I know who she is, Francie," the older woman interrupted, with a wave of her elephant-tusk cane. "I've probably heard more about Renata Desmond than the Great War, for heaven's sake. Well, *ma jeune fille,"* she said imperiously, raising a mother-of-pearl pince-nez, "come over here. Let me get a look at you."

"Yes, *madame."* Obediently, Renata scurried across the room.

"Hmm. Well." She scrutinized the girl's overdeveloped figure bulging under the blue and white cotton dress. "You will learn much in Paris this summer, Renata. Particularly in the area of fashion. I shall see to it."

"Yes, *madame.* Thank you." She did a quick little curtsy.

"Ahh!" Aunt Clarissa grimaced in distaste. "Totally inappropriate, my dear. Curtsies are always inappropriate unless one is being introduced to royalty. Please make it your last. Such an antiquated, superfluous gesture. I always resented having to curtsy when I was a girl. Time was when—"

"Yes, Auntie," Francine interrupted, with a conspiratorial wink to her friend.

During the long train ride from Switzerland, Francine had warned Renata of Aunt Clarissa's garrulity. "She's quite sharp, really. But sometimes she just rambles on and on. She's also rather, ahh, *opiniâtre*—opinionated. Don't ever bother disagreeing. Trying to convince her she's wrong is a waste of time."

"Well, young ladies, let us be comfortable," Aunt Clarissa ordered.

Renata watched as Francine guided the frail septuagenarian Frenchwoman toward a velvet settee. Despite her age and the inconvenience of a cane, Clarissa Devereaux maintained an elegant presence.

Her long hair, dyed jet-black and impeccably coiffured, was piled high on her tiny head. Her perfectly oval face, etched with numerous fine lines, had been carefully made up in the brilliant reds and pinks of the day. Giving her the appearance of a wizened china doll.

Aunt Clarissa wore a floor-length gown of pale green silk-satin, specially designed for her delicate frame by her good friend Madeleine Vionnet. And when she sat, she crossed her thin ankles in the same ladylike manner Renata had learned at school.

"You are here for the entire summer, aren't you, my dear?"

"Yes, *madame,"* Renata nodded.

"Imagine how much she will digest, Francie. Where better to study the history of art than in the cosmic labyrinth of the Louvre? Or during a visit to our magnificent Opéra, with its splendid gold dome. She must see it all, Francie. The Grand Palais, Napoleon's tomb, Place Vendôme, the Tuileries, so gorgeous in the summer. They tell me that the people actually outnumber the statues there this time of year. And the *bâteaux mouches.* We must schedule a cruise along the Seine at once."

"Of course, Auntie," Francine agreed patiently, patting Clarissa's hand. "First thing tomorrow."

And so it went during Renata's first week in Paris. Day after day she was caught up in a veritable whirlwind of sightseeing activities.

Each morning Victor, the Devereauxes' silver-haired chauffeur, would bring the cobalt-blue Mercedes-Benz 500 around front for Renata, Francine, and her prim English governess, Winifred Jones. Off they would go, sometimes visiting as many as three tourist attractions in one afternoon.

Renata blinked in amazement at the spectacular view from the top of the Eiffel Tower. She raced breathlessly with Francine up the steep stone steps of Montmartre leading to the alabaster-white Sacré Coeur basilica. And she stood transfixed in the history-steeped Place de la Concorde.

In Paris, just getting up in the morning was exhilarating because Renata never knew what to expect. Each day was different. And the best days were the ones during which the two girls managed to slip away unchaperoned. These clandestine excursions always took place on Winifred's day off. Under the pretense that they were about to spend the afternoon at the Louvre or in the Tuileries Gardens, they'd have Victor drop them off for several hours. Then they'd scamper away to the nearest métro station and take a train to parts unknown.

One morning Francine decided to surprise her friend with a mystery trip. After Victor had deposited them at the Carnavalet Museum, they watched the Mercedes turn the corner and disappear. Then Francine grabbed Renata's hand and hailed a cab.

They drove for a very long time, through dozens of arrondissements, and Renata kept pestering Francine, asking her where in the world they were headed.

"You'll see soon enough" was all Francine would say.

Finally the cab pulled up in front of a very large, very busy square.

"Place de la Nation," the driver announced as they got out.

At first Renata couldn't believe her eyes. It wasn't the square that was such a surprise, it was what was happening in and around it.

Dozens of street tents and stages had been erected for live shows. There was a calliope, colorfully dressed musicians everywhere, and improvisational dancers whirling freely about.

Renata spotted a wheel of fortune, a merry-go-round, and even a Ferris wheel. Everywhere she looked she saw vendors offering ice cream and thin crèpes dusted with powdered sugar. And there was a big booth where a chubby woman in a flowered dress was selling pig-shaped gingerbread cookies.

"What is this, a carnival?" asked Renata excitedly.

"That's close. Welcome to the Gingerbread Fair," said Francine, beaming. "Have you ever seen anything like this in your life?"

"Yes. My father once—"

"Once what?" Francine yelled above the sound of the calliope.

"Never mind," Renata murmured, averting her eyes. The painful memory of Cappy Desmond had diminished somewhat that summer. And this boisterous, frolicsome celebration of life was a stinging reminder of his free-spirited joie de vivre.

"What's wrong?" Francine inquired, concerned.

"Nothing. Come, let's see the lion show," Renata urged, tugging on the older girl's arm.

Francine wouldn't budge.

"Come on," Renata repeated, with a questioning glance.

Francine's dark eyes were full of tenderness. "I am sorry for you, ma chère."

"But it's nothing," Renata insisted.

"Yes it is, and a very big something. I know these things." Francine recognized her friend's strained smile and hoped that it would pass.

By late afternoon it had. Stuffed with gingerbread cookies and reeling from too many Ferris wheel rides, Renata was laughing once again.

As the summer progressed, she made a concerted effort not to think about her father. Why should she? He didn't care about her anymore. He never wrote. The only times she ever heard anything about him were during those awful visits to Dr. Bruener's office in Geneva.

"Well, you seem to be doing quite well, my dear," the gynecologist had concluded after a recent examination. "Your father will be pleased to hear that, won't he?"

"I wouldn't know," Renata said sulkily. "We don't correspond."

"You don't?" he asked, with a momentary lift of his wiry eyebrows. "Well, I send Mr. Desmond a complete report after each visit. And I'm sure he'll be happy to see you're coming along so well."

"What does that mean, doctor?" she inquired sarcastically. "Does that mean I'll be normal soon?"

"*Soon* is a relative word, my dear," he replied with a weary sigh. "And you must not think of yourself as abnormal. Let me just say that you are a very healthy young woman. And that there is no indication that you will not fill out proportionately just as most young women do when you—"

"I have already filled out, Dr. Bruener."

"Yes," he said, leaning back in his chair uneasily. "Yes, you have, a bit prematurely. But let's just look at it as though you've had a . . . ah, head start, Renata. There is no reason for concern. Madame Rouard tells me you've adjusted quite nicely at L'École Sumaar and—"

"How long, Dr. Bruener?"

Jacques Bruener tightened his jaw and stared at the impertinent young woman seated across from him for a long moment. He found her disrespectful tongue quite disturbing. She'd become more cantankerous with each succeeding visit. And for the briefest second he considered dismissing her permanently.

But that would mean passing up a phenomenal amount of money. Thirty francs per session. Imagine! Three times his usual fee. And nothing was expected of him. In these cases of precocious puberty, there was no reliable treatment and no positive method of predicting when the patient would revert to normalcy.

"How long?" she demanded once more. Was she sneering at him? Or had he just imagined that?

"A few years perhaps, Renata. Four, or possibly five. Certainly by the time you're—"

"Seventeen?" It seemed a lifetime. "Thank you," she said in an icy voice.

"I'll see you again in six months," he reminded her as she left the office.

More than anything Renata hated those trips to Geneva. With Dr. Bruener poking and probing and mumbling to himself as he made notations on an extensive checklist. It was embarrassing and degrading. And the very thought of having to slip her feet into those unbearable stirrups once again was enough to reduce her to tears.

But in Paris during the remainder of that summer Renata managed to submerge all thoughts of Dr. Bruener and her father quite successfully. Distracting herself was never a problem. There were always so many things to see and do.

By late August her French was near-perfect. And she could easily find her way around most parts of the city. It seemed to Renata as though she'd learned more in those six short weeks in France than in her entire lifetime. And when she first set eyes on the University of Paris, she made an instantaneous decision. It was there that she would spend her college years.

"I think it's a grand idea," Francine agreed, stirring a *café au lait* as the two watched the hazy purple sun begin to sink behind dusty clouds.

It was a humid, sultry afternoon and they were sitting at a small round table just outside the Dôme, a popular spot frequented by the writers, artists, and models of Montparnasse.

Although Aunt Clarissa had not yet been apprised, Francine intended to study painting at the School of Fine Arts once she'd completed her curriculum at L'École Sumaar. And she found this exposure to the bohemian life-style in Montparnasse much to her liking.

She also found the thought of Renata attending college in Paris most pleasant. At her advanced age (Francine was now fourteen) she had tried "doing it" with two different boys. But her disappointment with those experiences had only served to heighten her desire for Renata. It was, therefore, most comforting to know that even after boarding school, the enticing American girl would still be hers.

Francine's passion for Renata had increased considerably over the summer. There was a certain allure about the younger girl now. Something Francine couldn't quite define. A sophistication that had been missing before. A newfound self-confidence perhaps.

Renata was taller, by at least an inch. She had a new wardrobe from the house of Vionnet. Aunt Clarissa had insisted upon it. And the new frocks had transformed her from an oddly shaped schoolgirl into a mysteriously scintillating young woman.

Madeleine Vionnet's expertise was in the use of the bias, or fabric cut on the cross, giving it a pull and a fall. On Renata the crepes and wools and silks all fell in exactly the right places, giving her a lissome, graceful appearance that Francine found irresistible.

"Do you think you can convince your father about college here, Reny?" Francine inquired, straining to catch a glimpse of a gorgeous dark-haired woman across the street. It was Kiki, the celebrated model and undisputed queen of Montparnasse.

"Lovely, isn't she?" Renata sighed wistfully.

"Not as lovely as you'll be, my sweet." Francine comforted, touching her friend's hand affectionately.

Renata smiled into the French girl's deep black eyes. She was more than fond of Francine Devereaux. She deeply admired the older girl. And she felt a tremendous sense of gratitude toward her for this enriching summer in Paris.

In the three years they had known each other, a unique symbiotic closeness had developed between them. Francine Devereaux and Renata Desmond met each other's needs completely. They were each other's parent, teacher, lover, and best friend. Soul mates.

Separation seemed unthinkable.

The years they were together passed quickly at L'École Sumaar. Renata excelled in her studies. All of her summers and holidays were spent in Paris with Francine. She rarely returned to Shangri-la.

By the time Renata was fifteen, Cappy Desmond had become a vague memory buried deep within the inner recesses of her mind. She chose not to remember her father. It was far less painful that way. By denying her feelings for him, she could pretend he did not exist.

And it was relatively easy to do that, since he rarely wrote to her.

When he did, the letter was always short, terse, and to the point—usually concerning money.

She never had to ask him for anything. He saw to her every financial need and sent a two-hundred-dollar check each Christmas.

He provided for her. But he did not love her. She had accepted that long ago.

Francine Devereaux was the closest thing Renata had to family. The two were inseparable at school. The older girl was graduated in 1935 and remained in Paris that fall.

Returning to L'École Sumaar, Renata felt quite lost and alone. She missed her friend terribly. And she had no idea what an impact the separation would have on both their lives.

September 28, 1935

Dearest Francie,

It is so dreadfully dull without you here at school. I don't think I shall ever get used to it. It just doesn't seem possible that we won't see each other again until Christmas.

We had such a wonderful summer, didn't we? I still can't believe we actually climbed up to the top of Nôtre Dame that night. I told Jeanette and Constance all about it. But they didn't believe me. They think I'm lying about the whole thing. Especially the eternal steps up that endless spiral staircase.

But what a glorious view when we reached the top, remember? So eerie, with the scarcely discernible Hôtel-Dieu, the Quartier Latin and the Sorbonne. How truly beautiful Paris is. Someday it will be my home.

I told Jeanette and Constance all about our evenings at the *bals musettes,* too. Constance is so dense she didn't even know what I was talking about. What can you expect from someone raised in Yorkshire? Anyway, I explained about the dance halls on the Rue de Lappe and told them some nights we visited as many as four of them.

What was the name of the one where you almost got caught for being under age? Le Petit Balcon? Or was it La Boule Rouge? Imagine what would have happened if the owner had really called the police. Can you picture Aunt Clarissa's face if she had seen us all decked out in those spit curls and suspendered skirts?

Of course Jeanette and Constance didn't believe any of that, either. I'm convinced they are just jealous. I'm sure they both had perfectly horrendous summers at the shore.

I must close now, as the lights are about to go out. Please write soon, my darling, and tell me all about your classes at the School of Fine Arts. I miss you so.

All my love,
Renata

October 15, 1935

Dear Francine,

I am amazed not to have heard from you by now. It has been more than two weeks since my letter. I pray that you and Aunt Clarissa are well. Perhaps your letter to me was lost in the mail. Surely that must be it.

I thought of you yesterday in the gymnasium. Mademoiselle Verette had removed her shoes in order to demonstrate an exercise. When she wasn't looking, Jeanette snuck up and slathered goose grease all over the soles. You should have seen the look on Verette's fat face when she took a step and slid halfway across the floor. It was so funny but would have been much more fun had you been there.

It the meantime, I am working very hard on my studies, especially history, which, as you know, I plan to study in college. I just wish good grades would get me out of here a year earlier so I could start at the University of Paris next fall. Waiting until 1937 seems an eternity.

I hope that your art classes are much to your liking and look forward to learning about them in your letters.

With much love,
Renata

October 23, 1935

Francine,

I can't imagine what the problem is. Still I have not heard from you, and I am now very concerned. If your letter does not arrive later this week, I shall telephone you from Madame

Rouard's office. I hope that I am not forced to do that. As you know, we are only allowed to call family from the premises. And Rouard is always there snooping around and listening in.

Yours,
Renata

October 28, 1935

My dear Reny,

Forgive me, *ma chère,* for not writing sooner. Classes have kept me so busy that I barely have a moment these days. And what a wonderful choice I have made. Each day at the School of Fine Arts is a spectacular new adventure. I am learning so much so fast that I can hardly keep up with myself.

My instructor's name is Eric Jeunotte. He is terribly attractive and equally talented. He had a showing himself at the Galerie Manois on the Avenue Bosquet in the *très chic* École Militaire district. And the entire class attended. We are sixteen all together. Some of us frequent the cafés of Montparnasse after classes. The Dôme and the Select. And now I know many of the regulars by name. They are a boisterous bunch, I tell you. You will meet them all during the holidays.

Oh, yes, how could I forget? There is a new bar that we must visit. It is called the Monocle, on the Boulevard Édgar-Quinet. The newspaper describes it as a "temple of Sapphic love." It is owned by a fascinating-sounding woman named Lulu de Montparnasse.

And here is the very best part—all of the women who go there wear tuxedos. Yes, it is a bar especially for lesbians. Isn't that wild? Arranging for tuxedos may be a bit difficult, but once we solve that we should have no problem. Slipping into the Monocle unnoticed should be a lot easier than sneaking into a *bal musette.*

Oh my, time has elapsed too quickly. It is now almost midnight and I still have some sketches to work on for tomorrow. *Au revoir. Au revoir,* my Reny. Auntie sends her best. We both miss you.

Love always,
Francie

November 15, 1935

Dearest Francie,

I can't tell you how relieved I was to hear from you today. I am so glad that you are well. And that you are happy with your classes. It sounds as though you are having a great deal of fun indeed. And I look forward to meeting your friends.

The Monocle sounds quite wonderful. We must try it, of course. Is there, perhaps, a second-hand men's store where we might buy tuxedos, then have them altered?

Did I tell you I read about yet another *bal musette*? This one quite brazen and licentious. It's on the Boulevard Montparnasse and it's called the Jungle. Let's go there over the holidays as well. My, we will be busy won't we!

I shall write to you many more times before then, my dearest Francie. Because I miss you so.

My love to Aunt Clarissa, but most of it to you.

Yours forever,
Renata

November 30, 1935

My dear Reny,

I apologize for my penmanship. But I am scribbling this in class as Monsieur Jeunotte lectures (my least favorite part of the day).

You won't believe this, but I finally caught a glimpse of our heroine, Marlene Dietrich. Remember all the hours we spent sitting around that Hungarian restaurant on the Rue de Surène, last summer, just waiting for her to show up? I was beginning to think that column in *The New Yorker* was total fiction and that Dietrich never went there at all.

But just last week I happened to be passing by that very restaurant. And, *voilà,* there was our Marlene in the flesh. And what marvelous flesh it is too. She looked absolutely divine, wearing trousers of course. (I'm just dying to have some made for class, but Auntie would be outraged.) Her jacket was tweedy, her blouse silk. And the way she carried herself! It was heaven, *ma chère*! I only wish you could have shared the sight of her with me.

Take care and think of me.

Love,
Francine

July 8, 1936

Dear Mr. Desmond,

You must pardon the personal nature of this letter, but I find it my duty to write to you concerning your daughter, Renata.

It is not her health that troubles me, for she is quite well. And her disposition could not be sweeter. A very remarkable girl, I would say. And a very lonely one.

I have held my tongue (or my pen, in this case) for a number of years about this matter. But at this point I do feel that it is time for you to become a stronger presence in your daughter's life.

This summer with us here in Paris has been rather difficult for her, I'm afraid. My niece Francine is quite distracted with her new set of friends. And Renata clearly does not feel wanted.

This situation manifested itself on your daughter's sixteenth birthday. I took her to Maxim's for dinner, as is my habit on special occasions. But Francine was unable to join us. Renata and I talked about you, Mr. Desmond.

It was not a long talk. Far be it from me to pry into other people's lives. But I got the distinct impression that she has never felt close to you. And from what little she told me, she has little reason to.

I know it is not my place to interfere. However, when a father neglects his daughter so consistently, not even bothering to remember her birthday, I do feel it merits mentioning.

That is all I am doing, Mr. Desmond—bringing to your attention the fact that your daughter needs you. I hope I have not offended you by doing so. I hope too that this letter finds you in good health.

Cordially,
Clarissa Devereaux

August 1, 1936

Dear Miss Devereaux,

I read your recent letter with great interest. And I must thank you for your concern about Renata.

You are correct in your assumption that ours is not the typical father-daughter relationship. But as a bachelor it is impossible for me to provide the kind of family atmosphere necessary to nurture a young girl. And the situation at L'École Sumaar seems to be working out extremely well. Renata receives excellent grades, and I also understand that she has become somewhat of a class leader.

This pleases me very much. And, as I have indicated in the past, I am deeply grateful for your presence in her life. It is apparent that she treasures her visits to your home in Paris as well as her friendship with your niece, Francine.

I am quite certain that any discontent you may have observed in Renata over this past summer is merely the result of a normal maturation process. Growing up is not an easy task, Madame Devereaux, as we both know. Youngsters must learn to take what life offers and make the best of it.

Enclosed is a check in the amount of five hundred dollars to cover the expense of some new frocks for Renata. I would be most appreciative if you would accompany her when she selects them, as I know you are a woman of exquisite taste.

Again, many thanks for your concern.

Sincerely,
Charles Wentworth Desmond

October 21, 1936

My dear Reny,

Why have you not yet answered my letter of late September? It has been almost two months since you returned to L'École Sumaar, and I am beginning to believe that you are angry with me.

It is true you were quite cold when we parted at the train station. But I attributed that to one of your passing moods. Now I am almost convinced that I have hurt you in some way, and my heart is heavy with the thought.

I know you did not thoroughly enjoy the summer. I just wish

you had made more of an effort to enjoy my new friends. But I can understand that some of them put you off with their affectation. Such is the artistic bent.

You cannot say it was a terrible vacation, however. After all, we were together many evenings. And that was wonderful, *ma chère*.

Have you told Jeanette and Constance about our escapade at the Hôtel Chabanais? Did you know that it is the most famous of all Parisian brothels? That is what my English classmate, Justine Langston, told me she'd read somewhere.

When I explained to Justine how we'd managed to sneak into the hotel as maids, she said it was the "cheekiest" thing she'd ever heard of. She was absolutely enthralled with my descriptions of the "theme" rooms, especially the Chinese pagoda and the Moorish hall. I thought she would go absolutely wild with envy when I told her about the torture chamber with all the hunting crops and flails.

Such sensational adventures we have had together, *ma chère* Reny. How can you be so cool to me? You know I adore you, precious one. Merely looking at you makes me happy. For your beauty increases with each passing year.

Even Auntie can't believe how tall you've grown. You must tower over Madame Rouard by now. And when Professor Jeunotte saw me working on your portrait in class, he was intrigued by your "scintillating beauty." I swear that is what he said. The portrait, by the way, is almost finished. It will be my gift to you this Christmas.

Please write soon, *ma chère*. I miss you.

All my love,
Francie

November 3, 1936

Dear Reny,

I am anxious because I have not heard from you. And I do not wish to write this, but write it I must. For I know something is troubling you.

There is only one reason I can think of that you might be angry. And I don't even want to consider it because the very thought is so silly. But it occurs to me that Henri Descannet might be at the root of the problem.

Is it true? Are you unhappy because I slept with him this past summer? Don't you know it makes no difference, and that my feelings for you remain the same?

Henri is attractive and quite affluent, and we both know that Auntie would be in heaven if he asked for my hand. But he is very busy with medical school now, striving to become as famous a surgeon as his father, I suppose.

I rarely see Henri anymore. Besides, my heart beats for you, *ma chère,* So please do not be jealous of my brief dalliance. It was merely a fling.

What is life unless we can drink in all of its wines, sample all of its pleasures? How else can we be certain of our true feelings, except through experimentation?

My love for you has not lessened, but increased.

I long to hear from you. My thoughts are with you always.

Love forever,
Francie

November 14, 1936

Dear Francine,

I've been terribly busy here at school, or I'd have written sooner. Thank you for your three letters, each of which I have read several times.

Of course I understand about Henri and hope you realize that I am far too mature to be jealous over something so meaningless.

This year, my last at L'École Sumaar, promises to be my most fulfilling. I had no idea I would be voted in as president of the student body. But it happened just two weeks after school began. And I have been swept up in a tempest of activities ever since.

There are so many committees to oversee that I've lost track of what each of them does. Did you know we have two hundred fifty-three girls here now? I can hear the construction crew working on the new wing as I write this.

Most exciting is the senior-class play. I know I didn't mention that I was going to try out, but I did and I got the part I wanted. Ophelia! I am absolutely delighted too that Rachel O'Neill is playing Hamlet. She is three inches taller than I am, so we are well matched. I'll have to memorize my lines over the winter holidays, but we'll find lots of time for fun too.

Until then,
Renata

April 20, 1937

My dearest Reny,

I am dancing on air. So thrilled. So excited. You will never guess what has happened. Yes, perhaps you will, for you are always so intuitive.

Well, here it is—Henri Descannet has proposed. And I have accepted. Dear Auntie is delirious with joy. But the wedding is not planned until the fall of next year. So we will have our usual wonderful summer together, *ma chère*.

This one will be far better, however. For we travel to the Côte d'Azur. Henri's parents have a splendid resort home in Nice. You will adore it, I promise you.

And Henri has a cousin named Philippe who will also be vacationing there. Philippe is a first-year law student and quite handsome. I am certain he will fall crazy in love with you.

Oh, I am so rhapsodic and so very much in love. Imagine, soon I will be addressed as Madame Descannet. We've hardly discussed details, but we plan to hold the reception at the Plaza Athénée. I will wear a traditional gown with a massive train. Auntie has already asked Madame Vionnet to commence sketching.

And you will be my maid of honor, or course. Isn't it grand? I am flying on a cloud pillow and cannot wait to tell you all of the glorious details in person.

I am so glad we had our talk over the spring holiday. My heart is full, knowing you understand my feelings for Henri. It was you, after all, who predicted we would marry. I wondered, at the time, if you really meant it. Certainly you couldn't have imagined it would happen this fast.

And the wonderful part is that, even though I will be a married lady and having babies (very soon I hope), my new circumstance will not come between us. What we had as young girls we will carry with us forever. It will always be our special secret to look back on with joy.

Now we must go forward as women. Who knows, *ma chère* Reny, perhaps you will fall in love with Philippe this summer and we will have a double wedding.

All my love,
Francine

April 29, 1937

Dear Francine,

Your engagement news came as a surprise. I am very happy for you and Henri. And I hope that you will have a wonderful life together. I know being married to a doctor will suit you very well, and I'm sure Henri will be just as successful as his father is.

I have recently heard from my father, who insists that I summer at home in California. There is really no way I can refuse to go, as I have not seen him in many years.

I am sorry that I will not be able to join you on the Côte d'Azur, which I have heard is very lovely indeed. Perhaps another summer. I shall return to Paris in the fall, in time to enroll at the University. And father insists that I take an apartment, as he feels I have relied on your generous hospitality far too long.

My best to Aunt Clarissa.

Renata

18

■ Kate's mind was a jumble. Intellectually she knew there was no one man for her. No Mr. Right. Love was a matter of circumstance. Timing. Environment. So many things came into play before two people came together.

There would be other men in her life, she realized that. And in her heart she knew she should wait it out, find someone appropriate. More established. Closer to her age.

But she could not let go of Seth Arnold. She'd tied herself up in emotional knots over him. Trying to forget him. Thinking that her work in California would help sever the bond. Yet there was something inevitable about their relationship. Something she could no longer deny.

She had fought it for weeks. She couldn't explain it, let alone understand it. All she knew was that what they had was instinctual and not without a hint of déjà vu. Kate Brannigan and Seth Arnold could have existed on two different planets and still have found each other.

Kate had felt this way when they had first made love, more than a year ago. And now, holding Seth so close, her face pressed up against the yellow cashmere of his sweater, she savored the memory. She felt weak in his arms. Happy to be with him. Uncertain she should be. But very much aware that she'd had no choice.

Yet she had put herself through tremendous angst, trying to decide. Only minutes earlier she had been walking aimlessly around the grounds of the Bel Air Hotel, replaying the same internal argument that had been plaguing her for days. Should she see him? Make love with him? Marry him?

Sara's incessant warnings kept echoing in her mind: *He's wrong for you, Kate. You'll only be hurting yourself. Don't do this. You're going to regret it!*

Walking around weighing the options had only confused Kate further, magnified her quandary. By the time she approached the garden bungalow her legs were trembling. And when he opened the door, she still had no idea what she was going to do.

"Hello, sweetheart," he said softly, smiling down at her. Reaching for her.

His touch was like an electric shock. She felt her throat tighten with desire. The heat rushing to her face. At the same time she was overcome by an amazing sense of relief. They were together now. She had come back to him. That was all that mattered.

"You're so beautiful." His husky voice made her shiver.

She looked at him through sparkling eyes, her soft red curls glistening in the late afternoon sunlight. Her face tilted upward, expectantly.

His mouth came down on her anxious lips and held them with such fervor that it took her breath away. She kissed him back greedily, reaching up to clutch his broad shoulders and gently massage the back of his muscular neck. She could feel his coiled strength pressing into her, just as she had so many times before.

Kate had forgotten, or merely managed to block out, her overpowering visceral response to Seth Arnold. She was, quite simply, entranced by his sheer physicality. His hard, well-toned body. His ruggedly handsome face. There was a sexual magnetism that radiated from him with such force it made her feel dependent and helpless. Even when she didn't want to feel that way.

She wrapped her arms around his waist, burying her head in his massive chest. Losing herself in his powerful physique. And for the first time in months she felt safe, protected, content.

"I . . . I missed you," she almost purred, basking in the cocoon of his long, muscular arms.

"Should have called me sooner," he teased, tightening his embrace, holding her so close she felt he would crush her into him. Make her a part of his body.

And she wanted that. More than anything at this moment she wanted to be his. To feel his strength around her, on top of her, deep within her.

"I thought I'd never see you again," he whispered, picking her up quickly and carrying her across the room. "I fell asleep thinking about you, wanting you. You know that?" he asked, placing her gently on the bed.

"I know that," she answered with an ebullient smile as she touched his bronzed, virile face.

He caught her wrist and lovingly ran his tongue over the palm of her hand. Their eyes locked. And she could feel him drinking her in, devouring her with his penetrating look.

A sudden surge of longing came over her, quickening her pulse and bathing her in a radiant glow. And a sigh of deep passion escaped her lips. "I . . . oh, Seth. I need you," she gasped. Then, unexpectedly, her eyes filled with tears.

"It's all right, baby. I'm here now. And I'm not going anywhere," he soothed, running his hands through her soft fluff of curls and down over the two faint spots of color in her cheeks. "I'd do anything for you, sweetheart. Anything," he repeated, brushing his lips past her forehead, over her eyes, down to the tip of her pert nose.

Then he drew back, his expression full of adoration. But uncertain, somehow. And she returned his gaze, her magnificent blue-violet eyes exuding tenderness and desire.

"Yes, I love you," she said, answering his silent question. Knowing the words were superfluous.

He held her eyes with his for a long moment and his sensuous mouth curved into a gentle smile. "And how many children do you want, Mrs. Arnold?"

Her stomach did a little flip as she replied, "How many are you prepared to give me?"

"Oh, a half dozen or so."

"Can we pare that down to two?" She laughed.

"Three!" he joked authoritatively. "And that's a compromise."

"I think we're in for a lot of compromising."

"We can handle it." He tickled her ear playfully. "Can't we?"

"I guess so."

"When's the wedding," he inquired, watching her face carefully.

"When do you suggest?" she heard herself say. Was she really going to do this? Marry him? Have his children?

"I suggest the sooner the better," he said firmly. As if the engagement was a fait accompli.

"Well . . . I have the piece for *World* to finish up and—"

"How long?"

"Three weeks—a month, tops."

"Good. Maybe we'll have a Christmas wedding."

"Christmas, what happened to Hanukkah?" she teased.

"Hanukkah, Rosh Hashanah, Shavous, who cares? As long as you're with me," he said, taking her long, graceful hands in his own. Then his face turned thoughtful and his eyes were full of tenderness as he told her, "You know there's been no one else, Kate. I couldn't stop thinking about you. It's always been you."

"I know. Me too." She sighed, drawing him down on top of her once again. Welcoming the weight of his body. The urgency of his hardness against her thighs. She felt pinioned, riveted to the bed. As if he owned her, possessed her.

He slipped his hand under her cable-knit sweater and began a gentle caress that made her start to tremble. Her eyes were closed, her face flushed, and he could see a pulse beating furiously on her neck.

He tugged the sweater up, lifting it over her head. Then he unzipped her beige gabardine slacks and inched them slowly downward, following the shapely curve of her leg with his tongue.

When she was fully undressed, he stood up and hastily stripped off his sweater and jeans. She watched him silently, her eyes moving over his well-muscled athlete's body. And she thrilled to the sight of him.

His chest, thickly covered with dark hair, always seemed more immense naked than clothed. His waist and hips were narrow, above long, sinewy legs. There was a grace and symmetry about his body that reminded her of a racehorse. So perfectly were the muscles delineated and toned.

That body, she thought to herself with a luxurious stretch, *is going to be mine for the rest of my life.*

The instant she felt his hot flesh against her she was submerged in her own concupiscent trance. She closed her eyes and ran her fingernails lightly down his back. Eager to feel his large hands roaming over her bare skin. His strong fingers caressing her. Exploring the innermost recesses of her being.

He wrapped himself around her. "I love you, Kate," he said. "Everything is better with you in my life."

And then they began to make love, longingly, leisurely, as though they'd been created by some higher power specifically for this union. For theirs was a primal bonding. Magnetic in its intensity. Animalistic in its fusion. So natural and uninhibited that it seemed as if they had been together forever. Perhaps over a period of centuries and through many different lives. Their bodies fashioned for the exclusive purpose of pleasuring each other.

"Seth. Oh, Seth. Darling!" she whimpered.

Her body quivered in sudden little contractions and she moaned with pleasure, arching her back.

"I'm yours, baby," he murmured, swept up in the libidinous delirium only she could trigger.

She was like a blazing fire beneath him. Searing into his very soul. A coursing molten heat that grew more intense with every second. And he had to take her harder, loving her savagely and with abandon. Releasing all the frustration that had been pent up within him for these many weeks.

His body stiffened as her arms tightened against the small of his back. and she enveloped him with her legs, pulling him closer to her, deeper inside her.

"I'm never going to let you go, Kate Brannigan. Never."

She looked up at him, overwhelmed with the rapture of their passion. Knowing he was right there with her. Floating. Soaring. Drifting in that special place where only they could take each other. That labyrinth of supreme ecstasy. Reaching beyond whatever limits of physical joy they ever dreamed existed.

The white-hot lights in the television studio shone with a penetrating glare. Brandy could feel her skin growing taut from the scorching incandescence.

"Three minutes," the floor director called out.

Not soon enough, she thought, recrossing her legs for the second time. She tugged nervously on the vermilion Yves St. Laurent suit jacket. Brushed back a wisp of blond hair. And sat up ramrod-straight on the tweed sectional couch.

Out of the corner of her eye she could see the studio audience filing in. Staring down at the living room set. Examining her curiously. Making her feel even more conspicuous.

Never mind. You'll get through it. Pull yourself together.

Setting her mouth in a tight-lipped smile, Brandy observed the man directly across from her.

Pete Landry, the most popular television personality in greater Chicago, was shuffling through a handful of three-by-five cards. Making mental notes. Paying little attention to Brandy.

He didn't have to. She needed him more than he needed her. That's the way he saw it. Like all the guests who appeared on his show, she was there to sell something. And he was there to deliver what the viewers tuned in for. Sensational television. He never let them down.

With his sharp, often caustic, sense of humor. His penetrating gray eyes. And his uncanny ability to probe the psyches of the haughtiest of stars, Pete Landry had held his enviable position, high in the catbird seat of Chicago television, for twelve years.

He was a household word, with a national profile. His incisive interviews often made headlines. *USA Today, World,* and *People* had all run features on him more than once. His fans sent homemade cookies, knitted sweaters for him, chased him through the men's department of Marshall Field.

They admired him because he did what they didn't have the courage to do. Pete Landry went for the jugular. Not in an offensive way. He was an incredibly smooth interviewer. Like a fine chef, hovering lovingly over a delicate Bavarian cream. Stirring it. Coaxing it gently. Then suddenly bringing it to a boil, without once raising the flame.

Brandy was well aware of Pete Landry's tactics. Monica had warned her.

"But you haven't a thing to worry about, my pet," the protective agent had added hastily. "Not after the way you came through in New York."

The TV and radio shows there had gone extremely well. Brandy had floated through each interview with stunning adroitness. She'd seemed to blossom. Fielding the difficult questions dexterously. Often turning them around to her own advantage. Even coming up with some spontaneous, funny anecdotes about life in Hollywood.

"Keep doing that, honey," Monica had urged. "Remember, nothing wins an audience over faster than laughter—or tears."

At the moment, Brandy was somewhere between the two. Landry's reputation as an interviewer automatically made her apprehensive. On the other hand, she was amused by him. He was so, well, unusual-looking.

"Mort? Let's stretch this first segment to ten, buddy." Landry was on the phone, talking to his director in the control booth. "What? How should I know from commercial times? You figure it out."

He slammed the receiver down huffily. And gave Brandy a plastic smile. "All set, sweetie?"

She nodded, wondering how Landry had ever gotten into television in the first place. It certainly wasn't looks. Or sex appeal.

Landry was fifty-two, with shock-white hair and sallow skin. He had a big bulbous nose. Small gray eyes. A squarish head that was too large for his body. And an ego to match.

"Quiet in the studio, please," called the floor director. "Thirty seconds to air."

A hush fell over the audience. Seventy-five eager women settled into their thinly-cushioned chairs. And smiled in recognition at the sound of the show's familiar theme song. All eyes were riveted to the monitors on either side of the set.

Huge orange letters, spelling out THE PETE LANDRY SHOW, flashed onto the screen. Then a series of quick cuts. Landry on his country French living-room set. Chatting with Dionne Warwick. Laughing with Sylvester Stallone. Looking serious with Meryl Streep. Instantly the montage dissolved to reveal the popular host in the same living room, this time with Brandy St. John.

He introduced her rapidly, made some flattering remarks about her burgeoning career. Asked why she had changed her name from Brenda Vreesen. Said he thought she looked much more like a saint than a john. The tasteless joke brought color to Brandy's face. A roar of laughter from the audience.

He wondered about her busy schedule. And about acting. How challenging was it for her? How satisfying?

Answering these questions, she began to feel more comfortable. leaning back, draping her arm over the couch.

The floor director was signaling five minutes. The interview was half over. And it was going well. She could afford to relax.

"Your biography says you're from Denver," Landry was saying. "What part?"

"Uhh—Lakewood, the, uhh, suburbs," she answered, silently cursing herself for stumbling. "But actually I was born in Stockholm. My father was a Swedish exporter. He died when I was quite young, and Mother and I moved to Colorado."

"And what was it like, growing up in Denver?"

"Oh, nothing unusual," she said with a pleasant smile. "I guess you'd say I had a pretty normal childhood."

"Would you say that, Brandy?" he inquired, leaning in closer to her. His tone was serious. And so was his expression.

A blank look swept over her face. And she searched his eyes for some clue. What was he getting at?

"Did you have a normal childhood?" he probed in a gentle voice.

"Why, yes. Yes, certainly," she repeated, flustered. Thinking of something poignant to say. "Except, of course, for my mother's death. I was only seventeen at the time. And I moved to New York after that."

"After her death or before her death?"

Brandy's azure eyes went huge with disbelief. He'd caught her off guard. "I . . . I don't understand."

"Oh, but I think you do." His voice was soft, but his gray eyes turned flinty as he continued. "Tell me, Brandy, do you consider yourself an honest young woman?"

"Of . . . of course." Her voice cracked on the words.

"Yes. I'm sure you do. And I'm certain you had your reasons for doing what you did," he said, reaching for something next to him on the couch. "You must forgive me, Brandy, as I clearly have the advantage. I don't suppose you've spoken with anyone on the West Coast this morning, have you?"

"N-no, I h-h-haven't," she stuttered. Her hands were shaking. She clasped them together, the fingernails digging into her palms.

"Then you obviously have not heard about this morning's edition of *The Hollywood Daily.*" Landry held the trade paper up for the camera. "I had this copy flown in, special."

There were whispers in the audience as row upon row of curious housewives strained to read the fine print on the monitors.

"There's a front-page story on you in here, Brandy. All about your mysterious past. The past you say you spent in Denver. But, as it turns out, you never got close to Denver. You actually grew up in Atlanta. Your real name is Grace Bjorling, not Brenda Vreesen. At age sixteen you ran away from home and posed for some pretty shocking pornographic pictures. You were also picked up for shoplifting. Your mother died in her downtown Atlanta apartment—alone."

Brandy's skin was as white as bleached linen. She stared at Landry aghast, so stunned she was uncomprehending. He was looking at her, waiting for her to say something.

Her mouth opened, formed a perfect O. But nothing came out.

"Now I realize you're very upset at this moment, Brandy," he said, with fraudulent sympathy. "And I want you to take your time. We all have skeletons in the closet. But what you have here today is a chance to wipe the slate clean. Tell me why you—"

"There . . . there must be some mistake," she forced herself to say.

"No, I don't think so," Landry replied evenly. "I made some calls. The story checks out. *Penthouse, Hustler,* and several tabloids are already bidding to publish those photographs."

She could barely hear what he was saying. His voice was dim. Overpowered by the terrible silent scream within her.

No. No, it can't be true. The series. My career.

Her body was chill. Hot and cold. Bathed in sweat. She felt dizzy. Unable to breathe. Wild, convoluted thoughts jostled chaotically in her brain.

"So if you'll just start at the beginning, Brandy . . ." the tenacious talk show host urged in a fatherly manner.

She stared at him without really seeing him. Willing herself to move. She had to get out of there. Run—run fast. Escape.

"Brandy, there's really no need to—"

He tried to stop her, but she was standing now. Taking a wobbly step. The floor was spinning. The black linoleum. Why was it coming toward her?

"My God, call a doctor," someone screamed.

Quintana worked with furious precision. Reaching up to lift the copper bowls from their individual gold-plated wall hooks. Wrapping each one carefully in tissue. Then placing it in a Bekins box. Her hands and arms moved swiftly, automatically. With assembly-line exactitude.

She'd been in the vast custom-designed kitchen for three hours. Emptying drawers and cupboards. Lovingly packing up her collection of Henkels knives, an assortment of whisks and measuring spoons. Her favorite iron skillet. The citrus press she'd brought back from Italy. The K-Five Mixer. Quarry tiles. Baking dishes. Dozens of aluminum and Teflon pans. The tools of her trade.

Quintana had worked out of this kitchen for nineteen years. Launched her catering business here. Watched it flourish. The thirty-three heavy boxes stacked neatly on the terra-cotta tile floor were bulging with memories. She could trace her emergence as a creative spirit back to the first French porcelain quiche pan she had ever purchased. Renata had encouraged it. Had encouraged her to begin cooking professionally.

But there was no room for sentiment or nostalgia as Quintana continued packing determinedly. She had made up her mind. And her attorney had emphasized the importance of haste. She was to remove all her belongings from the house immediately. Before Renata found out.

It was amazing how smoothly everything had gone. Within forty-eight hours Quintana had managed to sublet a furnished house in the flats of Beverly Hills. The kitchen there wasn't nearly as elaborate as this one. But it would do, temporarily. Par Excellence would continue to thrive.

She paused for a moment, wiping her brow with a paper towel. Almost done, she thought. And ahead of schedule. The movers were due at four o'clock. There was just enough time for a quick look around the house. An "idiot check." To make sure she'd left nothing behind.

Quintana used her foot to shove the last box across the floor. She was on her way to the dining room when she stopped suddenly. Listening. She was certain she'd heard a car door slam. Odd. The housekeeper and both maids were upstairs. Her assistant, Janet, was at the new house, organizing. And Renata had a late-afternoon appointment with Templeton Haight.

Unless it had been canceled.

Quintana's chest tightened, and her heart began pounding at an accelerated rate. The last thing she wanted was a confrontation.

But there were footsteps now. High heels slapping against the cement walkway. That familiar gait. Moving closer.

Quintana peered out the window near the refrigerator. Renata was strolling toward the kitchen entrance. Elegant in a turquoise wool suit with heavily padded shoulders, a nipped waist, and a flared skirt.

She stepped inside the screen door. "Oh, Quin, I forgot my—" Renata stopped midsentence. Her emerald eyes swept over the barren room and focused on the boxes. A shocked expression crept over her face. "Whatever is going on here?" she demanded imperiously.

"What does it look like?" Quintana said, gazing at the splendid creature before her. Renata's clear, milk-white complexion looked almost iridescent in the afternoon sunlight. A touch of turquoise shadow made her eyes seem even more green. And a bit of rose blush accentuated her exquisite high cheekbones.

For a split second Quintana lost her courage. Perhaps she was being too hasty. Overreacting.

"I asked a question," Renata said slowly in a glacial, throaty voice. "I assume you have an explanation?"

"I don't think I need one," Quintana snapped. Bristling at the condescension of Renata's tone. "It's fairly obvious, isn't it? I'm leaving. If I must spell it out, Renata, three's a crowd."

"That's ridiculous," Renata objected, removing her pillbox hat. "She's not here permanently. You know that. Just until—"

"Until you're tired of her, as you have become of me?" Quintana heard herself say and regretted it instantly. She was determined not to play the victim.

"You are simply carrying this too far, Quin," Renata admonished, gently placing the hat on the white Corian countertop. "Michelle is merely—"

"A passing fling? A fleeting affair? Yes, I know. You explained it all to me at La Costa. But sometimes one must lift the blackened crust under the apple pie to see all is not as it appears, Renata. Such is the case with your nubile darling. She *is* living here, under your roof. My roof—as it were. And I leave you to her."

Quintana spun around abruptly and marched into the dining room.

"You'll regret this, Quin," Renata shouted, following her. "You won't last long on your own. And just where do you think you're taking all of this, anyway? Need I remind you that Par Excellence is half mine? That includes the overhead. What you're doing constitutes theft."

"What I am doing," Quintana called back as she quickened her stride, "constitutes the dissolution of a partnership. Talk to my lawyer." She hurried through the dining room, down the hall, across the foyer, and started up the steep marble staircase.

"You will not get away with this," Renata threatened, scurrying up the steps behind her.

"Oh, but I will, my sweet," Quintana said breathlessly as she reached the top. "For I have had a very good teacher. I've watched you for many years, Renata. And I've learned a great deal. By the time I'm through with you, I'll own not only Par Excellence but a tidy portion of your estate, as well."

Renata's spiraling laughter echoed through the enormous house. They were facing each other now. Eyes locked in anger.

"You're full of it," Renata said with a derisive smile.

"Full of what, my pet?" Quintana asked, adopting a saccharine tone. "Spunk? Spirit? Panache? Yes, indeed, I'll grant you that. But I have something much more valuable, Renata. Ammunition. And lots of it."

"Such as?"

"Such as," Quintana repeated, a cunning lilt to her voice. "I know who you tried to seduce last night. And how you went about it. Really, my dear, I thought you had more class."

"What are you talking about?" Renata asked with icy tonality.

"You know perfectly well. Taylor Evans. His trailer. For a little over an hour. I have witnesses," Quintana recounted smugly.

Renata's cold green eyes were set in a penetrating glare. Three deep wrinkles merged to form a frown on her forehead. "And what is that supposed to prove?" she asked through clenched jaws.

"Prove?" Quintana asked vaguely. "Why nothing condemning, darling. Merely that, just as I know about your abortive encounter with Mr. Evans, I know everything about you. All of your little secrets. My stockpile spilleth over."

"I am warning you, Quin," Renata said, her words simmering in the air. "You will lose. Everything. Par Excellence. Your reputation. Your—"

"Why, Renata, has it come to this?" Quintana asked, feigning surprise. "You threatening me? The one person you allowed inside the castle walls. The only person who has ever gotten close to you. Don't I deserve better, after all these years?"

"Quit that damn simpering. You know I despise it."

"And do you know what I despise?" Quintana asked, hands on hips. Her face fiery hot. "You. Yes, I have come to despise you, Renata. You and your sad, wretched little world. Always plotting and scheming. Playing the puppeteer with other people's lives. Constantly pulling their strings."

"Shut up!" Renata hissed.

"No, I will not shut up. And I will not stand idly by and watch you manipulate my life. Ruin it. Steamroll over me as you have over so many others in your megalomaniacal path. Like that poor soul, Brandy St. John. Did you enjoy that, Renata? Did it give you great pleasure to ruin that young girl's career. To drag her—"

"I did not—"

"Yes, you did. You wanted her out of the way so you could have Taylor Evans. But you lost in the end, didn't you? Better get used to it, Renata. You're going to lose again. Only bigger this time, much bigger. Because I know all about your . . . ahh, shall we be delicate and say *shady* activities?"

"Meaning what?" Renata insisted furiously.

Quintana's crimson lips were set in a taunting smile.

"You're bluffing."

"Am I? Well, let's just say I've got *my* signals straight." she replied and disappeared into her room.

Taylor eased himself up out of the steaming Jacuzzi and sighed heavily. "I'm cooked. Want a beer?"

"Talking my language, brother," R.B. drawled. His body felt fluid in the hot, soporific wetness. He leaned back, allowing his head to rest on the hand-painted Spanish tiles. Two hot jets pummeled at his shoulder blades, rendering him absolutely limp.

He looked up at the cloudless black sky. It was an unseasonably balmy night in Los Angeles. Just the hint of a breeze and the acute redolence of eucalyptus wafting through Taylor's verdant backyard.

"Rough trip, huh?"

R.B. accepted the ice-cold Beck's. "Might say that. Feel like I left my body back in Tokyo. Negotiated a deal to buy an electronics firm over too much sake last night. Woke up this morning with a headache that should have been wished only on Hitler."

"Rigors of the game."

R.B. looked up at his friend thoughtfully. "Nothing like yours, though, old buddy."

"Yeah." Taylor sat down, his long, muscular legs dangling in the Jacuzzi. A forlorn expression on his face.

"I saw the pictures in *The Star*. Disgusting stuff. Like to get my hands on the bastard who took them."

Taylor nodded.

"You still got the hots for her?" R.B. swigged the beer, savoring its pungent coolness.

"Affirmative." Taylor stared into the swirling water.

"Well then, listen, my man, you got to find that li'l gal. Now's the time she needs you."

Taylor shook his head, morose. " 'Fraid not, R.B. If it would do any good, believe me, I'd go after her. God knows I've thought about it enough—"

"Thought about it?" R.B. bellowed, bringing his arm down with a big splash. "Trouble with you is you're too damned analytical. Sometimes you have to jump right in. Do it!"

"No use, I'm telling you," Taylor argued. "First of all, I have no idea where to find her. After that talk show in Chicago she just disappeared and—"

"And that's a bunch of crap," R.B. said vociferously. "She's in New York, probably in her apartment. And at her wits' end. Where else is she going to be?"

"I tried calling," Taylor objected with mounting agitation. "Monica's already been there. Did everything but break the door down."

R.B. moved his head slowly back and forth, baffled. "You've got to start understanding the female psyche, brother. That li'l gal hears your voice, she'll probably open the door."

"And what if she does?" Taylor said heatedly. "What the hell am I going to tell her? That I'm sorry the network is canceling her series?"

"I hadn't heard that," R.B. said, surprised.

"Still unofficial, but imminent. Sara is beside herself."

"And it's all because of that slithery Desmond viper," R.B. added, with disgust. "Dammit to hell. Woman has fangs would intimidate a saber-toothed tiger." A sudden look of rage swept over his face. "Makes me absolutely furious I'm going to have to write her a check for twenty big ones!"

"You what?" Taylor gasped. Then, "Oh, that's right. The Longhorns won yesterday."

"Their fifth game. But I gotta tell you, brother, I think something funny's going on there."

"What do you mean?"

"You see the game?"

"No."

"Longhorns were favored to win by twelve points at the kickoff. Only won by three. But the way they've been playing this season, they shoulda beaten the shit out of the Oilers."

"So they had a bad game."

R.B. scrunched up his face. "Maybe more than that."

"Like what?"

"I don't know exactly. But a pal of mine—name's Barry Jennings —manages the Longhorns. And he tells me the team's morale is subzero these days. Just doesn't make sense. First winning season, and they're all in the dumper?"

"I still don't understand what you're getting at, R.B."

"Hell, neither do I," the Texan admitted, wiping a wet hand over his face. "Who cares, anyway? Real problem's that damned viper, Desmond. She still coming on to you?"

Taylor's lips twisted into a conspiratorial smirk. "Not anymore. She dropped in unexpectedly over at the studio the other night. But I scared her off. Told her I had an outbreak of herpes."

R.B. threw his head back and roared with laughter. "And what'd the old bitch say—that she'd take a rain check?"

"No, she said something like 'Surely you're not serious?' And I said, 'Lady, you're never going to have the opportunity to find out.'"

R.B.'s laughter spiraled down to a chortle. And his expression turned pensive as he said, "Guess that's why I read all about your low ratings in today's *Daily*."

"At least it wasn't a cover story," Taylor muttered, then purposely changed the subject. "I didn't know you made a habit of reading the trades."

"Got to, brother," R.B. said, finishing the beer. "Now that I'm going to run a studio."

"Is that moving along?"

"Not fast enough for me. Nothing ever does. But, we're getting there. Just swung a deal with a snooty faggot in New York. Archie Komack. Bought him out of a huge block of Selwyn. I own seven percent of the company now. Next step's the road show."

"The what?" Taylor asked with a soft chuckle. A vision of R.B. playing *The Music Man* at a suburban dinner theater flashed through his brain.

"Road show. In financial jargon that means traveling all over, meeting with various institutional investors. Banks, mutual funds, insurance companies. Of course, my show has to be clandestine, so Teddy won't find out."

"How are you going to manage that?"

"By setting up some surreptitious meetings with key portfolio managers. The ones who control a lot of Selwyn. About sixty percent of the stock is tied up in institutions. And I mean to have those votes in my hip pocket well before proxy time."

"And when's that?"

"December, with any luck," R.B. said, finally climbing out of the Jacuzzi. "Come to think of it, brother, you ought to snap up a little Selwyn stock. It's at eight now. Way I figure, it'll triple within the month."

Sara charged through the doors of the Hamburger Hamlet like a human cyclone. Her upper lip curled back in a snarl. Her hazel eyes hard and narrow. Her scarlet face a sharp contrast to the black velour warm-up suit she was wearing. In a word, she was furious.

She marched determinedly past the counter, quickly scanning a long line of red leatherette booths. Searching the faces. Ready to pounce. And within seconds she found her target.

"Kate!" Sara shouted, so loudly that a nearby waiter lost his balance and dropped his overladen tray.

Four heavy china plates, two orders of lobster bisque, three number elevens, a side of chicken wings, and a chocolate milkshake went clattering to the floor.

The waiter was near tears.

Sara was completely oblivious.

She quickened her stride, neatly sidestepped the mess, and disregarded the curious stares coming her way.

"What the hell do you think you're doing?" Sara hissed when she got to the booth. "Just what is going on?"

"We're having brunch," Kate said in a small, innocent voice, gesturing toward the twins across from her.

Jennifer was looking down at her plate, moving the french fries around in a pool of catsup, like dead toy soldiers. Jackie fidgeted self-consciously in her seat.

"Mom, will you sit down?" she whispered. "You're causing a scene."

"I don't care what the hell I'm causing," Sara said sharply, sliding in beside Kate. "Look at me, dammit." Kate did. "I want to know where you come off canceling my appointment."

"What appointment?" Jennifer squealed.

"Her doctor's appointment," Kate said softly. "And I did it for your own good, Sara."

"For my own good? And how did you determine that, Miss Peabrain?"

"By using my judgment, which in this particular case, is a whole lot better than yours."

"Oh, is that so? What do you think, you're God or something, deciding I can't have surgery?"

"Surgery? Mom, what's wrong with you?" Jackie cried anxiously.

"Nothing, honey," Sara answered in a reassuring voice.

"That's right. Nothing at all," Kate added. "Your mother is fine. Just a little preoccupied with her looks."

"You're full of it, Kate," Sara countered defensively. "You don't even know—"

"I know more than you do about how you look, Sara. That's the point here. You look terrific. Didn't you tell me you'd lost six pounds already? And you're finally dressing like a human being again, thanks to Harding Johnson."

"Let's hear it for Harding!" Jennifer interjected, raising her Coke in a toast.

"Yeah, good ol' Hard-on Johnson," Jackie joined in, making her sister laugh.

"Hush! Both of you!" Sara ordered. "Harding Johnson has nothing to do with this, Kate!"

"Oh, yes, he does. He's the reason you dropped Pelo Nafti flat on his bloated face. Thank God! And I'm sure he's the reason you decided to see Dr. Naddleson. you probably thought Harding would be impressed if you had your thighs suc—"

"Dammit, Kate," Sara yelled angrily. "I was not going to get sucked!"

A hush fell over the surrounding booths.

Sara's mouth snapped shut, as she realized her faux pas.

What seemed like a hundred pairs of eyes focused on her as her face changed colors from bright- to beet-red. She looked down at her hands in her lap, trying to let the moment pass gracefully.

"Jeez, Mom! Keep it down, will you?" Jackie pleaded in an urgent whisper. "Ricky Shroder's over there."

Sara gave her daughter a withering look.

"Well, then, what was the appointment for?" Kate inquired with an incredulous expression.

"Why didn't you ask the nurse when you called to cancel?" Sara fumed.

"I just assumed that—"

"You assumed wrong. You're some journalist, Kate. Where'd you acquire your research skills, Disneyland or Sea World?"

The twins giggled in unison.

"I'm sorry," Kate said, chagrined.

"You should be," Sara admonished. "It'll be two weeks before Naddleson can fit me in again."

"Mom," Jennifer groaned. "What was the stupid appointment for, anyway?"

"These!" Sara said, leaning over the table and pointing toward her face. "These two ugly sandbags under by eyes. they've got to go. Doctor Naddleson says—"

"Gee whiz, Mom," Jackie complained, "you're going to have more incisions than Phyllis Diller."

"No. I think you mother's right," Kate offered, coming to Sara's defense. "Without the dark circles she'll probably look younger and feel better."

"How generous!" Sara said, still bristling. She picked a soggy french fry off Jennifer's plate and popped it into her mouth.

"You know, Mom," Jackie began, eager to change the subject, "we want to go to Aunt Kate's wedding."

"Hmmm. I'm not sure," Sara said testily. "When is it?"

Kate shrugged.

"You don't know yet?" she asked, as though Kate should.

"We've just decided to get married."

"So? Weddings take time. You can't plan too soon."

"Well, Seth has to tell his parents first. He's in Bermuda with them now and—"

"Bermuda?"

"A family vacation. They have a condo there."

"And his folks don't know about the wedding?" Sara asked skeptically.

"Maybe they do by now," Kate replied in an irritated voice. "What difference does it make?"

"A big difference if you think you're getting married in December. From what you've told me, the Arnolds are pretty traditional people and—"

"Sara, could we just drop it for now?" Kate said hotly.

"Sure, sure." She studied her friend's face for a moment. "I must say love agrees with you, though. I haven't seen you look this good in months."

It was true. There was a special glow about Kate. A striking brightness in her blue-violet eyes. An unusual rosiness to her smooth, flawless skin. And she seemed to have a new sense of herself. For the last few days Sara had noticed a distinct improvement in her friend's disposition.

"Thank you," Kate said softly, giving Sara's arm a little squeeze. "When's Harding coming back to L.A.?"

"Next week." Sara's mouth curled into a girlish grin. "Well, San Diego, actually. ICN has a new TV station there. He should be in California for about a month."

"I'm glad you're happy."

"Happier!" Sara corrected. "I still have my moments."

"Lordie, I'll say," Jennifer complained with a moan.

Sara reached across the table and tweaked her daughter's cheek affectionately.

When they all got up to leave, Kate took Sara aside. "I'm sorry again about canceling your appointment, kiddo."

"No problem, sweets," Sara replied good-naturedly. "Of course," she added, on the way to the cashier, "there is something you could do to make up for the, ahh, inconvenience."

"And what's that?" Kate asked warily.

"R.B.'s in town. Have dinner with him. Or at least a drink."

"Sa-ra," Kate warned in a singsong voice.

"Kay-ate," Sara mimicked.

"I can't have dinner with him. I'm engaged."

"So? You're not dead yet!"

"Heard from Mark lately?" Kate asked, deliberately changing the subject.

Sara handed her ticket to the valet. "Not *from* him—*about* him," she whispered, making sure the twins couldn't hear.

"What do you mean?"

"He's still slumming around with that twit, Niki Erickson."

"How do you know?"

"Phone call from a friend of mine last night. She was in New York earlier this week. Saw Mark with Niki Erickson, having a wonderful time at the Russian Tea Room."

"Alone?"

"I didn't ask. At this point, it hardly matters."

19

■ Teddy Selwyn raised a chubby pink foot from the sudsy water and appraised it affectionately. He adored pedicures. Especially in his office. And Friday mornings were reserved for the ritual visit from Tiana Ky, the meticulous Vietnamese manicurist who tended to the studio chief's extremities.

Quite often he would take meetings when she was there. Teddy always enjoyed an audience. It gave him great pleasure to bark orders at the dimwits who worked for him while having his toenails clipped.

This morning three of his staff members were lined up at attention before him. Tim Hudson, his private secretary. Richmond Billings, studio vice-president. And Jeffrey Clements, chief financial officer.

They'd been waiting for fifteen minutes. Perched uncomfortably on identical chrome-and-leather Wassily chairs. Anxiously anticipating the interrogation.

"I think perhaps the pearlized pink," Teddy was saying to Tiana, who proffered a selection of polishes. "Yes, that one, in the center. Very nice."

As the manicurist gently inserted foam rubber separators between his pudgy toes, Teddy reached for the morning trades.

He scanned the *Daily* and *Variety* quickly. Then turned to the last page of *The Hollywood Reporter* and surveyed his favorite column with keen interest. George Christy's "The Great Life."

Teddy never tired of Christy's witty social meanderings. The snappy narrative and repartee from all the "A" parties. Quotes from the most quotable people in town. And, best of all, there were pictures.

Teddy's eager eyes darted up to the top of the page searching for his own face. It wasn't there.

Annoyed, he tossed the *Reporter* aside and glanced around his gargantuan office.

The oval room was exquisitely decorated with ultramodern furniture and priceless works of art. Teddy's desk being the cynosure. It was distinctly high tech. A half-moon of black lacquer, specifically designed for him. And intentionally positioned in the center of the room on an impressive Italian marble platform.

Teddy Selwyn spent his days elevated three feet from the floor. It gave him a distinct advantage.

"So what's with Gobbles, Rich?" he asked, peering down at his high-strung vice-president. "Any feedback on the new ad campaign?"

Richmond Billings's trembling hands began flipping frantically through a pile of papers. He'd learned long ago that his boss was apt to ask anything at these dreaded Friday meetings. And he was always armed with a battery of memos and reports.

"Come on, come on—can't you just tell me off the top of your head?" Teddy complained, an amused glint in his ferret eyes. Watching an employee grovel was his favorite spectator sport.

Billings was perspiring now. Sweat glistening on his nose.

"Speed it up, huh, Rich," Teddy goaded. "Take an entire month to go through all those damn files?"

"I've got it, sir. right here," Billings exclaimed breathlessly. Wielding the report overhead, like a tennis trophy.

"Yes, yes," he went on, reading as he spoke. "According to this, the animated turkey commercials are doing quite well in Minneapolis, where they're being test-marketed. There's a breakdown here of children, females eighteen to forty—"

"I don't want an asinine breakdown, you dunderhead. I want to know about sales. Sales, Rich. You know, as in money!"

"Sorry, ahh, the campaign isn't that far along, sir, and we—"

"Okay, okay. Fade out, Rich. Just do me a favor and call the ad agency. Breathe down their necks a little, got it?"

When Richmond Billings nodded he reminded Teddy of one of those toy dogs that bobbed from the neck.

"Tim! What about my autobiography? Is Lutz ready to go on that?"

"I think so, Mr. Selwyn," replied the thin, angular young man, in a well-modulated voice. He had bright red hair, severely chiseled cheekbones, and a highly expressive mouth. Teddy thought he looked like Rita Hayworth. Everyone else thought he looked like Maggie Smith.

"So when do I meet the ghost writer?" Teddy persisted.

"They're working on that, Mr. Selwyn. The last time I spoke with Mr. Lutz he—"

"Lutz! Lutz the *putz,*" Teddy interjected, laughing at his own joke. "Can't believe I own a publishing firm and the jerky guy who runs it isn't able to come up with a heavy hitter to write my story. What about Sidney Sheldon or Irving Wallace?"

"They write fiction, Mr. Selwyn," Tim replied, aghast.

"I know that. But what I've got to say is better than fiction. And money's no problem. Maybe we can work a deal."

"I'll tell Mr. Lutz to look into it," Tim said, making a hasty note on his steno pad.

"You do that." Teddy swung his glance to the right. "Clements, everything in order now at Diamond?"

Jeffrey Clements rearranged his cumbersome girth in the slant-back chair. He'd known the question of the record company would come up. In all his years as chief financial officer he'd never had to deal with such chaos.

The books at Diamond Records were so discombobulated it had taken three months just to unscramble the first quarter of 1983. And it was becoming increasingly apparent to Clements that purchasing the company had been a colossal mistake. He was smart enough, however, not to impart that information to his boss.

"We're still straightening things out, sir. Coming along nicely, I'd say. Should be finishing up by the end of the year," he lied.

"Good," Teddy said, glancing down to scrutinize his newly pearl-ized toenails. His face immediately clouded over.

"Is that a smudge, Tiana?" It was more an accusation than a question.

Tiana's hands flew. She swooped up the nail polish and went to work. Smoothing. Retouching. Adding another coat.

Teddy watched with mounting impatience, his pasty-white skin assuming a crimson glow.

"No, no, no," he chastised angrily. "Can't you see that toe doesn't match the others? You're going to have to start all over."

A disgusted sigh escaped Teddy's puffy lips as he turned back to his apprehensive triumvirate. "That will be all for now. I'm leaving at noon, as usual, for the desert," he concluded, waving a fleshy hand in dismissal.

"Mr. Selwyn, if I may speak with you about one matter, please . . ." It was Clements, approaching the platform as the other two filed out.

"Yes, what is it?" Teddy snapped.

"I was just wondering, sir, if you'd seen the stock report this morning?" He held up a copy of *The Wall Street Journal.*

A strawberry-blond eyebrow arched curiously as Teddy leaned over to accept the paper from Clements. His small dark eyes traveled down the New York Stock Exchange listings until they reached the line the CFO had marked in red.

Teddy studied the figures incredulously. His mouth dropped open. His loose jowls caressed his flabby neck.

Within seconds he had his broker on the phone. "Garth? Listen, the stupid stock is moving like crazy all of a sudden. Up to twelve yesterday, according to the *Journal.* That's three points in two days. Is this a misprint, or what?"

Halfway across town at Merrill Lynch in Century City, Garth Woodman stubbed out his freshly lit cigarette. And punched up Selwyn Studios on his Quotron. "No misprint, Teddy. The stock's at thirteen right now."

"Sonofabitch!" Teddy gasped. "And there's a marked increase in trading. Four hundred thousand shares yesterday. Who the hell is doing the volume?"

Woodman's laugh was low and raspy. "I wish I knew."

"Don't *wish,* Garth. *Do!* Find out who's buying."

"That'll take a little time, Teddy. I'll have to—"

"I don't care what you have to do. I don't care if you have to pay off the entire Securities Exchange Commission, you *putz.* Just do it and do it fast."

Teddy hung up the phone in a fury and glared at his CFO.

"And what the hell's with you, Clements? What are you standing around smirking at? Get to work, for God's sake. Do I have to do everything around here?"

When Taylor arrived in New York he was still telling himself it was useless. First of all, she probably wasn't there. Even if she were, she wouldn't want to see him.

The doorman at her building was wearing a dark green uniform with "Mel" embroidered on the pocket. He was tall, slump-shouldered, and officious.

"Miss St. John isn't in, sir. Hasn't been for weeks. Don't know when to expect her either. Only thing I can tell you is to try and get in touch with her agent," he announced automatically, as though he'd repeated the lines before.

"Why don't you ring up anyway, Mel, just to make sure?" Taylor urged in his friendliest tone.

"Oh, no need for that. I am sure, all right. I know Miss—" He paused to examine the twenty-dollar bill Taylor was pressing into his hand.

"Well, I guess it won't hurt to check." Mel reached for the phone. "Evans, was it?"

Taylor nodded, smiling affably.

She answered on the third ring. And he edged a little closer, eavesdropping. But the doorman shot him a disdainful look and turned away.

Several seconds later Mel hung up. There was a puzzled expression on his face. And he was pulling pensively on his chin. "Well, I'm not certain I understand all this." He paused, as though trying to piece the missing facts together. "But I definitely know she said for you to come up."

Taylor grinned, his eyes crinkling with surprise and relief.

"Thanks. Thanks again, Mel," he called back as he hustled toward the elevators.

When he got to the penthouse he didn't know what to expect. He could hear his heart thumping in his ears. He pressed the doorbell button. And, to his annoyance, his hand was trembling.

When she opened the door he started to speak. But couldn't. He felt paralyzed—or was it dumbfounded?

She was dressed in a white toweling robe, looking tired and pale.

Her trademark mass of golden hair hung limp around her exquisite face. And he could see tiny red lines in her sad azure eyes.

Such a pathetic sight, he thought. *Like a frightened, lost child.* And he ached to reach out for her, wrap her in his arms, assure her that everything would be all right.

"I'm sorry" was all he managed.

"I know," she murmured, fighting back tears. "I mean, I know you . . . you—"

"Come on, let's sit down," he said, guiding her to the ottoman near the window.

Her apartment was all black and white. Expensively decorated. Sparsely furnished. Spacious and airy. *Architectural Digest*—perfect.

But there was something rigid about the overall design. A certain coldness that dominated the elegant living room, much like the woman herself.

"I brought some sandwiches," Taylor said lightly, placing the paper bag on the onyx coffee table. "Doesn't look like you've been taking very good care of yourself."

They sat at opposite ends of the ottoman. Saying little at first. He nibbled on a pastrami without tasting it. She sipped black coffee from a paper cup, rarely looking up at him. But there was comfort in the silence for them both.

She'd been hoping he would come. As soon as he'd walked in the door she'd felt better. Peaceful, somehow. He had a tranquilizing effect on her. And she wanted desperately to open up to him. Tell him everything. All the reasons she'd been afraid for so long. Just as she had wanted to tell him that horrible night after Teddy Selwyn's party.

But the words had stuck in her throat then, just as they were doing now. All the secret fears she'd kept locked up for so many years. Welling up inside her. Clamoring to push their way out. Choking her with despair.

Taylor put the half-eaten sandwich down and gazed out the window. His amber eyes focusing distractedly on an enormous glass-and-chrome high rise, not seeing it at all.

Then he turned back to her.

"Brandy," he said in a gentle voice, "I can't imagine what you've been going through. Only that it's probably been excruciating. We don't have to talk about it if you—"

"No. Yes, I do want to." She glanced up at him briefly. "But I just . . . I don't know how to—"

"Listen, it's okay," he soothed. "Whatever you want to say, love." the word had slipped out, startling him. *What the hell,* he thought, *she knows how much I care about her.* "Whatever you want to say," he repeated softly. "Start at the beginning."

"There's so much," she sighed tentatively. "Too much to—"

"I have plenty of time to listen," he smiled, holding her eyes for a long moment. "And there is nothing I would rather do."

A sigh of deep sadness escaped Brandy's lips. Minutes passed before she said anything. He could tell how difficult it was for her.

When she began, she spoke slowly in halting half-sentences. Struggling to dredge up the painful memories. The anger, hurt, and bitterness she'd so carefully and deliberately buried in the innermost recesses of her mind.

"It's all true. What you've read. Grace Bjorling. That's my real name. I was born in Stockholm. And lived there until my father . . . He died. Shot himself. He'd gone bankrupt and we had very little. Mother took me to her hometown. Atlanta. She borrowed money and opened a clothing store. A boutique. But things didn't go well. She lost the store and we had to move to a small apartment. And . . . that's—"

Brandy stopped for a moment and brought her hands to her face as though the pressure of her fingertips would release the agonizing remembrances and set her free.

Taylor leaned over and touched her frail shoulder gently. "You don't have to continue if you—"

"I'm okay, really," she said, brushing a tumble of blond hair from her cheek. "That's when it started. When we moved, I mean. That's when mother—Penelope was her name, and she was very beautiful —she began working in a cocktail lounge. And drinking. A lot of drinking. Then, that summer . . . Mother became very distant. We fought a great deal. And she would hit me sometimes. Slap me, you know? But one time, when I'd come home late from school, it was pretty awful and she was sorry afterward. Put ice on my black eye, and everything. I thought maybe that was the end of it. That she'd gotten the anger out of her system."

"But it happened again?" Taylor asked softly.

"Yes. Many times. And then she met this guy," Brandy said with a shudder. "Matt. I guess he picked her up at the cocktail lounge. She never said. But he moved in with us. And, at night sometimes, when she would be working . . . he'd be there at home with me. And he . . . he—"

The image of Matt Benson and his stout, hairy body was so vivid in Brandy's mind that a wave of nausea overtook her. She could see him unzipping his jeans. Sitting on the bed. His thick arms forcing her down to her knees. His strong hands shoving her face into his lap.

Taylor's expression turned somber. He could feel his jaws tightening as he asked the question he did not want to hear the answer to. "What did he do? Touch you? Take advantage of you?"

She nodded. "He . . . he made me do things to him. I told Mother about it. I begged her to make him move out. But she said I was lying. At the time I was doing some modeling at a local clothing store. Just weekends, but she knew how much I enjoyed it. And she threatened to make me quit unless I stopped making up stories."

"And is that when you ran away?"

"That was the first time, yes. To Nashville. I met Derreck there, the . . . uhh, photographer."

She paused, remembering that first night in Nashville. The smeared glass doors of the bleak bus station. The smell of sizzling grease from the snack bar.

She'd stood there, clutching her small brown overnight bag. Feeling quite lost. With nowhere to go. Hardly any money.

Derreck Reiger had been leaning up against the candy machine.

"Looking for work?" he'd asked nonchalantly as she deposited the quarter she had allotted herself for dinner.

She'd regarded him warily, rescuing her Clark bar, saying nothing.

"Ever done any modeling?" He'd followed her over to a wooden bench and watched her gulp down the candy. "Jeez, you must be starving. Lemme get you a hamburger."

He was tall, with thinning, flyaway hair and small, active eyes like matching ball bearings, constantly in motion.

Eventually he wore her down with his friendliness. She went home with him. Home, such as it was. A small, untidy photographic studio.

She wasn't happy there. But she stayed because she felt safe. Derreck paid her five dollars an hour to model lingerie. Catalogue work, he said. And she didn't mind.

"Just pretend you're wearing a bathing suit," he advised.

He never touched her. She slept in a small twin bed near the makeshift kitchen. And used the bathroom to change clothes.

It was when he brought the other man around that she became suspicious. Mr. Saperstein. Middle-aged, balding and unctuous. He wore a black pinstriped suit and smelled of too much after-shave.

"He's rich, honey. Big publisher from New York. Two hundred dollars for this job. Be nice," Derreck had warned with a wink.

She didn't like what they asked her to do. She'd cried, thrown a tantrum, locked herself in the bathroom.

But Derreck had coaxed her out and had given her a small pink pill to "relax," he'd said. The pill had had a marvelous effect. she'd felt weightless, as though she were drifting through space. Dreaming. Going through the motions, but not really there.

It wasn't until afterward that she realized what kind of a performance she'd given, and for whom.

"Saperstein likes it that way, what can I tell you?" Derreck had explained over Chinese food that night.

He'd taken her out for dinner. A treat, he'd said since she'd been such a "good girl." But she hadn't been able to eat. She couldn't stop thinking about what she had done.

She could see herself clearly, lying on that Oriental rug. Naked except for the thin gold chain around her waist. Moving her legs to the rhythm of the soothing instrumental music flowing from the stereo.

"Great, great. That's very good, sweetie," Derreck had encouraged, clicking away with his Leica.

She had hardly noticed the blinding strobe lights. The studio seemed hazy. Everything was diffused. The two men like abstract shadows moving in and out of the dimness. Nothing to do with her.

She'd draped herself over a green velvet chair. Her legs falling to either side. Her arms extended. An elusive smile on her face.

She'd stood on one leg, kicked the other to the side. And held her balance. Like a ballerina in a hallucinatory trance.

And then there was another girl. A petite brunette with large turquoise eyes. Also naked. Leading her back to the rug. Lying next to her, touching her, making her turn over, and—

"Just stop thinking about it, will you?" Derreck had complained in an irritated voice as he finished the chow mein. "A few pictures. Who cares what you had to do. Or how Saperstein gets his rocks off, for that matter. You made two hundred smackeroos, honey. That's all that counts."

"When do I get the money?" she'd asked dubiously.

"End of the month, with the rest that I owe you. What's the matter, don't you trust me?"

She didn't. But she'd had no choice. And when Derreck insisted that she learn to shoplift she had gone along with it. Promising herself she would leave just as soon as she got the money.

But two weeks later she was arrested in a large department store. The police sent her back home to Atlanta.

Taylor was watching Brandy's face intently as she finished her story. Even though he'd heard her utter the words, he couldn't imagine how she'd managed to survive such a devastating childhood. That this fragile young woman had gotten as far as she had despite the obstacles she'd faced amazed him.

He had a new sense of respect for her.

A new feeling of compassion.

"I'm . . . I'm not proud of anything I did, you know," she apologized, looking down at her long, thin hands.

"I know you're not," was all he could manage to say at first. Then he inched closer to her on the ottoman and touched her shoulder with his hand. "You know, Brandy, none of us are entirely pleased with our pasts. We all have secrets. But your burden has been excessive. And you're paying for it now. More than you thought you'd ever have to. I think you're doing a remarkable job of holding yourself together."

Taylor stayed in New York for three days, sleeping in Brandy's guest bedroom at first. During the days, they took long walks together, carefully disguising themselves in order to avoid the paparazzi. They talked for hours, ordering food in from local delis. They listened to classical music, watched movies on HBO. And the night before he left, they made love for the very first time.

It happened quite spontaneously, shortly after the phone call from Monica. *Vs. the Odds* had been canceled, but Brandy shouldn't give up, the loyal agent had said. After all, she still had her modeling career and. .

"And nothing," Brandy replied despondently. When she hung up the phone, her eyes were moist with tears. And it was Taylor who brushed them away.

"Listen to me, my love," he'd said softly, holding her in his arms. "I know you feel as though your life is over and it's useless to go on. And you have a right to that for a while. So indulge yourself. Go ahead. Cry. Let it all out. But if I know anything about you, I know you're not a quitter. You're going to be right back on top again, no matter what you choose to do. And it doesn't matter to me what that is. I love you, Brandy St. John," he said, gazing deep into her azure eyes. "And the only thing that really matters is that we stay together."

The next morning, when Taylor flew back to California, it was with little enthusiasm. He knew Brandy wouldn't be ready for a trip to Los Angeles for some time, unless her career did a drastic turn-around. And that was too much to hope for.

Unless . . .

Taylor had been toying with the idea for the past couple of days. It was a long shot. But in his estimation it was definitely worth a try. And he couldn't imagine Kate Brannigan turning him down. Not after she'd heard Brandy's whole story. Of course, that would be the tough part, convincing Brandy to do an interview with Kate. An interview for *World* magazine. One that, if handled correctly, could put Brandy back in the spotlight again, clear her name, and give her a fresh start.

The visitors' locker room of the Pontiac Silverdome reverberated with postgame euphoria.

"Way to go, Bro'!"

"Man, we busted their balls, didn't we?"

"Play—offs . . . play—offs . . . play—offs . . . ."

The chorus of low, husky voices grew in intensity and speed until little else could be heard. Waves of euphonious enthusiasm swept through the capacious room, bounced off the lockers, and finally crescendoed in a rally of cheers for the star quarterback.

Don Brocato's ears were still ringing with the frenzied applause of the fans outside. Thousands of astounded, ecstatic fans. Calling his name, rooting for him.

Triumph flickered in his expressive dark eyes as he thought about what those fans had just witnessed.

Surely it would become the most celebrated play of his football career.

There were bloodstains on the white adhesive tape around his wrists. And the lampblack under his eyes had creased and smudged. He looked haggard and exhausted. But he felt energized enough to play the entire game again.

Without warning, and with an eagerness that caught him off guard, a half dozen of his teammates lifted the two-hundred-pound quarterback up onto their shoulders. Just as they had minutes earlier on the field.

But this time they were all in various stages of undress. And totally uninhibited. An overly enthusiastic wide receiver tossed his helmet in the air, smashing a fluorescent light. The halfback next to him hurled a shoe across the room, denting a locker. One thickly built, naked, tight end twirled a damp jockstrap on his muddied index finger.

"Bro—ca—to . . . Bro—ca—to . . . Bro—ca—to," they sang out, rejoicing in the Longhorns' last-second victory.

Max Dunphy observed the flagrant burst of revelry through eyes of stone. After a few minutes he swung out of the glassed-in office reserved for the visiting coach and approached his fevered players.

"Brocato! In here!" he bellowed, shattering the jubilation with his gruff tone and angry glare.

For a brief moment the locker room was absolutely silent.

"Your arm all right?" Dunphy asked as the quarterback followed him into the fishbowl office.

"Yeah. Sure. Just a bump."

Dunphy closed the door and leaned against it. He was a big, feisty

Irishman. A former all-pro lineman. Six feet five inches tall. Two hundred and forty pounds. He'd been on the sidelines for fifteen years. But he worked out regularly. And his enormous body rippled with the muscular definition of a much younger athlete.

When Max Dunphy talked to his players, he commanded and got respect.

"Sit down," he ordered.

Brocato, still in football pants, pads, and a sweat-stained gray T-shirt, flopped onto the tan leather couch.

A self-assured, fiercely determined product of Notre Dame, he had star quality on the field and off. "Brocato looks like a larger version of Tony Danza," a sports columnist had once written, referring to the quarterback's ethnic good looks. And his straightforward manner.

But Don Brocato had no regard for the media. He knew all the glowing adjectives in the world couldn't get him what he wanted most. A shot at the play-offs. During his five years as a pro, he'd never been more confident about getting that shot than he was right now.

Max Dunphy sat down in a swivel chair behind the metal desk, folded his arms, and stared at his star quarterback for a long moment.

"What the hell were you doing out there?" he said slowly, measuring his words.

Brocato brushed a wisp of moist black hair from his forehead and grinned back at his coach. "What do you mean, what was I doing?" he asked good-naturedly.

Dunphy's brow furrowed over. "The straight drop-back Z—OUT. That's what I mean."

"Yeah, worked pretty good, didn't it?"

"I sent in fifty-one counter pass left," Dunphy complained, raising his voice. "What the hell you doing, changing the call?"

"Hold on, Max!" Brocato jumped up off the couch. "Are you off your rocker? The Lions were keying on the halfback and rolling their coverage to the wide side of the field. There's no way in hell that play would ever have gone two inches. And—"

"And you listen to me, Brocato," Dunphy shouted furiously. "I call the plays for this team. Not you. And I've got coaches up in the booth. Professionals, Brocato. You ever hear the word?"

"Max, what—"

"Quiet! We've scouted these guys heavily see? And we know how the Lions' defense will react. It's all worked out. Kinda scientific. What the quarterback is supposed to do is cooperate and call the plays as we signal 'em in. Understand? Pulling a stupid stunt like today could have cost us the game, but instead—"

"Max, you can't be serious—"

"But instead," Dunphy repeated hotly, "it's going to cost you a one-thousand-dollar fine."

Brocato put his hands on the desk and leaned in toward the silver-haired Irishman. Dunphy's face was red with rage and peppered with a roadmap of tiny blue veins. His breath reeked of whiskey.

"What do you mean *fine,* Max? Is this your first day on your new brain, or your last day on your old one? You know damn well I saved that game. I pulled it out of my ass and you ought to be kissing it."

He turned to leave, then added, "And don't start spending that thousand bucks until you get it out of my attorney."

"Your attorney might be keeping you company on the bench, pal," Dunphy said calmly, pouring Bushmills into a plastic cup.

"Don't try and bluff me, Max. You wouldn't do that. You're not that dumb."

Dunphy swallowed hard on the whiskey. "Neither are you, Brocato. You'll pay the fine. And you'll play by my rules. Because otherwise you won't play at all. Now go take your shower."

Kate woke up with a start when the phone rang. But the sound of Seth's voice soothed her back into a dreamy mood.

"Sorry to call you so early, sweetheart. But I'm leaving for New York with my dad in a few minutes."

"It's okay. I'd rather talk to you than sleep."

She snuggled back down into the cushy pillows, and her mind danced with the prospect of a December wedding.

Soon it would be a reality.

Ever since she'd agreed to marry Seth, Kate's life had taken on a new dimension. The gray cloud of depression she'd been battling suddenly disappeared. She seemed to float through the days, feeling more purposeful and self-confident than she had in a long time. Nothing bothered her. Even the normal frustrations of her work.

The piece for *World* seemed less important now. She had failed to come up with a startling hook. But she had given it her best shot. And in a couple of weeks she'd be able to wrap it up.

Only the interview with Renata remained. Something Kate wasn't looking forward to. But she'd get through it. Six months from now it wouldn't matter at all.

At the moment the only thing that did matter to Kate was her future with Seth. She'd tossed and turned most of the night, anticipating his call. Running down the list of things she wanted to discuss with him. Fantasizing about their life together. Their children. Their family.

She had made the decision to convert to Judaism. And knew how pleased he would be.

Sara had been wary.

"What's the rush?" she'd asked the night before. "Jewish is more than seder and Hanukkah, you know, Kate. You might wake up some morning and want to burn his yarmulke. Give it some time."

Kate didn't have to. She knew. She felt so strongly about her commitment to Seth Arnold that sometimes it astonished even her. But she had no doubts. In fact she'd never been more sure of herself in her life.

"I miss you," she murmured into the phone, with a lazy stretch.

"Me too," he said softly.

"Have a good time in Bermuda?"

"Yes. Sure. Always do. Courtney got a little too much sun, and Dad sprained his ankle playing tennis. But that's par for the course."

"I guess," she chuckled lightly, warming to the sound of his deep, husky voice. Wishing he were with her now, in bed.

"Remember the Bel Air Hotel?" she teased, a sultry lilt to her tone.

"I remember," he answered laconically.

"Seth, is someone there?"

"No. I'm alone. Why?"

"You seem sort of, well, I don't know, distant."

"By about three thousand miles. It's a little difficult being intimate on the phone."

"Sorry. I guess I'm imagining things."

"How's it going?" he asked quickly. "Did you ever track down that columnist?"

"Sammy Rollins? 'Fraid not. I tried everything. His health club. His barber. Even staked him out in the *Daily*'s parking lot. Talk about elusive, I don't think the guy exists."

"Any more leads on the dragon lady?"

"No. And to tell you the truth, I don't care. It doesn't matter anyway. I'd rather talk about us." She shifted onto her side, waiting for him to say something.

"Seth?"

"What, sweetheart?"

"There is something wrong, isn't there?"

It was only a matter of seconds, but to Kate it seemed like an hour went by before he spoke.

"Kate, I—"

She sat straight up in the darkness. Instinctively aware that she would not like what she was about to hear.

"What is it, Seth? You have to tell me," she demanded, annoyed with the urgency in her voice.

"Sweetheart, I . . . I can't marry you."

The words froze like ice in her mind. And as much as she wanted to deny their presence, tell herself she hadn't heard them, they remained there. Echoing over and over again. *I can't marry you.* Glacial words. Shattering her heart and dissolving all her dreams.

"What? What do you mean, Seth? I . . . I don't understand." Her throat ached with suppressed tears, but she choked them back, willing herself to stay in control.

"This is very hard for me, sweetheart." His voice quavered, and she thought he was about to cry. "I talked it over, us, I mean, with my folks and—"

"And they told you not to marry me?" she said icily. "You let your parents—"

"No. Let me finish, Kate. Listen to me. I'm not saying we're not going to see each other again. Or maybe get married someday. What

I'm saying is, I'm not ready yet. I need time to feel more established. You know as well as I do that I've never really held down a job—"

"But you work for your father, Seth. What kind of excuses are you trying to—"

"I'm not making excuses, sweetheart. I just want you to know how much I love you. But you . . . please try to understand that it's going to take some time before I feel I'm ready to have a wife and family. That's a lot of responsibility and—"

"And you should have thought about that before we planned to get married," she shot back defensively. "You're the one who kept pushing for it, you know. You're the one who—"

"Yes. Yes, I know that. It was wrong of me. But I don't want to lose you, sweetheart. Right now, though, I just . . . I can't marry you right now."

Kate was silent for a moment. She tried to think. But her thoughts were confused, running rampant through her befuddled brain.

His parents. That was it. But why? They'd always seemed to like her. Inviting her to all the family gatherings. Birthdays. Holidays. Kate had even joined the Arnolds, Seth and his two sisters, at temple on Rosh Hashanah.

And she'd been touched by his family's closeness. Their strong sense of tradition. Being with them on those occasions had given her a great sense of belonging. Something that had eluded her most of her adult life. Something she was looking forward to, once she and Seth were married.

"It's religion, isn't it? And my age?" she gasped brokenly. Her breath strangled in her throat.

"No," Seth insisted. "You're wrong, sweetheart. My folks think you're terrific. And you know I love you. It's me, Kate. I have to be able to stand on my own two feet before I get married. You're so much farther along than I am. I can't start off being dependent on you."

Lies, she thought to herself. *All lies so he won't hurt my feelings. The truth is I was an illusion. A fantasy he created in his mind. When I disappeared, he couldn't wait to get me back. Now that he knows I'm his, he doesn't want me.*

He wants the perfect young Jewish woman. Someone his parents will approve of. Men, what miserable bastards!

She was angry now. Angry and hurt and disappointed. Dimly, through the pounding in her head, she heard Seth's voice.

"Sweetheart, I'm sorry I had to tell you like this—"

"Over the phone, you mean? Oh, why not, Seth? It's easier that way, isn't it? And you always take the easy way out."

"That's not true, Kate. I love you and I always will. It's just that I'm so torn . . ."

His voice trailed off. She could tell he was fighting back tears. And somewhere deep within her she took pleasure in his pain. She wanted him to hurt just as much as he'd hurt her.

"Say whatever you like, Seth," she said, gathering up all her strength. "But the fact is that you led me on. And you let your parents make up your mind. That isn't love—it's infancy. I can't imagine why I wanted to marry you in the first place. You don't have the balls to make a commitment."

She cut him off before he had a chance to speak. And quickly hung up the phone. Then she shrugged into her velour robe and wandered aimlessly around Sara's enormous house, thankful that everyone else was still asleep.

And somehow she managed to block the ripping pain inside her long enough to concentrate on the litany running through her mind. She kept telling herself she had done the right thing. That there was no going back. She'd been a fool to think it would work.

It wasn't until much later in the morning that Kate allowed herself to cry. She threw herself down on the bed and closed her eyes, remembering all his promises. All the wonderful moments they'd shared.

Then she felt the scalding tears well up in her eyes. And the sobs came gushing out with such force that her entire body began to shake.

She cried for a very long time. And as the agonizing minutes ticked by, Kate was gripped with the terrifying sensation that the tears would never stop.

That her insatiable longing for Seth and what they once had would never cease.

That as long as she lived she would never be able to wrench this cavernous pit of emptiness from her soul.

* * *

Teddy Selwyn's stretch limousine was opulence on wheels. A specially designed Rolls-Royce, brown and gold, with a tiger-head grille, and an interior of mahogany and crushed brown velvet.

The passenger area included a tambour bar, foldout tables for gourmet snacks, a television set and VCR, a compact-disc sound system, and a vibrating pillow, which the driver always positioned under the studio chief's silk-stockinged feet.

Teddy adored being driven around when he had nothing better to do. Which was most of the time. He especially liked cruising West Hollywood, also known as "Boytown." The perfect place to ogle a tantalizing display of male anatomy. Most of it for sale.

Sometimes he just looked. Other times he sampled. On rare occasions he made a major purchase and went home with the goods.

Today he was undecided. He'd lunched at the Palm and spent the last ten minutes surveying the Santa Monica Boulevard flesh parade. So far, nothing of interest.

But what was that sauntering past the Safeway?

Teddy pressed his face up against the tinted glass window, peering out at an enticing bleached-blond waif. He was tall, skeleton-thin, and walked with the grace of an alley cat. A silver-plated drop-earring dangled from his right ear. His faded Levi's jeans were skin-tight, with a rip in the back and an obvious bulge in the front.

The boy couldn't have been more than sixteen.

Young and vaguely innocent-looking. Just the way the studio chief liked them.

Teddy was in paradise. Twitching with excitement.

"Pull up here, Bruce, in the Safeway lot," he ordered, wasting no time. "See the one in the ripped—"

"Excuse me, sir," the driver apologized, "but the emergency line is—"

Teddy glanced down at the flashing light on the slender red telephone next to him.

He yanked it up to his mouth, ferret eyes still tracking his blond dreamchild. "Yeah, what is it?" he grunted.

"Woodman here, Teddy. Sorry to interrupt, I wanted to let you know we've finally nailed down who's been buying all that Selwyn stock."

"About time," Teddy grumbled, as the Rolls slid into a parking space.

Bruce sprang from behind the wheel and fled like lightning, in hot pursuit of the bleached-blond kid.

"It seems that the brokerage house doing the volume is Bear Stearns," Woodman was explaining from Century City.

"What do you mean 'seems,' Garth?" Teddy snapped.

"Well, there's no way of being absolutely certain in a case like this. All we really have to go on are the paper transactions. And Bear Stearns has definitely been doing a great deal of trading on Selwyn."

"But who, Garth. Who is the broker at Bear Stearns? And, more important, who is his client?"

"I don't know."

"Well, find out, dammit! How many times do I have to tell you?"

"Teddy, you have to understand something here," Woodman replied evenly. "There are no individuals named on these transactions. Just the firm's name. Finding out who is actually putting up the money is virtually impossible."

"Garth, let me tell you something, old man," Teddy hissed. "Nothing is impossible. For instance, it is very possible that I will pull my account out of Merrill Lynch. And that I will make it very clear to your superior why I did so. You have until tomorrow."

Teddy hung up just in time to see Bruce come trotting back toward the limo. His face was grim as he opened the door.

"No luck, Mr. Selwyn. I'm afraid the young man got away."

Story of my life, Teddy thought with a despondent shrug. But it was just as well. His carnal appetite had subsided considerably.

The conversation with Garth Woodman had vexed him. Selwyn stock was moving quicker than a horny jackrabbit, and the jerk couldn't figure out why.

"Imbeciles," Teddy muttered to himself. "The world abounds with them."

As the Rolls slipped back onto Santa Monica Boulevard, the corpulent studio chief settled into the commodious brown velvet seat and pondered the remainder of the afternoon.

He could return to the office and screen the first cut of the new Alisa Hudson film.

Or stop at Bijan and buy a new suit.

At the moment, however, a steam and a massage seemed much more appealing.

Sara tottered toward the double glass doors marked *World,* feeling like one of the Marx Brothers on a highwire. Her short arms were extended unsteadily, balancing a heavy picnic basket and three bags of food in one hand. A bottle of wine, a stadium-sized Thermos, and a box marked L.A. Desserts in the other.

Her feet moved slowly, uncertainly, ankles wobbling with each step. Her small frame teetered back and forth.

She was afraid to look down. And she couldn't see anything but packages when she looked up.

"What the hell am I doing *schlepping* all this *chazzerai*?" she grumbled aloud to herself, finally reaching the entrance.

Visiting your friend, a little voice answered. *So be nice.*

With an audible groan, Sara sagged against the sturdy plate glass and jabbed the night-bell with her elbow.

It had been a lousy day. Meetings since nine o'clock. Lunch with a tyrannical network executive who'd announced over dessert that two of her studio's series were being canceled. A long confrontation with an actress who was refusing to accept the fact she'd been fired. And a call from Mark, asking when he could see the twins.

She'd left the office at eight, reeling from the pressures of the day and the automatic angst that her estranged husband's voice always triggered.

She hadn't felt like driving all over town, picking up food. But she had promised. Kate was on a deadline, pulling an all-nighter. Sara knew that otherwise she probably wouldn't eat. She also knew how desperately her friend needed cheering up.

She hoped this would help. But she doubted it.

Kate had lapsed into a devastating depression. As high as she'd been when the wedding was on, that's as low as she was now. She'd said nothing about what had happened with Seth. Just that the engagement was off.

It was unusual for Kate to keep her feelings bottled up inside. And Sara could tell by her friend's despondency that this malaise was something she was not going to snap out of quickly.

Thank God she has a new assignment, Sara was thinking, as she watched Kate approach the door. *Maybe it'll help keep her mind off Seth.*

Kate was wearing a rumpled ankle-length army-green dress. Looking pale and drawn. Her eyes narrow and tired.

She reached up to shove a pencil into her frizzy red ponytail, then unlocked the door. Sara could tell her smile was false.

"Aha, the rescue squad. And none too soon," Kate said, with forced enthusiasm.

"How's it going, Ace?" Sara asked, handing her the picnic basket.

"Okay. Not great. Let's take this stuff into the office."

"What do you mean, *stuff*?" Sara objected, with mock indignation. "Chinese chicken salad from Ports. Mushroom pâté from the Irvine Ranch Market. Brie and fruit from Gelson's. And chocolate cheesecake from L.A. Desserts. That's *stuff*?"

"Enough stuff to make me feel stuffed," Kate replied, trying to be funny, but realizing it was a futile charade. She felt as though she were in a coma. Her mind trapped somewhere in a steel vault.

A noon deadline tomorrow, and she hadn't written a usable word. The thought of food revolted her. She wasn't hungry. She hadn't been hungry in days.

With a thud, Kate placed the picnic basket on a walnut coffee table.

"Not to mention the Soave from Vendome and the cappuccino à la Café Silverstein," Sara continued, waving the Thermos in the air.

"You didn't!" Kate's forced smile became a wide grin. "You're just too good to me."

"Somebody has to be. You've had to deal with enough *tsuris beliten* to last a century."

"Sympathy I don't need."

"Part of the package. Take it or leave it." Sara uncorked the wine.

Kate watched the clear liquid splash into the glasses, and her troubled eyes flickered with affection.

"This is really nice," she said, sipping the Soave.

"The wine or the TLC?" Sara teased as their glasses clinked in a toast.

"TLC, smartass," Kate answered, strolling over to her desk. "But the wine doesn't hurt." She stared down at the computer screen. "I seem to have brain-drain tonight."

"But you just got started," Sara said encouragingly. "Doesn't it always take a little while to get your lead?"

"Five hours is more than a little while, Sara. And I didn't tell you the latest. Russ Stevens called from New York tonight. Seems he's decided to bump this up from a Q & A to a feature-length profile."

Sara's face lit up. "That means three pages, doesn't it? My God, Kate, that's terrific. Imagine what a break this could be. Not just for you but for Brandy too. You said yourself her interview was wonderful. The piece might even turn the network's thinking around."

"I know. That's what Taylor's hoping," Kate said glumly. She sat down and scowled at the words on the screen. "Do you think he'd like to write the story for me?"

"You're perfectly capable and you know it," Sara protested, peering over her shoulder. "Let me see what you've got so far."

"Nothing readable," Kate said, punching the scroll button.

Sara's hazel eyes traveled quickly down the screen over Kate's attempted leads.

> Brandy St. John aka Brenda Vreesen aka Grace Bjorling. Three identities. One young woman. A tragic life.

> Brandy St. John. She had the kind of fairytale career little girls fantasize about back in Atlanta. But growing up in Atlanta was really a nightmare for the . . .

> She was a dreamlike figure floating through the fast-paced, glamorous world of modeling and show business. A starlet on her way to the top. Then the bottom dropped out.

When the words stopped, Sara was silent for a long moment. Wondering what to say. How do you tell your best friend her writing is dreadful?

"So, you have a little block," she offered finally. "Happens to all writers, doesn't it?"

"Not to me. Never like this." Kate shoved the chair back and got up. Her face a mask of frustration.

Arm in arm, they walked toward the coffee table.

"Look, you're probably just worn out, and hungry—"

"That's not the problem, Sara. And you know it."

"Yes. I do know it." She took a seat on a barrel chair opposite Kate. "I also know you won't do anything about it. You won't talk about it. You won't even return Seth's calls."

"There's no use in returning his calls," Kate said wearily. "Nothing he can say is going to make a difference."

Sara leaned forward and observed her forlorn friend for several seconds.

"But you love him, Kate."

"Past tense."

"And I don't believe that for a minute, Kate Brannigan. You can't just snap your fingers and stop caring for someone. Give him a little time. Probably he just got cold feet and—"

Kate shook her head slowly. "No, Sara. It's more than cold feet. It's . . . well, it's an impossible situation."

"You didn't feel that way a week ago."

"A week ago I was fooling myself."

"About what?"

"Seth, his age, his—"

"What kind of cockamamy talk is that? Age doesn't mean *bupkes* anymore. Look at Mary Tyler Moore and that young doctor she married. Debra Winger and Timothy Hutton. Juliet Mills and Maxwell Caulfield—"

"This is different, Sara . . . Look, I've never told you this before. Probably because I knew what you'd say. And I didn't want anyone to burst my bubble."

A troubled expression swept over Sara's face as she listened. She could tell Kate was embarrassed.

"Seth isn't just young in years, Sara. He's terribly immature in so many ways. In fact . . . in fact, he still lives with his parents," she admitted with a sigh, anticipating Sara's reaction.

"But I thought he lived with you!"

"For several months. Then it was back to Mom and Dad."

"You mean at twenty-five he's never had his own apartment?" Sara reiterated incredulously. "Never been on his own?"

"Never."

"Oy, vey!" Sara exclaimed, beginning to understand. "Honey, that should have been your first warning. Only child?"

"Two sisters. Both older," Kate replied, aware of what she was thinking.

"And he's close to the folks?"

"Like glue."

"They broke the engagement?"

"Right on."

Sara shook her head slowly and said in a gentle voice, "You might not want to hear this, sweetie pie. But it sounds to me as though Seth is a real prince. Probably a mama's boy to boot. And if that's the case, no woman is ever going to be good enough for him."

"I know." Kate's voice cracked with emotion. "I mean, I think I know that now. But I miss him, Sara. I really did love him so very much. And for such a long time I thought he loved me."

"Well . . . I'm sure he does . . . in his own way," Sara soothed, feeling inadequate. Trying to find the right words.

"If he loved me he'd have married me." Kate's chin trembled and her blue-violet eyes turned misty.

"Don't be so hard on yourself, hon. Can't you see he couldn't marry you? Not because he didn't love you, but because his love wasn't mature enough or strong enough. He's like a child, Kate. Still letting his parents make his decisions."

"I wanted it to work, Sara. I tried so hard," Kate whimpered, tears trickling down her pale cheeks.

"Ah, *bubuleh,* I'm so sorry for you," Sara comforted, wrapping her arm around Kate's shoulder. "But you're really so much better off without him. His family would always be there, you know. Interfering. Mucking things up. Someday you'll realize that."

"I guess," Kate murmured, choking back a sob. "I just can't stop thinking about him. Even in my sleep. I wake up in the middle of the night, wishing he were there, just to hold me. And tell me everything is okay."

"I'm sure that's very normal," Sara sympathized, handing her a paper napkin.

Kate dried her eyes, but instantly they were moist again. "Oh, Sara, I just feel so lost. And I don't know what to do."

"Time, sugar," Sara sympathized. "It's going to take time. All I can tell you is what my mom used to say. 'A door is closed and a window opens.' I wish I could do more than that."

"You can't, I know," Kate said through her tears. "And it's my own fault, really. I had this little fantasy and it just didn't work out."

"Nothing wrong with reaching for rainbows, Kate. That's the only way to get what you want. But sometimes—"

"You fall on your face," Kate concluded, with a watery smile.

"Yes. And then somebody comes along to pick you up. This time it's me."

20
Beverly Hills, California 1937

■ Cappy Desmond grimaced into the blinding California sunlight and stared out at the topiary gracing his magnificent backyard.

He had no desire to meet his daughter's train. The station was all the way downtown, far too long a drive. And he'd already made several social commitments for that particular Sunday afternoon.

Higgens would have to fetch her, in the Duesenberg.

"She's a rather, ahh, well-built teenager," Cappy explained to the chauffeur. "Dark hair. Green eyes. She'll have a trunk or two. For God's sake, be careful. I would hate to see any nicks on the car."

Her train was due at eleven A.M.

With any luck it will be late, Cappy thought, ambling across the patio to the breakfast table. Neither the blueberry muffins nor the morning paper tempted him.

He was far too preoccupied with his daughter's impending visit. And the deleterious effect it would have on his usual freewheeling social life.

He couldn't imagine why she'd decided to return to Shangri-la for the summer. She could hardly consider it home anymore. She hadn't been back in years. Her nanny, Consuela, was no longer on staff. So what was there for her to return to? Certainly the girl had no delusions about his affection for her.

Or maybe she did. If so, he held Clarissa Devereaux responsible. Meddlesome busybody, with her presumptuous letters. What business was it of hers telling him how to run his life, as long as he paid the bills?

Each summer Cappy had wired two thousand dollars to Madame Devereaux, more than enough to cover Renata's expenses. The old woman had refused the money at first, but he'd insisted.

Now he would gladly write a check for three times that amount if only it would ensure his daughter's indefinite residence abroad.

Cappy unfolded the *Los Angeles Times* and examined the headlines distractedly. His manipulative mind humming with possibilities.

Perhaps she'll find it terribly unappealing here and reconsider, he thought, smiling. *Yes, perhaps she'll find it so distasteful that she'll want to rejoin the Devereauxes in France immediately.*

"Coffee, sir?" the maid inquired meekly.

"Of course," Cappy snapped. He took coffee every morning with breakfast. Why did the lamebrain always have to ask?

"Will Miss Desmond be wanting breakfast, sir?"

"No. She'll be too late. Lunch perhaps, but I won't be here."

If he had to face Renata, far better to do it late in the day, after a couple of belts of gin. Make that several belts.

Cappy leaned back in his chair and stretched. Well, he would make the best of it. She was almost an adult now. If she insisted on staying, surely she would find her own friends and not interfere with his life. He'd be away for several weeks anyway, making arrangements for the New York bureau of *The Hollywood Daily.*

The trade paper was doing remarkably well, better than he'd expected. Better than anyone expected. They'd all laughed at first. Not one studio had been willing to purchase an ad. But Cappy had been determined.

He was convinced he had a phenomenal idea. Since the onset of the talkies, more and more attention had been focused on Hollywood. What the town needed was its own newspaper for and about the entertainment community. What could have been more logical?

It was an expensive endeavor, at first. He knew he'd be operating in the red. But the money was incidental. Cappy Desmond was already worth millions.

Since he'd never invested in the stock market, the crash of 1929 hadn't affected him. All his money was tied up in California land. And with his real estate empire thriving, Cappy was ready to diversify. He needed a project. A new challenge. He needed to take a risk.

Launching a newspaper would certainly be risky. But he felt, instinctively, that a no-nonsense daily, printing accurate news about what went on behind the scenes in show business was bound to be a success.

The premiere issue of *The Hollywood Daily,* featuring endorsements from many of Cappy's celebrity friends, rolled off the presses on December 4, 1929. His plan was to deliver the trade paper free of charge for the first year.

Within six months it began to catch on. The studio chiefs, directors, producers, and actors who had resisted at first started talking among themselves. They liked what they read in the *Daily* because they were reading about themselves—and each other.

For the first time in the history of motion pictures, Hollywood had a clearinghouse for information. A newspaper that went behind studio gates to get the inside story. The deal-making, the scandals, the glamorous lives of the stars, and the all-too-frequent heartbreaks that accompanied celebrity—it was all in Cappy Desmond's fledgling trade paper.

"Why buy the *Times*?" he was fond of saying. "If anything newsworthy happens, you'll read it in the *Daily.*"

His peripatetic reporters were omnipresent, infiltrating every movie location, party, nightclub, and private conversation in town.

The Hollywood Daily began turning a profit in the spring of 1931. And by that time the trade's publisher was well entrenched in the show business community. Studio moguls such as M-G-M's Louis B. Mayer and Columbia Pictures' Harry Cohn made it a point to socialize with Cappy Desmond. Big box-office stars, such as Greta Garbo, William Powell, and even the Marx Brothers, sought him out at parties and restaurants.

Aligning oneself with Cappy was considered a very clever move in the thirties. He was a man of great vision and power. He had an uncanny overview of the entire movie industry. His daily editorials were discussed over lunch at the Brown Derby and over drinks at the Carleton Café.

Cappy had created his own showcase, and cast himself as the central player. By establishing *The Hollywood Daily,* he'd changed his image from a frivolous bon vivant to a shrewd and fearless impresario. And that was just the way he wanted it.

Of course, he had competition. Two more trade papers had sprung up since the *Daily*'s inception—*The Hollywood Reporter* and *Daily Variety.* But Cappy welcomed the rivalry. He always moved a little faster when someone was nipping at his heels.

Secretly, he admired Billy Wilkerson, publisher and editor in chief of *The Reporter.* Wilkerson was a tough, self-made entrepreneur. Resilient and stubborn, but honest. And Cappy respected that.

He wasn't sure he'd feel the same way if Wilkerson's circulation were larger than the *Daily*'s. But he wasn't worried. *The Hollywood Daily* consistently outgrossed both of its rivals. Cappy Desmond didn't foresee that changing.

Savoring the last swallow of coffee, Cappy reached inside the pocket of his hand-tailored trousers and extracted a neatly typed list of the day's activities. First, a formal luncheon at the home of studio chief Jake Selwyn, followed by an afternoon of tennis. Later, drinks with his good friend Will Rogers. And, finally, a festive dinner for twenty at Cappy's favorite restaurant, Chasen's.

He'd be escorting the sensational-looking young starlet, Sunny O'Day. Their first date. She'd been playing hard to get, and he was looking forward to finding out whether she was worth all the trouble. Probably she wasn't. They seldom were.

His sexual appetite was notoriously insatiable. He had bedded almost all of the town's most glamorous women. The others, he just hadn't gotten around to yet. His affairs were always brief. His love-making technically perfect. His dialogue always in check.

Cappy was a man who never discussed his feelings. Love was a word he never used. An emotion he chose not to remember.

"Well, we're a bit ahead of schedule," said Higgens as he wheeled the silver Duesenberg up the steep, winding, palm tree–lined private road. "I imagine your father will be surprised."

Yes, won't he though, thought Renata, reaching for her red-leather handbag. She extracted a small compact and checked her appearance, wondering what he would think.

She had matured into a strikingly beautiful young woman. Creamy-white, luminous skin. Widely set, magnetic emerald eyes. Thick blue-black hair cascading over her erect shoulders and down her long, shapely back.

The curves of her graceful body belied the odd shape of her youth. She was tall—five feet eight inches. And lissome. And there was a presence about her. A certain aristocratic gentility in her manner. An aloofness. An arrogance in the way she carried herself.

Would he be surprised at how much she had changed? He had no way of knowing what to expect. She certainly hadn't sent him any pictures. And she'd stopped seeing Dr. Bruener when she was fourteen. What was the point? Her father hadn't objected. He hadn't cared.

Higgens brought the car to a stop in the cobblestoned forecourt. "Why, there's Mr. Desmond now," he announced cheerily.

Renata felt a burning sensation in her stomach. Odd. She hadn't been nervous earlier. All of a sudden she was trembling.

He was walking toward her now. White trousers. A navy blue jacket. Gray spats. That tight, priggish smile and curlicue mustache. The same buoyant steps she remembered so well.

"Welcome home," Cappy said flatly as Higgens opened the door for her. And then his expression changed ever so slightly. "My . . . my, but you've grown up."

"Yes. The Ugly Duckling returns," she replied, green eyes mocking him.

"Well, now, that's a bit harsh," he laughed uneasily as Higgens struggled with the trunks in the back of the car. "Come." He took her arm and guided her up the steps to the house. "Your room is all ready. Would you like breakfast?"

She could feel his eyes on her as they walked into the foyer.

"No, thank you. I'm not hungry. I think I'll just unpack."

"The maid will see to that, Renata. I, ahh, was just on my way to a luncheon," he said, a look of mild astonishment still on his face. "Don't suppose you'd like to join me?"

"No."

"Well, then, I'll be off. There's a dinner at Chasen's tonight, though. You must come. Seven o'clock. I'll be back to pick you up."

He brushed his lips against her cheek and turned to leave. But he paused at the doorway and looked back dubiously, as though gazing at a vision that would swiftly disappear.

Renata stood in the foyer for several moments after her father had left. And a smug smile of satisfaction crossed her mouth. It would be easier than she had thought. He was captivated, already under her spell. Within time she could probably get anything she wanted from him. And make his life miserable, as well. Spending the summer at Shangri-la was definitely going to be enjoyable.

* * *

The Venetian-style dinner dance that Cappy staged in Renata's honor three weeks later was ostensibly a belated birthday party.

"Seventeen. A very special age. We must celebrate," he'd announced one morning.

She knew it was just his way of showing her off. Now that she was presentable again, he was proud of her. A beautiful bauble to brag about. Just as he had when she was a child.

The party took place on a balmy evening in late June. And Renata waited an hour before making her entrance, mainly to irritate her father.

She'd chosen a ravishing floor-length gown of emerald-green taffeta. The vivid color intensified the shade of her extraordinary eyes. The massive hoop skirt emphasized her small waist. The scoop neckline showed off her firm, rounded breasts.

Cocktails were well under way when she swept down the winding staircase. And the moment she stepped inside the triple-arched entrance to the ballroom, a hush fell over the room. The music softened. Conversations dwindled. And heads turned. It was immediately apparent to all one hundred fifty guests that Cappy Desmond's daughter was a show-stopper. She didn't so much enter a room as she overwhelmed it.

Cappy was at her side immediately. "My darling, you're tardy. Our friends have been waiting," he whispered, kissing her lightly on the cheek.

She shot him a derisive look. "Come, come, Father. You're perfectly capable of handling a crowd like this. You did it for years without me."

Cappy flushed hotly for a second and felt the lines of his face grooved to the bone. She was constantly making those cutting remarks. Chastising him. Mocking him. The meek child he had sent away to Switzerland had returned a saucy, sophisticated, condescending young woman. Her flip attitude and caustic comments absolutely infuriated him.

At the same time, he liked it. Cappy admired women with spunk. Especially a tantalizingly beautiful woman who had the courage to defy him with her tongue. It wasn't often he found a female of such single-mindedness and self-assurance. Now he had found one under his own roof.

Since the first day of her return to Shangri-la, Renata had managed to set her father off balance. Her presence frustrated him. Confounded him. And aroused him.

He could feel his pulse race now at the mere touch of her skin. The delicate scent of lilacs in her thick, dark hair.

Arm in arm, they circled the room, greeting guests. She danced with a number of young men who asked if they might call on her. Whenever she noticed Cappy watching her on the dance floor, she would purposely throw her head back and smile, aware of how sensational she looked. The dazzling debutante, enjoying herself to the hilt.

And why shouldn't she? This celebration was, after all, the payoff. Her night in the spotlight. Her reward for all the years her father had neglected her.

She would make him regret it.

She had decided to avoid him the entire evening, and had no trouble doing so. When she wasn't dancing, she was engaged in conversation, playing the femme fatale.

She knew her behavior irritated him. That was precisely the point. As the night went on, his fury increased. And Renata reveled in her triumph.

It was two in the morning when the band finally stopped playing. Relieved, she excused herself and retired to her bedroom before Cappy noticed.

He was leaning up against the redwood bar, telling a long story in a loud voice, and gesticulating boisterously. A smattering of guests stood by, smiling politely. Cappy Desmond had consumed far too many double gins. It was quite obvious. But it was not unusual.

Upstairs in her newly decorated room, Renata kicked off her high heels, unzipped her constricting ballgown, and watched it fall in a heap at her feet. With a sigh of relief, she stripped off her underwear, slipped into an ivory silk robe, and reclined on the velvet-covered Regency chaise longue near the window.

She was exhausted, yet exhilarated. Transcendent. Overcome with a pleasant rush of excitement. Her limbs felt fluid. But her mind raced, reviewing the events of the evening.

Everything had happened just as she had intended.

She had timed things perfectly. She had made a spectacular im-

pression on her father's friends. She had been invited to several
parties and luncheons within the next few weeks. She had felt like a
princess swirling about the dance floor in her magnificent green
gown.

Yet somehow, sitting here alone in her room, none of it seemed
real.

It is real, she reminded herself, closing her eyes, dreamily. *You
were the star tonight. Nobody can take that away from you. You've
earned it.*

With a graceful cat-like stretch, she opened her eyes again and
gazed at the frilly, feminine bedroom. It was done in shades of lavender and pink. Eclectically decorated. There was an oblong etched
mirror. A chubby club chair. An art-nouveau writing table. And a
big double bed covered in pink satin. Huge, fluffy pillows sat like
lavender clouds at its head. Renata had supervised the decorating
herself.

Francine would adore it.

Damn Francine, who cares about her?

You do. You want her back and you know it.

I do not! She's getting married.

*So what? She hasn't marched down the aisle yet. You know you're
hoping she'll get good and tired of Henri over the summer. That's why
you haven't written. You want her to miss you so much she'll come
running back.*

If she has any sense, she will.

Renata moved over to the bed, dropped her robe, and slipped
between the cool, freshly laundered sheets. She tossed and turned for
a while. When she finally dozed off she could feel Francine's arms
encircling her.

It was four in the morning when the bedroom door opened.

She didn't hear it. She didn't hear his heavy footsteps. Or the
sound of his belabored breathing. She was still asleep when he slid
under the satin coverlet next to her. But when she felt his hot, moist
chest pressing up against her back, she woke up. And gasped.

Her body stiffened in terror.

He flung his arm across her, pinning her to the mattress.

"Don't—" she pleaded.

But he covered her mouth with his hand and moved on top of her.

In the darkness she could barely see his face. When his mouth came down upon hers she wanted to scream. But he kissed her harshly, with such intensity that she could barely breathe.

"I won't hurt you," he whispered.

His hands roamed eagerly over the gentle curves of her bare silky skin. And he moaned his pleasure in quick, excited gasps, kissing her again and again.

Then he eased himself downward. His hands caressing her long, graceful torso. His tongue tracing a line from her breastbone, past her slender waist, over her flat stomach. Enrapt in his own sybaritic delirium, he forced her thighs open. Then quickly plunged his tongue down deep into the folds of her moist, tender flesh.

She writhed, attempting to twist away from his insatiable passion. But his hands anchored her firmly in place, and his tongue dipped deeper, stroking the very depths of her being.

She started to scream but held back. She knew she was hopelessly under his power. Dominated by his viselike grip. Controlled by his lusty strength.

And so she would submit to him. Allow him to take her. To pleasure her. To adore the body he'd once so carelessly rejected. Yes, she would be his, this time. And the next time. For she knew he would want her again.

But she would use his passion to her own advantage. Giving him just enough to make him hunger for more.

Renata relaxed her hips, undulating to his rhythm. She bent her knees slightly, contracted her abdomen, and arched her back.

He moved up farther, holding her tight. The air was heavy with the commingling of their bodies, the musky smell of sex.

She closed her eyes and envisioned Francine. Francine making her tingle, urging her on. And soon she began to feel it. That overwhelming surge of excitement. The sudden burst of unbridled passion she'd experienced so many times before.

But she knew immediately that this was different. Stronger, more intense. This was magnificent. Exquisite. Achingly, almost painfully, erotic. An incomparable rolling, rippling release that seemed as though it would never end.

"Oh, oh, my God!" she cried out.

Renata was exploding, floating, soaring, orbiting in some unbelievably thrilling ionosphere she'd never visited before.

And Cappy Desmond was right there with her.

He never mentioned it. Neither did she. But he came to her room as often as twice a week that summer. Each time, he was inebriated. And each time she would resist his advances at first, knowing that her cool restraint further aroused his lasciviousness.

He never forced intercourse upon her. She assumed it was because he thought she was still a virgin. She wasn't. She'd made love with several young men and had found it far less enjoyable than she'd hoped.

Yet heterosexual sex did have its advantages. There was a certain sense of omnipotence in allowing a man to touch you all over, even undress you, and still not let him have you. Watching a man work himself into a frenzy gave Renata tremendous pleasure. And she relished the manipulative powers of sex.

That summer she acquired many beaux and went out to dinner, movies, or parties almost every night. Although Cappy was caught up in his usual social whirl, he was frequently in the library around eight o'clock. Just in time to meet Renata's date.

On those occasions her father's cordiality bordered on the solicitous. He would go out of his way to make her young man feel comfortable. Inquiring about his work or schooling. Offering a sherry. A cruise on his yacht some Sunday, perhaps?

Renata knew it was all an act. He was jealous. He wanted her for himself. She could see it in his eyes.

And she could tell by his lavish gifts just how desperate he was to keep her. At least once a week a package wrapped in frilly pink paper would arrive by messenger.

The first time it was a bottle of Chanel No. 5. The next, a pair of hand-tooled, imported-leather, high-heeled shoes. And another week, an elegant necklace of diamonds and silver, with delicate drop earrings to match.

By the end of the summer he was sending her satin negligees, fine, handmade lace bras and panties, and silk slips in a variety of styles and colors.

Renata adored being pampered. Each time the messenger arrived, a little thrill of exhilaration would rush through her. And she could never wait to take the package upstairs, always tearing into it immediately in the middle of the foyer.

But she never thanked him. Only when he noticed her wearing one of the gifts would she show any sign of gratitude. Even the day he found her posing in front of a mirror, admiring the Norwegian blue fox jacket he'd selected, Renata's only comment was, "Nice, Father. But fox . . . it's so pedestrian, don't you think?"

If her chilly behavior bothered him, he never let on. Cappy was far too enamored with Renata to question her attitude. In fact, he rather enjoyed the challenge of trying to please her. And the more he was around her, the more he wanted her.

One morning at breakfast he casually suggested that she consider attending college in California. He was skimming through a copy of the *Daily* at the time, so he didn't notice the satisfied smile that crossed her lips.

"No, Father. Really, France is the place to be, you know. The people there are so, ahh, how can I explain it? So *soigné*, sophisticated. So refined."

"Still, you have spent so much of your youth in Europe, Renata—"

"Because you shipped me off, like so much damaged goods, Father. You remember?" she said icily. "I do."

He did not respond. Nor did he raise the subject again.

He did not object when she told him of her plan to rent an apartment in Paris. He arranged for her to receive a monthly allowance of fifteen hundred dollars, far more than she'd requested.

The week before she left, he insisted on accompanying her on an all-day shopping spree, which resulted in a three-thousand-dollar fall wardrobe.

She was surprised when he didn't come to her room the night before her departure. She was even more surprised when he offered to drive her to the train station the next morning.

They took his new white Cadillac and said very little on the way. As she was about to board the train, he put his arms around her and held her close for a few seconds. Then he kissed her fully on the lips, stepped back, and studied her face.

"I want you back with me soon," he said determinedly.

Their eyes locked as if in combat.

And then she was gone.

21

■ Kate sat down. Took a deep breath. And gazed at the distinguished-looking woman across from her. Doctor Laura Bernstein's face was long and sharp-featured. She had striking silver hair swept up in a pompadour. A small moonstone pin on the lapel of her raw-silk suit jacket. And the most intriguing eyes Kate had ever seen.

They were a mystifying blue, the color of lapis lazuli. Deeply set and warm. Almost charismatic, Kate thought as the session began.

She was feeling distinctly more comfortable this time. During her initial appointment, Kate had done more crying than talking. And the forty-five-minute session had quickly dissolved into a very expensive half-box of Kleenex.

Afterward, feeling frustrated and foolish, she'd written a check for eighty dollars and left. Convinced a shrink was not her answer.

But Sara had urged her to try it once more. And here Kate was, searching for the right words to convey all the anger and confusion she'd been harboring. There were fewer tears this time. But the pain was still there gnawing at her.

Laura Bernstein observed the troubled journalist with keen interest, nodding occasionally. Her handsome face was impassive, But her mind worked quickly and precisely. Like a computer. Inputting, storing, comparing, and sometimes discarding information.

She'd been practicing psychology in Beverly Hills for some twenty years. And for the past decade she'd specialized in upwardly mobile female professionals.

Many of them, she had found, shared the same predicament. On the way to the top of their professions they'd sacrificed a personal life. Those who had husbands or lovers usually discovered they'd chosen the wrong kind of man.

Kate Brannigan's story was unique in circumstance, typical in nature. And like a number of Dr. Bernstein's other patients, she had begun to dabble in self-analysis.

"I just don't know," Kate concluded, as she finished capsulizing the last few years of her life. "I think I'm addicted to him."

Laura Bernstein's smile was as warm as her mystifying eyes.

"No. I don't believe that's the case, Kate. Oh, don't get me wrong. I'm certain that breaking off with Seth is triggering your depression. But you are not addicted to him. He is not your problem. He's merely a symptom of something that goes much deeper. The real problem, Kate, lies within. Seth can't fix that. Only you can."

Kate stared at her blankly. "I . . . I don't understand."

"I didn't expect you to. That's what we have to work on. Tell me, Kate, what are your feelings about Seth? How do you see him now, as a person?"

Kate's tired blue-violet eyes shifted to the right and focused on an ormolu clock on the mantel. Her face turned pensive.

"I see him as . . . as a very young man, struggling to find his way. Sort of lost. Unsure of himself. Learning what it's like to be an adult."

"And what can he offer you?" Dr. Bernstein asked in a gentle voice.

"Nothing," Kate replied laconically.

"That's right, nothing but some occasional sexual energy and empty promises."

Kate's eyes moistened and she reached for a tissue. "But I miss him so much. And I'm sure he loves me."

"He does love you," Dr. Bernstein said emphatically. "But that doesn't change anything, does it?"

"No."

"So what are your choices, Kate?"

"To go crazy or get through this somehow," she answered, looking down at her clenched, white-knuckled hands. She felt absolutely helpless, like a little girl who couldn't find her way home.

A subtle tone of authority entered Dr. Bernstein's voice. "I'm certain you won't go crazy. But how do you intend to get through this trying time?"

"I was hoping you'd tell me," Kate answered despondently.

"I would like to do that. And I want you to know you are not alone. Many women your age are facing similar situations. I have more than a dozen patients much like you. They're finally ready to marry and have children but find themselves in relationships with inappropriate men. There are ways of looking for the right kind of relationship, Kate."

"But how can you tell a relationship is wrong when you're in it and enjoying it?" she inquired, disconcerted.

"You have to ask yourself what it is you're enjoying. Part of the reason you stayed with Seth was because you could control him."

A look not unlike anger fell over Kate's face. "But I *didn't* try to do that. He was just always around."

"I'm not accusing you of anything, Kate," the analyst continued calmly. "You didn't set out to run Seth's life. But he was there whenever you needed him. And you grew to depend on him. He became your 'warm fuzzy.' Someone you could lean on. He was loving and kind. And he took care of you. Better than you'd ever taken care of yourself. It isn't so much Seth that you're missing now, Kate, but the nurturing he provided for so long."

Kate considered Laura Bernstein's words in perplexed silence.

"A few minutes ago," the doctor continued, "you told me that you are a workaholic. And I believe you are. Most people look forward to a time to kick back. They plan vacations. You're more likely to plan your next writing assignment. Am I right?"

Kate nodded. the truth was she'd never planned a vacation for herself.

"Before Seth came along, your life was out of sync. You probably never took time off to enjoy yourself—to play. He balanced things by sharing his 'child' with you. When you were with him everything seemed more fun. Seth was your instant vacation. He provided you with the emotional stability you've never been able to give yourself. Now you're going to have to start doing that."

"How?" Kate asked dubiously.

"Slowly. But realize something first. You are suffering from mild depression. You're in what we refer to as a survival state at the moment. It's as though you are swimming in the middle of the ocean. So far out you can't see the shore. All you can do is keep stroking."

"You mean working, functioning? I manage," Kate replied curtly.

"Yes, I'm sure you manage. But you don't feel very good about yourself, do you? What we need to do is to get you to a place where you can accept what's going on in your life and make the best of it, not drag yourself down by looking over your shoulder at the past. Eventually you'll be able to put more energy into expanding your horizons socially. Make an effort to get out and do things other than work. When you feel you are ready, start dating."

Kate sighed heavily and crossed her arms.

"But none of this is going to happen overnight, Kate. And the very best thing you can do right now is keep telling yourself that it's all right to be alone. You don't need Seth, or anyone, to make you whole. The sooner you accept that, the better off you'll be."

"But I want a relationship. I don't want to be alone the rest of my life."

"And you won't be," Dr. Bernstein reassured her. "That small dark cloud you've been towing around is not going to attract a desirable man very quickly, though. And, were a desirable man attracted to you at the moment, I don't think you'd recognize it—not even if he hit you over the head with a baseball bat."

An amused smile crossed Kate's lips.

"You see, you almost laughed," Dr. Bernstein said lightly. "One more thing before we stop for today, Kate. I'd like to leave you with a visual to think about."

"What?" Kate asked, puzzled.

"A mental picture of the way things are inside you. Right now you are like a two-story house in total chaos. It's a mess in there, with furniture, dishes, linens, silverware, everything flying around hitting you in the face. Slapping you in the back. Tripping you. It's a horrible place to be, but there is nowhere else to go except the attic. Now, what do you see up there?"

"It's light," Kate answered instinctively, "airy, and calm—very peaceful."

"Exactly," the psychologist agreed with an encouraging smile. "The attic is the only place you can find solace and tranquillity. You can totally relax there, and that makes you very happy. For the past year, Kate, your only way up to the attic has been Seth. Now he's gone and there is no ladder. You're going to have to climb back up there all by yourself."

* * *

The Epicurean was Muffet Selwyn's favorite restaurant in all of Palm Beach. She loved going there. She especially loved sitting in one of the private rooms for two. And she loved it even more when her date happened to be good-looking, macho, and sexy.

This one was. Too bad he was all business.

Muffet poked at the half-eaten filet mignon with her fork and glanced up from her plate.

He was certainly a turn-on, this tall Texan who'd flown all the way from New York to take her to dinner. She just wished he'd quit yakking about the dumb stock.

Muffet knew nothing about stock, except the kind her mother-in-law used to make chicken soup from. And she'd never really mastered that, either.

All the financial mumbo-jumbo Tex had been throwing around the past couple of hours made absolutely no sense to her. But she was listening enthusiastically. Nodding every so often. Pretending to understand.

What Muffet really needed was a hit of coke. But that was out of the question. She didn't want to risk what it might do to her senses. Besides, Tex was too much of a hunk to be left alone.

So she was biding her time. Trying to be patient. Hoping he'd ease up a little and enjoy the moment. Notice how terrific she looked in the new Kamali. Didn't he see how great the lavender silk played up her eyes?

"Now, little lady, what do you think?" Tex was saying as he leaned in toward her.

The closer, the better, she thought, shifting slightly so that the lavender décolletage fell away from her glorious bosom.

"Gee," she purred sensually, blinking at him through a tangle of long brown lashes, "It's like I'd do anything to screw Teddy over, you know? I mean, I really hate the fucker."

R. B. McDevitt suppressed a laugh and gulped some ice water. She was a character, this one. Not that he hadn't been warned.

"A cute little wacko with a magnificent upper torso, a baby face, and no class," was how his financial consultant, Miles Durville, had described her. "Best thing we've got going is she loathes her ex."

R.B. had assumed Muffet would be a pushover. So far, however, the little minx had been evasively noncommittal. And something was telling him there was a strain of street-smarts beneath that unruly mass of frosted frizz. Either that or she was just too dumb to comprehend what he was offering her.

He pondered his next move and decided on assuming an air of confidentiality. "Well, Muffet, I can certainly sympathize with your feelings about Teddy. From what I've heard, he didn't treat you too well—"

"Wow! That's an understatement!" she yelped, reaching for a Salem and watching him light it for her. "Do you know what the sleazebag used to do? He'd bring a couple of his weirdo boyfriends around and make me watch."

R.B. shot her an incredulous look.

"No kidding. He'd tie me to a chair. It was disgusting. And sometimes it went on for hours."

Muffet took a long drag on the cigarette and blew three angry smoke rings into the air, as though she were trying to expel whatever tainted essence Teddy Selwyn had left within her.

After a few moments, R.B. asked, "How long were you married?"

"Too long. Eight years. I must have been drugged." A slight smile crossed her hot-pink lips. "Come to think of it, I was most of the time," she added, with a high-pitched ripple of laughter. It sounded like breaking glass.

Muffet exhaled a few more rings and sipped on the remains of her third martini. "I just can't imagine why I married the pervert in the first place."

R.B. cleared his throat, considering his words. His dream of owning a Hollywood studio rested entirely on the whim of this embittered, top-heavy temptress. She owned five percent of Selwyn Studios' stock. Swing shares.

No matter how many shareholder votes R.B. was able to accumulate, it would be impossible to win a proxy fight unless she was on his side.

He couldn't afford to say the wrong thing.

"Well, now," he began, compassion oozing from his voice, "you sure did get a bad deal there with Teddy. But you can't blame yourself for marrying him, you know. Life's funny. We all make mistakes. We all get hurt and we all get angry. Trick is to turn that hurt and anger into something positive. And with what I'm offering, you could do that, sure as shootin'."

Muffet stubbed out the cigarette and swung her eyes up to study his uncertainly. "What do you mean?"

"Well, for starters, when I take over Selwyn Studios, first thing I'm going to do is give Teddy the old heave-ho."

She threw him a look of ecstatic disbelief. "You mean you could actually fire the bastard?"

R.B.'s bushy eyebrows shot up involuntarily. *Street-smart she isn't. Just plain dumb. New game plan.*

He moved in a bit closer. Gave her his most alluring grin. Lowered his voice seductively.

"Of course I'll be able to fire him, Muffet. See, that's the whole idea of taking over the company, to change everything, including management. And in this case—"

Muffet's mind raced with the possibility of what she'd envisioned so many times. Even had dreams about. Teddy lying helplessly on the ground. Flailing his porky arms and legs. Pleading for mercy. A colossal steel container hovering overhead. All of a sudden, it opens, releasing an entire ton of fetid, squishy, dark brown globs.

Teddy Selwyn buried in turkey turds. Just what he deserved.

But losing his job to a handsome Texas hunk. That was even better.

"So what do I have to do?" she asked, indigo eyes glazed with triumph.

R.B. touched her bejeweled hand gently. "All you have to do is vote for me. That's it. I know you signed some papers that prohibit you from selling your stock. But I want you to know that once I'm in, Muffet, I'm going to make you a very rich lady. And I'm going to make you a promise right here and now. What I'm going to do when I'm running the studio is give you an option on one million shares at eight dollars per. Do you know how much money you could make on that?"

She shook her head, blinking up at him adoringly. His strong fingers on her hand released a hundred fluttering butterflies in her stomach.

"Four million dollars, based on the current price of the stock. What do you think of that?"

"I think I'd like you to take me home for a nightcap so we can get to know each other better," she sighed suggestively.

"I suppose that could be arranged," he drawled, motioning for the check.

Muffet Selwyn's skin went all tingly with anticipation.

Her heart palpitated uncontrollably.

When she stood up her legs went weak, for she imagined the virile Texan between them.

The phone call from the portfolio manager at Updike Mutual had come as a complete surprise. And it took Teddy Selwyn three days to recover.

He'd gone off on a tirade at first. Firing a half-dozen employees, just for the hell of it. Then he'd holed up in his geodesic-domed house for two days, ordering deli from Nate n Al's.

The onion bagels, Nova Scotia, and cream cheese always had a tranquilizing effect on him. The noodle kugel and the potato knishes did wonders for his attitude. There was something about the satisfying, leaden food that made Teddy feel all was right with the world.

He felt the same way whenever he stepped into his executive bathroom, which was where he was now. Pacing back and forth across the marble floor. Feeling stronger but still working on control. Control would be essential in the meeting.

He'd already lost some leverage by agreeing to a neutral location. A suite at the L'Ermitage Hotel.

But he planned to win some back by being late.

Besides, he needed time to think. And this was the perfect place to mull over his plan.

The executive bathroom adjoining Teddy's office was immense, and luxuriously decorated with an abundance of malachite.

The lustrous, silky green ore was everywhere. Covering the tissue box. Embellishing the toilet seat. Framing the pictures of Teddy as a boy with George Burns and Jack Benny. Even the marble floor and sink were resplendent with traces of the extravagant virid mineral.

Malachite soothed Teddy. It had been the predominant theme in his mother's bedroom, where he'd spent many happy hours as a child. He found its presence both calming and reassuring.

Whenever depressed, it was to his lavish malachite bathroom that

Teddy retreated. Here, the most difficult situations came into focus. Decisions were made. Problems seemed less severe.

Today was different. The longer he paced, the more agitated he became. What Teddy was about to do absolutely infuriated him. All that money. Twenty-five, no, probably closer to thirty million. Robbery, that's what it was. Upscale robbery!

If only Garth Woodman, that imbecilic excuse for a stockbroker, had done his homework it wouldn't have come to this.

But there was nothing Teddy could do about that now. He didn't have a choice. He had to make the offer.

The alternative was unthinkable.

Happiness was nonstop activity. And Kate was certainly getting her share.

She sped across town in the Peugeot, reflecting on the past few days. And wondering about the most recent development.

She couldn't make sense of it. Alisa Hudson wanted to talk to her.

"This is an exclusive, Ms. Brannigan," Hillary Stone, publicist, had explained on the phone. "I assume you are aware of Miss Hudson's low profile. In the thirty years our firm has represented her, we've set up fewer than a dozen interviews. Yours is one of them. The only thing I ask is that you run the story in *World* immediately. Is that possible?"

"Yes, yes, or course," Kate stammered excitedly. "But what is the nature of—"

"I'd rather leave that up to Miss Hudson," Stone replied crisply. "Suffice it to say the subject is newsworthy. By the way, Miss Hudson requested you because of your fine work on the Brandy St. John article."

"Why . . . ahh . . . thank you," Kate replied, too overwhelmed to ask the publicist why she had never returned her calls before.

For weeks Kate had been phoning Hillary Stone in a futile attempt to set up an interview with Alisa Hudson. Hoping the reclusive actress would agree to read Letty Molloy's cryptic letter and answer some questions about Renata Desmond.

Now, by some strange quirk of fate, Alisa Hudson, four-time Oscar winner, was asking for Kate. It was the best news she'd had in weeks. Exciting enough to make her spirits soar as she raced along Sunset Boulevard to meet Sara.

Kate was late. But Sara didn't mind. She was enjoying herself, sitting in the sunny front-porch section of Le Dôme. Watching the steady stream of Hollywood's elite pour through the enormous glass doors. Nodding to some. Chatting with others. Holding her own little private court.

Everyone who was anyone in Hollywood did lunch at the elegant French restaurant. Studio executives. Producers. Directors. Writers. There was usually a smattering of celebrities. And always a gaggle of MAWs (models, actresses, whatever) draping themselves around the circular bar.

There were three main dining areas. Each one bulging with enormous egos and buzzing with talk of deals. Here, dealing had been refined to a cliquish art form. Over iced tea and Shelly Berger salads, projects were set. Fees negotiated. Secrets traded. Careers made and broken.

It was the kind of place where rumors traveled like sand gnats.

And Sara loved it all. Lunch at Le Dôme always made her adrenaline surge. Today it was doing double time. Because she had something to celebrate.

"Sorry to keep you waiting, kiddo," Kate apologized as she approached the table. "Had to make some last-minute calls to New York."

"No problem, Ace." Sara said, nodding at a waiter to pour some champagne. "What's up?"

"Weird stuff," Kate answered, sitting down.

"Beats depression all to hell," Sara replied with a wink. "How are things in the attic?"

Kate laughed gently, watching the bubbling white foam rise to the top of her glass. "Haven't quite made it up there yet. But I am seeing Dr. Bernstein again next week."

"Glad to hear it," Sara said enthusiastically. "So, what's weird?"

"Cary called this morning."

"Cary? As in Eckhart? As in your former New York roomie?" Sara asked, astonished.

"One and the same."

"What for?"

"To congratulate me on the Brandy St. John piece."

"And well he should," Sara said, lifting her glass in a toast. "You notice we're drinking Taittinger Blanc de Blancs? The network's going with *Vs. the Odds,* after all, Kate. Starting next week. And your piece did the trick."

"You're kidding! Oh, Sara, that's terrific! How absolutely fabulous for Brandy!"

"And for your reputation at *World,* I should think. I drafted a letter to your editor, Russ Stevens, in New York this morning, telling him what a fabulous journalist you are."

"Sara, you didn't—"

"I most certainly did. Least I can do, considering you helped save Brandy's career. I can't believe the attention she's getting. Even *60 Minutes* is after her."

"I know. Monica told me. She's thrilled."

"She should be. Think of the zillions the old broad is going to reel in," Sara laughed, scanning the menu. "By the way there's a party for Brandy on Monday night. Chasen's, at seven. But I wouldn't show until eight if I were you. The press is invited for cocktails, and I'm sure it will be a zoo."

"Will Harding be there?" Kate asked offhandedly.

Sara peered up over the menu, scrutinizing her friend's face. "Why?"

Kate shrugged. "Just wondered. You haven't said much about him lately."

"He's in town," Sara replied vaguely, without looking at Kate.

"That much I know."

"And his divorce is final."

"And?"

"And he's talking serious, Kate. Like living together," Sara said softly. "I'm not up for it."

"You're not?" Kate asked, surprised. "But I thought that—"

"So did I," Sara replied, shaking her head back and forth. Not anymore, though. Not for me, anyway. I don't know what it is, but all of a sudden he's lost his charm."

"Maybe you're just frightened of making another serious commitment so soon," Kate suggested.

"Well, it would be nice to have the ink dry on my divorce papers before I have to make any decisions," Sara said with a sigh.

"What's the status there?"

"Who knows! Mark's lawyer keeps haggling about community property, holding up the works. At this rate, we'll still be married in the year two thousand."

Kate pondered what she was about to say for a moment. Then asked, "Could Mark be having second thoughts?"

"Are you joking? Our phone conversations last about three seconds. And most of that is dead air. If he was thinking about a reconciliation, he'd have a little more to say" She sighed. "Could we please change the subject?"

"Sure."

"So what's with Cary?"

"I don't know."

"He called because he's ready to rekindle the old flame?" Sara suggested mischievously.

"He didn't say so. But . . . he is separated."

"Aha! He's ready, all right. What about you?"

"Mixed," Kate answered. "He asked if we could have dinner sometime soon."

"And?"

"And I said I'd have to think about it."

"Smart," Sara agreed. "Better talk to Laura first."

"Good God, Sara! I don't have to consult with my shrink about every little decision."

"Can't hurt," Sara replied, beckoning the waiter. "How's the Renata piece coming along? Almost done?"

"I wish!" Kate answered with a pensive look. "Actually I just called New York to ask for an extension. I have something lined up next week that might change the course of the story."

"Oh? Like what?"

"Can't say." Kate's smile was smug.

"To your best friend, you can't say?" Sara complained.

"Only that it involves an interview with Alisa Hudson."

"Alisa Hudson?" Sara gasped. "What a coup. You ought to be leaping through the air right now. I'd think just that would be enough to send you straight to the attic."

"It did, for about five minutes." Kate took another sip of champagne. "I'm working toward a lifetime pass."

Teddy Selwyn and R. B. McDevitt were about as compatible as a rattlesnake and a mountain lion. That was apparent within seconds of their meeting in the split-level suite at the L'Ermitage Hotel.

Neither of them saw any reason for pretense.

An inaudible hiss and an imperceptible snarl hung heavily in the air. Rancor and repulsion radiated from their brief hellos.

They did not shake hands but sat down abruptly. And the meeting commenced, with a conspicuous absence of cordiality.

As host, Teddy spoke first.

"You were smart to accept my invitation, McDevitt. You're going to save yourself a lot of trouble this way. And make some money besides." He shook his head in a disgusted manner. "You guys are something, you know."

"How's that, Teddy?" R.B. asked, with feigned naïveté.

"Cut the crap, McDevitt. I'm on to you, see? And I know what you want. My sources tell me you've accumulated eleven percent of my company's stock and—"

"Check that, Teddy," R.B. interrupted with a stiff grin. "Twelve percent, as of this morning." He crossed his arms neatly over his pinstriped suit jacket. And stared back into the studio chief's small, dark eyes.

"All right, twelve," Teddy repeated impatiently. "I also understand you've been visiting banks and mutual funds, talking about launching a takeover—"

R.B. held up a long-fingered, deeply tanned hand. "Wrong again, Teddy. I'm not just talking about it. I'm doing it. With the help of those nice people at the institutional houses you just mentioned, I've been able to get thirty-six percent of the stock committed my way. Now thirty-six plus twelve gives me—"

"I know how to add, McDevitt," Teddy snapped, doing some fast mental arithmetic. *Forty . . . forty-eight percent. Holy shit! The fucker's moving faster than I thought he was.*

R.B. recrossed his arms, watching Teddy's jaw tighten. Wondering what thoughts were warring in the fat man's warped little mind. He had a pretty good idea.

"Listen, McDevitt," Teddy said finally, in a confidential, almost friendly, tone. "You know as well as I do that forty-eight percent isn't enough for a takeover."

"I'm working on that," R.B. replied placidly.

"Well, you can stop. Because I'm going to give you what you want, pal." Teddy droned the last word as though he'd like to chew it up and spit it out. "So you listen carefully, because this is a take-it-or-leave-it offer."

R.B. sat in silence, thoroughly enjoying the intensity of the moment. Teddy Selwyn was wasting his time. But it was sure fun watching him do a slow burn. He wondered how fractious the bloated scumbag would get.

"What I'm prepared to give you," Teddy was saying, "is two dollars over the current price of the stock. And the way I figure it, McDevitt, you stand to make a profit of close to fifty million."

The studio chief's puffy lips drew back in an uneven, self-congratulatory smile. It was going to cost more than he'd figured. But worth every penny if it meant cutting this *putz* loose.

"Sorry, Teddy. No sale."

R.B. watched his adversary's tiny brown eyes widen in his fleshy face.

"You see, greenmail isn't my game," the Texan explained further. "I'm not out to grab a quick profit like Saul Steinberg did from Disney. Or T. Boone Pickens from Unocal. I don't rape companies, Teddy, I regenerate them. And that's exactly what I intend to do with Selwyn Studios. Restructure. Reorganize. Turn it back into the winner it was before you got hold of it."

Teddy's blood pressure soared. His pasty-white face turned bright pink.

"There is no way in hell you'll ever get your greedy hands on my studio, McDevitt," he hissed with a venomous look. "So hop off the damn soap box and take the money, if you want to play it smart."

"Smart?" R.B. asked with a cunning smile. "Why don't *you* play it smart for once, Teddy? You've spent five years running Selwyn into the ground. Now that I own such a chunk of it, you'd be real smart to give me representation on the board. Save yourself some trouble, and some money. Three seats will do nicely, for a start."

Teddy was tongue-tied with rage. So angry he could barely think.

His mind a tangled web of virulence. He wanted to scream. He wanted to strangle R. B. McDevitt. He wanted to kick him in the groin.

Instead, he forced himself to count to ten slowly and silently.

Then he stood up. Adjusted his Nino Cerruti velvet jacket. And said in an impassive, well-modulated voice, "Your suggestion is so ludicrous that it does not merit comment."

R.B. watched as Teddy did a dramatic ninety-degree turn on his imported Bally heels and marched toward the door.

"Is that right?" he called out cheerfully. "Well, I'm not so sure about that, Teddy. I guess we'll just have to let the shareholders decide."

Quintana was fuming as she sat down on the Breuer chair in the reception area of Swerdloff, Waxman, and Jacobs. She yanked a copy of *Esquire* off a glass-and-chrome side table. Flipped through it quickly. Checked her Patek Philippe watch. And silently cursed herself for being early.

An entire hour early. What could she have been thinking of?

Who knew? Quintana's life seemed a series of wrong turns these days. Her mind was on overload. running rampant with a stupefying conglomeration of hopes and fears. Leaving little room for order.

Her nerves were fried. And threatening a complete blowout.

Running Par Excellence out of the house she'd rented in Beverly Hills had become increasingly difficult. People were always underfoot. Except for Sundays, Quintana had absolutely no privacy.

The truth was, she could not concentrate.

Somehow she got through it all. Supervising her staff. Planning parties and dinners. Meeting with clients. Smiling and laughing at the appropriate times. She operated on automatic, like a fast-paced culinary robot.

No one suspected the anxiety that swirled up inside her. The sleepless nights. The devastating turbulence of mixed emotions, from longing and loneliness to jealousy and rage.

No one, that is, except for Sam Waxman. Sam had been Quintana's attorney for fifteen years. He was the one person she trusted with her innermost thoughts. And the only person capable of convincing her she could survive without Renata Desmond.

So it was with tremendous relief that Quintana finally bustled into Sam's office, sweat glistening on her overheated face.

He met her at the doorway and planted a fatherly kiss on her moist cheek.

"How's my girl?"

"Better now," she said tersely, settling into the maroon leather chair across from his desk.

He sat down to face her.

"What's wrong," she asked suspiciously. "Why are you looking at me like that?"

"Like what?" he said with a short laugh. "You walk into my office and already I'm offending you?"

"Sam, you know what I mean. You look distracted. Upset. What is it?"

"Quin, please. Quit overreacting," he soothed in a gentle voice. "I'm, ahh, just a little perplexed."

"I knew it. What's gone wrong? We're still going to win the palimony suit, aren't we? I'm still going to get half the estate?"

"Quintana," Sam said sternly, "I never promised half."

"Well, a third, then—"

"I hope so, my dear." Sam stroked his salt-and-pepper goatee. "But there is a bit of a complication that I—"

"What complication?" Quintana interrupted anxiously.

He reached for a pile of correspondence on his right and pulled out a thin manila folder.

Quintana's cinnamon-colored eyebrows arched curiously.

"This," he said, extracting a yellowed parchment document and handing it to her. "I received it yesterday from Alf Bendel, Renata's attorney."

Quintana's eyes grew wide with disbelief as they flickered over the neatly typed paragraphs.

"What the hell is this?" She looked up at him, dumbfounded.

"Something you signed a long time ago, apparently," Sam explained. "I thought you told me you had no living agreement with Renata. But according to this, she's exempt from giving you a nickel, should you walk out on her."

"But . . . but . . ." Quintana sputtered angrily. "I never signed anything of the sort. This is a forgery, Sam."

"Are you sure about that?" he asked warily. "Take a moment to think. It is dated 1968, you know. A very long time ago. Perhaps it merely slipped your mind and—"

"Not *my* mind, Sam. I did not sign it. There is no question."

His crystal eyes studied her for a long moment. "Well, that's perturbing. As you can see, the document has been notarized. Now I suppose I could put a trace on the notary records and—"

"Yes. Why don't you do that, Sam? The sooner, the better. Meanwhile tell Bendel we're not backing down so easily," Quintana ordered, hoisting herself out of the chair.

"Very well, Quin." He got up and escorted her to the door. "I'll phone you tomorrow. And just remember, you're one resilient lady. Everything is going to work out all right," he said, giving her arm a quick squeeze.

Quintana was shaking by the time she got to her gold Mercedes. And for a while she just sat there in the bleak underground parking garage, assimilating all Sam had told her. Sifting through her frantic thoughts. Searching for an idea.

She wasn't going to give up. She knew too much about Renata Desmond to let her deal the last card. There had to be a way.

22

■ Brandy had been standing for so long in the spiky satin sandals that her feet were throbbing with pain. But she looked like a storybook princess in the shimmering white beaded gown. And her exquisite face mirrored the merriment of the party-goers surrounding her.

For two hours they'd been pouring into Chasen's festive California Room. Which had been strewn with tinsel and colorful balloons for the occasion. A four-foot ice sculpture spelling out Brandy's name dominated the sumptuous buffet table. And each guest had been given a T-shirt with *Vs. the Odds* emblazoned on the front.

All of Hollywood loved a celebration. Especially a free one. And this spectacular promotional party, bankrolled by Culver Studios, had drawn not only an admirable showing of movers and shakers but a wildly enthusiastic throng of reporters and television crews as well.

Overwhelmed by the nonstop interviews and accolades from the media, Brandy stood near the back of the room. Chatting with reporters. Posing for stills. Smiling effervescently into the blaze of hot television lights.

Every so often she would sneak a glance to the right, where Taylor stood watching. Nodding his approval.

Over the past several weeks Brandy and Taylor's relationship had changed drastically. She'd begun to rely on him as a source of strength. He'd become more than a friend. Taylor had taken on the roles of protector, mentor, and lover as well.

The press had made much of their union. Some columnists predicted marriage. Others speculated that they were merely living together.

They weren't. Not yet. But Brandy and Taylor refused to comment. They were well aware of the value of conjecture in the media. One thing was quite obvious, however. The two were inseparable, spending as much of their free time together as possible. Speaking on the phone at least four times a day.

They were more than a media couple. Brandy and Taylor had a relationship that Monica Chase described as "rock-solid."

The motherly agent observed the two now, as she reached for a piece of cracked crab from a mountainous platter of succulent seafood.

"What a blessing, my dear," she whispered to Sara, "that your handsome brother has taken our Brandy under his wing."

"Works both ways," Sara pointed out. "Now maybe he'll finally settle down and get married."

"Marriage!" Harding remarked with a mischievous grin. "Let's drink to that." He handed Sara a glass of red wine.

"Ohhh? Are wedding bells in the air?" Monica quipped insinuatingly.

Sara smiled evasively.

"Did I mention that you look spectacular tonight?" Harding whispered in Sara's ear as Monica disappeared into the crowd.

"Not bad for a conservative old broad, huh?" Sara extended her arms, flaunting the buff-pink charmeuse Adolfo.

She was pleased with her new look. Which was basically her old look. Expensive, classic designs. Understated elegance. A noticeable lack of rhinestones and sequins. Sleek, tasteful shoes. Her natural soft, sandy-blond hair.

Gone were the hair ornaments. And Pelo Nafti. She could thank Kate for that.

The split with Nafti had been a bitter one. With him threatening lawsuits. And swearing he'd send her "before" and "after" shots to *Vogue* to prove his point.

Kate had laughed, wanting to know which before and which after.

Sara sipped the Zinfandel and surveyed the fanny-bumper scene at hand. The room was jammed with network and studio VIPs. All reveling in the unrealized success of a television series that had yet to make the air. But was bound to be a hit.

It had to be. She'd just dumped a negative fifty thousand into promotion.

Sara sighed, surrendered her wineglass to a passing waiter, and gave Harding a tired smile.

"Duty calls. Gotta work the room," she announced, moving away from him.

He caught her hand and held it. "What about later? Your place or mine?"

"Please, hon," she said, with a hint of irritation. "It's been an awfully long day."

"Yes, but it could be an even longer night."

"We'll see," she answered and turned to greet a CNN reporter.

Chasen's powder room was hardly intimate, with the presence of a watchful attendant. But Monica was glad to have a moment with Brandy.

"Terrific. You're doing just terrific," the agent enthused watching her glamorous client in the mirror. "Taylor says you're carrying it off like a real pro tonight."

"Thanks, Monica," the lissome blonde replied, dusting on a touch of mauve blush. "He's just so sweet. I only wonder . . ."

An anxious frown fell over Brandy's enchanting face.

"What is it, dear?"

"Monica, how do you think Taylor feels? I mean, he never complains. But after all, I'm the one getting the attention. His series isn't doing so well and—"

"Ah, but you must remember, pet, that he's getting his fair share of publicity by just being here with you. *Entertainment Tonight. People.* Margo Green with her camera crew. Not to mention the local press. Nothing to sniff at for an actor on his way up."

"I guess you're right," Brandy agreed, reaching for her lip gloss.

"I am. Believe it," Monica said with finality. "Just don't worry your pretty head about him. Especially not tonight. Tonight is just for you, Brandy. It's your official launching. You'll see. I told you you'd be a star."

She planted an affectionate kiss on her protégée's cheek and was off.

"Now don't dawdle. I'll see you inside."

Brandy stood before the mirror, fluffing her hair. Staring into her own azure eyes. Wondering how it had all happened.

A star. A media darling. Reinstated in the public eye.

Overnight she'd gone from a shamed, out-of-work model to a

highly sought-after actress. With her own show. And more money than she'd ever dreamed of making.

Monica had seen to that. A tough negotiator, the crusty agent had held her ground, demanding thirty thousand dollars per episode. Twice what Brandy had been making before the network canceled her series.

No, it wasn't a fantasy, Brandy thought, giving herself a final check in the mirror. It was her life. A wonderful life to be lived and enjoyed.

Chance, she mused as she opened the door. How uncanny the role it plays in the whole scheme of things. If it hadn't been for Kate Brannigan's extraordinarily sympathetic piece in *World,* none of this could have happened.

Brandy's mind traveled back to the harrowing night when she'd first met Kate, quite by chance. In the ladies' room of that Greenwich Village restaurant. So many miles away.

That they had stayed in touch all these years was remarkable.

That their paths had crossed again at this propitious time in Brandy's career was a twist of fate for which the actress knew she would be eternally grateful.

Taylor's face froze in an expression of disbelief. His fingers tightened, threatening to crush the cut-glass tumbler of orange juice in his right hand. "Omigod," he exclaimed in a harsh whisper. "Who let her in?"

Sara turned slightly to trace the direction of her brother's stunned stare. Past a throng of celebratory journalists, to the entrance of the California Room.

The cause of Taylor's irritation was immediately apparent.

Sara gasped.

And a momentary hush fell over the party.

Renata Desmond had arrived, quite unexpectedly.

At the moment she was gliding past the balloon-festooned reception table. Making one of her show-stopper entrances. Elegantly attired in a stunning black velvet suit. Broad at the shoulders. Nipped at the waist. An exquisite sapphire-and-diamond choker around her slender neck.

As a grinning publicist thrust a press kit and a T-shirt into

Renata's long, gloved hand, the imperial publisher's penetrating green eyes searched the crowd. Glancing over dozens of faces. Finally settling on the most handsome one of all.

Taylor Evans's.

He shot her a look of unmistakable hostility. And turned back to his sister.

"You didn't invite *her,* did you?"

"What?" Sara snapped. "What do you think, I'm *meshuggeneh* or something? I specifically kept her off the guest list."

"Well, here she comes," Taylor said anxiously. "What the hell do I do now?"

"Smile. Be charming. Give it your best performance. And get the conniving backbiter out of here before Brandy sees her," Sara instructed, eyeing Renata's choker.

The large sapphire was emerald-cut. Seven carats at least, Sara calculated. There were cultured pearls, too. And pavé diamonds, studded with cabochon sapphires.

"Renata, lovely to see you. And how distinctly elegant you look. Glorious necklace. Van Cleef?" Sara chirped enthusiastically.

"Cartier, darling. And how kind of you to comment."

Renata's smile was deliberately calculating. She looked up at Taylor and their eyes locked in cold war.

"Such a surprise to see you, Renata," he managed. "Delighted you could make it."

"Yes," she agreed, accepting a glass of Dom Perignon from a circulating waiter. "Normally I don't bother with the promotional treadmill. But this is an occasion, after all."

She held the champagne flute up in a singular toast. Her sultry eyes studying his face. The finely chiseled nose and jawline. The neatly trimmed wheat-gold mustache. The angry amber eyes, blazing rockets of hostility.

"I'm terribly sorry, but you must excuse me," Sara was saying. "It's showtime!"

Taylor watched his sister step up to the nearby podium.

Renata watched Taylor with increasing anticipation. She had never noticed the strength of his profile. He had an ascetic, keenly etched bone structure no woman could ignore. And she didn't intend to.

She wanted this man. Had never wanted a man so much. And the more difficult he made it for her, the more determined she became.

"Time to introduce the guest of honor, I suspect," she commented dryly, hoping to distract him from Sara's speech.

"That's right," he said, eyes riveted on his sister.

There was a wave of thunderous applause as Brandy stepped up to the microphone.

"Such an angelic child, isn't she?" Renata commented in a syrupy voice. "And talented, too, from what I read. That was quite an article in *World,* Taylor. I understand you engineered the whole thing."

"Not really."

"Oh? Well, then, I am disappointed. I was hoping that little publicity scam had been your brainstorm. And that you were working on another one, equally good, to save your own career."

Despite himself, Taylor turned to face her.

"Meaning?" he said hotly.

"Meaning that your show is headed for disaster, my sweet," Renata purred. She traced a line up the sleeve of his tuxedo with her finger as she continued.

"But it isn't too late, Taylor. I could still provide you with a nice spread in the *Daily.* A little vote of confidence, if you know what I mean."

Her tone was so insinuating that it sickened him. He knew he should not react. A week later he would not be able to articulate why he did what he did. But at the moment it seemed the only thing to do.

With the swiftness of someone disengaging a tarantula, Taylor reached for Renata's hand and removed it from his arm. Then he raised his cut-glass tumbler in the air and quickly upended it.

Suddenly there were ice cubes bouncing from her padded shoulders. Freshly squeezed orange juice trickled down her haughty face. Renata gasped, too shocked to say anything. And by the time she recovered, Taylor Evans was nowhere in sight.

"Brandy, you . . . you shouldn't have!" Kate exclaimed, examining the gold-embossed envelope she'd just received from her friend. "It's far too generous and—"

"Nonsense," the actress countered affectionately. "It's the very least I could do. Treat yourself, Kate. You deserve it."

"But five thousand dollars? That's more than—"

"Forget comparisons. We're talking Neiman-Marcus. This gift certificate probably won't cover more than than two designer outfits. And maybe half a pair of shoes," she giggled.

"No, please, Brandy. Really, I can't. It's just . . . well, it's totally unethical. Tell you what, take me to dinner instead, okay?"

"Girl talk?" Taylor asked, joining them. He slipped his arm protectively around Brandy's waist.

"Sort of," she replied genially. "The journalist is objecting to my thank-you note. Where'd you disappear to?"

"Oh, I've been around, Cinderella," he said. "Watching you. Your speech was great. Warm. Touching. Just long enough."

"I'll second that," Kate offered.

"Thanks," Brandy said, beaming at both of them.

Taylor gazed off into the distance for a moment, a puzzled expression crossing his face.

"Kate, I . . . ahh . . . think you have an admirer," he said with an amused smile. "There's a weird-looking guy with a monocle over near the bar. Keeps eyeing you."

"Oh, Lord," Kate shuddered, with a little laugh. "Jerry Lindner, I'm afraid. My commander-in-chief. Fresh from Europe. Better go roll out the welcome mat. See you two later."

When R. B. McDevitt arrived at Chasen's he did a double take.

Renata Desmond was standing outside, waiting for her limousine. Her expression was grim. Her hair was drenched, hanging around her sour face in lank, wet bunches.

"Nice look, Renata," R.B. guffawed as he passed by. "Tell me, is the sprinkler system on inside, or did you just stick your head into the toilet?"

"Up yours, McDevitt," she hissed, sailing toward her limo.

Chuckling to himself, R.B. swaggered into the festive party room like a stallion primed for a race. He waved to Taylor. Caught Sara's eye. Then scanned the flurry of unfamiliar faces. Searching for Kate.

He spotted her chatting with two men near the bar. And took off in that direction.

R.B. had called Kate Brannigan a number of times since her visit to his ranch. In fact, almost every time he was in Los Angeles. Asking her to lunch, dinner, a football game.

She'd refused each invitation. But that hadn't stopped him from thinking about her. And remembering the way she'd looked the last time he saw her. Dressed in that short, quilted bathrobe. Showing off long, shapely legs. Whenever this image flickered in R.B.'s mind, an undulating feeling rippled through his groin.

He had that feeling now, walking toward her.

It was a visceral response. One he did not question. But one that he knew, instinctively, merited further investigation.

That was the only reason he'd taken time to drop in on Brandy St. John's party. R.B. was wondering whether the elusive journalist would live up to his expectations. By the time he was within three feet of her there was no question in his mind.

Kate was elegantly dressed in a classic royal-blue cashmere suit, with a gold satin camisole and an artistic swirl of copper at her throat.

When she turned to R.B. he noticed that the camisole fell away ever so slightly to reveal a perfectly round beauty mark centered between her breasts.

She offered a cool hello, but not her hand.

After the obligatory introductions, the two men—both of whom the opinionated Texan had pegged as fags—slipped into the crowd. Leaving Kate and R.B. standing side by side.

She was feeling distinctly uncomfortable. Trying to think of something to say as her eyes roamed the room. After a few moments she said, perfunctorily, "Nice party, isn't it?"

"Sure is. And I understand you helped make it happen."

Reluctantly, Kate turned his way. "Well, I wouldn't go quite that far—"

"You don't have to. Everybody else did. That was some writing job, Kate. Fine story."

"Thank you."

"How's your schedule these days?" R.B. teased, watching her face carefully.

"Busy, as usual."

"Seems to me you're always busy. At least every time I call."

"It's my nature."

R.B. laughed and said that reminded him of the story he'd heard a long time ago about the frog and the scorpion. He wondered whether Kate had heard it too.

She hadn't. She was certain she didn't want to. But she didn't have much of a choice.

"Well, it was raining and the pond was flooding over, see?" R.B. began with a devilish flicker in his eyes. "And this frog was struggling to make it to shore before things got worse. He's paddling along like a bandit. *Glub, glub, glub. Glub, glub, glub.*"

Kate stared in amazement as R.B. flailed his arms to the beat of the frog sounds. And she laughed in spite of herself. This was a side of the pompous Texan she couldn't have imagined.

"The frog's swimming along, huffing and puffing. All of a sudden he hears, 'Help me, help me!' It's a scorpion, stranded on a rock. 'Please, frog,' the scorpion begs, 'let me hop on your back and take me to shore. Otherwise I'll drown out here.' "

"But the frog won't let him?" Kate asked, amused.

R.B. shook his head. "The frog wasn't dumb. He knew the danger involved. 'Listen, scorpion,' he says. 'What do you think, I'm crazy? If I let you get on my back, you'll sting me and I'll drown.'

" 'No, no, no! That's simply ridiculous,' the scorpion quickly points out. 'Because if you go down, I'll go down with you. So why would I want to sting you?' "

R.B. paused dramatically before continuing. "The frog thinks about that for a while. And it seems to make sense. So he says, 'Okay.' And the scorpion swoops onto his back.

"They move along for several minutes. Then, all of a sudden, the frog feels this agonizing pain in his back. He shakes and quivers. And there's no doubt about it—he knows he's been stung.

"Now the two of them start sinking. The frog just can't believe it. And with his dying breath, he asks, 'Scorpion, why . . . why did you do it?'

"The scorpion is struggling to stay afloat. But he knows he's a goner too. And just before he drowns he finally sputters, 'I couldn't help it. It's my nature.' "

Kate chuckled, feeling a bit foolish because she knew the joke was on her.

"I see your point," she admitted affably.

"I thought you would." He held her eyes for a long, perceptive moment. Until Kate felt anxious and shifted her glance away.

"You know I, ahh, heard something today that might interest you —about the Longhorns," R.B. announced to her profile.

Kate's blue-violet eyes swiveled back up to his. "And what is that?"

"Seems a rule's come down about interviews. Basically, management put a muzzle on all the players. Nobody talks to the press unless Renata's chief gofer is on hand. Guy's name is Templeton Haight. He's—"

"I know who he is," Kate interrupted. "Since when is this in effect?"

"Today. Tonight. I just spoke with an old pal of mine, Barry Jennings. Team's manager. Seems there's a lot of strange stuff coming down. Ever since the Silverdome game. You ought to talk to Jennings. He might—"

But Kate was no longer listening. She was too busy thinking about the clandestine interview she'd arranged at Will Rogers State Park for the next morning. And wondering whether Don Brocato would show up.

It was one-thirty in the morning by the time the gleaming white limousine rolled down Beverly Boulevard, heading for the Hollywood Hills.

Brandy swung her legs up onto the luxurious European mohair seat and snuggled against Taylor's shoulder. Half-asleep.

"How's the rest of your week, princess?" he asked softly.

She turned and offered her lips for a kiss. "Impossible. And yours?"

"The same. But there's a small dinner party Friday night. A little publicity gathering for *Ki & Company.* Upstairs at the Bistro. And I was hoping you'd come."

"Oh, Taylor, I'm sorry," she said sleepily, "but Nita is flying in from New York. You know, Monica's right hand. There's an agency party for her that night. At Morton's. Maybe we could meet later and—"

"No. No, that's okay. Let's just settle for the rest of the weekend. If we get an early start on Saturday—"

"Saturday?" Brandy said, surprised. She shifted in the seat to change her position and looked directly at Taylor. "But I thought we discussed this before. I'm doing the cover shots for *Glamour* all day Saturday. Didn't I tell you last week? Oh, Lord," she said with a tired sigh. "I guess I forgot. I'm sorry. It just seems like it's one thing after another and—"

He was silent for a few moments, staring out the window at a Pia Zadora billboard. "Hey, it's all right," he said in a low voice.

"No, it isn't. I'm really sorry, Taylor. I—"

"Listen," he said, slipping his arm around her once again. "I know how demanding schedules can be. Maybe you did tell me. Probably just slipped my mind. No problem. We'll go to Westwinds on Sunday."

It was at least a minute before Brandy gathered the courage to tell him. And she felt absolutely lousy doing so, as though she'd actually calculated ways to make him think she didn't want to spend time with him. But she had to tell him. After all, she'd already blocked out three hours on Sunday afternoon for the *Entertainment Tonight* interview. An important profile piece. Five minutes of airtime, minimum. Marvelous publicity. She couldn't afford to cancel.

"I, uhh, Taylor . . . I won't be able to get away on Sunday either." And then she explained.

She couldn't see the disappointment on his face in the darkness. But she didn't have to. She knew how bad he felt.

"Oh" was all he said.

When the limo pulled up in front of Monica's house, he got out and walked her to the door. But there was something missing in his touch. And in their good-night kiss.

On the ride back to his house in West Los Angeles, Taylor kept telling himself it didn't matter. So she was busier than he was. So what? Her career came first. He'd probably do the same thing, if he had the choice.

But that was the problem. He didn't.

Sara was in a dour mood. She placed her elbows on her desk and cradled her chin in her hands. Her forehead felt as though a jackhammer was ripping through it. Her neck ached. She'd been queasy since she woke up.

Shouldn't have come to work, she thought, eyeing the stacks of untouched correspondence and contracts in front of her.

Lousy, rotten hangover!

And she had only herself to blame. Too much red wine. And champagne. And Courvoisier later, at Spago.

Why? she asked herself, taking a gulp of steaming black coffee. *Why the self-destructive act? What the hell do I have to prove?*

Sara heaved a disgusted sigh. And rolled the questions over in her troubled mind. She knew the answers. Had known them all along.

Mark. She missed him. She loved him.

Harding. Sometimes she liked him. Other times she wished he'd get lost.

Transportation. That's what Harding was to her. A cold, clinical, word. Shrink talk. But what better way to describe it? Somebody new to move you away from the person you'd been involved with. Somebody to help bridge the gap and make you feel whole again. At least temporarily.

And that's exactly what Harding Johnson had done. He'd transported Sara from the depth of depression back to a place where she could recognize herself.

She still liked Harding. But she wasn't in love with him. And that bothered her. Made her feel guilty. Like a user, which the whole cockamamy town was full of. But which Sara Evans Silverstein had promised herself she would never become.

So what could she do? Let Harding down easy? Over dinner somewhere or at his Beverly Hills Hotel bungalow? No! Why should she? He was good company. And a loyal friend. There had to be a way to work it out and not hurt him. He was too nice a person for that. Besides, she wasn't ready to let go completely.

The phone blinked and buzzed once, jarring Sara out of her melancholy.

"Your brother is here," her secretary announced.

"What?" Panic crossed Sara's face as she glanced at her date book. Taylor's name was neatly printed next to eleven o'clock. "Well, ahh, of course, Laurie. Send him in."

"Oy, vey, the day isn't bad enough," she mumbled to herself as she got up. "Now I have to contend with this."

Taylor was all smiles. "Sister executive," he teased, walking over to kiss her. "To what do I owe this exclusive audience?"

"Sibling adoration," she said lightly as they strolled over to the sitting area and settled across from each other on a beige and brown striped couch. "We don't see enough of each other."

"Wasn't that you I was talking to at Chasen's?"

Sara shook her head and took off her dark glasses. "I was clearly not in my right mind last night. As my entire system is telling me this morning."

"Overdid it, huh? What time did you two leave?"

"Too late."

"Maybe you should check out of here early. Go home and get some rest."

"No. No. We really . . . ahh, we really have to talk, Taylor."

"About what?"

"The show," she said glumly.

"I figured," he replied, expressionless.

The recent Nielsen's showed *Ki & Company* with an eleven rating and a sixteen share. Bottom of the barrel. Out of the sixty-one programs on the air, it ranked fifty-ninth.

"Don't look so miserable. I didn't say you'd been canned."

"You might as well. The way we keep bouncing around the schedule, it's a wonder anyone can find us."

"Taylor, that happens with new shows all the time. It's part of the—"

"I don't care what it's part of," he complained. All I know is that *Ki & Company*'s time slot has been switched twice over the last four weeks. There's nothing wrong with the show, Sara. It's the network's fault that we're losing viewers. You know that as well as I do."

"Yes," she agreed tentatively. "You may be right. But at least they believe in the show, Taylor. And they're willing to leave it on the air, provided we make certain changes."

Taylor's amber eyes searched hers questioningly. "What kind of changes?"

Sara took a deep breath. "Major. Specifically with the cast. We're adding a couple of actresses. The Saunders sisters. They'll be—"

A shocked expression of disbelief fell over Taylor's face. "The Saunders sisters? My God! They haven't got enough talent between the two of them to fill up a flea's navel. Sara, is this some sort of joke?"

" 'Fraid not." Her smile was forced. "Taylor, what can I tell you? The producers are grasping at straws, trying to come up with a way to save the show. The network went for the idea of Cassie and Karen Saunders as regulars. Sort of helpmates for the Justin Kane character—"

"Helpmates? Sara, *Ki & Company* is a tastefully executed drama about a fairly sensitive private detective. Not the T & A follies. I just don't see how I'm going to play off of a couple of gyrating bimbos."

"You'll see soon enough. The new script should be here any minute."

"And what does that mean? That I have to read it, swallow hard, and say 'okay'?"

He sprang off the couch and started pacing back and forth on the Oriental rug like a caged tiger.

"Calm down. You're overreacting. Where's that even-tempered guru I used to know and love? You have no idea whether you'll like the script or not."

Taylor stood perfectly still and gave his sister a long, penetrating look. "Oh, yes, I do. And I'm telling you, Sara, if I don't like it, I won't do it."

She marched across the room to face him. Full of authority.

"Well, then, little brother. I will just have to remind you that you have a contract. A binding contract that you cannot break."

"Is that right?" he snapped emphatically. "Well, you just watch me."

It was almost dusk. And the sun had slipped behind a muted purplish haze so glorious that Kate felt compelled to keep glancing up at the sky as she strolled down Little Santa Monica Boulevard. She was on her way to meet R. B. McDevitt at Harry's Bar & Grill. And silently cursing herself for having made the date.

Disastrous timing. After spending the last forty-five minutes with

Dr. Laura Bernstein, Kate was hardly in the mood for a drink with the overbearing Texan. She wished now that she hadn't let him talk her into it.

But she couldn't very well stand him up. And the walk would do her good. It had rained earlier, bringing the temperature down to a cool sixty degrees. And the fresh air felt good against Kate's flushed face.

She slipped her hands into the pockets of her green gabardine slacks and moved along automatically. Eyes straight ahead now. But her mind was far away. Drifting back over the session with Dr. Bernstein.

There was so much to grasp that Kate had felt a bit overwhelmed. As though she'd just been handed a thick volume of James Joyce to digest overnight. She wasn't sure she was up to it. But she didn't doubt Laura Bernstein's analysis for a moment.

"At this point, Kate," the psychologist had explained, "you are at war within yourself. And a great deal of that relates back to your mother and her illness. You felt stifled staying at home in Rochester, watching her slip away, and working for that weekly newspaper."

"But I didn't have a choice. I had to. It was the only paper in town that would allow me to work part-time."

"I realize that," Dr. Bernstein said patiently. "Nevertheless, you resented it. You knew you were far too talented for that job. You felt confined—frustrated. And ever since your mother's death you've been trying to play catch-up. Striving for the success that you think passed you by while you wasted your time at home."

Kate's face turned ponderous. She studied the marbleized pencil holder on Dr. Bernstein's desk, listening.

"The problem is that even though you've moved very quickly, making great strides in both the journalistic and political arenas, you have yet to realize it. You don't believe in your own success, Kate. And that reveals itself in the relationships you choose."

"How's that?" Kate inquired, swinging her glance up to meet the psychologist's intriguing lapis-lazuli eyes.

"Quite simply, you don't feel worthy of the kind of man you should be with. That is, someone who can help support you financially as well as emotionally. You're too busy trying to do it all yourself. And as a result, you feel oppressed and lonely most of the time. As though your life is one long, isolated uphill struggle."

"Are you saying I don't want a man around to share my life with?"

"You do and you don't. The romantic notion of love and commitment appeals to you. But inside, you can't allow a man to get too close because he might endanger your chances of proving yourself. Seth was safe as long as he was noncommittal. Even when you agreed to marry him, in your heart you knew it would never work out."

"And Cary?" Kate asked dubiously.

"That didn't work out either, did it?"

"No."

"And why do you think that was?"

Kate thought for a long moment. "I loved him, I guess. But I felt I had to compete with him."

Dr. Bernstein nodded. "Exactly. You see, Kate. You are so terrified of the male being dominant, of having to give up that independence which you missed early on, that whenever a man starts getting serious, it's as though a huge vise is coming at you. Threatening to immobilize you, snuff out your identity."

"So how do I proceed? What in the world can I do about it?"

"I can't give you any quick fixes. It's a long process. But you can start by not being so hard on yourself. Realize what you've accomplished. Reiterate it daily, if you have to. Run down the checklist of all the prestigious magazines you've been published in. Don't let the fear of failure threaten you any longer, Kate. You have been successful. You will be more successful. Now it's time to relax a little and start enjoying your life."

Easily said, Kate was thinking as she swung through the double brass-and-glass doors of Harry's. It was still early. The bar was dimly lit, quiet, almost empty. As soon as her eyes adjusted, she spotted R.B. at a corner table.

This better be good, she told herself, remembering how he'd conned her into meeting him.

"I've run across something about Renata Desmond you might find real helpful, Kate," R.B. had explained over the phone. "Something we ought to discuss in person."

So she'd agreed. Anxious for anything that might spice up the piece.

Now that she'd asked for an extension on her deadline, *World*'s managing editor, Russ Stevens, was expecting major revelations. And she was feeling rather desperate. Hoping that Alisa Hudson would provide some clues. Eager for whatever else she could dig up.

"Glad you could make it." R.B. stood up as Kate settled into a chair.

"Yes, good to see you," she replied, stealing a glance at her Piaget watch. *One hour. That's all he gets.* "How go the takeover wars?"

"On the record, or off?" he chuckled.

"Off, if you like."

"Smooth. Bumpy. Peaks and valleys. Like anything worth fighting for. Teddy Selwyn is one slimy son of a gun. But we're making some progress. Just filed with the SEC today. Unfriendly takeover. Proxy vote comes up in mid-December," R.B. concluded as the waiter approached. "What'll it be, Kate?"

"A wine spritzer, please."

"Say, did you ever get in touch with my pal Barry Jennings?"

"No. He had a publicist return my call."

"That right? Probably wouldn't hurt to try again. If it'd help, I'd be happy to give Jennings a ring myself."

"That isn't necessary, R.B. I've sort of given up on the Longhorns' angle," she said without elaborating. Why tell him that Don Brocato hadn't shown up for their interview in Will Rogers State Park? It was only an admission of defeat.

"How's the piece coming along? Getting anything juicy?"

"A couple of things, yes," she fibbed. "And some very good leads. But from what you said over the phone, I've missed something."

R.B. poured the rest of the Corona into his pilsner glass. And glanced up at Kate's blue-violet eyes. Yes, she was worth it, he convinced himself for the third time that day.

What had it cost him? A few thousand. Odds were she'd be impressed. Maybe even warm up a little. *Not half as tough as she seems,* he calculated, watching Kate bring the wineglass to her glossy lips. *Brightest woman I've met since Lalli. And the most challenging.*

R.B. raised his glass in a toast and Kate reciprocated, without smiling.

"So what is it that you've discovered?" she asked matter-of-factly. *No use wasting time. Especially on him.*

"Something I sure can't make heads or tails of," he began. "Maybe you'll have more luck. It seems our favorite dragon lady's been doing a little traveling. To Bakersfield. She goes there regularly, twice a week."

"For what purpose?"

"I'm not exactly sure. But the interesting part is that she always uses a rented car for these little getaways. Which indicates she doesn't want anyone to catch on. Even more perplexing is her destination," he added in a conspiratorial voice. "St. Dominic's. An exclusive private-care facility."

"For what kind of patients?"

"Mainly mental cases."

"How odd," Kate said, running down the possibilities. "Could it be a relative? Renata doesn't have family, does she? I thought she was orphaned before Cappy Desmond adopted her."

"So the story goes. One thing's for sure, there aren't any clues at St. Dominic's. No records of any Desmond staying there. And as far as my . . . ahh, as far as I could determine, no indication that Renata ever visits."

"You checked?" Kate asked, astonished.

"Well, ahh, yes. I was kind of intrigued with the whole thing. Figured it was worth finding out."

Kate searched his eyes for a clue. Found none. And decided she might as well be straightforward. "Let me ask you a question, R.B. Exactly how did you come across this information?"

R. B. McDevitt had a policy. He never lied. Even when he knew the truth wouldn't necessarily work to his advantage. He knew that now. All he could do was hope that the attractive redhead wouldn't take his answer the wrong way.

"Private detective," he said candidly.

"What?" Her face registered total surprise.

"Hired him several weeks ago. Not long after you came down to my ranch. Couple of reasons," R.B. explained. "First, I had cause to believe that everything wasn't on the up-and-up with Renata and the Longhorns. Second, I wanted to help you."

"Well," Kate said huffily, "that's all very nice. But you really have no business—"

"Hang on there a minute, killer," R.B. ordered, silencing her. "I'm a free citizen, aren't I? I can hire a private investigator anytime and for whatever reason I want to—"

"Yes, but—"

"Let me finish," he insisted without raising his voice. "In this case my motivation involved you. I'll admit it. Couldn't get to first base. Every time I called, you were busy. Even after you broke your engagement."

R.B. watched the color blossom in Kate's cheeks and smiled, unabashedly, as he continued. "Just figured a friendly gesture might do me some good."

"Well," Kate said, struggling to suppress her rage. "I am genuinely flattered, R.B. But you must look at it from my point of view. As a journalist, paying a private detective for information is just, well, it's just unscrupulous."

"You don't have to worry about that. You didn't pay. I did."

"It's the same thing. What am I to do if this comes to something and my sources are questioned?"

"Exactly what Woodward and Bernstein did. Only give me a different name, will you. I don't see myself as the Deep Throat type."

Kate bit back the sarcastic answer on the tip of her tongue. And tapped nervously on her wineglass with a neatly tapered fingernail. Thinking about the arrogant Texan sitting across from her.

What had he done, really? He'd helped her. More than just about anybody else had. As for his intentions, so what if she was feeling a bit manipulated?

The fact was, Kate knew more about Renata Desmond right now than she had an hour ago. That in itself was worth having had a drink with R. B. McDevitt.

"Well, I guess there's nothing more I can say, except thank you," Kate announced, finally, in a calm voice. "But if your bloodhounds are still sniffing around on my account, please call them off immediately."

"Already have."

She watched him finish the Corona. And in that few seconds she made up her mind. She'd tell him. She'd thought about it before, but to do so now made perfect sense. It would be a reciprocal gesture, considering the fact he'd gone out of his way to help her. More than that, it would even the score. If she could provide R.B. with some equally exclusive information, she wouldn't owe him anything.

Yes. Certainly. There was no question.

"R.B.," she asked, in a friendly, lighthearted voice, "do you have time for another drink?"

"Why . . . ahh, sure," he replied, baffled.

"Good." Her smile was radiant. "I have something to share with you about Teddy Selwyn. It's a true story about his filmmaking career. His early filmmaking career."

23

■ Alisa Hudson was smaller than Kate had imagined. The renowned septuagenarian actress couldn't have been more than five feet three inches tall. and she looked diminutive in the baggy denim overalls, which she wore rolled up at the ankles over thick black rubber boots.

"My gardening attire," Alisa announced matter-of-factly. "Come, sit down," she ordered, taking a seat at the sturdy oak table in the center of her large rustic kitchen. "Sorry I kept you waiting. But my roses always come first. Therapy, you know. And these days I need it."

Kate, more than a little ill at ease, simply nodded and settled into the straight-backed wooden chair. Staring at Alisa Hudson. The famous, wrinkled, pixyish face. The sharp and dazzling jade-green eyes.The infectious smile, which had won audiences the world over for more than three decades.

To her surprise and irritation Kate felt tongue-tied. Panic washed over her like a flash flood. If she couldn't get a sentence out, how in the world was she going to ask Alisa Hudson to read Letty Molloy's letter? And how was she going to approach that delicate subject in the first place? Earlier, Kate had imagined it would all just work itself out naturally.

Now she had grave doubts.

Kate was awestruck.

Meeting Alisa Hudson had temporarily robbed her of her faculties. Except her ability to gawk. She'd never thought of herself as a run-of-the-mill fan. But in this case she most certainly was.

Since childhood, Kate had idolized Alisa Hudson. She'd seen all her movies, from *Darling Daughter,* the black-and-white classic, which had won Alisa an Oscar nomination at the age of twelve. To her most recent, *Golden Years,* in which she starred as an aging tap dancer whose career is suddenly revived.

Aside from the presumptuous ramblings of gossip columnists, little had been written about the actress. In movie-making circles she was known to be straightforward and feisty, feared both for her high energy and low boiling point. Like Garbo, she'd assiduously avoided the press. Automatically refusing all social invitations. And never letting on why she hadn't married.

Everyone knew about Alisa's longtime affair with Armand Renaud, though. He was a very wealthy, very married, French industrialist whom the actress had met in her late thirties. And remained faithful to until his death in 1983.

Since then she'd relocated from London to Los Angeles. Her five-bedroom ranch-style home was perched high in the hills of Topanga Canyon, surrounded by thousands of brilliantly colored flowers, including ten different varieties of roses. There was only one servant. Alisa's loyal British housekeeper, Geraldine.

"Will you have tea, Miss Brannigan?" the actress inquired politely, while pulling off her heavy boots.

"Yes, please," Kate said quickly. Relieved to find her tongue at last.

"Now then," Alisa announced, as Geraldine poured the steaming brew into identical red mugs, "I'll get right to the point. I'm suing Teddy Selwyn next week. And I want your article to precede the filing."

Kate's blue-violet eyes widened curiously. "But . . . but, why?"

"Because I want to watch him squirm, that's why. The more publicity I can stir up on this, the better. Your magazine is the most prestigious of all. I want everyone to know, before the fact, why I am going to drag that maniacal pervert through the courts."

"And why are you?" Kate flipped to the first page of her slender reporter's notebook.

"Breach of contract and defamation of character," Alisa said slowly, watching Kate's shorthand. "I'm suing the little weasel for sixty million dollars, only because my attorney refused to go for more. In my entire career, Miss Brannigan, I have never filed a lawsuit. I've had my differences, of course. But never, never anything this outrageous."

"What did he do to instill such hostility in you?" Kate asked as her hand flew across the page.

"I'll tell you what he did," Alisa replied, measuring her words as though they had been scripted. Cognizant of the import of a sizzling quote.

"That young whippersnapper sweet-talked me into doing a film at his studio. And I let him. I knew I shouldn't have. Almost all my film work has been with Lardner Studios in London. Never did trust the Hollywood chieftains. And I certainly shouldn't have trusted that snake Selwyn. But it was such a wonderful part, you see, and a lovely script that I'd optioned. *Transcendence*. All about reincarnation. And my role was a spirit who kept being reborn into different bodies during different time periods. It was Oscar-winning stuff, not that I care about that rot."

Alisa continued her tirade for the next five minutes. Flailing her arms and pounding the table animatedly. Giving, Kate mused, possibly one of the best performances of her career.

She talked about the way she'd fought for two years to interest Lardner Studios in doing *Transcendence*. But ultimately failed. Because the head of production was convinced the movie wasn't commercial enough.

Then along came Teddy Selwyn, offering to take on the project and pay Alisa's standard three million, plus points. She'd agreed, overjoyed to be able to tackle the challenging role at last.

"Never did I even suspect," Alisa went on, lowering her resonant voice dramatically, "that Teddy Selwyn would do what he did. That unscrupulous manipulator had the audacity to rework the script after I'd finished shooting. He had new scenes written. Disgusting, depraved scenes full of sex and violence. And they were cut into my film. Can you believe it, Miss Brannigan? Can you believe the grandson of Jake Selwyn, the most trustworthy studio owner in the history of film, would do a thing like that? Turn *Transcendence* into an X-rated piece of sleaze? Teddy Selwyn ought to be more than sued. He ought to be shot!"

Kate looked up from her notebook and studied the fury in Alisa's small, round face. "It sounds to me as though you have a very good case, Miss Hudson," she said evenly. Keeping her overwhelming excitement in check.

Inside, Kate was jubilant. Overjoyed. Cartwheels of confidence danced in her head.

She had a terrific story here. Russ Stevens would be ecstatic. Maybe he'd even up the ante on the staff job he'd offered her after the Brandy St. John piece.

More than that, Kate was now quite certain that she could convince Alisa to read Letty Molloy's letter. Although it would take some very fast talking, since her hour with the actress was swiftly running out.

Geraldine had already begun clearing the table. And Alisa was on her feet, waiting for Kate to get up.

"I think you have it all now, Miss Brannigan," she said, with a spritely smile. "And I know you'll report it, just as I've enunciated it."

"Yes, yes, of course I will, Miss Hudson," Kate agreed as they walked toward the front entrance. "There is one thing, though, that I think might be of interest to you. A friend of mine, an outstanding businessman named R. B. McDevitt, is attempting to take over Selwyn Studios. Perhaps you've read about it in the trades."

Alisa nodded thoughtfully.

"And it occurred to me—forgive me if this seems bold, Miss Hudson—but I thought you might be interested in meeting Mr. McDevitt. That between the two of you—"

"We might manage to put Teddy Selwyn in some deep shit, as they say?" Alisa asked gleefully.

"Something like that."

"Certainly, my dear. You tell your Mr. McDevitt to call whenever he likes. Any enemy of Teddy Selwyn's is an automatic friend of mine."

Kate paused at the doorway and smiled. *It's now or never time. Do it.*

With one swift move, she reached into her handbag and extracted Letty Molloy's letter.

Alisa Hudson observed her curiously.

"Miss Hudson," she began, "I wonder if you could spare just a few more minutes . . ."

* * *

"Okay, first team," the assistant director bellowed.

A hush fell over Soundstage 12.

Taylor found his chalk mark on the floor and placed his feet behind it. He was standing in an elegantly decorated hallway directly in front of a closed pine door.

Sara had all but begged him. And he'd agreed to stay with the series, despite the cast changes.

"Ready, Taylor?" the director asked. "All right, then, action!"

Taylor, as Justin Kane, knocked on the door. Waited. Knocked again. Glanced down the hallway furtively as though someone were following him. Then knocked a third time.

Karen Saunders, as Laurie Robinson, finally opened the door a crack and peeked out suspiciously. "Oh it's you!" she exclaimed in a syrupy voice. "Come on in."

The door swung open.

"Want to borrow a cup of sugar—or something?" she teased, blinking up at him.

Kane was too stunned to move. He stood there dumbfounded. Staring in delight and disbelief at Laurie Robinson's scantily clad voluptuous body. The gorgeous brunette was dripping wet. And the towel she held in front of her barely covered the essentials.

Taylor's mind was working overtime. He was wondering whether this scene would ever get past the censors. And hoping it wouldn't. He groaned inside, thinking about what came next.

"Ahh . . . Lynne?" he asked witlessly.

"Bad guess, Supersleuth. I'm Laurie. And I was just taking a shower." She took a beat, then added playfully, "Want to join me?"

Not in a million years, slut, Taylor thought to himself.

Kane stood rigidly in the doorway, saying nothing.

Laurie waited a few moments, her face radiating panic. She searched Taylor's stony eyes. Could he have forgotten his next line? She decided to ad lib.

"Come on . . . it'll be fun!" She lunged for his hand. And inadvertently dropped her towel.

"Cut!" shouted the director.

A chorus of wolf whistles punctuated his command.

The wardrobe mistress wrapped the abashed actress in a terrycloth robe.

The crew hustled to reset the shot.

The director threw Taylor a disgusted look. "Tess," he yelled at the script girl, "line for Mr. Evans, please."

"Never mind, Tess," Taylor interrupted, moving quickly toward his director. "I know the line, Barney. That's not the problem."

"Then what is?" Barney shot back with a tired look.

"It's not that I can't remember the line," Taylor repeated. "It's the line itself. Barney, listen, I tried. But I just can't do it. As Justin Kane, I cannot find the motivation to follow Laurie Robinson into the shower. It is totally out of character and I—"

"Screw character, Evans," Barney shouted, silencing everyone within a hundred feet. "You don't like the lines, you talk to the writers—before you show up here, see? Not now. Not when I'm finally getting to the first shot of the day at eleven A.M."

Taylor's face turned an angry shade of red. "I'm sorry if I'm holding you up, Barney," he apologized automatically. "But I really think we need a rewrite here. Let's call the production office and—"

"No way. Forget it," the director vociferated. "The script's approved. We're ready to shoot. Now get back there on your mark and deliver the damn lines, or one of us is going to be walking off this soundstage in less than a minute."

"Is that a threat, Barney?" Taylor shouted. "I'm asking you, is that a threat?"

Barney nodded to his assistant director who called, "First team, places, please."

The cinematographer double-checked his shot in the lens.

The head gaffer finished adjusting a gel on a Five-K light.

The sound technician stepped in, holding a boom mike.

Karen Saunders scampered to her mark behind the closed door.

Taylor didn't move an inch.

He glared down into Barney Klein's myopic eyes for a long moment. Then he turned and walked determinedly off the set.

Teddy Selwyn raised his porcine face to the late morning sun and smiled contentedly. He was stretched out on a blue and white striped chaise longue in the center of his red-oak bedroom terrace. Wrapped in a baby-blue velour bathrobe. Sipping a frothy cappuccino. And paging through a copy of *Gentlemen's Quarterly.*

Waking up California-style, Teddy called it. Something he usually reserved for weekends. But by his reckoning, he deserved this leisurely Wednesday morning. He was rewarding himself for hard work. The hardest work he'd ever endured.

It had been a rigorous couple of weeks, fraught with nonstop activity. His daily calendar chockablock with appointments. On two occasions he'd been so busy he'd actually skipped lunch. And the previous Friday he'd been forced to cancel his pedicure.

Unheard-of sacrifices, never to be repeated, Teddy had promised himself. But, looking back, he had to admit that his efforts had paid off.

Teddy had saved Selwyn Studios. And he was proud of himself. Basking in his own glory. Marveling at the ingenious way he'd turned the tables on R. B. McDevitt.

It hadn't been easy. According to all his advisers, the only way to thwart McDevitt's efforts would be to comb the world of high finance and come up with a "white knight." An investor. Preferably one who already owned a hefty block of Selwyn stock and was willing to purchase more. An investor Teddy could trust. One he could invite to join the board of directors. An investor he could be certain would vote his shares management's way in December.

George Thornton, an Australian financier with major holdings in several American companies and a fascination with Hollywood, fit the bill perfectly.

Flying to Sydney was more than Teddy had bargained for. But he'd found Thornton extremely affable and bright. The Aussie had listened attentively to Teddy's scheme. They'd negotiated half the night. And finalized the deal the next morning.

Thornton already owned ten percent of Selwyn Studios' stock. That, coupled with Teddy's twenty-five percent, gave them a substantial base. Now Teddy would issue twenty-five million new shares, which his "white knight" would swiftly purchase. But not before he signed a "stand-still" agreement, prohibiting him from further Selwyn stock acquisitions or any takeover attempt.

In return, Teddy had promised to install Thornton on the board. And appoint him Vice-President of Acquisitions. A nebulous title, signifying very little, least of all what kind of acquisitions. But Teddy would worry about that later.

The point was, he had Thornton on his side. And the Australian was a valuable asset indeed. Not only because of the proxy votes he would control. But because of his reputation.

George Thornton enjoyed a high profile as an astute, discerning businessman who'd been instrumental in the rebirth of several major corporations. Early in his career, he'd purchased a fledgling monthly magazine called *Australian National* and, in one year's time, turned it into a popular weekly. He'd performed similar transformations on a furniture company, a cosmetics firm, and a Melbourne-based department store chain.

In the United States, Thornton sat on the board of two major corporations. Jetstream Aeronautics, which he'd once helped rescue from bankruptcy. And Baskin Foods, which had increased its profits to the multimillion dollar category, thanks to an acquisition plan the Australian had helped engineer.

George Thornton's presence on the Selwyn Studios' board of directors would be more than a feather in Teddy Selwyn's cap. It would be a crown of considerable glory. One which would instill confidence in his shareholders and encourage them to vote management's way.

Nor had Teddy overlooked the institutional houses. The banks, mutual funds, and insurance companies that R. B. McDevitt claimed to have locked up. The studio chief planned to call on each portfolio manager R.B. had spoken with. And win each one over. A simple enough task, Teddy calculated, once he mentioned George Thornton's name.

As the noontime sun centered overhead, Teddy guzzled the last drop of cappuccino from his favorite glass mug. Closed his eyes dreamily. And visualized his "white knight." George Thornton was suited in shining armor. Mounted on a fierce white steed. Galloping valiantly toward Selwyn Studios. Brandishing his sharp iron lance. Swinging it low and quite effortlessly decapitating R. B. McDevitt.

It was almost two A.M. at Chez Jay, a popular beach bar in Santa Monica. The noisy crowd had long since thinned out. But Taylor was still perched on a barstool, slumped over a bottle of Cuervo Gold.

He had no idea where he was. Or that he was drunk. Inebriation was an unfamiliar sensation. One he hadn't experienced since his college years. He'd never even liked the taste of liquor.

But that didn't matter now. All Taylor wanted to do was forget. And a rapid succession of tequila shooters was making that possible.

He knocked back another and continued talking to the screenwriter next to him. The one who'd left five minutes earlier.

"So I just walked off the set. Just like that. And I'm never going back, either. Show business stinks. Everybody's got an ego as big as that stuffed fish hanging up there. You agree with that, Bill? Or was it Benny?" Taylor asked, glancing to the left, where the writer had been sitting.

He blinked several times in surprise at the empty stool. And wondered what was wrong with his vision.

"Not a thing," he told himself in a loud voice. Poured another shooter. Drank it quickly. And noticed the bartender staring at him. But paid no attention.

Let him look. Who cares? Who cares about anything? Let them all stare, and let them talk. Nothing anybody thought or said could bother Taylor Evans. He was too strong and too smart. He knew who he was. And who he wasn't.

He was not an actor. He was never going back to Culver Studios, no matter what Sara said. And he wouldn't go running to Brandy, either.

She was doing just fine on her own. Headed for superstardom. Quite clearly, she didn't need him around. He wasn't right for her. Their worlds were just too different. He could never adapt to the kind of glamorous life-style she thrived on. Why had it taken him so long to come to his senses?

"Last call," the bartender announced, glancing toward the entrance.

A tall woman with spiky orange hair and a man in jeans, about a foot shorter, had just walked in.

"Sorry, buddy, last . . . hey, Mark, is that you?" the bartender asked excitedly. "What a surprise! Where the hell you been?"

Mark Silverstein smiled affably as he and the woman situated themselves at the bar. "Taking care of business, Charlie. Out of the country. Too late for a little Jack Daniel's?"

"Not for you, it isn't. So what's shaking? Where, out of the country?" Charlie asked, reaching for the whiskey bottle.

"Oh, here—there. Been playing games and making lots of money. You know Niki Erickson, right?"

"*The* Niki Erickson?" Charlie asked, impressed. "Hey, this is turning out to be a better night than I thought. I have all your albums on tape, Niki. And they're terrific."

"Thanks," the singer replied without smiling. Her heavily made-up almond-shaped eyes swept beyond Charlie and focused on the man sitting alone at the end of the bar.

"Who's your late customer?" she asked in a low, sensuous voice.

"Damned if I know. But whoever he is, he's in for a hell of a tomorrow. Guy's been belting shooters all night. I lost count."

Mark glanced down the bar. Stared in astonishment. Rubbed his eyes and looked again.

"What the hell's wrong with you?" Niki inquired.

"That's . . . that's my brother-in-law."

"The actor?"

Taylor sat there, nursing his Cuervo Gold. Oblivious of the three pairs of prying eyes.

"I'd better go over," Mark told Niki as he slipped off the barstool. He cast Taylor a giant smile. "Hey, how you doing, pal?"

Taylor's face registered nothing at first. It took him several seconds to recognize Mark.

"How you doing?" Mark repeated, sitting down next to him. "What brings you over to this part of town?"

"None of your damn business," Taylor sneered.

"Hey, come on. Let's be friends, huh? Nothing's changed between us. Now, gimme some skin," Mark urged, holding out his hand.

Taylor recognized the crude emotion welling up inside him. Rage. A burning, blistering rage.

"Screw you, Silverstein."

"Okay, okay. I just thought maybe we could go somewhere. Get a cup of coffee. You look like you could use some."

"Yeah?" Taylor asked, standing up and steadying himself against the bar. "Well, I don't need your help. Nothing you can do will make up for what you've already done to my sister, you bastard."

"Listen, Taylor, that's between Sara and me—"

"Says who?" Taylor shouted. He was weaving back and forth like a solitary blade of grass in the wind. "Sara doesn't like the way you're using her money to buy drugs for that whore you're living with."

Niki Erickson shot Taylor an icy glare.

Mark jumped off the barstool, his eyes spewing anger. "That was uncalled for, Taylor. You know the money is just as much mine as Sara's. What I do with it is my own affair. And you owe Niki an apology."

"Oh, I do, huh? Well, why don't you just give it to her for me?" Taylor asked, hurling a shaky karate chop in his brother-in-law's direction.

Mark dodged quickly. And Taylor went sprawling onto the sawdust-covered floor.

"Is he okay?" Charlie asked from behind the bar.

"Yeah, just dazed," Mark mumbled.

"Who cares?" Niki said, heading for the entrance. "You coming, Mark?"

"In a sec," he answered, looking down at Taylor and shaking his head. It was the first time Mark could ever remember feeling sorry for his brother-in-law. But there was an accompanying twinge of satisfaction in seeing the high priest of inner peace lying there helpless. And in knowing just how far out of control he'd allowed himself to stray.

It was a one-hundred-ten-mile drive from Bel Air to Bakersfield. Two and a half hours on the Golden State Freeway.

The return trip seemed twice that long.

"Worthless, absolutely worthless," Kate muttered to herself as she flicked on the headlights. "A total waste of time."

She'd spent the entire afternoon at St. Dominic's Home and Hospital for the Mentally Disturbed. On the guise of writing a piece about privately funded sanitariums, she had finagled an interview with the supervising director, Sister Mary Theresa.

Afterward, a nurse had escorted Kate on a VIP tour of the facilities. Later she had roamed the impeccably manicured grounds alone. Scanning the faces of patients and visitors. Eavesdropping on conversations. Hoping to come up with some clue. Specifically a name.

A face. The missing link between Renata Desmond and this quiet, oppressive institution.

Feeling increasingly desperate as the afternoon wore on, Kate had summoned all her moxie and returned to the supervising director's office.

"Sorry to disturb you, Sister. But I forgot one thing during our interview. I was wondering whether you keep any records of the visitors here."

"Whatever for, if I may ask?" Sister Mary Theresa had replied, eyebrows arching over her wire-rimmed glasses.

"For the sidebar. That's an insert that runs along with a story," Kate explained, trying to sound nonchalant. "And for this one we want to determine the number of times a week a patient is visited by a family member, a friend. I'm doing a routine check at all the homes and hospitals that will appear in the piece."

"Well, I'm very sorry, Miss Brannigan. But that information must remain private at St. Dominic's. However, I could have one of the sisters take a look and come up with some figures for you. Would that suffice?"

"Ahh . . . yes, certainly. That would be fine," Kate answered automatically. And said good-bye.

Brannigan, you fleabrain, she thought now in the car. *Why couldn't you have pressed a little harder? Come up with something better? Have you no imagination? And you call yourself a reporter!*

Frustration. It seemed the one constant in her life. The sessions with Dr. Bernstein were helping. But not enough. If Kate wasn't fighting her anger and loneliness for Seth, she was berating herself about her work. Always anxious. Never satisfied. Continuously thinking she could be more productive. Particularly when it came to the Renata Desmond story.

She'd set out for Bakersfield feeling optimistic. Telling herself something would come of it. Fate had sent R.B. and his private detective her way. Fate was drawing her to St. Dominic's, where she would discover a tantalizingly vile secret about Renata that the nation deserved to read about.

Having failed, she was filled with an overwhelming sense of futility and exhaustion. As though she'd been on an interminable journey through the desert and couldn't go a step farther. Kate felt so tired that she was tempted to pull the Peugeot off the freeway and go to sleep.

It was the kind of physical surrender that her mind would never accept. Only her determination to think through the problem at hand kept her eyes glued to the road. Time. She was running out of it.

She'd managed to put the interview with Renata Desmond off as long as possible. But now it was firmly set for the following week. And, still, Kate had nothing substantial. Not one hook. Nothing "juicy," as R.B. would put it. At least nothing she could use.

If only Alisa Hudson would . . .

Oh, hell, Kate argued with herself. *Don't even think about it. Alisa has already refused. And she's not going to change her mind. Forget her and forget Letty Molloy. That's never going to work.*

But try as she might, Kate could not convince herself to stop reviewing her final few minutes with the actress. Alisa's reaction to Letty's letter had been so baffling that Kate had replayed the conversation in her mind dozens of times. Hoping to make some sense of it.

She could still see Alisa, standing in front of the red-brick fireplace in her living room, holding the thick envelope in her thin, withered hand.

"I'll read this, but on one condition only," the veteran performer had announced with a stone-faced stare. "That any response will be off the record. Is that understood?"

"Yes, of course," Kate replied eagerly.

She watched as Alisa settled into an overstuffed calico couch, propped her feet up on a hassock, and yanked a pair of bifocals from her overalls pocket. It took her fifteen minutes to read and then reread the six pages of Letty Molloy's spidery longhand. When she'd finished, she folded the letter carefully, placed it back in the envelope, and handed it to Kate.

"It's true. All of it," she said simply, a look of nostalgia in her sharp green eyes. "Funny, too, I always suspected Letty would be the one to tell. She was in love with Cappy Desmond, you know. And I think she always resented Renata's presence."

"And is that why—"

But Alisa held up a wrinkled hand before Kate could finish her question.

"Oh, my dear girl," she said, smiling impishly, "wouldn't you like to know? A fascinating story, that one. Beguiling set of characters. Heady times for us all. But it's not my place to tell you, Miss Brannigan," she said, pushing herself up off the couch abruptly. "Trust me, my dear, you're far better off not opening that can of worms. Too many slimy creatures to deal with."

I'll take them, Kate thought, as she wheeled the car along Stone Canyon Drive toward Sara's house. *At this point I'll take anything.*

But her gut instinct told her it was hopeless. The puzzle would remain unsolved. The pieces were there, but none of them fit. And Kate hadn't the time or the energy to try to force them together.

"One puff piece on Renata Desmond, coming up," she muttered, pulling the Peugeot into the garage.

24
Paris, France
1938

■ It was Francine Devereaux's habit to stop by her friend Renata Desmond's apartment overlooking the Seine at least two or three times a week. She'd been doing this since the fall of 1937, when Renata had begun classes at the University of Paris. And she always looked forward to the visits.

But on this particular balmy spring afternoon neither of the young women was in good humor. Francine held the reason in her slender ivory hands. It was a single sheet of beige parchment stationery.

The Frenchwoman's black eyes narrowed with anger as she scanned the expansive masculine scrawl. But she held her tongue until she reached the last paragraph.

"What?" she objected indignantly. "He wouldn't dare!"

"I'm afraid he would—and will very soon, if I don't capitulate," Renata replied, frowning.

"But we cannot cancel now," Francine complained, handing the letter back to her friend. "We have reservations at the finest hotels. All of our transportation has been paid for. Renata, you must not allow him to do this. Forget about it. Pretend you never received the stupid letter."

"I wish I could."

Renata sighed heavily as she glanced down at her father's fashionably embossed stationery. They'd already argued extensively over the phone. And this was the third time he'd written in recent weeks ordering her back to Los Angeles. She'd managed to ignore the other letters. This one she could not.

May 4, 1938

Dear Renata,

Your stubbornness astounds me. How can you insist on remaining in France? Worse yet, embarking on a sightseeing vacation?

Surely you read the newspapers. You must be aware of the highly volatile political situation abroad. This is no time to travel through Europe. With that madman Hitler on the loose, any atrocity is possible. The French are blind to his power. They think their Maginot Line will deter him. But my understanding is that the German troops are highly mobile and Hitler capable of anything.

I fear for your life, Renata. And I must insist that you return to California at once. I shall expect to see you no later than the end of the month. Otherwise, I shall be forced to take matters into my own hands.

If you do not return, I swear I shall cut off your expense money immediately and make arrangements to disinherit you. Drastic steps, perhaps. But you leave me with no alternative.

Please, my darling, come home.

Your loving father,
Charles Wentworth Desmond

Francine got up off the maroon velvet couch and paced the parquet floor of Renata's tastefully decorated living room. She paused at the marble mantelpiece, reached for a slender onyx-and-gold box, and extracted a cigarette.

"All that rhetoric about the Germans is garbage. You know why he's doing this," she said, accepting a small silver-plated lighter from Renata. "He just wants to get his hands on you again, the incestuous old lecher."

"I told you before, Francine, it is not incest," Renata insisted. "I'm adopted."

"Well, he's just making idle threats to scare you. Money. Who cares? I'll pay for everything. It is, after all, my last adventure as a single woman. And the least I can do for my bridesmaid."

"I can't allow that."

"Why not?"

"I just can't, that's all."

But it was tempting. For months Renata had been looking forward to traveling with Francine. It would be like old times, just the two of them, exploring together. London. Rome. Madrid. Romantic places where, she'd hoped, Francine's feelings for her would be re-awakened.

Aside from an occasional hug, there had been no sign of physical affection between the two young women since Francine's engagement. And although she was too proud to admit it, Renata was extremely unhappy with this arrangement. She longed for the complete abandon of their lovemaking, the fusion of their passions, the spontaneous combustion of their desire.

Early in the year, she had suggested the summer trip, hoping it would rekindle their closeness. Perhaps, under the right circumstances, Francine would change her mind and decide not to marry Henri Descannet.

But by now Renata knew in her heart that she had already lost that battle. Francine spoke of nothing but Henri and the wedding. The only reason she'd agreed to the trip was because he would be busy interning. By fall he would be a full-fledged surgeon and she would be Madame Descannet. It was already a fait accompli.

"So what are you going to do, *ma chère*?" Francine urged, sitting down again.

Renata looked at her friend for a long moment. So lovely in her fitted vermilion suit. Curly chestnut hair brushed and gleaming. Wide-set black eyes, perfectly made up. There was nothing she wanted more than Francine Devereaux. But she knew she could not have her. Not the way she wanted her. Not anymore.

And she had her own future to consider. A future that was totally dependent on the whim of Cappy Desmond. Fickle as he was, she knew he could very well disinherit her, just like that. And then where would she be?

Renata wasn't about to risk staying in Europe. She had to go back and reestablish her presence in her father's life.

"I must return to California, Francine," she said, finally. "I have no choice."

"But that is ridiculous. Of course you have a choice. You can—"

"No. I can do nothing. No matter where we go, he will track us down and drag me back. Once he makes up his mind, he is apt to do anything to get his way. I know him."

"And you are afraid of him?"

"Not afraid. I just know how he reacts."

"I think you like how he reacts," Francine said cunningly. "I think you want to be with him. Ogre that he is, I think you like what he does to you."

Renata's emerald eyes turned flinty with anger. "Think what you wish," she said heatedly. "But you will not alter my decision."

When Cappy Desmond first caught sight of his daughter at the train station he could feel his heart thumping in his head, his ribs, his ears. Renata was breathtaking. More beautiful than he remembered.

Her silky black hair was swept back and coiled in a chignon at the nape of her slender neck. The severity of the coiffure only served to intensify the exquisite shape of her face, the elegance of her high cheekbones, the magnetism of her wondrous green eyes.

As she strolled toward him with that confident, imperious gait, he could imagine the soft curves of her naked body under the chic linen suit. And he was struck with a passion so great, so primitive in nature, that he could barely enunciate the words that clung to his throat.

"My darling," he murmured, planting a fatherly kiss on her cheek. "You've been gone far too long."

"So it seems," she replied haughtily, shrugging from his embrace. "Where's Higgens?"

"My, but that's an unusual greeting. Away almost a year and all you can say is 'Where's Higgens?' "

"What do you expect me to say, Father, that I'm overjoyed to be home?"

Her tone was sarcastic. Her demeanor petulant. She said nothing as he guided her toward the car.

It was a long drive from the train station to Shangri-la. And for more than half of the trip they didn't speak. But as the Duesenberg slipped into Beverly Hills, Cappy broke the silence.

"I've a surprise, darling. A new yacht, named after you. The *Regina Renata.* What do you think of that?" he asked, with a proud smile.

"Very nice," she answered crisply. "Is that my reward for missing my European vacation?"

"Now, Renata, you know perfectly well that I—"

"That you have no regard for what I want to do," she interrupted, her voice bordering on fury. "You needn't have summoned me home like a wayward child, you know, Father. I am perfectly capable of taking care of myself."

"Not abroad, you aren't. Not at this time. It is far too dangerous over there for two young women to be gallivanting about. I truly feared for your life, Renata."

She believed him. But she knew it would work in her favor to sulk for a while. So she did. As the days went by, nothing Cappy could say or do brought a smile to her face. The fancy dinners in the finest restaurants. the elaborate parties he threw and escorted her to. The continuous stream of pink frilly packages, which arrived by messenger.

He did not come to her bedroom during the first two weeks, which concerned her. For she knew his sexual obsession was a valuable asset. One to be cultivated and exploited.

She was confident that he had not lost interest, however. For when they were together, she could feel his intense brown eyes peering into her. And it seemed, whenever she caught him staring, that he was not just interested, but intrigued. At those moments Cappy Desmond looked like a man possessed. A man who wanted to devour her.

It was as though he couldn't let her out of his sight. He became despondent when she went out on a date. So he tried to keep her busy by taking her to dinner or a party every night. He even started including her in his daily activities, inviting her to business luncheons and meetings.

Reluctantly, she would accompany him, acting as though she were doing him a favor. But secretly Renata was enjoying this exposure to Cappy's friends and business associates. It gave her a vantage point from which to observe the extent of her father's power. And the base from which it emanated.

It did not take her long to ascertain what it was that made Cappy Desmond a force to be reckoned with in southern California. It was not his millionaire status or his real estate empire or his reputation as a bon vivant that provided him with entrée into the homes of politicians, celebrities, and studio moguls. It was the trade paper that set him apart. Made him a king in his own community. A leader. Someone to be emulated. And feared. And desired.

She asked him for a tour of *The Hollywood Daily* and spent the morning watching him in action. Discussing stories with his managing editor. Chatting with reporters. Putting the finishing touches on an editorial about studio-player contracts.

They lunched at the Brown Derby with Carole Lombard, who couldn't stop talking about the house she was having built for her mother. Several stars, including Betty Grable, stopped by to say hello. And each one commented on how John Wayne had upped and left Universal to sign a contract with Republic for eight films.

Later that afternoon, Renata met the *Daily*'s gossip columnist, Letty Molloy, who told her that Ronald Reagan had been spotted out on the town with Susan Hayward.

"Just a publicity stunt, nothing serious," Letty added offhandedly, snuffing out a Camel and lighting another one.

"What's been the most exciting event of the year, so far?" Renata wanted to know.

"Oh, that's easy," Letty chuckled. "Joan Crawford's birthday party at the Trocadero. The most elegant soiree I've seen in a long time. All arranged by her second husband, Franchot Tone, you know. Joanie looked glorious. Wore that fabulous ring he gave her. The one with the seven-carat emerald-cut diamond. Goodness, that woman has style!"

"Is she your favorite actress?"

"Just about. Course, there's Marlene . . . Dietrich, you know. Word is, she's just ga-ga over Doug Fairbanks, Jr. But everybody knows he's carrying a torch for Loretta . . . that's Loretta Young, you know."

"Of course," Renata agreed, even though she hadn't the slightest.

"What time is it getting to be, anyway?" Letty asked, glancing at her watch. "Yikes, four o'clock! Got to get to work."

She reached for a sheet of paper and rolled it into her Underwood. "Nasty little story today. Follow-up on Jackie Coogan filing a lawsuit against his mother and stepfather. Can you believe that? Claims they robbed him of more than four million dollars he earned as a juvenile star. Sometimes even I can't believe what goes on in this town."

Renata sat, captivated, for the next hour watching Letty. And intermittently browsing through some of her columns. She was fascinated with the chain-smoking gossip. Not with her appearance, for Letty was a big woman without a flair for fashion.

The drab green suit did nothing for her ungainly frame. The wide-brimmed straw hat looked totally out of place. And her flyaway brown hair had a habit of leaping into her mouth at the oddest times, so that she was constantly fanning at her face. As though shooing flies.

Nevertheless, Renata admired this hard-driven woman for her obvious stamina and enthusiasm. Apparently Letty knew all the stars she talked about. Dined with them. Visited them on sets. Even partied with them.

How someone who looked like Letty had managed to work her way into such charmed circles was beyond Renata's imagination. But the more she watched the columnist plunking away at her typewriter keys, fighting a five-thirty deadline, the more intrigued she became with the idea of working for the *Daily* herself.

The thought of a career had never crossed Renata's mind. She didn't know any women who worked and had never imagined trying to follow in her father's footsteps. But now it seemed like a perfectly legitimate prospect. And by the time Cappy emerged from his office, ready to take her home, she'd made the decision that would ultimately change the course of her life.

"And how's my lovely daughter doing, Letty? Not pestering you, I hope?" Cappy was joking, as he strolled across the room.

"Not in the slightest, boss. She's welcome anytime," Letty replied quickly. Her pale cheeks brightened to a rosy red as she glanced up into his mischievous brown eyes.

"All finished?" he inquired.

"You betcha," she said, yanking her column out of the typewriter. "There's a little shindig for Helen Hayes at Norma Shearer's tonight and I don't want to be tardy."

Letty spoke rapidly, rushing her words together as she swung around in her swivel chair. Then, just as she was about to get up, her elbow hit a pencil holder and sent it flying.

"Well, darn it to heck," Letty exclaimed, bending over to scoop up a handful of pens and pencils. But the chair rolled back. She lost her balance and was soon surging forward toward the floor.

If Cappy hadn't caught her, she might have broken her arm. Renata watched in amazement as he lunged to help steady the large woman and pull her to her feet.

"Too much work, Letty? Or too much partying?" he teased with an amused smile.

"A little of each, I suppose," she giggled.

He raised her chin with his fingertips. An innocent gesture. But Renata did not miss the look that passed between them. It was instantaneous but unmistakable. A fleeting look of understanding, familiarity, of—yes, even intimacy.

Renata spent the entire drive back to Shangri-la wondering what her father could possibly see in Letty Molloy. And convincing herself that, surely, he hadn't slept with her. But, instinctively, she knew he had.

Francine wrote several times and telephoned twice. But Renata could not be persuaded. She had made up her mind. She would not go back to Paris. Not even for the wedding. She couldn't bear it.

She knew she had lost Francine. And the best thing to do now was to stay in California, where it would be easier to forget.

Already time and distance had helped ease the pain. She missed her dear friend but not nearly as much as she'd anticipated. And as the days slipped by, memories of Francine subsided. For Renata had something else to concentrate on.

She had become almost totally preoccupied with her future. For the first time in her life, she had a direction. She had decided to carve out a new identity as a career woman. Her goal was to become as successful and powerful as Cappy himself.

The only problem was that she needed his cooperation. And she was quite certain she would not get it. Not if she asked directly. Like most men of his day, Cappy Desmond was a staunch chauvinist. Women who worked were oddities, to be tolerated, not encouraged. Women who tried to compete with men in the business world were definitely to be discouraged.

Letty Molloy was an exception. And Renata had thought about

asking the veteran gossip to talk to Cappy on her behalf. But then she'd come up with a far better idea.

It was a foolproof plan. One that was totally dependent on her feminine wiles. And her patience. For if the plan were to work, Renata would have to wait. As long as it took for him to approach her.

The fact that he hadn't yet come to her bedroom was mildly disturbing. And despite herself, Renata had begun wondering whom else he was sleeping with besides Letty Molloy.

She wasn't jealous of his other women, at least that's what she told herself. But somewhere in the depths of her being, buried under the multiple layers of anger and hatred, there was an inexplicable longing for him. A longing that Renata managed to submerge with little effort. For she had become an expert at denial. And now more than ever before, it behooved her to deny her feelings for her father.

Once he discovered her vulnerability he could destroy her. She would become his prisoner, his slave. By remaining aloof and petulant, she could control her own destiny.

And he would come to her eventually—she was certain of it. It had taken her almost eighteen years to get to this point. A few more weeks wouldn't matter.

It was one in the morning and Cappy was in a foul mood when he left the Café Trocadero. He'd dined at the Vendôme, become bored with his date, taken her home early, joined some friends at the Troc, had too many gins, clumsily knocked over a bottle of claret, and left in a huff, without even saying good-bye.

Now he was cooling his heels, waiting for the parking attendant and wondering where to go next. The *Rex*? Sure, why not? The night was still young. And it was the only place in town that might lift his spirits.

The *Rex* was Cappy's favorite all-night playground. A twenty-four-hour gambling ship owned by his good friend Tony Cornero, it was anchored off Santa Monica, three miles out, just beyond the legal limit. And on most evenings Cappy liked nothing better than to drive to the beach, hop on a water taxi, ride out to the luxury liner, climb aboard, and gamble until dawn.

Gambling was Cappy's aphrodisiac. He was a risk-taker at heart.

And once he sat down at the roulette table, he couldn't get enough. He would stay there for hours. Transfixed. Captivated. Totally immersed. So swept up in the game that nothing else mattered. Not even Renata.

This particular Saturday night was going to be different. Cappy knew that as soon as he strolled into the casino. For despite the conviviality of the tuxedoed men and bejeweled women playing baccarat or keno, despite the cacophony of their discordant voices, the shrieks of surprise from the winners, Cappy Desmond was oblivious.

He walked through the room as though in a trance. Aware of nothing but the deafening sound reverberating in his head. The sound of his daughter's laughter. Taunting him. Mocking him. Enraging him, as it had all night. Making him wild with anger—and salacity.

"Her fault, all her fault," he muttered to himself, taking a seat at his usual roulette table.

"What was that, sir?" the croupier inquired.

"Nothing. Ten on nineteen," Cappy said, slapping down a handful of black chips.

The wheel spun. The ball hopped and skipped. His eyes traveled the circumference expectantly, watching the ball flip from number to number. Until finally the wheel slowed. And the ball dropped to rest. On four.

Cappy ordered a double gin, shoved ten more chips on nineteen and glanced up at the group of excited faces gathered around the table.

But all he could see was Renata. As she'd looked earlier in the evening. So striking in that bright red off-the-shoulder dress. On her way to a formal dinner party with that pretentious attorney, Alphonse Morrow. It was the third time that week she'd seen the ineffectual wimp. What was she doing, sleeping with him?

Cappy grimaced and watched the ball settle on fifteen. The mere thought of Renata with someone else enraged him. He'd waited. He'd been patient. Forcing himself to repress his desire for her. Thinking that eventually she would settle down. Forgive him for dragging her back from Europe. Need him. Want him as much as he wanted her.

But now he realized he'd been deluding himself. For what was she doing, really? Acting vindictive and unappreciative. Flaunting a series of men in front of him. A parade of eligible bachelors. Each one well educated, reasonably attractive, and rich.

She was trying to make him jealous and she was succeeding. But not for long, Cappy told himself, reaching into his tuxedo pocket. He extracted ten more chips.

"Sorry, sir, no more bets," the croupier warned, watching Cappy's hand.

"But I didn't get a chance to—"

The croupier ignored him and spun the wheel.

Defiantly, Cappy shoved his chips on number nineteen. "There, I'm in," he shouted with a spiteful smirk.

A hush fell over the table as the wheel turned and the small white ball danced in circles, flipping around from number to number, then slowly came to rest. On nineteen.

"Aha!" Cappy exclaimed victoriously. "I've won!"

"No, sir. I'm sorry, but you haven't," the croupier disagreed in a low voice, raking the chips off the table.

"Yes, I have, you idiot. I've won fair and square, dammit." Cappy jumped up, lunged at the croupier, and caught him by the shoulder. "Now give me my chips."

Within seconds the pit boss appeared. A balding, rotund man, talking fast through a cloud of cigar smoke. His badge read "Louie."

"What seems to be the problem, Mr. Desmond? What can I do to help?"

"I'll tell you what you can do. You can fire this dimwit and get a competent croupier. Then you can kindly pay me the thousand dollars I've just won."

Louie glanced nervously around at the crowd that was gathering. Fifty people at least, each one waiting eagerly for a fight. Then he flung his arm over Cappy's shoulder in a brotherly fashion and smiled affably, displaying several gold teeth.

"Sure thing, Mr. Desmond. Why don't we just step over here to the saloon and discuss the matter."

Cappy shot Louie an indignant look, removed the man's arm as though it had a distinct malodor, and grabbed him by the lapels. "Now you listen to me, fatso. I don't want to discuss anything. I want my money and I want it now. And if—"

Suddenly Cappy felt two crushing weights on either side of his neck. The hands of the Deacon, chief bouncer on the *Rex.*

A few minutes later, the crowd had dispersed, the croupier was back at work, and Louie was calmly strolling around the casino, puffing on his imported Havana cigar.

Cappy Desmond was crouched in the corner of a water taxi, gently massaging his own neck. And moving slowly toward shore.

Somehow he managed to weave his way back to Beverly Hills in the Cadillac, all the while cursing at the top of his lungs.

"Damn them, damn them all. I'll show them. I'll write a scathing editorial all about Tony Cornero and his two-bit floating gyp joint. That'll fix 'em. That'll fix 'em good."

When he got home, he went directly to the billiard room, yanked a bottle of gin off the bar, and walked unsteadily up the winding staircase to Renata's bedroom.

He wasn't surprised that her door was closed. But locked? He tried to jiggle the doorknob with his free hand. It wouldn't budge.

"Renata . . . Renata," he whispered urgently.

She awoke with a start and sat straight up in bed, listening. For a moment there was no sound, and yet she knew it was he. Silently, she tiptoed across the hardwood floor and put her ear to the door.

Just then he knocked again, calling her name impatiently. His voice was louder now and full of anger.

He paused for a second to take a swig of gin.

As he did so, she moved to one side of a nearby chest of drawers and used all her strength to shove it against the door.

The scraping noise startled Cappy. He staggered two steps backward, a befuddled expression on his face.

"I know you're awake in there," he slurred through a mouthful of gin. "Come on, open up."

Renata scampered back to bed, propped herself up on a huge lavender pillow, folded her long graceful arms, and waited, triumphant in her little scheme.

"Dammit to hell, Renata." He was furious now, shaking the door on its hinges, sending a great clattering noise through the house.

Renata caught her breath. *My God,* she thought frantically, *maybe he's angry and drunk enough to break the door down.*

She heard the dull thud of his shoulder against the solid oak. Then another thud. And finally the shattering sound of breaking glass as the gin bottle crashed to the hallway floor and scattered in jagged pieces.

Renata's heart raced as she groped for alternatives.

There was only one.

She glanced at the double glass doors to the terrace. As a child, she had once sprung from the edge of that terrace into the thick ivy and climbed down the side of the house. But if she did that now he would only run after her and—

Wait a minute. Had he stopped? All of a sudden she could hear nothing. Except for the sound of her own breathing. And his footsteps. Moving heavily down the stairs.

After a few seconds it was perfectly quiet.

When she realized he was gone, a smug smile of self-satisfaction slipped across her lips. And a huge sense of relief washed over her as she sat there in the darkness, waiting for her thundering heartbeat to subside.

So she had won. And she wasn't surprised. It had gone exactly as she had planned.

Let it be the first in a series of victories, Renata thought with a lazy yawn. Then she stretched luxuriously. Nestled back under the cool pink sheets. And several minutes later she was fast asleep.

The next morning she arose early. Slipped into a crimson silk dressing gown. Adjusted the front folds to reveal a tempting portion of her bosom. And joined him on the patio for breakfast.

"Good morning," she said cheerily, sitting down.

"Morning," he mumbled, without looking up from the *Los Angeles Times.*

"Sleep well?"

"Fine," he lied, still reading.

"You know," she said, taking a sip of freshly squeezed orange juice, "I've been thinking about what I want to do."

"What do you mean?"

"I'm rather bored with school, Father. Perhaps it's time for me to start working."

"What for?" he asked, turning a page. "You don't need the money."

"Well, I certainly will if you decide to disinherit me."

"You know I didn't mean that."

"Nevertheless," she persisted, "you could if you wanted to."

He peered up over the paper, frowning at her. "Renata, you are generously provided for in my will. I shall never disinherit you. Now stop this nonsense about working."

"But I'm very serious about this, Father. I want to go to work. I want to be a reporter for *The Hollywood Daily.*"

He threw back his head, laughing uproariously. "And what else do you want to do, pilot an airplane?"

"Not just yet," she replied caustically, reaching for the cream. "I can't imagine what could be wrong with me working for the *Daily.* And it certainly shouldn't be too difficult for you to arrange."

"Impossible," he replied stonily.

"Why?" she prodded.

"Man's work."

"You have female reporters."

"Just Letty Molloy," he said with a little smile. "And only because she's got the best connections in town."

"I could establish connections. I could learn."

"You haven't the slightest idea how to go about it."

"She could teach me."

He studied her face for a moment, then asked, "Renata, are you telling me that you want to work for Letty? Do you really want to go slinking around private dinner parties and studio dressing rooms, groveling, waiting for someone to toss you a crumb?"

"If that's what it takes, yes," she said firmly.

Cappy folded the newspaper meticulously and placed it on the chair beside him. His expression was intense. "Well, if you are so eager to learn," he said in a low, penetrating voice, "why don't you start by learning how to leave the bolt off your door at night?"

Renata's emerald eyes flashed invitingly. "Promise me I'll be editor in chief by this time next year and I'll do that. In fact," she added, leaning toward him, "I'll do that every night."

Furious, he shoved back his chair, stood up, and hastily bounded from the table.

"Father, dear, whatever is wrong?" Renata called after him in dulcet tones. "You haven't finished your omelet."

25

■ It was late Wednesday night when Teddy placed the call to Palm Beach.

"I have to talk to you, Muffet," he insisted with urgency.

"No way, jerk-off. I got no time for losers." She hung up.

He dialed back immediately.

"Look, Muffie . . . please, sweetie, stay on the line. Hear me out. I . . . well . . . I just can't believe what you're doing."

"Can't, huh?" she sneered. "Better check today's *Wall Street Journal* and—"

"I know. I saw it. I was hoping you'd—"

"And I'm gonna be quoted in *Forbes,* too. You know, that magazine you always said I was too dumb to understand? Well, the reporter who came to interview me thought I was pretty damn smart."

"Muffie, I—"

"Don't call me Muffie, you bloated sybarite. You don't care one bit about what happens to me. You only call when you want something."

"Oh, but that's not true. You have no idea—"

"Cut the crap, Teddy. You got one more minute and I pull the plug. So talk fast. I'm listening."

"Okay. First off, you're making a big mistake aligning yourself with R. B. McDevitt. I don't know what he told you, but he's dangerous, Muffet. A corporate raider. I know the type. If he does take over, believe me, he'll destroy the studio."

"Now how the hell can he do that, Teddy, when you already have? You've run Selwyn Studios straight down the tubes. The way I look at it, the stockholders are pretty damn lucky R.B. came along."

"Muffet, I'm warning you, if he takes over we'll all lose."

"Wrong," she insisted. "You'll lose, Teddy. And you'll lose big. If R.B. throws you out, you might not have enough money left to keep your stable of hot little bumboys flaunting around the guest rooms anymore. But I'll be sitting pretty with my five percent. And the additional shares R.B. promised me."

"Additional shares?" he yelped. "What's that overblown braggart been telling you? He's lying, Muffet—"

"Can it, *putz,*" she interrupted. "Time's up. Sorry you weren't very convincing, Teddy. Why don't you try me again sometime, say, like in about fifty years?"

"Wait! Please, please, Muffet, don't cut me off," he pleaded, a desperate edge to his voice. "I need to speak with you and—"

"You just did."

"No, I mean face to face. I'll leave for the airport now. We can—"

"No we can't. And we won't. My mind's made up, Teddy. I don't want to see you. And if you dare show up here, I'll have you booted out."

She hung up. And quickly disconnected her red and white striped telephone.

"Conniving slut!" Teddy screamed at the top of his lungs.

Then he stood up. Washed his hands meticulously. Walked out of his malachite bathroom. Stepped up to his half-moon desk. And buzzed for Tim, his Maggie Smith look-alike secretary.

"Book me on the next flight to Palm Beach," Teddy yelled into the speaker phone.

He was pacing back and forth on his Italian marble platform. Thinking about Muffet Baker Selwyn. The white-bread nympho fruitcake he'd been crazy enough to marry at the tender age of twenty-three. Long before he'd had the courage to come out of the closet.

The wedding itself had been a major extravaganza. Five hundred people at his father's Bel Air estate. Twelve bridesmaids in pink peau de soie. Muffet, an angelic Goldilocks in white antique lace. Teddy lusting after her teenage brother. Fighting himself. Determined to extinguish the unnatural urges that had plagued him since puberty. Hoping marriage would help. Knowing it wouldn't.

Months before the ceremony, Teddy had realized that marrying Muffet would be a big mistake. But he couldn't have imagined that years later it would come to this.

The dumb broad could ruin him. And all it would take was her flaky, featherweight signature.

He'd been counting on Muffet, taking her for granted. Well aware that she held the swing shares. And assuming she'd vote his way.

If she didn't, Teddy could very well lose the proxy fight. George Thornton, his white knight, was well aware of that. The Aussie financier had already called, threatening to bail out unless Teddy did something to change Muffet's mind.

Well, he was going to try. And he didn't care what it might cost him. Cocaine was cheap compared to the ultimate loss of his studio. Once Muffet saw the quantity of coke he was willing to provide on a monthly basis, maybe she'd weaken and start leaning his way.

If not, there was another alternative. A riskier plan. One he hadn't thought through completely. But he didn't have to. That's what old pals like Angelo DiSappio were for.

Angelo Augustus DiSappio, Teddy's roommate at Harvard. A law student. And for the past decade, the notorious *consigliere* for the powerful Borrelli family of New York.

Angelo owed Teddy a favor. And the studio chief might soon be in a position to call it in.

Muffet Selwyn's opulent Mediterranean mansion on North Ocean Boulevard was completely protected by a nine-foot sandstone wall. A twenty-four-hour guard. An electronic security system hooked up to the Palm Beach police station. And two huge rottweilers, so ugly and vicious that even Muffet herself was terrified of them.

But the three men had no trouble slipping onto the estate totally undetected. They traveled in a truck marked Rocco's Fine Laundry. Two of them hid in the back.

The guard waved the truck through automatically. Barely glancing up from his Thermos of coffee. He poured the steaming brew into a chipped cup with one hand. Pressed a button on the panel in front of him with the other. And the massive wrought-iron gates sprang open. Just as they always did on Friday mornings, when a week's supply of towels and linens were delivered for Ms. Selwyn.

The three men had something else in mind for her.

And they had selected a perfect time. Not at random. For they had gone about their task methodically. Had known that the housekeeper would be off. And the maid out grocery shopping. They were also dead certain that the lady of the house would be on the premises.

She was. They found her lying next to her red-tiled, heart-shaped swimming pool. In a tiny string bikini. Magnificent bosoms tilted upward. A glistening, oleaginous offering to the sun.

Her eyes were closed. The acid rock blasting from her portable radio was so loud that she didn't hear the men at first. She didn't hear them at all. One of them had to nudge her with his heavy, rubber-soled shoe.

"Hey, Miss Muffet, time to wake up," he ordered in a raspy voice. "We got a delivery for ya!"

Muffet's indigo eyes fluttered open. And closed immediately. It had to be a nightmare. Two grisly-looking thugs dressed in black and sporting handguns staring down at her? *Must have been the smack last night,* she thought. *Shouldn't have touched the stuff. Better go back to sleep.*

"Hey, princess, I'm talking to you, get it?" asked the one with the scar on his face. He leaned over and gave her reddened cheek a slap.

"Ow! What the hell are you doing?" Muffet yelped, eyes popping open. She caught her breath as the hideous face came into focus.

The scar was a purplish shade. And long. It ran all the way from his right temple to the tip of his chin. She could see it pulsating as he stooped down next to her. Twirling the gun in his hand. Smelling profusely of sweat and garlic.

"Hi ya, sweetlips, my name's Sal," he announced with a surly smile.

A glacial chill crept over Muffet's sunbaked body as a million tiny goose bumps bloomed on her skin. Fear coursed through her veins like ice water.

She wanted to scream. She wanted to run. But she could do neither. Muffet was so scared that she was completely immobilized. Trapped. Pinioned. Limbs locked in place.

Don't panic, she told herself. *If you panic you're dead.*

"Who . . . who let you in?" she stammered through quivering lips.

"The guard, cupcake," Sal chortled. "Real nice guy."

She inched a towel up over her prodigious breasts.

Sal ripped it from her hands. "Now don't be shy, Miss Muffet. Tony and me were admiring the view. Right, Tony?"

The heavyset man with the dark, hooded eyes was pacing back and forth near the chaise longue. "Right, Sal," he agreed nervously. "So what do you say we just go inside and get this over? We're in here too long and the guard's gonna get wise."

"Tony. Tony. I just don't understand ya," Sal complained, shaking his head. "Ain't you never heard of enjoying your work?"

He grabbed Muffet's arm and jerked her to her feet.

"Okay, cuddlecakes. Show us to your bedroom. And make it fast, so's ol' Tony here won't get his nose outa joint."

"What about Joey?" Tony asked, glancing at the truck.

"Joey can wait!" Sal said, irritated. "Now put your gun away and do her wrists. Mouth, too. I gotcha covered."

Tony worked swiftly. Gagging Muffet with a wadded handkerchief and a black scarf. Extracting a piece of nylon parachute cord from the pants' pocket to bind her hands behind her back.

"All set, dollface? Forward march!" Sal commanded, following the two of them into the house.

The air-conditioning sent another cold tremor through Muffet's body. By the time she reached the top of the stairs she was trembling uncontrollably. So frightened she could barely walk. What were they going to do, shoot her? Was this one of those Mafia-style executions? Is that why the fat guy was insistent on getting it over with? And who the hell was Joey?

Sal shoved her through the bedroom doorway.

His dark eyes swept over the red and white polka dot, heart-shaped bed. "Ohhhh, real cute," he smirked. "A Mary Poppins bedroom. Bet you're really more like Madonna, though, huh, Miss Muffet?"

Muffet sank onto the bed and stared at the floor.

"Okay, truss her up!"

"Sal, come on. What are you talking about?" Tony complained. "Angelo said we weren't supposed to—"

"Screw Angelo! I'm the boss now. So get to it, on the double."

"But I already did her wrists—"

Sal's face contorted into rabid fury. "I know what you did. Now do more. The whole shebang. Come on, move it."

Reluctantly, Tony reached into his pocket for more parachute cord. "Ahhh . . . Muffet, I want you to, ah, kneel on the bed."

With Tony's help, Muffet shifted her weight to a kneeling position and raised herself slowly up on her haunches. She was choking on her tears. Struggling for breath. Her heart was pounding so hard she thought her chest would explode.

This is it, she thought. *This is where I'm going to spend the last few minutes of my life. They're going to rape me with my wrists tied. Both of them at once. One in front and one in back. Over and over, until I die. Then they'll cut me up and paint the walls with my blood. Christ, why don't they just shoot me and get it over with? Please, God. Please.*

"Now bend over," Tony was saying, giving her a little push.

Faster than she knew what was happening, he had her ankles tied to her wrists. So her shoulders and face were on the bed. And her bottom straight up in the air.

"Mfff . . . mfff," Muffet groaned, twisting back and forth.

"Now that's more like it," Sal said, excitedly, walking around the bed. He moved in closer and grazed his callused hand over her oily skin.

"Some nice stuff you got there, Miss Muffet. Some very nice stuff," Sal reiterated, giving her a little pinch. "So I guess you'd say we've got you in a compromising position, huh?"

"Mfff."

"That's right, babycakes. We sure do. And you're gonna see why in just a minute. Tony, you got those papers?"

"Right here," Tony said, extracting an envelope from his jacket pocket. "Want me to read what it says to her?"

"No, you rubberhead. That'd take about three years, at your remedial rate. Gimme it! Now be a good boy and go get Joey."

Sal held the contract in front of Muffet's face. "See this, honeybunch? This here's an agreement between you and Selwyn Studios. Basically it says you sign your voting power over to your ex-husband Teddy. Got that?"

"Mfff," Muffet moaned, nodding her head.

"Now if you sign this thing, me and Tony, we disappear. Poof! Outa your life like we never even been here. Just like magic. *Capisce?*"

"Mfff. Mfff."

"Good, babydoll. I love smart dames. Now, would you like to know what's going to happen if you decide not to sign this agreement?"

"Ummf," Muffet groaned, shaking her head back and forth.

"You wouldn't?" Sal chuckled. "Oh, but ya gotta listen, cutie pie," he taunted, running his index finger up her thigh. "I got to explain the whole package, see? And here's part of it. Come on in, Joey. I was just talkin' about you."

Muffet eyed Joey with apprehension. He looked like Sal, without the scar. Joey was younger, with a better build. But he had the same swagger to his step.

"Over here, Joey. So's Miss Muffet can see you," Sal instructed, waving his .38 Smith & Wesson.

Joey swung across the room toward the bed. It was then that Muffet noticed the thing hanging around his shoulders. It was long and brown and it looked like . . . it looked like rope.

A thick piece of rope!

Oh, Lord! Muffet clenched her teeth, picturing the inevitable. *They're going to hang me from the chandelier, that's what they're going to do. They're going to make a noose and string me up. Oh, no. Please, no!*

She was trembling and moaning as Joey came closer. She squeezed her eyes shut and listened to the thunder of her heartbeat. Praying to a God she barely remembered.

"Ummf," she murmured as Joey sat down heavily on the bed.

It took all her courage to open her eyes once more. At first she raised her lids just a bit. Everything looked fuzzy and out of focus.

Joey was removing the rope from his neck and placing it on the bed. The rope coming closer. It was moving. No, more like sliding. It was—

Muffet popped her eyes wide open just in time to see the rope slithering toward her.

She let out a high, keening wail.

She could see clearly now. It wasn't a rope at all. It was—a snake. A long, pale brown snake, with a yellow underbelly and a brick-red tail. Its head was hideous and full of scales. And it was almost touching her now. Just a moment more and—

Joey lunged and grabbed the snake.

Muffet froze, paralyzed with fear.

Sal twirled his gun, chuckling. "S'matter, Miss Muffet? You don'
like Joey's little friend? Come on now, be nice. This here's Sam. Jus
your average pet boa constrictor. Perfectly harmless—unless he'
hungry."

Joey smiled sadistically and held Sam's scaly head up next t(
Muffet's. The snake was two inches from her nose.

She didn't move. She didn't blink. Sam looked hungry.

"Well," Sal said, "I guess I can understand why you're not actin$
exactly cordial. Your ex-hubby told us you have this ah . . . what'$
that word he used? Oh, yeah, *aversion,* that's it. Teddy says you hav(
an aversion to snakes. Is that right, honeybunch?"

"Mfff," Muffet whimpered, ready to faint.

"Well, the way I see it then, sugar, you got two choices. Eithe≀
you sign this here agreement, or Joey lets loose with Sam. No⋈
which one's it gonna be, huh, Miss Muffet?"

The twins looked adorable in matching plaid skirts and sweaters
Their dispositions, though, were anything but sweet. And bringing
them to the Longhorns game had been a big mistake. They hadn'≀
stopped bickering since the kickoff.

Now, as the stadium clock counted down the final few minutes o∤
the intensely fought game, Kate was bordering on rage. And having
serious doubts about motherhood.

Her friend Sara's thirteen-year-old daughters were impossible. I≀
took all of her self-discipline not to haul off and slap them both.

"I wanna go home. I wanna go home. I wanna go home," Jennife⟍
kept chanting to the tune of the cheerleaders' fight song.

"Shut up dumbbell," Jackie protested, yanking on her sister's long
sandy-blond hair. "You're not going anywhere."

"Oh, yes, I am," Jennifer yelped, giving Jackie a shove. "I'm
going to the movies with Randy. At seven-thirty. So we have to
leave right now. Come on, Aunt Kate."

"Jenny, will you please stop?" Kate sighed, exasperated. "We're
not leaving until the game is over. And your mother said nothing to
me about the movies. You'll have to ask her first."

"But I never see her anymore," Jennifer whined. "She never even
comes home."

"Can it, puttyface," Jackie hissed. "You know very well that Mom's in Santa Barbara, trying to find Uncle Taylor. So—"

"Oh, yeah, sure," Jennifer interrupted, clasping her hand over Jackie's mouth. "A likely excuse. She's probably shacked up at the Biltmore, humping Hard-on Johnson! Ow! Damn you, Jackie. She bit me, Aunt Kate."

"Girls!" Kate gasped, with a furtive glance around the press box. Her face reddening with embarrassment. It was bad enough being with the twins. Worse when in the presence of her fellow journalists.

Kate had been the recipient of unfriendly glares and angry glowers all afternoon. At the moment, to her relief, no one seemed to be paying attention to the girls' Punch-and-Judy sideshow. All eyes were riveted to the television monitor as the players lined up at midfield, ready for action.

"This is it, Harry," a fat, cigar-chewing sports columnist told his best friend. "We're going to see the Rams pull themselves up by the short hairs now."

"Are you kidding, Len?" his sidekick replied. "With less than four minutes left? There's no way in hell the Rams are going to stop Brocato."

Down on the field, the irregular cadence of Don Brocato's husky voice pierced through the roaring crowd at Anaheim Stadium.

"Blue twenty-four. X-eighty. Hut-hut. Hut."

But the star quarterback barely heard the numbers that fell from his lips. His mind had frozen in crystal-clear intensity, focusing on the details of the upcoming play.

Suddenly a hush fell over the line of scrimmage as the assemblage of brawny, hulking bodies tensed for combat. And for a fleeting second it seemed as though both teams had stopped breathing.

"Hut!" Brocato took the snap.

Upstairs in the announcers' booth, Brad Hunter described the action for the national football audience.

"And Brocato is rolling to his right. Looking downfield. Good coverage by the Rams. Brocato's pulling the ball down. He's taking off. He's running up the right side. He's across the forty. And now he's down just inside the Rams' thirty-five-yard line. It'll be fourth and one as the official spots the ball at the Rams' thirty-five.

"Brocato made a nice move to avoid the first defensive back," added color commentator Woody Campbell. "And he's got it down well within field goal range for Longhorns' kicker Stanislaw Dupa."

"Hold on a second, Woody. I can't imagine why. But they're bringing in the punting team."

"Now why would the Longhorns punt in this situation, Brad?" asked the color commentator incredulously. "They're only two points up. And now they're going to give the Rams the ball back with plenty of time."

"Hard to believe. But that's exactly what they're doing. With three and a half left in the fourth quarter. I just don't understand why Fort Worth is giving the Rams a chance to win this game Woody. Christmas has definitely come early here in Anaheim. Stani slaw Dupa could kick a field goal from this range in his sleep."

"What do you think Coach Dunphy is up to?"

"Beats me. But right now it looks as though there's a little prob lem on the sidelines," said Brad, his voice rippling with excitement

"Maybe more than a little problem."

The camera followed Number 7 jogging toward the Longhorns bench.

"Apparently Don Brocato didn't like the call either," Woody con tinued. "He appears to be enraged. Making a beeline for Coach Ma Dunphy. Look at that! Got him good in the shoulder. Quarterback Don Brocato, clearly out of control. And here come some of hi teammates. They're trying to restrain him—"

Astounded by the sideline skirmish, Kate jumped up.

"Listen, you two," she told the twins sternly, "just sit here until come back. No funny stuff, understand? And for goodness sake, try to keep quiet."

Then she darted toward the door. Moving quickly and impatiently down an endless row of reporters.

"Whoops," she exclaimed, hooking her foot on a corpulent calf Before she knew it Kate had stumbled into the lap of the cigar chewing sports columnist.

She shuddered with humiliation.

Jennifer and Jackie doubled over with laughter.

"Terribly sorry," Kate apologized, pushing herself up off the man's humongous thighs.

He grunted an acknowledgment. Barely aware of her presence. Like everyone else in the stadium he was completely captivated by the fight. Stunned by the barrage of expletives the Longhorns' star quarterback was firing at his coach.

"You fucking mouthbreather," Brocato shouted, struggling to break away from the paralyzing embrace of two teammates. "What kind of a pussy call was that?"

Max Dunphy was seething. His scarlet face set in a stony glare. His jugular vein palpitating wildly. He wanted to rip into the defiant quarterback's flesh with his bare hands. Smash his perfect white teeth down his throat. Hear him beg for mercy. But Max Dunphy couldn't do that. He was on national television, for God's sake.

Three TV cameras ground away, covering the shocking confrontation from every angle.

Dunphy summoned every ounce of self-control.

"You're out of here, you asshole," the irritated Irishman hissed in a voice too low for audio pickup. Turning, he shouted at the punter, "Now get out there and kick the ball." Then he bent down and swooped his tan felt fedora up off the ground. And marched indignantly back toward the bench.

Relieved, the two players loosened their grasp on Brocato.

"Come on, Bro, put a lid on it," urged one.

"No way in hell," Brocato answered, shrugging them both off. And before they knew it, he was charging after Dunphy.

The camera crews followed in hot pursuit.

"You're not getting off that easy, pal," the strapping coach heard, just before his knees buckled.

Brocato was tackling him from behind. Wrestling him to the ground. Pouncing on him. Raising a fist to smash him in the mouth.

But Dunphy caught Brocato's arm in the descent. Used it to shift his weight. And rolled over on top of the surprised quarterback.

"I'm going to kill you, you little punk," sneered Dunphy, eyes inflamed with hostility. His massive fist smashed down on the handsome quarterback's mouth with a furious thud. Dunphy smiled triumphantly and drew back for another punch.

But someone grabbed his elbow. Then the other arm. All of a sudden four of the Longhorns were there. Jumping on top of the two men. Trying to pull them apart.

The television cameras zoomed in on the mountainous heap of gyrating flesh. Enormous arms and legs flailed about. For several moments it was impossible to tell which limb belonged to whom.

Brocato and Dunphy kept rolling around the ground. Clinging to each other like Velcro. There were grunts and groans. An endless bombardment of four-letter words from six different voices. Elbows jabbed into ribs. And knees plunged into groins.

Then finally it was over. The outraged coach and his pugnacious quarterback had been pried apart.

"Get offa me, goddammit!" Dunphy moaned. He was lying on his back, piniones by kicker Stanislaw Dupa and wide-receiver Dwight Smith.

Inches away Brocato was shackled in the iron clutches of a line-backer and an offensive guard.

Dunphy got up first and, with an indignant flourish, brushed off his slacks. Then he straightened his tweed jacket. "Get that bastard out of here," he ordered. "And I mean do it fast."

As Kate ran through the tunnel toward the field, her mind charged wildly ahead. Sifting through a maze of anxious thoughts. From the possibility of what the fight might mean to the prospect of an interview with Don Brocato.

What in the world was he doing out there? Pouncing on his coach in front of millions of people. Had he just gone berserk? Or was there . . . yes, of course, there had to be a better explanation. A young player like Brocato, with such a promising career, would never take this kind of risk, unless . . . unless his ethics were at stake.

Was that it? Was Don Brocato compromising his integrity by playing for the Longhorns? Was that the reason he'd agreed to an interview, then backed out at the last minute? Maybe he'd been scared then. Maybe he was ready to talk now.

Yes. Of course. That had to be it. Brocato had reached his limit, and he'd cracked.

Kate picked up her speed, thankful she'd had the good sense to wear a jumpsuit and Reeboks. She ran as though racing for her life. *Getting to Brocato could make all the difference. If he said something incriminating about the team. Or Templeton Haight. Or Renata—*

"Hold it right there, ma'am. You have a pass?" The beefy security guard stood at the entrance, blocking her.

Kate held up the laminated press credential hanging from a silver chain around her neck.

"That won't do you no good here," the guard said smugly. "Got to have field clearance to get inside."

Over his shoulder, Kate could see Number 7 limping toward the locker room.

Damn, she thought. *Brocato's getting away.*

"Listen," she tried to reason with the guard, "it's very important that I get in. You see I'm with *World* magazine and I'm doing a piece on—"

"Don't matter to me if you *own* six magazines, lady. You ain't going inside without a field pass, which I gather you don't have."

"No, but I—" She reached for her wallet and extracted a ten-dollar bill.

"Sister, how dumb do you think I am?" the guard sneered. "This ain't Hollywood. It's Anaheim. People got some decency here. Now why don't you just turn yourself around like a good girl and go back upstairs where you belong?"

Kate shot him a withering look. Did a half-turn as though leaving. Then made a quick last-ditch effort to sidestep him. But he was built like a stevedore. It was no use.

"Friggin' media," the guard muttered as she walked away. "Think they can do anything they damn well please."

Don Brocato was bleeding profusely from the mouth and grumbling to himself when he made his way back to the locker room. His swollen right knee throbbed with white-hot pain. His uniform was caked with dirt and covered with grass stains. His body glistened with sweat.

But he didn't bother to shower. Yanking his clothes from the locker and grabbing his leather bag, Brocato moved as quickly as he could toward the exit.

Once outside, he started limping in the direction of his rented black Mustang.

"Don. Don Brocato!"

The shout was female. He glanced back long enough to catch a glimpse of her, made a snap decision, and hailed a cab.

"Don, wait! Kate Brannigan. *World* magazine," she pleaded, running to catch up with him.

She was almost there. Just a few seconds more. Oh no, he's not going to—

Out of nowhere, a blue and white taxi squealed up to the curb. Before it came to a full stop, the door swung open, Brocato jumped in and sped away.

Kate was panting as she watched him disappear. So exhausted she had to sit down on the curb to catch her breath. And just as she felt a bit of strength trickling back into her limbs, she heard a faint rumbling sound from behind. Within seconds it had turned into a roar. A thunderous roar of applause. The tumultuous hoots and raucous cheers of more than sixty-five thousand fans coming from inside the stadium.

The L.A. Rams had just kicked their winning field goal. Beating the Longhorns, 20–19.

It took Kate more than a half hour to fight her way through the jubilant stadium crowd back to the press box. When she finally got there, everyone was gone. Including the twins.

"Good God, this is all I need," she muttered to herself, slumping into a seat. "First I lose Brocato. Now Jackie and Jennifer. Brannigan, you sure have a knack for mucking up a perfectly beautiful Sunday afternoon."

She sat there for a few minutes, as though in a trance. Unable to think clearly. She imagined the girls had gone to the car. But at the moment she felt as though she couldn't move another inch.

Her back hurt. Her feet hurt. Everything hurt. A vision of a steaming, hot bubble bath floated before her dull eyes. And she smiled dreamily. Wishing away the long, smoggy ride back to Bel Air.

"Aunt Kate! Where have you been?"

It was Jackie, bounding down the steep stadium steps. A frenzied expression on her small, round face.

"I might ask you the same question, young lady," Kate replied, forcing herself to her feet. "I thought I told you to stay here. Where's Jennifer?"

"Oh, Aunt Kate. I don't know," Jackie whimpered, throwing her arms around the weary journalist and holding her tight.

"What do you mean you don't know?" Kate asked with a rush of apprehension. She ran her hand over the girl's long, straight hair.

Jackie choked back a sob and loosened her grip on Kate. "I can't find her anywhere. Just before the game ended she went to the ladies' room. But she didn't come back. I got nervous and went looking. But she wasn't there."

Kate's chest tightened and her heart pounded at an accelerated rate. "Where else did you look?" she asked apprehensively.

"Everywhere! All over. For the last twenty minutes. But she's gone, Aunt Kate. I'm afraid she's been abducted. And—"

Kate struggled to remain calm. "Now, Jackie, don't jump to conclusions," she soothed in a gentle voice. "You're overreacting, just like your mother. I'm certain Jenny is perfectly all right. She's probably perched on the hood of the car waiting for us right now."

But as she took Jackie's hand and guided her toward the exit, Kate couldn't stop thinking she was to blame. And all the way to parking lot C she kept turning the same words over and over in her mind.

It's all my fault. It's all my fault. It's all my fault.

26

■ "It's all my fault," Sara blurted out when she finally reached Mark at one in the morning. She'd been trying his number for hours. Ever since she'd gotten back from Santa Barbara and found Kate in the living room. Her face ashen and grave.

"I'm sorry, Sara," her friend had begun.

Sara had listened intently, looking from Kate to Jackie. Unable to fully comprehend what she was being told at first. It just wasn't possible. Things like this happened to other people. Not her.

"I think we should drive to Anaheim right now and file a report with the police," Harding had offered officiously.

"I already did that," Kate replied.

Harding looked miffed, as though she weren't allowing him to be of help. "And what about here in town with the West Los Angeles Police?"

"Just got back from there."

Harding frowned.

Sara sank into a French bergère chair and tried to pull some clues together.

"Jackie, what's this about Jennifer having plans to go to the movies with Randy? Randy who?"

"I don't know, Mom," Jackie whimpered. "I've never heard of a guy called Randy. But Jenny does that all the time. She's constantly making up stories about new boys she's seeing. You know that."

Sara didn't. But she was beginning to realize there was probably a lot about Jennifer she didn't know. Maybe wouldn't ever have the chance to find out. Not now.

The next few hours unfolded like a bad dream. Harding insisted on staying. And made a scene, shouting at Sara when she finally forced him out the door.

Kate and Jackie refused to go to bed. Sara knew she couldn't possibly sleep. Or eat. In fact, she didn't know what to do, except cry.

And she did plenty of that. By the time she spoke with Mark, she was sobbing hysterically. Orbiting out of control. In desperate need of someone to calm her down.

"Mark, what are we going to do?" she heard herself plead in a frenzied voice. She felt so disconnected and out of sync, it was as though someone else were talking.

"Now just hold on, Sara," Mark ordered. "It's going to be all right. I want you to sit down and don't move. Don't do anything until I get there. Understand?"

He was at the front door within twenty minutes. And although Sara wouldn't admit it, just the sight of him made her feel better. After Kate and Jackie went upstairs to bed she sat down next to him on the couch. And they talked for several hours. Until she finally snuggled up against him and went to sleep.

They spent the next day together, visiting police stations. Talking to detectives in Anaheim and West Los Angeles. Answering dozens of questions about Jennifer. Filling out endless forms. Making certain that arrangements to distribute the bulletin with her picture were under way. Asking how soon they might know . . . anything.

They worked together effortlessly. Like a team. An efficient team. With a long track record. A firm belief in each other. And no problems, other than the tragedy of their missing daughter.

It was as though the crisis they were facing together had dissolved all the animosity between them. As though Jennifer's disappearance were, inadvertently, reuniting the two people who had met so many years ago on a Saturday night at a Princeton dance. And showing them why they'd decided to become a team in the first place.

By five in the afternoon they were back in the Bel Air house. Sitting at the kitchen table. Sharing an untouched turkey sandwich and sipping lukewarm coffee. Neither of them able to eat.

"Sara, you can't blame yourself for everything," Mark was saying. "It's as much my fault as—"

"No. No, it's not. You were there for her, Mark. You made an effort to see her, at least. I didn't. I neglected her needs. Just like Taylor's. I tried to make him into something he wasn't. And now he's gone too."

She pulled a tissue out of her pocket and dabbed her eyes. "Lord, I must look like a raccoon by now, the way I've been crying," she apologized, blowing her nose.

"Will you quit berating yourself, for God's sake?" he said, exasperated. "That's the trouble with you, you know. You always want to hog the guilt. It's as though nobody else has a right to feel as terrible as you do. Now why the hell is that?" he inquired with a little smile.

She looked up at him tentatively, then smiled back. "Because I'm a better Jew than you are?"

"No. I think it has something to do with you trying to justify your existence by being responsible for more than you can handle."

"You've been seeing a shrink?" she asked, surprised.

"If you can, I can. You're evading the issue, worrywart."

"But I am responsible," she said defensively. "It's just the way I . . . well, it's just the way I am."

"Yes, I know. But you have to realize that certain situations are beyond your control. Like Jennifer, for instance. You're not going to change anything by making yourself feel guilty."

"But I—"

"Sara, please. We're not even sure Jenny was abducted. She might have run away. You know she's threatened to leave home a couple of times lately."

"I know. I should have listened to her when—"

"Hush. We're doing what we can, Sara. We've gone to the police. They're sending out a bulletin. They're contacting all the units from here to Anaheim. Kate has already arranged for Jenny's picture to appear in the *Los Angeles Times* and the *Herald Examiner* tomorrow. There is nothing else we can do right now. And you have to live with that, Sara. You cannot blame yourself for everything that goes wrong."

"What about us?" she asked softly. "Who do I blame for that?"

Mark fell silent and tapped his finger on the coffee mug in front of him.

"Who do I blame, Mark?" Sara persisted. "Myself? Was I too capable? Too responsible? Is that why you left?"

"No," he replied in a low voice.

"Well, then, what was it? Maybe you should start enumerating the reasons and—"

"Sara, we've been through all of this before, dammit."

"No, we haven't. Not really. And I think I'm entitled."

"Look," he said, with a tired sigh, "there's nothing more I can say about it. I just need to be on my own for a while."

"On your own with that cheap trick Niki Erickson, you mean!"

Mark slammed his hand on the butcher-block table so hard it stung. "Shut up, Sara. You don't know what you're talking about, Niki and I are friends. And we share mutual friends. That's as far as it goes."

"You're living with her!"

"Are you crazy?" he shouted. "I've been alone since I moved out of here. You don't believe me? You want to come and see my place right now? Inspect the premises? Is that what you want?"

"No. I couldn't care less," she snapped.

"Good," he said, with finality. And after a few seconds, he added, "Sara, I have never lied to you. I told you I had to get out of this house because I needed time to—"

"Space was how you put it."

"Yes, *space.* And I still need it."

"You're going to have a lot of time and space, Mark," she reminded him in an icy voice. "As soon as the divorce goes through."

"I'm not the one pushing for that, and you know it."

"Well, I am," Sara insisted. "Somebody has to make a move. We can't just go on like this in . . . in some sort of limbo."

"Okay," he shrugged. "If that's what you want."

"It is!" she lied.

"Then let's stop talking about it, for chrissake." He got up and paced around the kitchen. "Why don't you go upstairs and get some rest?"

"Can't. Have to go to the studio."

"You're not serious?"

Sara nodded. " 'Fraid so. I took a three-day weekend and there's so much paperwork piled up on my desk the fire marshal is about to condemn my office."

"What about *Ki & Company?*"

She shrugged.

"No word on Taylor?"

"None."

"I hate to say this, Sara, but I think he'll be better off if he's canned."

"I know. It's all my—"

"No," Mark said, walking toward her. "No, it is not your fault. Why don't you start letting me take some of the blame?"

"But you didn't tell him to take the part."

"I encouraged it, though, didn't I?"

"So you did," she agreed with a faint smile. "All right, you can have half."

"That's better," Mark said firmly. And then, without warning, he leaned over and kissed her. Very warmly. Very gently. On the lips.

Sara could feel her mouth melting into his. Her heart pulsating furiously. She reached up to touch his cheek. And she was blinded by a sudden surge of tears, which spilled down her cheeks, moistening the kiss that sealed the fragile bond between them.

"I'll stay in one of the guest rooms tonight," he announced as he left. "Be here when you get back."

After she heard the door close, Sara sat at the kitchen table for several minutes. Staring into space.

She was shaken.

She was frightened.

She was in a state of shock.

Yet, somehow, she was ebullient.

And from the jumble of thoughts that tripped haltingly through her troubled mind, came the long-forgotten words of a favorite Shakespeare sonnet:

> ruin'd love, when it is built anew
> Grows fairer than at first, more strong, far greater.

Come off of it, Silverstein, she chastised herself as she marched up the stairs to change. *Don't get carried away. A mercy kiss. That's all it was. You're such a dumb, romantic wimp.*

Brandy had a six A.M. call. That meant waking up at four-thirty. She was still a bit groggy when she sat down in the makeup chair.

But the glaring headline on the front page of *The Hollywood Daily* jolted her to attention:

TAYLOR EVANS DISAPPEARS
Ki & Company Canceled

The scathing article portrayed Taylor as a preordained guru who should never have ventured forth from his Santa Barbara retreat. "An overrated hunk with a conspicuous absence of talent and a predilection for temper tantrums," it continued.

Brandy had to bite her lip when she read the last paragraph.

"Casting Taylor Evans in *Ki & Company* was a horrendous mistake. And Evans's presence on national television an embarrassment to the entire Hollywood community. Let it be a lesson to us all."

"Deanna, I just don't believe this," Brandy told her makeup artist in a shaken voice.

"What's that, honey? The piece on Taylor?" the attractive brunette asked, reaching for a lipbrush. "Pretty bad, huh?"

"Bad? It's appalling. Absolutely uncalled for. I can't imagine what he's going to do when he sees it."

"You still don't know where he is?"

"No. Well, yes. I mean, I think I do, but I—" Brandy sighed, obviously distraught.

"I know, honey. It's a tough one, isn't it?" the makeup artist said gently. Aware that she was treading on very sensitive turf.

Deanna knew how difficult it was for Brandy to discuss her personal life. But she also knew how much the young woman had opened up since her first day on the set. And it wasn't surprising. Quite often, actors and actresses shared more of their intimate thoughts with their makeup artist than they did with their best friends, or even their mates. All they needed was a little encouragement.

Over the years at the studio Deanna had become an expert listener. She'd had to. It came with the territory. The moment someone sat down in her chair she was a captive audience. Sometimes she was really interested in what she heard. Other times she just pretended to be.

But for Brandy St. John she'd felt an immediate affinity. Right from the start she'd sensed that the girl was troubled. Confused about her personal life. And probably in love with Taylor Evans, even though she wouldn't admit it.

"I'm not sure what will happen, even if I do find him," Brandy said after a long silence.

"You haven't heard from him at all?"

Brandy shook her head. "Not for a week. I telephoned several times and left messages."

"Well, maybe he's just out of sorts about his show and doesn't want to bother you. You know how men are."

"I'm not sure I do," Brandy said candidly. "And I'm certain I don't know what to do about Taylor." She thought for a moment, then added. "I never let on how much I cared about him, I told you that."

"Yes, you did. But now you seem to be telling me that you want this man back in your life."

"Do I?" Brandy asked, examining her own face in the mirror. "I guess so. But I'm . . . I feel so confused."

"Honey," Deanna said, whisking a powder brush over Brandy's forehead, "You know what I always say about something like this? If it's meant to be, it'll happen. All you have to do is follow your heart. Why don't you think about that for a while?"

Brandy did think about it for the rest of the day. She sailed through her scenes on automatic pilot. When she wasn't delivering lines she was weighing and balancing the odds of running after Taylor.

If she didn't run after him, what would happen? Nothing. She'd probably never see him again. If she did, what would he do? Would he want her back? Or was he too troubled right now? Too wrapped up in his own inner turmoil to care about anyone else? Worse yet, had he managed to forget her completely?

No. How could he? The thought of Taylor not caring anymore left Brandy shaken. Overcome by an unfamiliar emptiness. A longing she couldn't quite define. She missed him. Had missed him since the day he'd stopped calling her. She wanted to be near him. Needed him as she had never needed a man in her life. But at the same time she was frightened. Afraid to reach out. To let him know how deeply she cared.

"That's a wrap for you, Brandy," the assistant director told her at three o'clock. "Have a nice afternoon."

"Thanks, Mack,"

Brandy started wandering in the direction of the soundstage exit. Still lost in thought. But as she moved along her pace quickened. Soon she was mounting the steps to her dressing-room trailer. Changing into jeans and a sweatshirt. Grabbing her script and purse. Running out to her silver Maserati. Tearing past the studio gates like a fireball. And speeding over Beverly Glen to catch the Ventura Freeway north.

The drive took a little more than an hour. As soon as she saw the exit sign marked Seacliff, Brandy felt refreshed. Energized. And full of conviction.

She smiled as she turned onto the narrow dirt road. Seacliff was a small, private beach community tucked away just south of Santa Barbara. A half-mile strip of modest homes perched on a cluster of massive, craggy rocks overlooking the Pacific.

Not far away a railroad track ran parallel with the ocean. And after the summer months the exclusive colony took on the appearance of a ghost town. For there were few year-round residents. A modicum of activity. And aside from the roar of an occasional train on its way to or from Los Angeles, not an extraneous sound.

Yet the soothing lull of the ocean was all-pervasive. A constant reminder of the permanence of nature. The impermanence of everything else.

Seacliff was the most exhilarating yet serene setting Brandy had ever laid eyes on. The perfect place to block out the world. And she knew if Taylor were anywhere in California, it would be in this secluded enclave a short distance from Hollywood. Yet so removed from the deception and hypocrisy of the frenetic city, it seemed light-years away.

He'd brought her here just once before and shown her the rustic beachhouse he'd purchased several years earlier. Explaining that no one else knew about it, not even Sara. And confiding that, though he rarely used the house, it was like his "psychic insurance policy." A place where he could always come to sort things out.

Now, as Brandy took deep breaths of the cool, rejuvenating air, she wondered what he would say when he saw her. If he was there.

Of course he's there, she argued with herself, slowing down to fifteen miles an hour. Her anxious azure eyes scanned several empty driveways. And quickly spotted his blue BMW, parked behind the beige shingled house.

The side door was closed. She knocked tentatively.

No answer. Her heart quickened.

"Taylor. Taylor?" she called, walking toward the front deck.

There her voice was drowned out by the great roar of the ocean. But she saw him immediately, sitting high up on the rocks, watching the tide come in. His back was to her. And for a moment she just stood there on the redwood deck. Frozen in position.

She couldn't have predicted how she would feel at this moment. For she'd never had the feeling before. It was beyond joy. Beyond relief. Beyond ecstasy. A tingling exuberance radiated through her entire body. Like a series of quick electrical charges taking control. Commanding her to run. Spring. Fly across the front deck, over the sand, and up the crudely fashioned stone steps.

"Taylor. Taylor," she called, bounding toward him. Fighting the great sound barrier of the crashing waves.

"Taylor!" she shouted as she finally reached the top of the steps.

He turned to her. His face tired and bearded. His amber eyes reflecting an incongruous mix of disbelief and tenderness, anxiety and love.

When he stood up and reached for her she wrapped her graceful arms around his shoulders. Clinging to him with all her strength. As though her life were immutably entwined with his and letting go would be like giving up the most precious part of her very existence.

She could feel the soft cotton of his T-shirt rubbing against her face. The strength of his muscular arms encircling her.

"I . . . I wanted to come sooner," she said in an unsteady voice. "Wanted to tell you—"

"Yes," he asked gently. "Tell me what?"

"That . . . that you should call Sara. Jennifer's missing. She's been gone since Sunday. And . . . and your series—"

Taylor stepped back and examined her face. "I already know. I called Sara this morning. Is that all you wanted to tell me?"

Their eyes locked, and she felt a shiver run from the tip of her head to the bottom of her sandaled feet. "No."

"What else?" he asked expectantly.

"I wanted to tell you that I . . . I miss you. That I was worried about you. And that I'm . . . I . . . I love you, Taylor." Her voice cracked on the words.

He cupped her chin in his hands. Looking down at her exquisite face. Wanting so much to believe her.

"Brandy, you—"

"No. Please. Let me finish. I have to say it all at once, or I'll lose my nerve." She reached up for his hands and took them in her own. "I've been so selfish, Taylor. So insensitive. Taking you for granted. I knew what you were going through with *Ki & Company*. But I just, well, I just dismissed it, thinking that . . ." her voice trailed off and Taylor could see her eyes were moist with tears. "Thinking that I shouldn't be concerned with your career, because I hardly had the energy to devote to my own."

He pulled her closer to him, locking her in his arms. Wishing he could articulate what he was feeling. The myriad of emotions coursing through his being. But he couldn't find the words. Nothing he said could possibly convey the intensity of his connection with this woman. And what it meant to him to have her back. To know that this time she was truly his.

They sat down on the rocks and talked for a long time. Until the sky was shrouded in darkness and they could count the stars in the Big Dipper.

She told him how difficult it had been for her without him. That she was terrified of making a commitment—to any man. Especially now that her career was taking off. But that she was glad she'd been tested—if that's what this was. Happy she had come to recognize how much he meant to her.

When Taylor finally spoke, the words came slowly. "I just felt I was in the way," he admitted. "My series was going down the tubes. And I couldn't handle the rejection. I can't believe I fell into that trap," he admitted, shaking his head. "But that's exactly what happened. Six months as an actor and I turned into a total egomaniac. It's almost as if I became someone else when I started doing the series."

"I liked that someone else," Brandy said softly.

"I didn't. And you wouldn't have for long, believe me. I was jealous of you, Brandy. Can you understand that?"

She looked at him with questioning eyes.

"It was as if I had to compete with you, but couldn't. Don't you see? I couldn't measure up to you. So I just walked away. Telling myself that you'd rejected me."

"But that's not—"

"Hush," he said softly, squeezing her hand. "That's how I felt at the time. I've done a lot of sorting things out the past few days. And I think I've come to terms with who I am—and who I'm not. I'm not an actor, Brandy. I'm going back to Westwinds, where I belong."

"Full-time?"

"You bet, full-time. In fact, I'm considering building another retreat. Maybe in San Francisco."

"But you'll be so far away," she said softly, gazing out at the tranquilizing magnificence of the darkened sea.

"From you? Not that far. And we'll have weekends. Right here at Seacliff. Long, luxurious weekends together," he reiterated, drawing her closer to him. "If that's what you want."

"I want that, Taylor," she said, pressing her cheek against his. "I want that very much."

She found his lips in the moonlight and met them with her own. Kissing him gently at first. Then harder, with a fervor she had never felt before. Raising her hand to caress his face, his neck. Running her fingers through his thick wheat-gold hair.

"I love you, Taylor Evans," she murmured under her breath.

"That's good," he whispered back. "Because I'm never going to let you get away again."

The message from Miles Durville read: "Urgent. Ten P.M. Oak Room."

R. B. McDevitt thanked the desk clerk. Slipped him a five-dollar bill. Swung through the lobby of the Plaza Hotel. And moved quickly toward the soaring oak-and-glass doors. Growing more curious with every step.

He'd only just arrived in New York and couldn't imagine why his financial adviser wanted to meet at this time of night.

What could be so important that it couldn't wait until morning? When he found out, he was devastated.

All the lines of R.B.'s deeply tanned face seemed to converge at his brow, forming an angry frown of shock and disbelief.

"I . . . I just don't know what to say, Miles," he stammered. "I mean, are you sure?"

"Positively. One hundred percent certain," Miles replied poking his fork into a plate of cooling corned-beef hash.

"But this just does not make sense," R.B. objected. "She absolutely loathes Teddy. And there is no reason on this earth why she'd sign her votes over to him."

"What can I tell you, R.B.?" Miles shrugged. "I got it straight from her broker's lips. Apparently Teddy promised to give her the publishing company and a title at the studio."

"That's a bunch of crap, and you know it. Selwyn's a conniving weasel. He'll never come through."

"Nevertheless, she went for it."

"Well, this spells disaster, Miles. We can't let it happen. We've got to talk some sense into her head. Convince her our deal's better. Hell, make her a counteroffer. What about the record company? We could—"

"We could do a lot of things, but they won't do us any good," Miles warned with a discouraging look. "Muffet has an agreement with Teddy. All signed, sealed, and delivered. Besides, she's unavailable. Cruising around somewhere in the Caribbean, I'm told. Won't be back until after the proxy vote."

"All right, then. What are our options?" R.B. asked, thinking out loud. "To give up. Or to forge ahead with a little less than we'd planned, right?"

"A lot less," Miles said despondently. "I'm sorry to say this, R.B., but without Muffet's five percent, you don't have a chance."

"Well, that's pretty damn pessimistic of you, Miles. The vote isn't until December. We still have some time. And I can't imagine why, between the two of us, we can't come up with an alternative plan that—"

"It's no use, R.B. Teddy's already beat us to it."

"What the hell do you mean by that?" the Texan demanded.

"Listen, I didn't want to tell you this before because I didn't think it would amount to anything as long as we had Muffet's votes. But, Teddy's found a white knight. George Thornton. Ever heard of him?"

"From Australia? The guy who turned Jetstream Aeronautics around?" R.B. asked, impressed.

Miles nodded. "He owns ten percent of Selwyn. Teddy's just appointed him Vice-President of Acquisitions and plans to issue him twenty-five million new shares of stock."

"New shares? But . . . but that's illegal," R.B. blustered, almost knocking over his tall glass of Guinness Stout.

"No, it isn't really," Miles corrected. "The shareholders might object, though. What I'm saying is—"

Miles looked around to make sure no one was listening. Then he lowered his voice.

"What I'm saying is that you could file a class-action suit on the grounds that Teddy will basically be diluting all the stock with this new issue."

"And what would that get us?"

"Maybe a few votes. But more important, time. The suit could be held up in the courts for more than a year."

"And as long as it is held up, Teddy can't issue the twenty-five million new shares, right?"

"Exactly. And without those shares, Thornton doesn't really have the clout of a white knight. He can't do much to rescue Teddy."

"Good. We'll file tomorrow," R.B. grinned. "Miles, old buddy, you're a genius."

"Not so fast with the credit, please," Miles said, skeptically. "We still have only forty-eight percent. We're going to need more votes, R.B. A lot more votes."

"What about Alisa Hudson? We've got some major leverage there, Miles. She's gung-ho to send a letter to all the shareholders endorsing us."

"I know," the financial adviser mused with a chuckle. "She told me yesterday over the phone. Read me the part about Teddy's unethical behavior. Scathing stuff. Given half a chance I think the old gal would string the guy up by his balls."

"If she could find them." R.B. laughed and ordered another Guinness. "I don't know about you, Miles, but I've got a real strong feeling a personalized letter from Alisa Hudson will impress the hell out of the shareholders."

"No telling," Miles replied without enthusiasm. "We've come this far, though. Might as well give it a whirl. But I'm warning you, R.B. I wouldn't get my hopes up."

"Miles, old buddy," R.B. said, shaking his head. "You've got to understand one thing. I was born with my hopes up. Ain't nothing going to change that. Besides, I've got an ace up my sleeve on this takeover. Sort of a dirty ace."

"Like what?" Miles asked, surprised.

"Like an assignment for my pal Les Pimco. You remember him?"

"The sleazy-looking private dick you introduced me to in L.A.?"

"One and the same. He's got a counterpart working here on the East Coast as well."

"For you?"

R.B. nodded. "Kind of a clandestine 'Let's nail Teddy to the wall' movement."

"Any specifics?"

"Oh, it's a sordid little matter, too nauseating to discuss over supper. A real long shot. But I've taken plenty of those before. And you know something, Miles? Sometimes they work."

The moment Renata came marching into his office, Templeton Haight pressed the remote control button on the left side of his desk. And smiled gleefully.

Within seconds, his latest toy, a three-foot Super XXX Robot, was rolling across the thickly carpeted floor. Wielding a silver tray full of rhumaki and shrimp rolls.

"Champagne? Cocktail? Appetizer?" it asked in a tinny voice, rolling toward the statuesque woman in green.

"Templeton, lose the eunuch!" Renata demanded. "This is not a social call."

"But you're all dressed up," he replied, inspecting her velvet evening suit and matching veiled hat.

"I'm off to an awards dinner momentarily," she explained, sitting down on the wing chair across from him. "I just stopped by to get an update. Be brief. And be careful. Remember the walls have ears, just like telephones."

Templeton nodded, swallowed hard, and cleared his throat.

"Nothing yet," he said in a small voice.

Renata's perfectly plucked eyebrows arched indignantly. "But it's been more than twenty-four hours. What in God's name have you been doing?"

"Perhaps later tonight. I have a—"

"Templeton, do you realize how important this is? Are you aware of how dangerous he can be—to both of us?"

"Renata, I assure the matter is under control. I've done everything conceivable. Except," he added caustically, "to call the police."

She shot him a fearsome look. "Don't be so smug, Templeton. You're up to your eyeballs in this. You know it as well as I do. If I'm found out, you're as good as dead."

"Renata," he replied calmly, folding his chubby hands on the desk, "I do not mean to denigrate the seriousness of the situation. I merely wish to point out that I am doing my best. And if you can think of anything to speed things up, I most graciously invite you to do so."

Renata rose majestically to her feet. Emerald eyes flashing like green fire.

"Don't patronize me, Templeton. You got us into this. Now stop sitting around diddling your frigging robots and get us out of it."

27

Kate stormed out of the elevator and marched toward the *World* offices in a black mood. She detested pushy publicists. Especially young, dictatorial, pushy publicists with thick Brooklyn accents. Like Angelica Cohen, with whom she had just lunched.

Angelica worked for Laurence & Ferber, a top-notch public relations firm representing some of the most prestigious clients in the world. Among them, Renata Desmond. Rumor had it Renata was so demanding and uncooperative that she'd discarded more than a dozen publicists during her two years with the PR firm. Each time insisting on someone new.

Most recently, the burden had fallen upon twenty-eight-year-old Angelica Cohen, who'd been assigned to the Desmond account just three months earlier. And had obviously taken it on as a personal challenge. Reasoning, quite correctly, that she'd be fired if she didn't please Renata.

So perhaps the young woman should be forgiven for her rude behavior at lunch. But Kate didn't see it that way.

In the first place, she'd agreed to the meeting only as a courtesy, having called Angelica to postpone the Renata Desmond interview so many times. What she'd anticipated was a semi-boring meal at Jimmy's, peppered with light conversation and an occasional reference to Renata.

She had not expected a rapid-fire lecture on the do's and don'ts of interviewing from a supercilious young New Yorker. But that is exactly what she got.

Angelica Cohen had all the subtlety of a skunk at a garden party. She hadn't even waited for the main course to plunge into her monologue. Right in the middle of the endive salad, she was spewing Brooklynese faster than a jackhammer.

"Now, I'm not telling you what to say when you interview Miss

Desmond tomorrow, understand?" Angelica had begun in her whiny, nasal voice. "But I do have a few suggestions." She whipped a two-page memo out of her bag and handed it to Kate.

"You see, it has been my experience that avoiding certain types of questions is advantageous when dealing with Miss Desmond. And I've pointed out a number of them here. For instance, she does not enjoy conversing about her father. I'm sure you'll find the background I've provided you with on Charles Wentworth Desmond quite sufficient, anyway."

Kate was too surprised and irritated to say anything. She just sat there, glaring at Angelica, who didn't seem to notice.

"And about her personal life," the publicist jabbered on, "that is definitely off-limits. As we both know, Miss Desmond is invited to all of the major functions and is escorted by some of the most attractive available men in the world. There are constant rumors that she will marry. But we like to avoid direct questions about the men in her life, you understand."

What about the women? Kate wanted to ask. She couldn't believe her ears. Renata Desmond's bisexuality was no more a secret in Hollywood than Rock Hudson's homosexuality had been. Angelica's blatant deception wasn't just aggravating, it was ludicrous. Who did she think she was dealing with, Mary Hart?

"A nice approach, I think," Angelica continued, "would be to concentrate on Miss Desmond's image. She really has managed to carve out a name for herself in the community, you know. She's on the board of dozens of charities, including medical and educational organizations. I've included a list for you in the press packet. And you mustn't overlook her appearance, Kate. Women, in particular, are always fascinated with Miss Desmond's wardrobe. You might ask her for a little tour of her closets. She has so many of them, you know, all over the house, which is absolutely stunning, by the way. I'm sure you'll be impressed."

Kate was glad when the main course arrived, simply because Angelica would have to stop talking long enough to chew her poached salmon. But the garrulous young woman even managed to get in some more directives between bites.

"No tape recorder. Did I mention that over the phone?"

"You didn't," Kate answered crisply. Having to take notes would make her job twice as difficult. But she'd manage. At this point, getting anything worth recording out of Renata seemed impossible, anyway.

"And about Miss Desmond's other business activities, other than *The Hollywood Daily*, I mean. She would really prefer not to discuss any of her other professional involvements. If you have specific questions about her real estate holdings or the football team, for instance, I can arrange a brief interview for you with her vice-president, Templeton Haight. I'm certain he will be very helpful—"

"I don't understand," Kate interrupted. "Why didn't you tell me this a month ago?"

"Oh, I guess it just slipped my mind. But, anyway, you have plenty of lead time on the piece. So we can always work in a meeting with Mr. Haight, can't we? By the way, it would be very much to Miss Desmond's liking if you do not address her by her first name. She prefers the professional touch whenever possible."

Kate did not respond verbally. She merely nodded and continued listening to Angelica Cohen sing Renata Desmond's praises until the check came. She had no intention of avoiding any of the questions that the overbearing young woman had so audaciously referred to. But the worst thing she could do at the moment would be to announce the fact.

Instead, she kept smiling sweetly all the way to the door, where she said good-bye, shook Angelica's clammy hand, and began marching back toward Century City. Thankful she had at least a ten-minute walk to cool off.

It wasn't long enough, however. As Kate swung through the double glass doors to the *World* offices she was still furious. And not particularly pleased to find someone waiting for her.

"He's been here for more than an hour," the receptionist whispered, referring to the young man browsing through *Sports Illustrated* in the corner.

Kate shrugged and turned to face him. "Yes, can I help you?" she inquired in a bored monotone.

"Miss Brannigan?" the boy said politely.

He couldn't have been more than seventeen. And there was a familiarity about his face. The unruly black hair and dark eyes. Very ethnic. Italian-looking, Kate thought. Yet she couldn't quite place him.

"I'm Kevin Brocato," he said with a hearty handshake. "And I apologize for barging in on you like this, but I well . . . I wonder, Miss Brannigan, could we, ahh, talk privately for just a moment?"

"Of course," Kate said, with a curious twinge to her voice. She ushered him into the small office she'd been relegated to since Jerry Lindner's return. "Sit down, won't you?"

"No, I really can't stay, ma'am," he answered, making sure the door was closed. Then he lowered his voice to a conspiratorial whisper. "I've got a message for you from my brother, Don, Miss Brannigan. He's quit the team, you know. And disappeared. Nobody knows where he is, except me and my folks, so this has to be real confidential."

"Surely. I understand," Kate agreed. But she couldn't keep her heart from beating a little faster at the thought of what was coming next. Don Brocato was ready to talk, and she'd been chosen. Now the Longhorns' star quarterback needed her.

"What Don would like is for you to get on a plane to Phoenix. That's where he is right now, staying on a friend's ranch. If you tell me what flight you'll be on, I'll arrange for someone to meet you at the airport and take you to him. And one more thing, Miss Brannigan, Don says if you come he'll give you the best goddamned story of your career. Excuse my language, but that's exactly what he said."

"Yes. Yes, I'm sure it is," Kate replied distractedly, her mind spinning with excitement. "And this couldn't have been more perfectly timed."

"Pardon, ma'am?"

"Oh, nothing important, just talking to myself. Kevin, if you'll sit down for a moment, I'll start making the arrangements right now," she said, picking up the phone.

Kate smiled broadly as she dialed the offices of Laurence & Ferber. It was going to give her tremendous pleasure to disappoint Angelica Cohen by postponing the Renata Desmond interview once again.

* * *

R. B. McDevitt despised being late. At the moment he was an hour overdue for takeoff, which frustrated him no end.

It had been a morning of distractions at the ranch. And he was in no mood to accept another time-consuming call. But just as he wheeled his gunmetal-gray Jaguar into the fixed base operation where he kept his private plane, his car phone flashed and buzzed.

R.B. thought seriously about not answering it. Then picked it up.

"R.B.? Pimco here. Glad I caught you," the private detective announced in a strident voice.

"Yeah, me too, old buddy," R.B. said, as he brought the Jaguar to a stop next to his Falcon 50 jet. "But let's make this fast. I'm taking off for Los Angeles in a couple of minutes. What have you got for me?"

"More than you might think," Pimco said quickly. "But my advice is that you head east instead. I'm in New York right now. And I've got your man, R.B. Cameraman, that is. Name's Ted Nunes. Talked to him about two this morning."

R.B. stopped rifling through his briefcase and gave Pimco his full attention. "Outstanding, Les!" he exclaimed enthusiastically. "How the hell did you run him down?"

"Wasn't easy. Guy's pretty bummed out. Living at the West Side YMCA. Hasn't worked in months. Took three weeks to come up with a lead. Finally found him last night at a little bar he frequents in the Village. Show business hasn't been kind to Nunes. But he's got what you want, R.B. He's got a print of that film and, even better, he claims he's got a shot of your favorite director in action. Guess he figured it might be valuable someday."

"Hot damn!" R.B. said, flabbergasted. "Les, this is too good to be true. Are you sure this guy's not just crappin' around?"

"Sure as I can be before he actually delivers the film."

"And when's that?"

"Just as soon as you can get here. I'll arrange for a private screening room somewhere, and we'll have a little party."

"How much does he . . . what's his name—Nunes? How much does he want?"

"Peanuts," Pimco chuckled. "Ten thousand to talk. Another forty for the film."

"That's it?" R.B. asked, incredulous.

"Unless he wises up before you get here. And you ought to make it fast, R.B. We don't want to give Nunes any time to reconsider."

"Right, Les. I'll fly out of L.A. as soon as I finish up my afternoon meeting. Call me at the Plaza in the morning. Get Nunes to meet us around nine."

"You got it."

"And, Les. If this guy's legit, you've just earned yourself one hell of a bonus, old buddy."

"Mark! Mark!" Sara exclaimed excitedly, pounding on the guest-room door. When he didn't answer, she opened it a crack and peeked in. "Mark!" she shouted, at a glass-shattering pitch.

Mark rolled over in bed, rubbed his eyes, and looked at the clock radio. It was six A.M. "Reveille?" he inquired with a groggy yawn.

"No!" Sara shrieked, rushing over and handing him his robe. "It's Jennifer! She's home, she's here! Come on, get up!"

Mark bolted out of bed and darted across the floor. "The police brought her?" he asked, tugging clumsily on the robe.

"No," Sara said as they hustled down the hall together. "I don't know how she got here. I went down to get the *Times*, and when I passed Jackie's room on the way back, there was Jennifer, fast asleep."

Mark shot Sara a skeptical look. She'd been under a great deal of stress. But not enough to be hallucinating. At least he hoped not.

"You first," she said, shoving him into Jackie's room.

A look of utter amazement fell over Mark's face as his eyes shifted back and forth from left to right. Scrutinizing his daughters. Both of them. Yes, both of them. Propped up with pillows on separate twin beds. Wearing identical pajamas. And matching grins.

"Hi, Dad. Hi, Mom! What's shaking?" they yelped in unison.

Mark and Sara looked at each other and back at the twins. They didn't know whether to hug Jennifer or reprimand her.

So first they hugged her. Then the interrogation began.

"Jenny, where have you been? We were worried sick," Sara demanded frantically from one side of the bed.

"Who brought you home, sweetheart? Are you okay?" Mark asked simultaneously from the other side.

"Hold on, one at a time," Jennifer interrupted, stopping them. "The point is I'm home. Isn't that enough?"

Sara's face hardened into a fierce look of provocation. "It most certainly is not. Not after what we've been through. You've been gone for days, Jennifer. Now let's hear it. What happened?"

Jennifer gave her father a pleading, Do-I-have-to? look. He nodded.

"All right." She thought for a moment. Then rolled her eyes playfully and said, "Let's see, first I was molested in the ladies' room at Anaheim Stadium. Then I was drugged, thrown into the back of an old pickup truck, and left for dead in the Disneyland parking lot. How's that?"

"Jennifer!" Sara objected, glaring at her daughter's smirk.

"Okay, so it wasn't quite that sensational. What really happened was I got lost at the stadium until way after dark, started hitchhiking, and found I liked life on the road better than at home." She gave both of her parents a long, telling look. "Yeah, that one is pretty believable. Would you two accept that?"

"No, we wouldn't, Jenny," Mark said impatiently. "Sweetheart, you have to realize that this isn't the least bit funny. We were very concerned. Afraid we'd never see you again."

"Well, I hardly ever see either of you anymore, anyway. So I don't know what difference that would have made," she snapped.

"Jennifer, cut the bleeding-heart routine, will you?" Jackie complained. "Just get to the point and tell them."

"Why don't you tell them, smartmouth? I've already done enough for the cause."

"You mean, Jackie was in on this?" Sara asked, shocked.

"She certainly was," Jennifer said with a smug smile.

Sara and Mark turned to Jackie, who began fiddling nervously with the button on her pajama sleeve. "I . . . ahh . . . well, we . . . Oh, come on, Jennifer," she urged, glowering at her twin. "This isn't fair. It was your idea in the first place."

"Was not!"

"It was too, dammit," Jackie insisted, throwing a pillow at Jennifer.

Mark caught it in midair. "Hey, young lady, watch your language."

"Language, smanguage," Jackie yelled heatedly. "It's all her fault. And I knew she'd do this. I knew you'd do this, Jennifer. You're so damn two-faced."

"Am not," Jennifer shouted back.

"Girls!" Sara scolded. "Hush. Just hush. That's better. Now, which one of you is going to tell us what happened? Because if you don't, you're going to spend the rest of the day here in Jackie's room together. With no music!"

Jackie and Jennifer looked at each other in disgust.

"Bummer. Why live?" said one.

"Yeah. The pits. Worse than death," agreed the other.

"Jennifer!" Mark ordered in a stern voice.

"Okay. I'll tell you the truth," she relented. "But it's as much Jackie's fault as mine. If she hadn't—"

"Just begin at the beginning," Mark ordered.

Jennifer took a deep breath, clenched her hands in her lap, and stared down at them uncomfortably. "Well, see," she began, in a tiny voice, "neither of us likes it with you and Mom being separated. So we wanted to come up with some surefire way to get you back together. And," she said, raising her eyes to meet Mark's, "as you can see, it worked."

"What? You . . . you staged your own kidnapping just to—" Sara was so stunned she couldn't finish the sentence.

"Sure. Why not?" Jennifer asked belligerently. "We certainly weren't going to stand by and watch you two get a divorce without doing something. And the football game was perfect. My friend Sandy Meretsky's brother met me in the parking lot and drove me to their home in Beverly Hills. Mr. and Mrs. Meretsky are away in the Orient. So there's just a skeleton staff at the house. I could have stayed for weeks. And I was thinking about it. See, the original plan was not to come home until you two were sleeping together."

Mark sighed heavily and rubbed his forehead with his hand. Sara kept looking from Jennifer to Jackie, trying to figure out if this story was another ruse. Jennifer kept talking.

"But what the hell—I mean heck, Daddy. It could take another week for you and Mom to ahh . . . really get together. And I didn't want to stay at Sandy's that long. The food's much better here. Besides," Jennifer concluded with a smile, "I started to realize how much I really missed you guys. Yes, even you, spoilsport," she added, with a glance in Jackie's direction.

There was a vague expression on Mark's face. Somewhere between shock and disappointment. "So who's idea was it, anyway?" he asked, at a total loss for something else to say.

"It was mine, Daddy," Jennifer answered softly, a shade of guilt in her voice. "Jackie didn't want to cooperate at first. But I just knew we had to do something. So I . . . I told her if she didn't help me, then I really would run away."

"I see," Mark said, clearing his throat. He glanced at Sara, who didn't seem to know what to do either. "I think I'd better speak with Jennifer alone for a few minutes. Sara, Jackie, would you—"

"Mark, are you sure?" Sara asked. "Maybe we should wait until—"

"Sara. Please," he insisted.

"All right, we're going."

Jackie slipped solemnly into her paisley print robe and followed her mother downstairs for breakfast.

"Don't you think we should tell Aunt Kate?" she asked in an unsteady voice when they reached the kitchen.

"We can't," Sara replied, placing a box of Wheat Chex on the table. "Kate's out of town on a mystery trip. Made me swear I wouldn't tell where she went. But she'd probably have gotten more surprises if she'd stuck around."

"Yeah," Jackie agreed, slicing an English muffin. "She was sure upset about Jennifer. I think she felt it was all her fault."

"You girls owe Kate a big apology, you know."

"Yes, Mom."

"But to tell you the truth," Sara added with a devilish lilt to her voice. "It was a pretty clever idea."

"You think so?" Jackie asked, grinning.

"I sure do. Couldn't have pulled it off better myself. But for heaven's sake, don't tell your father."

"I won't," Jackie said gleefully. She rushed over to her mother's side and gave her a giant hug. "Mom?"

"Yes, honey?"

"Do you think it worked? I mean, is he going to stay?"

"I sure hope so, sweetie pie," Sara answered, holding her daughter close. "I sure do hope so."

Kate couldn't get to a pay phone fast enough. She'd spent three hours interviewing Don Brocato. And now all she could think about was to call Russ Stevens.

It was after hours at *World* headquarters in New York. But quite often Managing Editor Stevens stayed late.

Kate was hopeful that would be the case.

Please, God, just make him be there, she prayed silently as her fingers hit the buttons on the phone.

He had to be there. She had to talk to him. Kate Brannigan was sitting on the most sensational story of her career. And Russ Stevens was the only person in the world she dared share it with.

"Stevens here."

"Russ!" she exclaimed excitedly. "It's Kate. I'm at the airport in Phoenix. Just finished talking to Don Brocato. And we've got a real scoop here, Russ. You'd better save some room in Monday's issue for this one. Three pages, at least.

"Three pages? Kate, what the hell are you talking about?" Stevens yelped, perplexed.

"I'm talking about fixing games, Russ. Your Woman of the Year, Renata Desmond, has been doing just that. Betting against her own football team and making gobs of money."

"What? Brocato told you that?"

"And more," Kate continued. "He swears at least six of the Longhorns' games have been fixed this season. That's why he quit. Several of the other players know about it too, but he was the only one with guts enough to take a walk."

"The newspapers say otherwise, you know," Stevens argued. "Several sports columnists seem to think Brocato's developed an ego too big for his helmet. 'Angry Italian hothead' is what they're calling him."

"Don't believe it, Russ. What I'm telling you makes perfect sense if you look at the Longhorns' record so far."

"I'm not that familiar with it."

"You don't have to be. Brocato explained it in detail to me, all the specifics on games and plays. And everybody knows why he got so upset during the Rams game. Even your quotable sports columnists. Coach Dunphy had called for a punt when he should have gone for a field goal. Brocato told me that was the final straw. His ethics were at stake. He had to quit. Even if it meant jeopardizing his career."

"And what about Renata? Are you telling me she engineered all this?" Stevens inquired skeptically.

"Yes. Yes, I certainly am. Brocato overheard a conversation between coach Dunphy and her vice-president, Templeton Haight. Renata's name came up. According to Brocato, she's making millions with this highly sophisticated scam. It's all worked out between the coaches up in the booth and Dunphy. The players just carry out the calls and wind up blowing key plays. I'll make it all very clear in the piece."

"Not so fast, Kate," Stevens warned. "I find it hard to believe that Renata Desmond needs money badly enough to do something this unscrupulous, don't you?"

"No, I don't. It's greed, Russ. And an unquenchable thirst for power. She needs the money to help finance that monument she's building for herself. You know, *The Hollywood Daily* Center for Education and the Arts."

There was a conspicuous silence at the other end of the line as Stevens contemplated Kate's words. "And who told you that?" he asked finally.

"R. B. McDevitt, the Texas millionaire who used to own the Longhorns. He threw me a few hints about the team a while back."

"And you didn't follow through?"

"I did, but got nowhere. Until Brocato quit and contacted me. Russ, we're wasting time talking about this. You ought to be—"

"I ought to be listening to the tape. You did record Brocato's interview, didn't you?"

"Sure did," Kate said eagerly.

"Make a copy and send it to me. We'll need Renata's reaction. When are you meeting with her?"

"Friday afternoon at four. I've been told No questions about football. But I'll nail her with this at the end."

"Good girl. And Kate?"

"Yes?"

"I'll line up a second cover, just in case. Do we have Renata's photo here in New York?"

A smile of deep satisfaction spread across Kate's tired face. A cover story. *Her* cover story. "You should. I sent the head shot her publicist gave me last week. How about 'Hollywood's Darkest Secret' as a blurb?" she teased.

"Nice ring to it." Stevens laughed. Then his voice turned serious. "But I really have a problem now."

"What's that?" she asked apprehensively. Hoping whatever it was would not interfere with her cover story.

"Woman of the Year. Who the hell am I going to use at this late date?"

"I'll give it some thought on the way back to L.A.," Kate said, relieved.

"Never mind." he joked. "If we use Renata Desmond on next week's cover, maybe I'll just make you Woman of the Year."

R. B. McDevitt and Miles Durville were both naked and dripping with sweat. There was no one else in the steam room of the New York Athletic Club. But they kept their conversation to a whisper anyway.

Except in Miles's case, it was more of a hiss. "R.B. I just can't believe you're going to do this." He shook his head in disgust. "It's beneath you. It's . . . well, it's totally unethical. Worse even than greenmail."

"No it's not, Miles," R.B. assured his financial adviser. "We're talking about blackmail. And that's at least fifty percent better than greenmail. Don't you understand. I'm not stealing from Selwyn Studios, I'm just skinning the Black Prince alive. Beating Teddy at his own game. It's business, Miles. Happens all the time."

"Not with my clients," Miles snapped nervously. "My God, what if it leaks? What if the SEC gets word of it?"

"Who's going to tell them?" R.B. asked, oozing self-confidence. "You? Me? Teddy? I've got nothing to lose, Miles. Selwyn Studios virtually belongs to me already."

"Please, R.B., your proclivity for exaggeration is showing. You know he's not going to give up without a fight."

"There's no way Teddy can fight this one, Miles. I've got him boxed in and hog-tied. Of course, I'm going to buy him out, just to make it legitimate."

"For how much?"

"Oh, I expect he'll sell me all his shares at a dollar per."

"One dollar!" Miles exclaimed. "You're not serious? The stock is already up to twenty-one."

"Miles, you've got to calm down, old buddy," R.B. said in a low voice. "Once Teddy gets a glimpse of himself directing that snuff film, I'm going to have all the leverage. A young girl was murdered in that film, Miles. Strangled to death right on camera. I've got news photos of her body strung up on a tree in Central Park. Her picture was all over the papers the next day. The police labeled it an unsolved homicide. But Teddy Selwyn knows different."

"You're actually going to threaten him . . . about going to the police?" Miles asked, horrified.

"Damn right. And once he hears that, I calculate it'll take Teddy about half a second to sign Selwyn Studios over to me."

When Kate returned from Phoenix, she drove directly to the *World* office in Century City. Spirits soaring.

Tired as she was from lack of sleep, a surge of newfound energy charged through her system, filling her with an exhilaration that seemed almost superhuman. She was elated over the thought of a cover story. And full of enthusiasm about the next day's meeting with Renata Desmond.

How wonderful to have some leverage at last. Something to set Renata off-balance and show her as the perfidious power monger she really was.

I'll make her squirm, Kate thought, as she collected her messages at the reception desk. And it was with a triumphant gait that she swung down the hall to her small office.

There she stopped abruptly at the doorway. And a look of utter astonishment slipped onto her face.

Roses—a dozen, no make that two dozen—of the loveliest long-stemmed yellow roses Kate had ever seen were handsomely arranged in a huge cut-glass vase on her desk.

Her eyes filled with a special glow as she read the the accompanying card. And quickly buzzed the receptionist.

"Lynne, he was here? The guy with the flowers?"

"Well now, yes ma'am," Lynne drawled, feigning a Texas accent. "He most certainly was. Late yesterday. And a mighty good-looking hunk of a man too, I might add. Where've you been hiding that one, Miss Brannigan?"

"Way back in the Texas hills, honey," Kate chuckled. She read the scrawled note on the back of R. B. McDevitt's card once again.

With many thanks from your biggest fan. There's something to celebrate. Let's have dinner.

Well now, we just might do that, R.B., Kate thought to herself, as she moved the flowers to a side table and stepped back to admire them. Sending the roses was a very thoughtful gesture, whatever his motivation. So maybe there was more to R. B. McDevitt than she'd assumed. Maybe.

For a moment she wondered what it was he wanted to celebrate. But then she remembered the messages in her hand and began scanning them. She did so distractedly. Barely concentrating on the names or phone numbers. Until she came to the one with a 202 area code. And caught her breath when she read the name underneath it. *Seth Arnold.*

Kate's stomach fluttered. And her heart lodged somewhere near her throat, rendering her quite breathless for just a second. It was the first time she'd heard from Seth since he'd called to break their engagement. And she was quite unprepared for his sudden reappearance in her life. Just seeing his name spelled out was enough to leave her feeling shaken.

Her first reaction was to call him immediately. Then she thought further.

No. No, I will not give in to this, Kate told herself firmly as she sat down behind the desk. *I will not allow this man, this young man, whom Dr. Bernstein says I never really wanted to marry in the first place, to turn me into Silly Putty.*

Seth was a part of my life once. And I love him dearly. I always will. But I can't return the call. As much as I want to, I just can't. It would be like taking several giant steps backward. I've been struggling too hard to do that. And now my life is getting better. Maybe not great. But improving. I can feel it. I know it. I'm even entertaining the thought of seeing R.B., for heaven's sake. I must be making progress.

Still, the thought of talking to Seth, of seeing him, was tempting. The memories of their lovemaking, so achingly sweet, came flowing back. Filling Kate with a longing she'd so often surrendered to.

But she couldn't surrender now. She'd come too far for that.

Just be strong, she cautioned herself. *You're doing fine without him. And you're going to keep doing just fine.*

She sat there for more than ten minutes. Arms folded. A thoughtful expression on her weary face. Allowing the highs and the lows of the past few months to flash through her mind.

Her decision to visit Sara in Los Angeles. And the party that first night. Sitting next to R.B. at dinner. The lunch with Jerry Lindner the next day. The helplessness she'd felt those first few weeks in California. Missing Seth so much she couldn't think straight. Their reunion. Their breakup. And the tears.

All the time she'd spent crying. Carrying on like a deserted child. A thirty-five-year-old woman who had lost her way.

And now where are you, she asked herself, recrossing her arms. *Are you happy?*

Happier. Not overjoyed.

Challenged by your work?

At the moment, yes.

Optimistic about the future?

Well, I wouldn't go that far. Let's say hopeful.

And do you need Seth Arnold in your life to make it better? To help you climb up to the attic, where everything is lovely? Or can you make it there on your own?

I'm getting there. But it's not easy.

And what about Seth?

I love him. I'll always love him. But I guess I don't need him anymore.

Kate took another long look at the message, crumpled it up in the palm of her hand. And fired it into the wastebasket.

Then she reached for a legal pad and started jotting down questions for the Renata Desmond interview.

* * *

Later that night, when Kate returned to the Bel Air mansion, she found Sara sitting in the video room. Watching *Pee-wee's Big Adventure.*

"Infatuation?" Kate joked, glancing at the comical Pee-wee Herman as he flew down a hill on his bicycle.

"Work," Sara sighed, flicking off the VCR. "My boss thinks he'd be good for a series. Besides, I needed a distraction. How'd it go, Ace?"

Kate sank into a cushy leather chair. "Great. Better than great. Wonderful. I still can't talk about it, though," she added apologetically.

"Was I asking?" Sara teased. "Just as long as you're happy."

"And what about you, lady? You look a little blue."

"A lot blue."

Kate studied her friend's forlorn expression. "Sara, what's wrong. When I talked to you from Phoenix you were overjoyed about Jennifer coming back."

"I still am."

"Then what's the problem? Something at the studio?"

Sara shook her head. "No. Something here. Well, actually something that isn't here. It's Mark. He's gone."

"What do you mean?" Kate asked in a gentle voice.

"I mean he's off and running once again. Back to the apartment in Venice."

"But I don't understand, Sara. I thought that—"

"So did I. Especially when Jennifer told us why she'd run away."

"That's so odd," Kate said, puzzled. "I mean he seemed to really be back this time. What did he say when he left?"

"Oh, a lot of things," Sara sighed. "A bunch of *ferkochta* verbiage about really loving me but not being able to live with me. At least not right now."

"And what does that mean?"

Sara shrugged despondently. "Who knows? My head is spinning, I'm so confused. I'm beginning to think Harding is right. I should probably just press for the divorce and get it over with."

"Is that what you really want?"

"What does it matter what I want, Kate? How much longer am I going to have to live like this—in some sort of limbo? Wondering.

Hoping. Not knowing. It's futile. I'm ready to throw in the towel and give up the fight."

"I wouldn't do that just yet, Sara," Kate cautioned. "Give it a couple of months. Until the new year, at least. All right?"

"Maybe," Sara said with a tired half-smile. Then she reached over and squeezed her friend's hand. "Thanks, Kate, for being such a *mensch*. I'm not sure I could get through all this without dumping it on you. And I know it's a heavy load."

"Works both ways, you know, hon. At least we have each other. We can always count on that."

"Omigod, I forgot!" Sara yelped. "You're supposed to call Cary. He phoned when you were out of town. Said it's really urgent."

"Cary . . . Eckhardt?" Kate asked, stunned.

"No, Cary Grant," her friend deadpanned, getting up. She headed for the staircase.

"Where are you going?"

"To get the number. He's staying with a friend in Beverly Hills."

"I'll come with you," Kate said, following her. "Did he say what's so urgent?"

"No. But he sounded pretty depressed. I got the feeling he wants you back."

"What?" Kate said, astonished.

"Just something I picked up on my cupid antennae. Besides, he's just filed for divorce."

"And how do you know that?" Kate inquired, reaching the top step.

"I work fast, sweetie," Sara replied, strolling into her bedroom. "And, apparently, so does Mr. Eckhardt." She handed Kate the number. "He asked me a lot of questions about you."

"Like?"

"Like what you've been up to, who you've been seeing."

"What nerve! And you said . . . ?"

"And I said you'd been swept up in such a whirlwind of social activity that I hardly get to see you myself."

"Nice going," Kate stared at the slip of paper for a moment, then ripped it neatly in two.

"Kate what are you doing?" Sara objected.

"Building character," Kate replied, tearing the halves into tiny bits. "This is exactly what Mr. Cary Eckhardt once did to me."

·III
The Story

28

■ Kate leaned out of the car window and announced her name into a black speaker box. Seconds later, the opulent gold filigree gates sprang open.

She'd seen pictures of the magnificent Trousdale estate and knew that it stretched out over three acres. With two swimming pools, four tennis courts, several formal gardens, and a spacious guest house, which was rarely occupied.

Renata Desmond was not known for her hospitality. But she had insisted on being interviewed in her own home.

Kate pulled the Peugeot to a stop in the cobblestoned courtyard in front of Renata's imposing mansion. It was a massive, twelve-bedroom French chateau fashioned after the sturdy structures in the Loire Valley that were constructed during the seventeenth century.

She glanced at her watch. Ten minutes early. Perfect. She needed time to sit down and compose herself before the interview began. As self-confident as Kate was feeling about the forthcoming confrontation with Renata, she could not deny the churning sensation in her stomach. It had been there all morning, a raw, burning uneasiness, as if a hot coal were searing her insides.

Nerves, she told herself as she checked her appearance in the vanity mirror. *Nothing but nerves. Calm down. You have no reason to feel intimidated. The ball is in your court.*

But as Kate stepped out of the car and slipped into her turquoise suit jacket, she noticed her hands trembling slightly. And her steps were quick and anxious as she moved along the winding, flower-lined walkway toward the immense chateau.

All right, so you're scared, she thought, reaching for the doorbell. *You're about to take a risk. A tremendous risk and it could backfire right in your face. Don't do it if you're that frightened.*

But she knew she would. And as the butler led Kate across the cold gray marble foyer, she convinced herself once again to stick with her plan.

"Here we are, madam," he announced stiffly, pausing at the second door on the right. "Please make yourself comfortable. Miss Desmond will join you shortly."

Kate's blue-violet eyes swept over the library as she stepped inside. The room was quite large and paneled in a rich red maple, with a pleasing assortment of English and French antiques.

There was an Empire mahogany-and-ormolu desk situated at an angle in front of the built-in bookcases. An ornate Louis XV chinoiserie lacquer commode standing proudly near a floor-to-ceiling window. And a Bristol chandelier sparkling overhead. Four scroll-back chairs sat in a cluster just right of the entryway. And two English club chairs flanked the black marble fireplace to the left.

An intricately hand-carved rococo mantelpiece embellished the fireplace. And just above it hung a large portrait of Renata as a young girl. A haunting portrait, Kate decided at first glance. The smile was sweet enough. But there was something about the girl's deep-set green eyes. A brooding, lonely quality that dominated her expression, casting a certain melancholy over the entire room.

Kate stepped closer and scrutinized the bottom right-hand corner of the canvas. Francine Devereaux, it was signed. And below that, the year, 1936.

"Lovely, isn't it?"

The whiney Brooklyn accent caught Kate off guard. Angelica Cohen had made it very clear that she would be present at the interview. But secretly Kate had been hoping something would keep her away. Like a case of laryngitis or, better yet, lockjaw.

"Angelica, how nice to see you," she fibbed as she spun around.

The overbearing publicist was dressed in her usual glaring white. White silk blouse. White V-necked sweater. White raw silk pants. And white open-toed shoes with white opaque stockings.

"And how, ah, California, you look," Kate couldn't help offering.

"Thanks," Angelica replied, beaming. "I just love the casual aspect of the West Coast, don't you? By the way," she added, gliding toward Kate, "if you like, we will be able to take a little tour of Miss Desmond's fabulous closets. It took some doing, but it's all arranged. And I want you to know it will be an exclusive, Kate. We've been asked many times. But always refused, even the Sunday *Times.*"

Angelica announced this with such a rush of overdramatized excitement that Kate had to stifle a laugh before she said, "I really think I'd prefer just speaking with Miss Desmond. This is more of a personality profile than a fashion piece, you know."

Angelica's overly made-up face tightened with irritation. "Certainly," she said crisply. "After all, it is your story. Would you like coffee?" she added in a strident voice.

"Thank you, no." Kate sat down in a club chair in front of the fireplace.

Barely camouflaging her vexation, Angelica clomped across the room with the authority of a drill sergeant. She picked up one of the scroll-back chairs, carried it over and planted it next to Kate. Then she sat down and crossed her arms.

"It'll be just a few minutes," she announced perfunctorily.

"Fine."

They waited in silence until the sharp click of high heels on marble echoed down the hallway.

Angelica stood up automatically, eyes glued to the huge, arched, maple double doors. Kate, feeling foolish, did the same. It's only polite, she assured herself.

Polite nothing. You're turning this into an audience with the queen.

Renata's entrance was more than regal. She swept into the library with an extravagant air of elegance and vitality. Moving effortlessly toward Kate, a smug smile of arrogance ringing her flawless, bow-shaped lips.

She was dressed in a fitted scarlet suit with embroidered shoulders. Matching shoes. And a double strand of pearls at her throat.

"Please be seated, Miss Brannigan," Renata said as she eased herself into the club chair opposite Kate. "So nice to see you again."

"Yes, thank you," Kate replied, sitting down once more. Her stomach fluttered anxiously. *Am I really going to do this?* she thought. Then added, "I'm sorry I had to cancel so many times."

"Oh, but I understand perfectly," Renata responded, her voice oozing graciousness. "You reporters are so busy. I imagine you're juggling at least a half-dozen assignments right now."

"Not really. I mean not at the moment, anyway. I've been pretty much devoting my time to this piece on you."

"Well, I'm flattered," Renata said as she crossed her long, trim legs. "And I'm certain you have a number of things to ask me. So why don't we get started right away?"

"Miss Desmond has an early dinner engagement," Angelica interjected. "She must leave by six-fifteen."

"That will be just fine," Kate agreed, extracting a reporter's notebook from her bag. Two hours would be more than enough time to rake Renata Desmond over the coals. But Kate would tread lightly at first, leading with an inoffensive question.

She snapped her ballpoint pen and smiled at Renata with fraudulent sweetness. "Miss Desmond, you are one of the most powerful women in Hollywood. At least that is the way most of us see you. But I wonder, how do you see yourself? What image is it that you want to project?"

Renata glanced toward the window and thought for a moment, then turned her attention to Kate.

"I'll answer that in two parts, Miss Brannigan. First, my image as a woman. I'm very aware of that. It is extremely important, being a woman in business, to make a statement. And I've chosen to do that in two ways. By the way I dress and by the way I conduct myself. I like to label my approach as 'understated strength.' I try to be forceful without being oppressive. I choose clothing from my favorite designer period, the forties, not to be ostentatious but to reflect what I consider to be a period of substance and some of the most important years in my life."

"Why the forties?"

"Because that's when I entered the business world and ultimately found out how much I could accomplish. How much good I could do for others, as well."

"You mean charities, causes?"

"Indeed. That, in fact, is the second part of my answer to your question. You must understand, Miss Brannigan, that I do more than run a trade paper. In my position, lofty as some may see it, I am called on constantly to give of myself. It might surprise you to know that I spend half my time attending meetings or functions connected with the many organizations that are so dear to my heart.

The Women's Guild of Cedars-Sinai, of course. The Scott Newman Foundation for Drug Abuse. The Blue Ribbon Four Hundred at the Music Center. There are dozens. Angelica will supply you with a list."

"She already has."

"Good. My point is that, in terms of image, Miss Brannigan, one must be concerned with all aspects of one's life. And the philanthropic side of mine is of utmost importance."

"I see," Kate replied, pretending to take notes. *My God,* she thought, *how self-serving can you get?*

But her face was placid as she proceeded with the interview, asking several more innocuous questions. None of which she was interested in hearing the answer to. They were designed, as the first question had been, with one specific purpose: to flatter Renata Desmond's already overblown ego.

It was an old reporter's trick. Lead with puff questions; follow through with tough questions.

Half an hour of idle chatter later, Kate knew all about Renata's favorite celebrities: Carol Burnett and Robert Wagner. The actor who'd had the most influence on her life: Larry Hagman, because he'd urged her to stop smoking. How she enjoyed spending her spare time: she rarely had any but "adored" working out in her Nautilus room upstairs or swimming in the olympic-sized pool behind the house. Even in the winter.

By the time the butler wheeled a cart full of fresh fruit and macaroons into the library, Kate had decided that the timing was right. Renata was smiling affably, laughing at her own witty comments and sipping black coffee from a delicate Limoges cup. She seemed extremely relaxed and eager to answer Kate's questions.

At least for the time being.

"Let's get back to Renata Desmond the woman for a moment," Kate said. "You've been the publisher and editor in chief of *The Hollywood Daily* for more than forty years. There must have been some difficulties for you, at first, as a woman in a man's world. Can you tell me about the specific problems you faced during the early days, in the forties?"

"Problems?" Renata repeated as though she hadn't understood the word. "Why, there weren't any problems of that nature. You must understand, Miss Brannigan, that my father had already established the *Daily* as the industry's chief trade paper. And when I stepped in, everyone accepted me automatically. I'll admit that it was a bit difficult learning so much about publishing so quickly. But I managed. And within a very short time it was as though I'd been there all my life."

"Just how much did you know about running the *Daily* when you started? Had your father been training you to follow in his footsteps?"

"Well, I hadn't had much time to do that. You see, I was away at school in Switzerland and France most of my formative years. When Father died, I'd only begun to think about working for the paper."

"Oh? But shortly after he died, the newspapers quoted you as saying something like 'My father has been grooming me to take over the paper.' "

Renata's smile faded slightly. "Is that right?" she replied in a cool voice. "Yes, I suppose I did say something like that. However, I'd had very little experience at the time."

"The experience you did have, though—how much of it did you gain through your association with Letty Molloy?"

Renata's face went rigid at the mention of Letty's name. "Why, none," she said crisply. "I never worked with, or for, Letty Molloy, if that's what you mean. Although later she did work for me. Why do you ask?"

Okay, this is it, Kate told herself. And without looking down, she commanded her cold fingers to grasp the letter she'd sandwiched between the pages of her notebook.

"I happened to meet with Letty Molloy shortly before she died, Miss Desmond," Kate said in a grave voice. "And she told me something regarding your past that I feel obligated to ask you about."

"And what is that?" Renata snapped.

"Rather than having me explain it, I think you'd prefer to read what Letty said. She wrote it all down in a letter, you see. This is a copy that you may keep, if you like."

Renata snatched the letter from Kate's hand, unfolded it, and read quickly. Eyes skipping rapidly down each page. Her face impenetrable and emotionless, like an ice carving that would never melt. When she had finished, her lips curled into a condescending smile as she looked up at Kate.

"Why, this is nonsense," she said with great indifference. "The meanderings of a senile old woman. Miss Brannigan, it is difficult to believe that a reporter of your integrity would confront me with something so meaningless and yet so demeaning."

Kate took a deep breath and gathered her strength. "Forgive me for my curiosity," she replied evenly. "But I have reason to believe that it is all true."

A frigid silence fell over the room as Renata rose majestically to her feet. "I refuse to tolerate such a scathing accusation," she announced in a glacial voice. "The interview is over. Angelica, please show Miss Brannigan to the door."

The sycophant publicist shot out of her chair like a cannon. "Yes, ma'am," she agreed obediently.

Kate's agitated stomach churned unmercifully, as though it were going to bore a hole through her. *This can't be happening,* she told herself, with a frantic glance from Angelica to Renata. *I can't afford to lose the interview, not yet. Not like this. I shouldn't have tried, shouldn't have pressed it. Russ Stevens will have my head. He knows nothing of Letty Molloy.*

For a split second Kate felt limp and helpless, as every bit of her tenacity evaporated. Like the smallest drop of water vanishing into the scorching desert air. By the time she'd gathered the courage to speak, Renata had almost reached the doorway.

"I wouldn't be so hasty if I were you, Miss Desmond. I have witnesses, you know. Three of them."

Renata's body stiffened and she stopped for a moment, considering Kate's words. Then she turned slowly around, emerald eyes shooting daggers. "What witnesses?" she insisted.

"Alisa Hudson, among others," Kate lied. She was quivering inside. But her voice was full of confidence.

Angelica had heard enough. "Kate, the interview is over," she whined, tugging at the reporter's arm. "And it's really time for you to—"

"Angelica! I'll handle this," Renata interrupted, walking stoically toward her publicist. "You're dismissed."

"But . . . but, Miss Desmond," the frustrated Angelica stammered. "I really feel that in your own best interest—"

"Shut up and get out!"

"Yes, ma'am. Whatever you say," Angelica whimpered, retreating toward the doorway with measured, backward steps.

Once she'd disappeared, Renata turned to Kate. "And what of these witnesses?" she demanded.

"It's really quite simple," Kate answered matter-of-factly, handing her a slip of paper. "This is Alisa Hudson's home phone number. Call her if you like. She'll vouch for Sammy Rollins and Harvey Stinson too."

Renata's face hardened into an expression of disbelief and mild amusement. "Harvey and Sammy are going to accuse me . . . of . . . of this?" she said with a guttural laugh, brandishing the letter in the air. "You are deluding yourself."

"Apparently one of us is," Kate said tersely. "You can check by phoning Alisa."

Renata stared down at Kate with laserlike eyes. "I wouldn't dream of it."

"Suit yourself. But you can rest assured that since I have witnesses, certain parts of Letty's letter will be printed in *World* magazine with or without your side of the story."

My God, did I really say that? Kate's insides had turned to jelly. She was astonished at how well she could bluff. But terrified of what might happen. *Too far, you've really gone way too far now,* an inner voice warned.

Kate's eyes grew wide with apprehension.

Renata was walking over to the Empire desk and reaching for the phone.

She picked it up.

Kate couldn't breathe. The room seemed devoid of fresh air. And so quiet she could hear a fly buzzing in the distance. Her mind was spinning, racing, groping for ideas, excuses. The phone number she'd given Renata wasn't Alisa Hudson's at all. She'd written it down at random, on a hunch. A hunch that was about to boomerang, just as she'd feared it would.

Renata dialed three numbers with her long scarlet fingernail. Then she stopped abruptly. A foreboding look of doom crept onto her face. And she stood there for a few moments like an ominous marble statue rooted to the lustrous hardwood floor. Then, very slowly, she placed the receiver back in its cradle, walked over to Kate and sat down across from her.

"All right, Miss Brannigan," she said stonily. "Let's stop the game-playing. What is it that you want?"

An incomparable wave of relief surged through Kate's body. She felt as though a tremendous weight had been lifted from her, as though she could soar through the air.

But she maintained her placid expression as she said, "I want to know everything. The entire story. Everything Letty Molloy told me, from your point of view."

Renata was quiet for a long moment. And her tone was icy when she finally said, "On one condition. That what I tell you is off the record."

"No promises. I'm a reporter, Miss Desmond. And, excuse me for saying so, but at the moment I have you quite neatly boxed in."

Renata looked down at her own long, slender fingers and began twisting the heavy diamond ring on her right hand. After a few moments she met her adversary's penetrating eyes. "I sense the animosity in your voice, Miss Brannigan. And I assume it has something to do with the fact that you were fired from the *Daily.*"

"Not so," Kate replied in a strident voice. "I don't hold grudges, Renata. Although I must say I have little respect for your ruthlessness as publisher—specifically the way you tried to destroy Brandy St. John's career."

"Oh. So, it's poor dear Brandy I'm being paid back for?"

"Nothing of the sort. I am merely trying to get to the bottom of the story behind Letty Molloy's letter. Call it a case of extreme journalist inquisitiveness, if you like. But you might as well tell me your side, Renata. There is no way you can prevent this story from breaking. However, you may be able to soften it."

The room fell silent for a few moments as the two women glared at each other in nonverbal combat. Then Renata sprang abruptly to her feet.

"You must excuse me for a moment first," she said. And bounded from the room, high heels clicking noisily.

Kate jumped up, ready to run after her. But cautioned herself against it. She paced the floor anxiously. Wondering what the conniving woman was up to.

Calm down, calm down, she told herself, taking deep breaths. She moved back and forth in front of the fireplace, impatiently. Waiting. Wondering.

Then, all of a sudden, a chilling ripple of fear fought its way up her spine. And her pulse quickened as a vision of Renata brandishing a handgun flashed through her mind. *She wouldn't,* Kate thought, terrified. *She couldn't possibly—*

The click of high heels on marble pierced the solemn air.

An immovable lump lodged itself in Kate's throat as her eyes searched the library. Was there another exit? An open window? She had to get out of there. She had to escape. Rush back to her office and seal herself off from this volatile psychopath before it was too late.

Kate stared at the doorway, paralyzed with fear.

Within seconds Renata was there, clutching something in her right hand.

Kate's muscles went slack with relief.

It was not a gun.

Unsteadily, but with great determination, Renata marched over to Kate and handed her a single sheet of yellowing parchment stationery.

"I have some correspondence of my own, you see," she announced.

Kate studied the letter curiously. It was dated July 18, 1927. The letterhead read Charles Wentworth Desmond. And it was singed at the top, as though someone had once held a match to it.

"I found this two years after my father died," Renata explained as she sat down. "I was going through everything, preparing to move from our home on Angelo Drive. Needless to say, I was surprised when I fished this out of his wall safe. Go ahead, read it."

Kate sank into the club chair and did so.

My Dearest Daughter,

    I have no idea how to begin, but there is something I must tell you. And it is far easier to write this than attempt to explain in person. You are, after all, only seven years old, so you probably wouldn't comprehend all I have to say anyway. But I want you to know that all your fears are for naught, my darling. Daddy loves you like his own. Because you are his own, his flesh and blood. And he will never desert you.

Someday you will want to know about your mother. I can tell you she was the most beautiful woman in the world. Her name was Nadia Renata Melenz, and she emigrated to this country from Russia with her family in 1916. She was only eighteen when we met. She was working as a housekeeper for one of my friends. I fell instantly in love with her. I would have married her, I swear on your sweet life, my child. But dear Nadia died giving birth to you. And that is the sad state of affairs. I mourn for her always. And I cherish every moment I spend with you, Renata, for you are a part of my Nadia. It is my hope that you will grow up to look exactly like your lovely mother. You already resemble her in so many ways.

I am, I confess, a bit drunk at this moment. But the thought of something happening to me, and my own daughter never learning that I am indeed her true father, haunts me constantly. I cannot let another day go by without setting things right. I will leave this behind, my love, so that someday you will find it and know the truth.

> With everlasting love from your father,
> Charles Wentworth Desmond

When she had finished reading, Kate sat back, a puzzled expression on her face. "This is quite a revelation," she said, in a strained voice. "But what does it have to do with—"

"Everything," Renata interrupted impatiently. "Just sit back and listen, Miss Brannigan. The pieces will fall into place. You want to know how my father died. I hope that you are prepared for this explanation. It may shock you. But please be assured that what I'm about to say is the absolute truth. And it is my hope that once you've heard it, you will drop the notion of printing any of it."

Renata paused for a moment and straightened her back to an erect position against the club chair. As though by gathering all her dignity she could distance herself from the memories she was about to unravel.

She began slowly in a determined, steady voice. Her face set in stony expression.

"What I'm about to tell you remains a freakish nightmare, lodged in the dark crevices of my mind. You see, Miss Brannigan, I was a very troubled child and an equally unbalanced young woman. I want you to know exactly what I went through. And when you do, perhaps you will be able to understand why I . . . why I did what I did."

She continued to talk for the next fifteen minutes. And Kate listened with increasing amazement, her eyes fixed on the woman's granite face. For Renata's expression remained immobile as she invoked her ironlike will, uttering the words but not reacting to them.

She told Kate about her early years. The tremendous insecurity she'd suffered as the result of precocious puberty. The confusion and humiliation of living inside an adult body at the age of nine. The endless embarrassing doctor appointments. And the way her father had virtually disowned her and packed her off to boarding school.

"As if I were a freak he couldn't be bothered with," Renata said twisting the diamond ring around and around on her finger. "But things changed when I grew up," she added sarcastically. "And that, Miss Brannigan, has a great deal to do with what Letty Molloy told you."

Kate leaned forward in her chair and searched Renata's flinty eyes.

"My father abused me, Miss Brannigan," she said flatly, waiting for a response.

"He . . . he abused you physically, sexually?" Kate gasped, astonished.

"Yes, he did, on many occasions. Letty Molloy didn't know that, you see. Letty was quite taken with my father, in love with him, some said. But she had no idea what he was really like or that he was really my father. It is important for you to understand these facts before I go on and tell you how . . . how he died."

Kate swallowed hard and nodded. Wondering how much of this she could believe. It certainly sounded convincing. But she had to remind herself of Renata Desmond's manipulative nature. The woman was not to be trusted.

"As I developed into a shapely teenager, my father became quite taken with me," Renata went on. "Obviously, although I wasn't aware of it then, because I resembled my mother. He came to my bedroom many times during my summer vacations. I needn't tell you how shamed I was, Miss Brannigan. Or how confused."

As Renata continued to speak, her voice turned grainy and soft, as though it belonged to a much older woman. And Kate noticed a distinct change in her expression. Her emerald eyes, so hard just moments earlier, turned thoughtful and brooding, giving her a pathetic look of great sadness. A look not unlike the one of the teenage girl in the portrait over the fireplace.

What Kate did not know was that Renata was confronting that very girl for the first time in many years. Never since she had taken over *The Hollywood Daily* had Renata allowed herself a backward glance at her youth. The thought of revealing this much of herself to another person, particularly a reporter, had seemed inconceivable an hour earlier.

But as Kate Brannigan had reminded her, she was boxed in. She had little choice other than to play on the journalist's sympathies. And she was quite certain she could do that. The problem was going to be keeping herself in check. She had to assume the role of the victim, without losing control.

The longer she spoke, however, the more Renata became swept up in her own haunting memories. As the minutes ticked by, she began to relive every moment of anguish, of bewilderment, of pain. And by the time she began describing the events surrounding the fateful party aboard her father's yacht, Renata was all but in a trance. Trapped again in her own nightmarish past.

She spoke quickly, breathlessly, as though disgorging something poisonous.

"It was June of 1938, the weekend of my eighteenth birthday. And though my father and I had been at odds with each other for several days, he'd insisted that I join him and his eight invited guests on the *Regina Renata*."

Kate listened with keen interest, nodding spontaneously in agreement. *Yes, that was exactly what Letty had said, a party aboard the yacht.*

"I didn't really want to go. But he forced me to. That Friday morning we all set out for Tijuana, where we took in the late afternoon greyhound races and listened to mariachi music at a popular cantina. Unbeknownst to the rest of us, my father also arranged a little surprise for later that night.

"Most of the afternoon, he'd been guzzling double gins. By early evening, he was on the prowl, looking for me. And by the time he found me in my stateroom he was very, very drunk. He scolded me for not circulating among the guests and told me I was a terrible hostess.

"I paid no attention to him. I was lying on my bed at the time, paging through a copy of *Vogue.* I remember it as clearly as if it were yesterday. And as I said earlier, there was a great deal of friction between us that summer. My silence vexed him all the more, and before I knew what was happening he came flying across the room at me.

"He was in a rage, cursing me, ripping at my dressing gown. And . . . and then he was on top of me. He . . . He . . ." Renata's lips quivered involuntarily as she struggled to compose herself.

Kate sat captivated, totally immersed in what the older woman was saying.

"He . . . he raped me, Miss Brannigan," Renata finally admitted. Her shoulders were trembling now and her emerald eyes were wild with fury. "He'd never . . . never done that before. If you know what I mean?"

Kate nodded in silent understanding. Her face etched with the very empathy she'd been steeling herself against. Objective though she wanted to be, she could not help but feel sorry for the traumatized woman sitting across from her.

Renata's angry eyes had misted over by the time she spoke again. "Looking back, I suppose one could say I was in a state of shock after he . . . after it happened," she said. "I was horrified. So scared I could barely move. And desperately afraid that he would come back later and . . . and do it again.

"But there was no one I could confide in, you understand. And nothing I could do. I was all but captive at sea, and my own birthday party was in progress in the ship's ballroom. In fact, I remember that when he left my cabin he called to the maid and instructed her to make certain I was dressed for the celebration posthaste."

Kate could now sees tears welling up in Renata's eyes. Tears not of anger or revenge but of great remorse. Hot, briny tears. Splashing down her cheeks in a steady stream as she described the rest of the portentous evening.

Dressed in a stunning floor-length vermilion evening gown, she had joined her father and his guests for a six-course dinner in the dining room. Shortly after dessert, the entertainment had begun.

It was a tradition of these weekend excursions that each guest on board become part of the floor show. Fancying himself a sort of P.T. Barnum of the Pacific, Cappy delighted in goading each guest in turn to sing a song, do a scene, or perform a bit of comedy shtick. But he always saved his own special act for last. And it was certain to be the most outlandish, outrageous—and often scandalous—moment of the evening.

That night was no exception. After each guest had taken a turn at entertaining the group, Cappy, face flushed with excitement, staggered before them all and boozily announced his grand finale.

"Ladies and gentlemen, I give you . . . Rosa and Eduardo."

The guests began to clap politely, but suddenly they stopped. Instead of the expected flamenco dancers or perhaps a singing duo, they found themselves staring at a highly incongruous couple.

Rosa, a dark-haired, voluptuous woman, stood only inches away from what appeared to be a male dwarf. Eduardo was under four feet, with stubby limbs and a head too large for his body.

There was, however, something even more startling about the unseemly pair. They were dressed in next to nothing.

"What's this—a burlesque show?" one guest piped up, eyeing Rosa's enormous breasts.

"You'll see, Jeffrey. You'll see," Cappy chortled as the curvaceous woman circled the floor.

She was draped in a low-cut pink satin slip. Her partner wore skin-tight shorts and an open shirt. Within moments the two began a seductive dance as the sound of undulating jazz oozed from a nearby phonograph. Then, very slowly, they began to undress each other.

It was a captivatingly sensual bit of choreography. Unprecedented in its daring, even for this crowd. And not without a hint of perversion, which played well among Cappy's guests. They were appalled, though at the same time entranced. Eyes riveted on Rosa as she dropped to her knees before Eduardo.

What the dwarf lacked in physical stature he made up for in sexual prowess. For his size, he was extraordinarily well endowed. This became clear within seconds as Rose went about her business, leaving nothing to the imagination. And causing several of Cappy's female guests to not only gasp in revulsion but flee the room altogether.

The remainder of the audience remained fixed in their chairs. Wide-eyed with astonishment. Watching in stunned anticipation as Rosa and Eduardo performed their libidinous tasks.

What ensued was a hideous scene of unbridled debauchery. The two going at each other with such obvious delight and total abandon that it appeared they must have been drugged.

Cappy sat in the front row, reveling in every lewd second. Glancing from time to time at his guests. And growing more and more excited.

The titillating floor show continued for more than fifteen minutes.

Renata sat ramrod straight not far from her father. Shielding her eyes from the offending scene. Afraid to leave. Terrified of what Cappy might say or do.

When the performance ended, Rosa retrieved her satin slip and immediately disappeared behind an Oriental screen. But the dwarf remained center stage. He was dressed again in his shorts. And waiting, it seemed, for some sort of signal from the host.

The room was cloaked in heavy silence. There was, not surprisingly, no applause. Just a few throats being cleared. Followed by a smattering of muffled comments and anxious whispers.

At this point, Cappy, obviously inebriated beyond control, leapt to his feet and turned to his daughter.

"All right," he commanded, waving his arms about, "now let's see what *you* can do with Eduardo here." And with that, he pulled Renata from her chair and shoved her so forcefully in the again aroused dwarf's direction that she lost her balance and tumbled to the floor.

Gasps rose from the guests. Was Cappy Desmond insane? How could any man do such a thing to his daughter? One gentleman stepped forward to come to Renata's aid, but Cappy blocked his path and loudly ordered him back to his seat. The man glowered but did as he was told.

"I don't know how I managed," Renata now told Kate. "I was so frightened, you see. And I'd sprained an ankle in the fall. But from somewhere I summoned the strength to get up off that floor and . . . and defend myself. I had to. My father was totally out of control. No one else would go near him."

"As soon as I was on my feet, he was at it again. Lashing out at me. Hitting me, slapping me. He was like a madman, a savage, acting as though he wanted to kill me. He tore at my dress, ripped it halfway down the front. I kept trying to hold it up and fend him off at the same time. And then he went for my throat. I could feel his huge hands encircling my neck, and I knew what he was going to do. I knew he was going to strangle me."

"But just before his fingers dug into me, I turned slightly and grabbed a brass yachting trophy off the bar. I didn't stop to think you see. I didn't have time. The only thing I could concentrate on was protecting myself. And the trophy was the only object within reach . . ."

Renata's voice trailed off as the brutal scene replayed itself in her mind. She could see her father clearly. Dressed in a brand-new tuxedo. Drenched in sweat. His handsome face contorted in wantonness and rage.

The large blue vein on his left temple palpitated wildly as he leaned over her, eyes full of anger—and desire. His thick fingers pressed deeper and deeper into her flesh, bruising her skin, crushing her neck.

It took less than a second, and he didn't see it coming. The gleaming statuette. He'd won it the previous year. First place in an annual race from Los Angeles to Portland. How could he have known this same prestigious brass trophy would be used to destroy him?

She was gasping for breath when she swung it. And she did so with all her might. Raising it up in the air, then smashing it down into his face. Hitting him squarely between the eyes.

"He died instantly," Renata murmured as she muffled a sob with the back of her hand. And for a long moment she was silent, staring off in space, as she resumed turning the diamond ring around and around on her finger.

"And I must tell you, Miss Brannigan," she continued. "I've paid a terrible price. It was self-defense, of course. No one on board questioned that. But obviously none of them wanted to be associated with such a scandalous affair. So a pact of silence was agreed upon."

Kate's eyes filled with dawning comprehension as Renata explained.

"Some of the guests were greedier than others. Sammy Rollins, for one, demanding his own column. Harvey Stinson would never have lasted this long with the *Daily*, had he not been aboard. I've had to protect him, Miss Brannigan. Essentially, that is why you were fired," Renata concluded in a raspy voice.

Her large emerald eyes were liquid, still brimming with the tears that had continued to stream down her face, carving two sad white lines into her perfectly made-up cheeks.

Despite herself, Kate felt a tremendous surge of compassion. But she fought her first instinct, which was to console the grieving woman.

After all, Renata was still very dangerous. Convincing but calculating in the extreme. Kate didn't know what to think, but she had to keep her journalistic wits about her. She could not afford to appear too sympathetic. And there was another consideration. The Longhorns. She still had to confront Renata with that.

"You think I'm lying, don't you?" Renata asked before Kate could say anything. "Of course you do. But I have something else to share with you, Miss Brannigan. Something that will convince you that I am telling the truth. Please sit a moment longer."

She got up and walked slowly toward the desk, opened the bottom drawer, and extracted a leather-bound photo album.

"What's this?" asked Kate, accepting the album from Renata.

"Please look through it."

Kate began turning the pages. Her face set in a puzzled expression. The album was filled with dozens of snapshots of one person from infancy to manhood. A medium-sized man with dark hair and large green eyes. But Kate noticed something abnormal about him, particularly his face. The man's expression was always the same. Vague, glazed, and uncertain, with just the hint of a questioning smile.

In most of the snapshots he was sitting, but in several at the back of the album he was standing next to a building. And it was apparent that his spine was grotesquely curved.

"This is Eric," Renata said softly as Kate turned the last page. "My son . . . and my brother. He's in a private home for the mentally disturbed in Bakersfield. Despite my busy schedule, I try to visit him there twice a week. Aside from his doctors and the attendants at the home, no one knows about Eric. I am only telling you about him now, Miss Brannigan, as proof that everything I said about my father is true."

Kate sat there, stunned, And quite unable to assimilate what Renata was telling her at first. It just wasn't possible. The whole thing seemed too bizarre.

The lascivious sex show. A killing in self-defense. And now—now Eric. Cappy Desmond's son? Renata's son? That's who she'd been visiting at St. Dominic's in Bakersfield?

"You see, Miss Brannigan, almost all my life I hated my father," Renata was saying. "But once he was gone I realized how much of that hate was really love. And when I discovered I was pregnant with his child, I couldn't bring myself to abort."

Renata paused for a moment, searching Kate's blue-violet eyes for a sign of commiseration.

"And if this isn't proof enough, you are welcome to accompany me to Bakersfield to meet Eric. Miss Brannigan, what I am trying to make clear to you is that the crime that you are so anxious to report in your magazine was laid to rest years ago. What I did that night may not have been the right thing. But it was the only thing I could do at the time. And, believe me, there is never a day that I am not haunted by it."

"I'm . . . I'm certain it's been very difficult," Kate murmured, not sure of what to say next. She was deeply moved. But still skeptical, warning herself not to trust.

"Tell me then, Miss Brannigan, are you convinced of my innocence?" Renata inquired in a fragile voice. "Or are you still planning to expose me as a murderess?"

The words hung in the air as Kate wrestled with her conscience. And suddenly she was overwhelmed by a desire to get away, to run, to flee the thick cloud of emotion that was smothering her. Preventing her from seeing any of this with the clear, cool eye of a journalist. Quite simply, she could not think straight.

"Miss Desmond, I'll be honest with you," Kate replied unsteadily.

"It is impossible for me to make a decision at this moment. As a woman, I am tremendously sympathetic, of course. As a reporter, well, that is another matter."

Renata said nothing, but continued to look at Kate. Her weary emerald eyes imploring understanding and forgiveness.

Kate shifted in the club chair uncomfortably, wishing the interview were over so that she could walk away. But she could not. There was the matter of the Longhorns. She had to ask. Even though, at this moment, it was the last thing she wanted to do.

"There is something else I'd like to cover before I leave," she began haltingly, struggling to make the phrases seem as gentle as possible. "Your football team, the Longhorns. I have reason to believe that you and your vice-president, Templeton Haight, have been fixing the games."

Renata's face paled and her mouth dropped open to form a perfect O.

"The reason is Don Brocato, Miss Desmond," Kate continued, almost apologetically. "He told me everything. And before we print his story, I must ask you, is it . . . is it true? Have you been betting against your own team?"

Renata straightened herself in the chair, her face a cold, sinister mask of indignation.

"I'm . . . I'm sorry to have to press you with this right now," Kate explained. "But I really have to get a—"

"A statement?" Renata asked haughtily, raising an eyebrow. "Well, here it is," she announced, standing up. "I have never heard of anything so ridiculous. Miss Brannigan, you are a fool. And I am a bigger one for having deluded myself into thinking I could trust you. Now, good day!" she concluded. And strolled imperiously from the library.

Kate did not wait for the butler to show her out. Within seconds she was hustling down the hallway, through the foyer, and out the hand-carved double doors into the golden light of late afternoon.

She stood there for a moment, taking huge gulps of crisp autumn air, which did not help clear her head.

You're hyperventilating, she told herself. *Don't panic. Just get in the car and leave.* But by the time she slipped into the Peugeot, she was too dizzy to do anything but try to recover her breath.

A half hour later she marched determinedly into her office at *World* magazine. Locked the door behind her and withdrew a small tape recorder from her bag. She did a spot-check, making sure everything Renata Desmond had said was there.

Then she sat down and stared at her word processor. Her mind a jumble of incongruous thoughts. Her stomach quivering with excitement—and angst.

What was she going to do? She had a blockbuster of a story on her hands. A prize-winning investigative report. The stuff that books and miniseries were made of. With all the key ingredients: love, lust, power, incest, greed. Renata Desmond's shocking past ran the gamut. Russ Stevens would be ecstatic.

"But should I tell him?" Kate wondered aloud. "Should I tell anyone?"

She needed time to sort things out, time to think. Unfortunately, she didn't have that luxury. Stevens was expecting the story in New York by nine the next morning. Kate had to make up her mind and start writing immediately. But at the moment she could barely think.

With a weary sigh, she leaned forward and rested her head in her hands. She felt weak. She hadn't eaten since early that morning and knew she should put something in her stomach. But the thought of food nauseated her.

If only she could call someone and discuss the piece. Sara or Jerry Lindner, even Stevens himself. But that was impossible. She couldn't afford to disclose what Renata had told her, unless she was going to include it in the story.

Kate hadn't counted on this. She felt torn and utterly disconcerted. For the first time in her entire journalistic career, she had to admit that she did not know what to do.

At four that afternoon she had sat down to interview Renata Desmond. A true Hollywood villainess. A woman she clearly despised.

Now she found herself the arbiter of that woman's fate. In a way it was like playing God. And for Kate Brannigan there was no comfort in the role.

29

■ Quintana Jaye was up to her wrists in piecrust dough. As she worked away, gently blending the delicate mixture, she began humming her favorite melody. The title song from *The Way We Were*.

It had been a typically melancholy Saturday morning. With memories of Renata drifting through her mind. They'd been living separately for almost two months. But it seemed that everything in Quintana's house reminded her of her former lover. Weekends were always the worst.

This particular morning she'd been tempted to cry several times. That, in fact, was the very reason she'd taken refuge in her kitchen and was preparing some test recipes.

There was nothing quite like experimentation to get Quintana's mind off her troubles. At the moment she was fashioning a dietetic French chocolate-mousse pie for an upcoming party in Jane Fonda's honor. But the low-calorie crust she'd invented—a combination of flour, water, and a liquid butter substitute—was not cooperating. In fact, it was fighting back.

"Damn, damn, damn," Quintana yelped as she attempted to lift the thin layer of dough from the pastry cloth. Once again it fell apart in her hands.

With mounting impatience, she packed the belligerent dough into a ball, fired it into the wastebasket, reached for the flour, and measured one cupful into the sifter.

"I'll get this right if it takes the entire day," she muttered to herself, adding a tablespoon of water.

Just then the phone rang. Quintana paid no attention, intent on the task at hand. But the irritating jangle continued over and over again, vexing her to the point of total exasperation.

"Go away. Shut up. I'm not here," she shouted, attacking the new mixture with her fingers.

By the eighteenth ring she could tolerate the disturbance no longer.

"All right. All right. Hold your fire." she said, rubbing her sticky hands on her apron. She picked up the phone. "Hello?"

"Quin?" The voice was deep, throaty, and very familiar.

Quintana's legs went weak. She sank onto a nearby stool. "Yes?" she heard herself say.

"Quin, darling, it's Renata. I . . . I received your note. And I was very touched. I'm sorry it's taken me so long to call. But I . . ."

Quintana's grip tightened on the receiver. For a moment, she had the oddest sensation that she was acting out a dream. She'd waited so long for this, never really believing it would happen.

"Darling, I'll be very specific," Renata was saying. "Something's come up. I have to get away for a few days. And I was hoping that you'd be able to join me."

"Well, this is all very sudden," Quintana replied in a tremulous voice.

"Yes. Yes, I know it is, Quin. But, well, I'm in a bit of a spot. And I need you with me, Quintana. You are the only person I can trust."

Quintana's eyes widened suspiciously. "What kind of a spot?"

"I really can't explain over the phone. Suffice it to say that I received some rather bad news yesterday. And now I have to . . . well, recover. I was thinking of, ahh . . . Two Bunch Palms in the Springs."

"What about your paramour, little Michelle?" Quintana reported vindictively. "I'm sure she'd welcome a holiday."

"Quin, please, let's not bicker," Renata said anxiously. "Michelle has been gone for weeks. The point is, I want to be with you. Please, darling. I know it's short notice. But I really need you with me."

Quintana sat in ponderous silence. Watching the butcher-block clock. Glancing around her cluttered kitchen. Biding her time. She could afford to do that. After all, it was she who was being pursued. At last the tables had turned. And Renata was asking—no, it was more like begging, wasn't it? Yes, Renata Desmond was pleading for her affection. Let the bitch dangle a while. Let her know how it feels.

"Quin, what is it, darling?" Renata demanded after a few moments. "What's the problem?"

"Oh, just thinking," Quintana said in an airy voice. "About my schedule. And it doesn't look good, Renata. I've two parties to cater this weekend and five next week. Can't possibly get away. I know you understand. Perhaps another time."

When Renata spoke, it was as though she were breathing fire into the phone. "Quintana, I'm telling you. This is an emergency. There may not be another time."

"Well, then," Quintana said, weakening. "I guess, if you put it that way . . . Maybe I could join you tomorrow, once I finish up the—"

"No!" Renata interrupted. "It has to be today. You know perfectly well that Janet can carry on without you. She's done it before. Please, Quintana, just this once, be there for me."

Quintana could feel her heart hammering against her chest as her mind raced ahead to a long, romantic weekend of tender lovemaking with Renata. There was no one she would rather be with.

"Yes, all right," she agreed, finally. "I mean I'll go, but first I have to—"

"Good," Renata interjected. "I'll be by with the limo in two hours."

"That will be fine. Now, how long are we—"

But Renata had already hung up. Her next call was to Varig Airlines, where she reconfirmed first-class reservations on Flight 131 for Miss Marva Breemen and Miss Charlotte Wells. Yes, that was correct, open returns. The ladies would be staying in Buenos Aires indefinitely.

It was eight minutes past seven on Tuesday morning, and David Hartman was about to introduce his first guest. He caught the floor director's signal out of the corner of his eye, looked directly into the camera, and began talking to the six million viewers who were waking up with *Good Morning America.*

Among them, Kate Brannigan, Sara Evans Silverstein, and her twins. They sat in Sara's bedroom, dressed in bathrobes, eyes glued to the huge television screen before them.

"Aren't they going to show a picture of Aunt Kate?" Jackie yawned as Hartman began talking.

"Hush," Sara whispered. "Just listen."

"With me now," Hartman was saying, "is one quarterback who's been getting a great deal of attention lately. And if the current *World* magazine, which hits the stands this morning, has anything to do with it, it looks like he'll be getting a lot more."

As Hartman continued to speak, the *World* cover flashed on the screen. A three-quarter shot of Don Brocato's ruggedly handsome face smiled knowingly from beneath the magazine's logo. The blurb under his chin read: "Brocato Blasts the Longhorns."

"By Kate Brannigan!" Jennifer yelled, patting Kate on the back.

Now the cameras zoomed in on a close-up of Brocato in the studio.

"Wow, he's cute without his helmet," Jackie enthused.

"I'll say," her sister agreed.

"Jennifer, I can't hear!" Sara complained, punching up the volume.

Hartman was in the midst of introducing Brocato, who sat opposite him. The quarterback was dressed in a dark brown pinstriped suit, and looking more than a little uncomfortable. Tiny beads of sweat lined his wrinkled brow. His hands were clenched tightly in his lap. The knuckles were white.

"And after that nationally televised fight with Coach Max Dunphy at Anaheim Stadium," Hartman was saying, "Don Brocato quit the team and mysteriously disappeared. Now he's back with some stunning allegations, basically accusing Longhorns owner Renata Desmond and her vice-president, Templeton Haight, of fixing a number of Longhorns games this season."

Brocato cleared his throat and swallowed hard.

"Some pretty startling accusations in that interview, Don," Hartman probed.

"Yes, I guess you could say that," Brocato agreed with a stiff grin. "But it's the absolute truth, David. I mean I wasn't aware of it at first. A few games into the season, though, and I got the picture. I even tried to talk to Coach Dunphy, but he'd have none of it. So I got angrier and angrier and finally I had that, ahh . . . outburst, at the Rams game and then I had to take a walk. I mean when the team's owner is forcing your coach to make you blow key plays, you don't stand much of a chance."

"Before going any further," Hartman said, "I want to point out that we did attempt to contact Renata Desmond, Templeton Haight, and Coach Dunphy. In all cases, we were told, 'No comment.' "

"Yeah, I heard Renata Desmond left the country," Brocato said angrily. "But when the Los Angeles District Attorney's office launches an investigation, she'll be back."

"Is that what you understand is going to happen?" Hartman asked eagerly.

"You better believe it. I've already been contacted."

"So has Aunt Kate!" Jackie shouted at the screen.

"Jackie—shush!" her mother objected.

They watched in silence for the next four minutes as Don Brocato continued his tirade. He seemed perfectly at ease now, gesticulating animatedly as he described the bad calls, the key plays that had purposely been blown, the way Renata Desmond had sabotaged her own team.

"What about your career?" Hartman wanted to know. "You're taking a pretty big risk speaking out like this, aren't you?"

"Well, David, there are some things you just have to do." Brocato said firmly. "When you know you're right, there's no other way to go."

Seconds before Hartman was about to conclude the interview, the quarterback asked if he could say something else.

"Make it quick," Hartman urged, glancing at the time card in his floor director's hand. It said thirty seconds.

"I just want you to know," Brocato began, "that if it weren't for a crackerjack reporter named Kate Brannigan, I might not be sitting here. I still can't imagine how, but she picked up on the betting scam weeks ago. And she kept trying to get me to talk. In the end it was Kate who gave me the courage to tell the truth. That's her byline on the story."

"Yippee! Hooray! Good for Aunt Kate!" Jackie and Jennifer yelped in unison.

"Thanks, girls," Kate said modestly. She hadn't expected the accolade from Brocato and was very much surprised.

"Does this mean you're going to win the Pulitzer prize?" Jackie chirped excitedly.

"I don't think so," Kate laughed, shaking her head.

"Maybe not," Sara agreed. "But it does mean we're going to celebrate. Next weekend. A big party, right here. Say a couple hundred of our closest friends."

"Just make sure you invite Don Brocato," Jackie piped up.

"Yeah, he's gorgeous," Jennifer agreed.

"Sara, there's no need for a party," Kate said as the twins left the room. "Really, you know I've been thinking about getting away. Maybe to Hawaii."

"So wait a few days. We'll give you a fabulous send-off. With an 'A' list. So many famous faces George Christy will have to cover it."

"Now you're going overboard," Kate warned.

"Nothing's too much for my 'crackerjack' reporter," Sara teased as she sashayed toward the shower. "Face it, honey, you're hot stuff. Might as well get some mileage out of it."

Yes, I suppose I might as well, Kate thought, as she padded down the hall toward her room. She was smiling to herself when she climbed into bed. How luxurious to be able to go back to sleep at seven-thirty. What a triumph it was to be singled out as a top-notch journalist—on *Good Morning America,* yet. And how happy she was with the decision she'd made about Renata Desmond.

Good stories, exclusive stories, scandalous stories would come Kate's way again. Perhaps none of them would be as sensational as the one she could have written about Renata. But, ultimately, Kate had found she was incapable of writing it. Somehow doing so just didn't seem humane.

As Don Brocato had just pointed out, there were some things more important than getting ahead in one's chosen career. Kate was glad she'd been tested. And as she drifted back to sleep, the satin comforter pulled up to her chin, it was with the knowledge that from now on everything was going to be all right.

Dr. Laura Bernstein would have said that Kate Brannigan was beginning to believe in herself.

Templeton Haight's body was discovered at ten o'clock on Tuesday morning by his Oriental houseboy, Sho-Song.

It was not a routine suicide.

In his own inimitable style, Haight had engineered his death just as he had lived his life, with a flair for the dramatic.

At seven on Monday evening he'd showered, shaved, lavished

himself with an abundant splash of Paco Rabanne cologne, and slipped into his favorite dark blue cashmere suit. He'd descended to the first floor of his Beverly Hills mansion in the ornate elevator he'd purchased at a hotel auction in Paris ten years earlier.

Promptly at seven-thirty, he sat down to an elegant six-course meal, served by Reynolds, his longtime British butler. Templeton dined alone, savoring such delicacies as *pâté de brochet* and *donine de canard* while the haunting strains of Tchaikovsky's *1812 Overture* wafted through his cavernous formal dining room.

By the time the slender hands of his sleek Cartier watch reached nine o'clock, Templeton was finishing off the last cloyingly sweet spoonful of *coupé glacé baumanière*. He belched appreciatively then ascended once again to the second floor. There he paused in his magnificent master bathroom, brushed and flossed his teeth, tidied his hair, and splashed on a bit more Paco Rabanne.

Ablutions performed, Templeton proceeded to his study where he sat down in a brown leather wing chair, settled back comfortably, and peered knowingly at the contraption directly opposite him.

It was one of his latest anomalous mechanical toys. A remote-control crossbow, handmade in Germany to Templeton's specifications. A specially molded tip containing cyanide covered the arrowhead, assuring instant death.

The arrow was aimed directly at Templeton's heart and situated just three feet away from him.

Like a brave samurai committing hara-kiri, the ill-fated vice-president took his very last deep breath. Then he raised his chubby left index finger and resolutely pressed it to the small remote-control button on his lap.

In less than a second, the cold steel shaft plunged forward, pierced through his dark blue cashmere jacket, and swiftly snuffed out his life.

The next morning's *Herald Examiner* headlined the bizarre suicide. The accompanying article suggested Haight had killed himself fearing repercussions as a result of the current investigation into the fixing of several Longhorns games. The District Attorney was quoted as saying Coach Max Dunphy had already issued a statement, implicating Haight and his employer, Renata Desmond, in the betting scandal.

A sidebar story described the doomed executive's last wishes:

In a handwritten note found near the body, the 53-year-old bachelor requested that his entire net worth, estimated at seventy million dollars, be designated for the construction and operation of the Templeton Haight Gallery of Genius Gadgetry, where his extensive collection of eccentric paraphernalia will be on display. Included in this display, according to Haight's wishes, will be his death weapon, the remote-control crossbow, which at the press of a button will send an arrow flying through the air to neatly penetrate the heart of a mannequin in Templeton Haight's likeness.

30

■ It was a crisp, clear Saturday in November. A perfect afternoon for a party in Bel Air.

Kate was upstairs in her room, slipping into a new lilac Zandra Rhodes dress. And bubbling over with excitement about the upcoming celebration in her honor.

Sara was outside in the backyard, still in her jeans. And overwrought with anxiety. At the moment, she was standing next to the tennis courts, shouting at the tent man.

"I can't understand this," she complained pointing at the gigantic, sagging canvas, which the man was currently examining. "I've dealt with your company for years and not once have I been stuck with a faulty tent. This one collapsed like a sick popover right before my eyes."

The man assured her it could be fixed.

"How soon?" she demanded. "I have two hundred people arriving in less than an hour. What am I supposed to do, keep them circulating in a holding pattern on the street? You better—"

The high, keening screech of car brakes pierced the air. Then a crash, the mangling crunch of metal grinding into metal.

"What the hell was that?" Sara took off like a jackrabbit around the side of her rambling mansion. She arrived at the jammed circular front driveway just in time to see the flower delivery boy punch one of the caterer's assistants in the face.

Soon the two young men were rolling around on the ground. "You ruined my truck," yelled one.

"How'd I know you were backing up, asshole?" hissed the other.

"Stop, stop, stop!" shouted Sara at the top of her lungs. "Now get up and get to work. We'll settle all this later. You're both late, anyway. You," she said to the catering assistant, a good-looking Oriental lad. "Where's your other van?"

He stared at her blankly.

"Don't act dumb. I ordered a buffet for two hundred, and I know you can't squeeze all the food, serving dishes, and china into one of these." She pounded on the smashed front fender.

The young man's face went white. "I . . . we were told one hundred."

"Oy, vey!" Sara roared angrily. "Well, you'd better find your boss —and fast." She turned to the florist. "The centerpieces go on the tables under the tent, once the tent is up. Just stand by out there and—"

A loud honk from the street interrupted her. She glanced at the security guard at the end of the drive. He was opening the electric gates for an oddly shaped truck. It looked more like a square tank, with thick gray metal sides, a tinted windshield, and no windows.

"What's this, Brink's—or the Nazis?" Sara complained.

The truck lumbered up to the end of the driveway and stopped. A sheepish-looking man with salt-and-pepper whiskers got out.

"You Mrs. Silverstein?" he asked cautiously.

"Who the hell do I look like, Molly Goldberg?" Sara asked, marching toward him. "Sorry, nothing personal. Who are you?"

"Larry."

For a moment Sara showed no sign of recognition, and then: "Oh, yeah, sure." She smiled, checking her gold Rolex watch. "Good, right on time. Let's have a look." She walked briskly toward the back of the truck.

"Ahh . . . Mrs. Silverstein? I'd like to explain something first. ."

But Sara had already swung the heavy gray door open and was now peering inside. Her smile faded. "What happened?" she whimpered, in a tiny voice.

"I'm awful sorry, ma'am," Larry apologized, embarrassed. "See, this is a refrigerated truck, like I told you on the phone. But I drove in from Long Beach and, somewhere along the way, the, ahh, cooling mechanism failed and . . ."

Sara couldn't believe it. Her eyes crinkled up and for a moment she actually thought she was going to cry. *Hold on,* she told herself. *You're a grown woman. This is a tiny crisis, not the end of the world. You can handle it.*

She took a deep breath. "I ordered an ice sculpture," she said slowly, gritting her teeth. "You brought me a melted iceberg."

"It was gorgeous this morning, Mrs. Silverstein," Larry said defensively. "Of course I won't charge you—"

"Charge me? Charge me? I should charge you for ruining my party!" Sara shouted, glaring at the chagrined ice sculptor. "Why didn't I play it smart and use Chasen's like I always do?"

With that, she spun on her Adidas tennis shoes and ran toward the house.

It was then that she bumped smack into Mark, thumping him hard in the ribs.

"Hey, what am I, a punching bag?" he chuckled, wrapping his arms around her.

Sara fought him off and took a step backward, winded. "Mark!" she gasped. "What the hell are you doing here?"

"Partying. Wasn't invited, so I decided to crash. I didn't know it was a come-as-you-are affair, though," he said, eyeing her sweatshirt and jeans. "Or is this your dear friend Pelo's idea of casual chic?"

"Get lost," she muttered, moving toward the front door. "I've got problems up the kazoo."

"So I noticed," he replied, traipsing after her. "I just helped the boys out back secure the tent."

"It's up?" she asked anxiously. "To stay? What was wrong with it?"

"Nothing a Princeton graduate couldn't handle," he answered, feigning pomposity.

"So how are you with an ice pick?"

"You mean the sculpture? What was it supposed to be, anyway?"

"It was supposed to be a tribute to our guest of honor. 'Five Million Copies,' is what it was supposed to say," Sara fumed, hustling down the hall to the kitchen.

Mark let out a whistle. "The Brocato cover sold that many? Some kind of a record, isn't it? Kate's boss ought to be kissing her toes."

"He's done better than that. He's made her a fabulous offer and . . . Oh, Lord!"

Sara's eyes went wild at the sight of the Japanese caterer hunched over a platter of sushi. "Did your assistant talk to you?" she shouted in a loud voice, hoping he understood English. "Food," she repeated, stretching her arms out wide. "Lots of food."

The old man stared at her in amazement. But before he could respond, Mark swooped in front of her.

"Don't worry, madame," he began, in lopsided French. "Monsieur Mark has already contacted his favorite caterer, Rococo. A feast for one hundred, including chicken *piccante* with capers, poached salmon in dill sauce, Mediterranean artichoke salad, and a mouth-watering selection of miniature fruit tarts is on the way."

"How . . . how did you do that?" Sara asked, astounded.

"It was nothing, kid. Come on upstairs and I'll tell you all about it."

"Oh, no you don't, Mark. You just stay down here. I have to get dressed."

"Fine. I'll watch."

"Forget it!"

He followed her up the stairs.

"You're relentless," she sighed as they reached the bedroom. "So how did you get Rococo to deliver so fast?"

"Happen to know the owner," Mark said, flopping on the bed. "I can't understand why you didn't use them in the first place."

"Because I wanted to do something different for a change," she said, stepping into the bathroom. "There are times in your life when you want to shift gears. You, of all people, should know about that."

"Ouch! I think I'm under attack. Sara . . . Sara?"

The water in the shower drowned him out.

Several minutes later she emerged, wrapped in one of the matching terry cloth bathrobes they'd purchased at the Ritz Carlton in Laguna Niguel.

"Mmmm, nice robe," he said insinuatingly. "And as I recall, it was a very romantic rendezvous."

She tugged the robe tighter and crossed her arms firmly over her middle. "All right, Don Juan, just what are you up to? I've had enough of your mixed signals to last a lifetime. So why don't you just go ahead and level with me, Mark? What the hell do you want?"

His face turned serious as he slid off the bed and strolled across the room. When he reached for her, she withdrew, but he caught her chin in his fingertips and gently tilted her head so her eyes met his.

"You really want to know what I want, Sara?" he said in a tender voice. "I want you."

Sara's stomach did a flip-flop and her face turned bright pink. For a moment she just stood there, allowing the anger to churn inside her. When she spoke, her voice was full of bitterness.

"Oh, right! Sure! Just like that you decide to come back. And I'm supposed to throw up my hands and swoon. Saying, 'Take me, take me, I'm yours.' Well, not anymore. I've had enough of your jerking me around, Mark. Moving in, moving out. 'Sara, I love you. But, Sara, I can't live with you.' No! No, thank you. It's over, done, finished. And so are we."

"You don't mean that," he said, reaching for her once again.

"Yes, I do, dammit. Yes, I do." She shrugged him off and turned her head to hide the incipient tears.

"Sara, please, listen to me. I love you. I never stopped loving you," he said softly. "And now . . . now I can come back."

"No, you can't. You can't," she repeated in a trembling voice. "I just told you you couldn't."

"Darling," he urged, taking her hand. "Please. Just come sit down and hear me out. If you don't buy it, I'll walk. Scout's honor." He held up his hand.

"It's three fingers, not four. You always get it wrong," she mused.

"So, what's a *schlepper* from Hebrew school supposed to know?" he said, guiding her to the bed.

When they sat down, he reached inside his jacket pocket and extracted a deposit receipt from their joint bank account. It read three hundred thousand dollars.

"What's this?" she asked, suspicious.

"This," he paused dramatically, waving the receipt in the air, "is our money. Tucked away safely in our joint account. It replaces the huge sums I extracted."

"But that only added up to around a hundred and fifty thousand."

"To the penny. I knew you were keeping track." He kissed her on the cheek.

"Mark, cut it out. Tell me the rest."

"All right. But just listen. None of your wiseacre comments. Deal?"

She scrutinized his face for a moment. "Okay, okay. Deal."

"Now," he began, holding the desposit slip before her eyes. "This is the result of a game called Airplane."

"What are you talking about?" she scoffed.

"Sara!"

"Sorry."

"I first heard about Airplane through a friend of mine. Niki Erickson."

Sara's mouth popped open, ready to fire. But he clamped his hand over it.

"Niki—a platonic friend. A good contact. Nothing more."

Sara closed her mouth, giving his hand a little bite.

"Ouch! Watch it!" he said good-naturedly. "Anyway, Niki had already made a bundle—a couple hundred thousand, I guess—by playing Airplane here in L.A. And she was ready to do some globe-trotting in search of bigger stakes."

"But let me explain Airplane first. Basically it's a game of chance, a get-rich-quick, high-risk situation, not unlike the pyramid game that got so much publicity a few years back. Remember?"

Sara nodded. "Sure. The chain-letter scam where you'd get a list of names in the mail and send a couple of bucks to a bunch of people you didn't know."

"Yeah. And in return, if you were lucky, you'd get a whole bunch of money back because the more names added to the list, the more bucks those people would send you. Well, Airplane is similar, but it's set up so you actually meet the people you're dealing with."

"Where? At a party or something?"

"Exactly. And the more people who show up, the better off you are. It's all done on a first-come, first-served basis. Each guest pays a certain amount for a ticket on an imaginary airplane. Say, five thousand bucks."

"That much?"

"Sara, we're talking big returns here. Eight times that if you make pilot."

She gave him a quizzical look.

"It's really quite simple," Mark explained. "It takes fifteen people to make up an airplane. Eight passengers, four crew members, two copilots, and the pilot. Once the plane is full, the pilot gets all the money. Then the plane splits, with the two copilots each becoming pilots of their own planes."

"But then they have to fill their planes with more passengers before they get the big pay-off, right?"

"Right. So if it's a big Airplane party, with say a hundred people or so, and you get there early enough, you can't lose. In fact, the only way you can lose is if you're caught on a plane that just doesn't fill up."

"And you never were?"

"Not once." Mark beamed proudly. "I played all over the world, from Aspen to Zurich. Didn't lose a penny."

"For somebody who gets airsick, you did okay."

"Not bad," Mark agreed, pocketing the receipt. "But not as well as I'd intended."

"What do you mean?"

"I'd really hoped to raise enough to finance *Possessions.*"

"Mark! Were you delirious? That'll take millions."

"Exactly," he said with a smug smile. "And I have it."

"What? You have what?"

"The millions. I have the dough to back *Possessions,* Sara. Twenty-five big ones."

"You wha—? Oh, you're joking." She examined his face. "You're *not* joking. Twenty-five million dollars?" she repeated, incredulous. "How? Who?"

"Viscount Bryant Tremley III," Mark said through his best British accent. "Fascinating chap, really. Met him playing Airplane a while back in England. At his estate, in fact. And we became rather good chums."

"I guess," Sara said wearily. "So when did you hit him up for the twenty-five?"

"Two weeks ago, when he was in L.A. Bryant's family has been in the glass business forever. The guy's worth billions. He's a playboy of sorts. A shrewd playboy, with a keen eye for a deal. He'd visited Hollywood before. But knew little about the movie industry. So I showed him around, told him about *Possessions,* offered him a couple of points on the film. And—*bam*—I had a sale!"

"Hmmm. And how soon do you see the money?" she asked with a wry smile. "Or is the check in the mail?"

"No. It's here. In my corporation account. Or half of it is, anyway."

Sara just looked at Mark for a long moment. A stunned expression on her face. "Twelve million dollars?"

"Twelve and a half million. At Security Pacific, as we speak."

She shook her head, still digesting the influx of good news. Then asked, "What about the rest?"

"Bryant's got a group of friends he swears are good for it. An informal investment club. He's president."

Sara looked directly into her husband's twinkling eyes. "No hitches?"

"Not exactly a hitch—more of a condition."

"Uh-oh. I figured. What is it?"

"I have to make the film in Great Britain. At Shiffley Studios. One of Bryant's investor pals owns it."

Sara shrugged. "What's wrong with that?"

"Beats me," he enthused, leaning over to give her a hug. "Things are looking up, pal. Let's celebrate."

He nuzzled her on the neck.

She wanted to push him away but found herself kissing him back. "Mark, we have guests arriving," she murmured as he nibbled her lower lip.

"So? What are they, kinky? You think they want to watch?"

"No," she said, turning away slightly. "I mean, I'm not so sure I'm . . . well, ready for this again."

He was silent for a moment, looking at her through apologetic eyes.

"I mean it, Mark," she continued in a wounded voice. "You hurt me. You hurt me a lot."

"I know that, Sara. At least, I can imagine what you went through. And I'm sorry. Please believe me. I wish I could have done it differently. But at the time, there just seemed to be no other way."

"What about when Jennifer left? You came back then. How can I be sure you'll stay this time?"

"Sara . . . precious," he pleaded. "Listen to me. You can be sure. I guarantee it. Scout's—no, producer's honor. Oh look, you know why I left. I had to get out of this house because I couldn't stand being a failure. I was belly-up, Sara. Yesterday's news. You were the only one who believed in me, and sometimes I wasn't even sure of that. I had to find a way to make a comeback, to get *Possessions* off the ground. Because I knew if I did that I could go back. I could look everyone of those shithead studio executives in the eye. I could rejoin the human race."

"The inhuman race, I'm afraid," she corrected.

"You're right!" he said, kissing her softly. "Where did I get such an incisive, intelligent, beautiful woman? I think I'll marry her."

"You already have. Don't try it again—she couldn't handle it." Sara was silent for a few seconds. "God!" she exclaimed, chuckling to herself.

"What's so funny?"

"You. Airplane. Bags of money. An English viscount backing your films. Talk about creative financing!"

"I'd rather talk about creative something else," Mark said, inching her robe down her shoulders.

"Does it begin with an 'f'?" Sara sighed, running her fingers through his wavy hair.

"Yeah, you up for it?"

"I thought I was supposed to ask you that," she smirked.

"Wiseass . . . you always were a wiseass," he whispered, running his hand up her thigh.

"And the best one in town, honey," she added, reaching up to unbutton his shirt. "Better not stray too far."

Downstairs at the party, the guest of honor was in the midst of giving Brandy St. John a gigantic hug.

"It's so good to see you," Kate exclaimed, stepping back to admire her friend's fashionably appliquéd suede dress.

They were standing just inside the trellised entrance to the voluminous tent, through which an endless line of Hollywood notables continued to stream. Among them, a number of celebrities. Kate had already said hello to John Forsythe, Victoria Principal, and Julie Andrews.

"Isn't this terrific?" Brandy shouted, above the animated chatter of the convivial crowd. What a turnout. You're really a star."

"Oh, I wouldn't go that far," Kate chuckled modestly. But she couldn't deny the sheer force of exhilaration that had propelled her since the very first guests had begun to arrive.

They'd appeared at the stroke of five. Sauntering from their customized sports cars and limousines. Strolling through the backyard, past the lush rose and hydrangea gardens. Converging on the spectacular tent with a deliberate drift. That studied air of casual elegance reserved for the very successful. And the very rich.

They knew who they were. An impressive array of the town's top image-makers. The crème de la crème of the glittering heap. Producers, directors, gossipers and preeners, agents and publicists. All of them there to pay tribute to Kate.

And she was dazzled. Exuberant. Floating somewhere in a tantalizing paradise where the adrenaline ran high and joy was a given. The very air was charged with excitement and power. And Kate was the center of attention.

Over the years, she had attended dozens of Hollywood parties. But never one in her honor. And she hadn't been quite prepared for this. This sparking confabulation of VIPs, whose work commanded respect in the most charmed show-business circles. Who spoke of Jack and Angelica without bothering to add Nicholson or Huston. Who took "power-breakfast" meetings at the Bel Air Hotel, spent ten weekends out of the year at celebrity tennis tournaments, and didn't need a reservation at Le Dôme.

These people, congratulating her! Bussing her on the cheek. Fawning over her. Asking her questions as though they'd been waiting all their lives to hear the answers fall from her lips. Inquiring about her future plans. What other exposés she had up her sleeve. Telling her how glorious she looked. That Hollywood suited her. And insisting that she "must stay on the Coast."

It was pretty heady stuff. Like a drug, Kate thought as she watched Brandy disappear into the crowd. No, better than a drug. This was a high Kate knew she could deal with. Coming down would not be so difficult.

All she had to do was keep reminding herself not to believe any of it. Not one word. Oh, she knew that some of the accolades, especially those from her close friends, were well intended. But that was as far as it went. Two weeks from now, three quarters of the people standing here gushing over her wouldn't remember her name or what she'd written.

At a gathering of this nature, the level of duplicity ran cornstalk high. And Kate was well aware of that. So she listened with only half an ear. Taking everything with several grains of salt. To do otherwise would be complete delusion.

Still, she found playing the role of the journalist extraordinaire quite a kick. And she was enjoying this confluence of high-voltage, fraudulent enthusiasm. Why not? She deserved it. This was the ultimate social triumph. Tinsel Town at its best. And Kate Brannigan intended to indulge herself in every delicious second of it.

"Aunt Kate! Aunt Kate!"

She turned to see the twins tearing toward her, frantically elbowing their way through the tent's narrow, trellised entrance.

"He's here," Jennifer announced breathlessly, grasping Kate's arm. "Outside with the photographers. Let's go."

"What? Who's here?" Kate asked, confused.

"Don . . . Don Brocato. Mr. Gorgeous," Jackie chimed in. "Introduce us now, Aunt Kate. Before he disappears into the crowd."

"Well, wait until he gets inside, at least," Kate said, refusing to move. "Tell you what. I'll stand here and corner him, if you'll go find your mother. I haven't seen a sign of her."

"All right. But don't you let him go before we get back." Jackie agreed, grabbing her sister's hand.

Ten minutes later, Don Brocato had fought his way through the media circus, accepting a glass of ice-cold Cristal champagne from a circulating waiter, and located Kate.

"The paparazzi are in rare form out there, I understand," Kate chuckled as he approached.

"Worst I've ever seen. Must be fifty of them. I guess you're a hit," he said, raising his glass in a toast.

Kate smiled enthusiastically. "Couldn't have done it without you, if you'll pardon the cliché. And thanks for the national publicity the other morning, Don. It wasn't necessary you know."

"On *GMA*? Credit where credit's due is my motto, Kate. I meant what I said." He glanced around self-consciously. "Ahh . . . by the way, Margo Green is out there with her camera crew. Wants to do an interview with the two of us. I told her I'd have to check with you first."

"Well, of course," Kate agreed, flabbergasted. Margo Green's Wednesday night celebrity profile show was the hottest program on the air, often surpassing *60 Minutes* in the ratings.

"How about we do it in an hour or so?" he asked.

"Fine. Wonderful. I mean, that'll give me some time to compose myself. I hate to admit this, but I've never been on television before."

"That right?" Brocato said, surprised. "I figured you'd be making a move in that direction soon, crossing over to TV journalism."

"Not on your life," Kate exclaimed. "Archaic as it may sound, I harbor tremendous affection for the printed word. Besides, I'd be so nervous I probably wouldn't be able to speak."

"Well, I'm considering it—TV, that is," Brocato said, proudly.

"Yes? In what capacity?"

"Commentator, interviewer, reporter. I'm not real clear. But ESPN wants me to do my own show. At least that's what the Morris Agency tells me. I'll believe it when I see a contract."

"That's very exciting," Kate enthused. "But what about football? You aren't kissing the pigskin good-bye, are you?"

"No way. In fact, I've had a number of offers already. Funny, isn't it, how quickly you can turn into a star?"

"Tell me about it," she replied with a knowing look. "So what teams are offering? NFL or USFL?"

"Both!" Brocato beamed, reaching into his pants pocket. "And, just in case my favorite reporter wants to run a little blurb, I've got an exclusive press release right here."

"Great!" she said, unfolding the paper eagerly.

"You might have some trouble reading it, Kate," he laughed. "Typed it myself."

"No problem. I'll just have them run it as is," she joked as she read. "My, this is impressive. You're going to have your own line of sports clothes and a series of Pepsi commercials as well?"

"Yeah. Guess my ship's come in, huh?" he said, a bit embarrassed. "Say, have you heard anything more from the District Attorney's office?"

"I've met with them twice. They asked a lot of questions."

"I hear they've run into major problems tracking Renata Desmond down."

"Yes. At the moment it appears to be an endless quest. Uh-oh!" Kate said, glancing over the quarterback's broad shoulder. "Don, I'm not sure you're prepared for this, but two of your biggest fans are about to claim you and monopolize your entire evening."

After Kate had introduced the twins she turned to Jennifer and whispered, "Where in the world is your mother?"

Jennifer's face lit up like a neon sign. "Preoccupied . . . with Dad," she giggled.

Before Kate could question the twins further, Alisa Hudson appeared, locked her arm in Kate's, and drew her aside for a private chat.

"Miss Hudson! I'm so surprised," Kate exclaimed as soon as she could get a word in. "You never attend parties."

"Rarely, my dear. And please call me Alisa," the aging actress replied.

"But, I'm just so thrilled that you're—"

"Oh, poppycock. I wouldn't miss this. It's a special occasion. I wanted to be here to congratulate you personally, Kate. And I mean that sincerely, not like some of the two-faced chameleons around here. You did a fine job, exposing Renata for the contemptible creature that she is. I read your article thoroughly. And it is my pleasure to join in your celebration. Even though I had to dress up for it."

Kate's eyes swept over Alisa's conservative, dark green pantsuit.

"Anything other than denim is dress-up for me, dear," the animated septuagenarian explained. "And what about Renata? She'll be back, don't you think. Certainly she will. People that power-hungry can't lay low for long. But wasn't it a shame about her vice-president, that Haight fellow? Good he ended it all, I suppose. Poor man hadn't a chance. She'd have pinned the entire rap on him. No question about that."

Kate smiled with amusement as Alisa's vociferous monologue continued. There was no stopping her.

"And speaking of plunges," the actress was saying. "I've some absolutely delicious news about Teddy Selwyn. Off the record for the moment, my dear. Sorry, but the lawyers made me promise."

Kate nodded earnestly.

"Well, you can imagine how pleased I was when I heard this." Alisa lowered her voice and leaned closer to Kate. "The bastard is bankrupt."

"What?" Kate gasped, stunned. "But that's inconceivable. He just sold his interest in Selwyn to R. B. McDevitt."

Alisa shot Kate a conspiratorial look. "Yes, but for very little, I understand. A piddling ten million dollars. Barely grocery money for a sybarite like Selwyn. Now he's up to his fat pink ears in lawsuits. And if you'll pardon the expression, dear, the bugger doesn't have a pot to piss in."

"But that's impossible, Alisa. Surely Teddy has stocks, real estate. What about his fabulous multimillion dollar home in the Palisades?"

"All mortgaged to the hilt, I'm telling you. And I have this on very good authority. Teddy has thrown in the towel, filed for bankruptcy, Chapter Eleven. He had to. He couldn't afford to fight the lawsuits."

"Who's suing him, besides you?"

"Your friend Mr. McDevitt, for one."

"R.B.? But he just took over Selwyn. Why would he—"

"That's just it, my dear. It didn't take Mr. McDevitt long to figure out that Teddy had been borrowing heavily from the studio. Fifty million over the last five years, I believe. With no intention of paying it back. But then, he had no idea such a clever Texan would come along and beat him at his own game."

"That's . . . that's amazing," Kate stammered.

"Remember," Alisa warned, holding up an index finger, "keep it under your hat."

"Of course," Kate agreed. "I'm just so surprised. What's Teddy doing, liquidating everything?"

"Everything he owns, which isn't much, the way I hear it. Even some of his suits are being repossessed by the chichi haberdasheries on Rodeo Drive. I wouldn't be surprised to see him walking around downtown wearing a barrel," Alisa whooped, laughing at her own joke. "That is, if he could find one big enough."

Kate chuckled, picturing Teddy with a tin cup in his hand. *Divine justice,* she thought. *Sometimes things do happen for the best.*

"By the way, where is your fascinating Mr. McDevitt?" Alisa

wanted to know. "I must plant a mammoth kiss on his handsome cheek."

Kate raised her eyebrows in surprise.

"Not my style normally—the physical, I mean," Alisa explained with a devilish grin. "But he has been such a darling. You know that atrocious cut of *Transcendence* I told you about, the one I was suing Teddy over? Well, Mr. McDevitt has promised me that the entire abomination and any prints will be destroyed. 'We'll have a big Texas barbecue right here on the lot,' he said in that sultry drawl. Such a marvelous chap. Now where in the world is he?" Alisa asked, craning her wrinkled neck in search of him.

"I'm not sure," Kate replied, with a quick look around. "He was supposed—" She stopped talking abruptly, eyes fastened on something far away at the other end of the tent.

"What is it, my dear?" Alisa asked, following Kate's troubled gaze.

"That woman up there—on the platform near the band. The one picking up the microphone. Monica Chase, Brandy's agent."

"It looks like she's about to make an announcement," Alisa observed.

"But I can't imagine—"

"What's going on over there, a floor show?" came a spritely female voice from behind.

Kate whirled around. "Sara! Where've you been?"

"Tell you later," Sara whispered, with a wink. "Hello, Alisa. So glad you could join us. I'd really love to talk," she added, gliding away as she spoke, "but I think I'd better rescue Monica."

"Do that," Kate called after Sara, "before she makes a fool of herself."

"My," Alisa mused, scrutinizing Monica's unsteady gait. "She does look a bit tipsy, I daresay."

Up on the platform, Monica Chase was completely oblivious of the four double vodkas she'd just consumed. And she barely noticed the dizzying rush that buzzed in her head like a swarm of angry bumblebees as she teetered determinedly across the thick red carpet. She was totally preoccupied with the mission at hand.

News! Monica had the most marvelous news to share. And what a wonderful place to make the announcement. She peered out over the high-powered confabulation of creative genius before her. Front-runners, all. Trendsetters in multitude.

Won't they be delighted and surprised, she thought with increasing excitement. Then raising the microphone in her hand, she gave it a hearty tap.

The horrendous, deafening, boom that followed stopped every conversation. Heads turned. Mouths gaped. And suddenly more than two hundred pairs of eyes were riveted on the woman in black lace swaying back and forth on her perch.

Had she been sober Monica Chase would have trembled in fear. Since she was not, she simply smiled and plunged unabashedly ahead.

"Ladiesngenlemen," Monica slurred, in a blaring voice. "I have something verspecial and ver'exciting to share with you . . ."

Not far away, near a sumptuous buffet table, Brandy stiffened and reached for Taylor's arm. "Oh, no, she's bombed. And I think she's going to—"

"She's not!" Taylor exclaimed in disbelief. "She can't. I haven't even told Sara yet."

"I've juslearned," Monica continued, "that oneaHollywood's newest stars—"

She was totally unaware of the muffled laughs and whispers in the audience.

"thonly female performer witherown show consistently rated among the topfive. Yes, youguessed it, my client, Miss Brandy St. John, is engaged t'be married—no pleasdon clap yet. Our dear Brandy is gointamarry Taylor Evans at the enofthe year."

"My God, how embarrassing," Brandy shouted to Taylor over a wave of thunderous applause. "Poor Monica."

"Don't worry," he said, unable to submerge his laughter. "I see sister Sara's about to give her the hook."

Once Monica had tottered off, Sara took center stage, making an announcement of her own.

"I'll be brief. But I just want you all to know that our guest of honor, that highly talented crackerjack reporter, better known as 'Ace' around the Silverstein household, has not only managed to increase *World* magazine's sales substantially with her stunning cover story, but Kate has just landed herself an unprecedented contract. I won't be so gauche as to talk money. Suffice it to say that my favorite journalist has been offered a very sizable salary to become a special investigative reporter for *World*. And I think that's something to celebrate. So let's get to it. Thank you all for coming and enjoy . . . enjoy!"

The festivities went on for several hours. It was almost eleven-thirty by the time Kate finally said good night to Sara and Mark, then made her way up to her room. She was exhausted, but happily so. Trudging up the cool marble steps on weary feet, high heels dangling from her hand, she smiled to herself wistfully.

It had been a wonderful party, a dream of a night. And at the moment she was overcome with an odd mix of emotions. Wishing she could savor this giddy feeling of elation forever, yet anxious to move forward with her life and her new position with *World*.

One thing was certain—she'd imposed on Sara long enough. As soon as Kate returned from her vacation, she would rent an apartment. Or maybe a condo. *My God,* she thought, *a six-figure salary. With the money I'm going to be making, I could actually afford to buy a condo.*

Her face brightened with the idea of owning her own property. At last she was going to have the bucks she needed for the kind of security she'd always longed for.

"Independent, substantial, solid," she announced to herself in the bureau mirror, as the Zandra Rhodes dress dropped to her feet. "Finally, Brannigan, you're becoming an adult. Feels pretty damn good, doesn't it?"

Hours later, still far too excited to sleep, Kate stretched lazily in bed, waging a mental war. She kept telling herself it didn't matter about R. B. McDevitt. Who cared if he hadn't shown up at the party? His loss, not hers. The fact that he hadn't even phoned showed him for the jerk she always knew he was, anyway. And at this point in her life, Kate refused to allow any man to alter her spirits in the slightest. So he'd sent enough flowers to stock a mortuary. So what? Bottom line: R. B. McDevitt was totally unreliable and irresponsible. Just like all the other men she'd ever met.

Convinced at last that she'd have been a fool to give him a chance, Kate drifted off to a most pleasant, uninterrupted sleep.

31

■ It wasn't until the next day that R.B. finally made an appearance at the Silversteins' Bel Air mansion. His metallic gray stretch limousine rolled up in their circular driveway just before noon.

The chauffeur had barely parked before R.B. hopped out and sprang toward the front door. He was carrying a long white box under one arm and a small, exquisitely wrapped package in the other hand.

Sara answered the doorbell, still in her bathrobe.

"Maid's day off?" R.B. teased, stepping inside.

"After last night's fandango I wouldn't blame any of them for quitting," she laughed. Then added, "You're a bit late."

"Sorry. Business in Japan. Just got back. Is Kate around?" he asked anxiously.

Sara shook her head. "Not your day, R.B. She just left."

The handsome Texan's trademark grin faded noticeably.

"Why, ah do bahlieve the gentleman's uhpset," Sara chided, feigning a drawl.

"Where'd she—"

"Hawaii. The plane leaves at twelve forty-five. You might be able to—"

R.B. spun around and dashed toward the waiting limo.

"Hey, hang on a minute," Sara called, running after him.

He leaned out the window just in time to hear her shout, "Western Airlines, LAX. Maybe you'll get lucky and the flight will be late."

The flight was on time. R.B. arrived at the gate with three minutes to spare. Just long enough to purchase a ticket, which is exactly what he did.

His was first-class. Kate's wasn't. But he'd take care of that.

As soon as the wide-bodied jet reached cruising altitude he was on his feet, heading for the coach section. *Just my luck,* he thought when he got there, *a full house.* Almost every seat was taken.

R.B. summoned up his courage, dug his hands into his pockets, and began strolling down the aisle. He proceeded slowly, his keen blue eyes scanning each face. To all who observed, he appeared the epitome of self-confidence. Yet he felt like the ultimate fool.

What the hell am I doing up here on my way to Hawaii when I have an important meeting in Century City this afternoon, he asked himself with increasing irritation. *Dammit all! Maybe she isn't even here. Maybe she missed the flight.*

Then he saw her. Curled up in a window seat, reading a book. Lustrous red-gold curls cascading down over her shoulders, providing a sharp contrast to the royal blue jumpsuit she was wearing.

Kate Brannigan looked better than R. B. McDevitt could remember. Screw the meeting. She was more important.

"Ahh . . . Miss Brannigan?"

She recognized the drawl immediately, before she even looked up. And in that sliver of a second when she heard his voice, an instantaneous flash of hot mixed with cold, fire and ice, swept over her. Like a zillion infinitesimal tremors of apprehension.

Kate Brannigan was absolutely flustered.

"Yes?" she said, raising her blue-violet eyes to meet his.

He flashed a mischievous grin. "There's been a little mistake about seating, ma'am," he announced formally. "You're supposed to be up in first class."

"R.B., what are you talking about?" She started to laugh.

"No questions, please," he replied matter-of-factly. "If you'll just come with me."

"But I can't—" Kate glanced around at her curious fellow passengers and made a snap decision to cooperate. "Okay. Okay," she said, with a nervous chuckle, as she squeezed into the aisle.

"Right this way," he ordered, taking her hand.

Minutes later they were comfortably ensconced in the first-class section. Sitting next to each other in commodious, lush leather seats.

"Much better, don't you agree?" R.B. asked, beckoning the stewardess.

"R.B., what is going on?" Kate asked, baffled.

"We're celebrating. Two glasses of champagne, please," he told he flight attendant. Then he reached beneath the seat, pulled out the elongated white box, and handed it to Kate. "For you."

She raised the top and smiled in amusement. "More? Do you know how many of these you've sent me over the past week?"

"Not enough, I'm sure," he answered, as the stewardess poured champagne. "All the yellow roses in the world wouldn't be enough to thank you."

"To thank me for what? Maybe I'm dense, but I really don't understand."

"For Selwyn Studios. You helped me snare it away from Teddy's unctuous grasp." He raised his glass in a toast.

She clinked it with her own. "I did?" she asked, bewildered. "How?"

"That little tidbit about the snuff film you threw my way. I put it to good use."

Kate's eyes grew wide with amazement. "But how did you manage to—"

"Tell you later." He fished the small, gift-wrapped package from his briefcase. "First, open this."

"More presents?" she said evenly, camouflaging her excitement. "Aren't you carrying this a bit too far?"

"Just open it," he urged, watching her.

Kate's fingers felt as uncooperative as chopsticks as she struggled to remove the bow and strip off the silver paper. Once she'd done so, her face lit up in surprise.

"How . . . how did you know?" she asked, delighted.

"My usual informant—Sara," R.B. chuckled. "Besides, I like the name." He thought for a moment and his expression softened as he said, "I guess you might say it sums up the way I feel."

About you, he means, Kate told herself, eyes fixed on the small bottle of perfume in her hand. It was Calvin Klein's latest scent, Obsession.

R. B. McDevitt is obsessed with me, is that what he's saying? Kate was wondering whether she'd heard him correctly. Hoping she hadn't. Hoping she had.

"Oh," was all she managed.

"Anyway," R.B. continued, a bit awkwardly, "it's . . . ahh, just my way of congratulating you on your new job. You are taking it, aren't you?"

"Yes, absolutely." Something was churning inside her. Setting her off-balance. Making it difficult for her to speak.

"And where will you be located?" R.B. was asking. "Los Angeles?"

"Yes, at . . . at least I think so," she replied, haltingly. "I mean I can . . . ahh, live anywhere I choose." *Come on, just spit it out,* she chastised herself. *Why are you being so noncommittal?*

"Well, I'm glad to hear that," he said enthusiastically. "Because I'll be headquartering in L.A. myself soon. And I think it's about time we got to know each other."

"You do?" she asked, turning to him.

"Yes."

Their eyes locked in silent agreement. And automatically Kate began to relax.

"And why's that?"

"Let's just say it's my nature—to follow my instincts." He flashed a wide grin. "Any objections?"

Kate shook her head slowly. "None. But I would like to know what you're doing on this flight."

"Simply seeing that you have a safe journey, ma'am," he joked. "It's a little service we gallant Texas gents often perform. How long are you going to be in Hawaii?"

"Kauai, specifically. I'm meeting friends there. A week, maybe two."

"May I make a suggestion?" he asked playfully.

"A serious one?"

"Very. Why don't you cut it short over there and spend the following week in Texas?"

"Did you have any place special in mind?" she asked with a little smirk.

"Well, let's see, now. The hill country is always gorgeous this time of year. And there's the Clear Fork. Nicest ranch in the state."

"Run by that bashful tycoon who loathes publicity?" Kate chided. "The modest guy with the low profile, who never exaggerates?"

"You got it, gorgeous. What do you say?"

"At the moment, I'm not exactly sure," she replied lightly. "I'll have to think about it."

"A smart journalist like you ought to do better than that," he chided, gazing at her for a long moment. Then he leaned over and caught her cheek in his hand.

"I'm not so—"

His lips came down on hers before she could finish the sentence, which she couldn't remember anyway. It was a tender kiss. Almost ethereal, transcending anything Kate had ever experienced. His touch was so gentle at first, like the barest tickle of the lightest feather on her lips. Caressing her. Tempting her. Coaxing her.

Then his arms were around her and his mouth felt stronger, more intense, bearing down on her hungrily, demanding that she kiss him back.

And she did. Over and over again, until her limbs went fluid and she began to tremble with a longing so deliciously all-consuming that she didn't want him to stop.

"So," he murmured between kisses, "have you had enough time to think?"

"No," she said softly, touching his lips with her finger. "No, I haven't."

He drew back slightly and questioned her with uncertain eyes. It was the first time Kate had ever seen R. B. McDevitt look anything less than totally self-assured. And secretly she took pleasure in his expression. He seemed genuinely disappointed.

"You haven't given me nearly enough time," she said coyly after a few seconds. "But I have made a decision."

"And that is?"

"And that is . . . a yes," she said, raising her lips to meet his. "A definite yes."